Praise for the novels of Thomas A. Burns, Jr.

Stripper! A Natalie McMasters Mystery (2018)

***** - Extremely well written. The plot was very entertaining and the characters were well developed and likeable. Told from the first-person perspective of Natalie McMasters – the book is a real page turner. Great read! – Amazon review

***** - Excellent crime/mystery story, kept me turning the pages. Burns has created a fascinating lead character—Nattie McMasters. She's young, sexy and courageous. – Amazon review

Killers! A Natalie McMasters Mystery (2021)

***** - Chasing clues and serial killers, stumbling across more dead bodies, there will be gunfights and a look into the world of BDSM before it's all finished. And how does the murder of an aged Chinaman from Alabama fit in? Burns explores it all, as Tai Chi and southern culture collide with a maniacal killer, a sexual sadist known as The Marquis. But he's not the only sicko Natalie and her team will encounter. Graphic and all too real, Killers! explores a vastly different world with non-stop action. – Anthony and multiple award-winning author M. K. Graff

***** - Sultry tidewater Georgia provides an interesting locale for this tale. You can almost smell the brackish water and feel the heavy air. Burns's pacing and delivery surpass his previous novels, drawing the reader into the world of a psychotic mastermind who is unstoppable and whose deviant passions are unquenchable. – S.W. O'Connell, author of The Yankee Doodle Spies series

Sister! A Natalie McMasters Mystery (2022)

***** - Thomas Burns brings Natalie McMasters back in a hair-raising tale of mistaken identity. Natalie is waiting for her name to be called at her college graduation ceremony when police sweep in and arrest her. Some who could be her twin was captured on security cameras robbing a convenience store and killing one person. Only through the assistance of a friend, who is in the FBI, vouchers for her alibi. But, Natalie being Natalie, can't leave the investigation alone. She wants to know who this woman is and why she could be Natalie's twin sister. A quick visit to her mother only clouds the issue. The woman could indeed by her twin. Natalie and her extended family are up against power and money as the clues unravel. The tension is absolute, and the ending stunning. You might want to sleep with the lights on for a night or two. – Betsy Ashton, Author, *Mad Max Mysteries (Unintended Consequences, Uncharted Territory,* and *Unsafe Haven), Eyes Without A Face, Out of the Desert, Betrayal*

***** - Sister!, the latest installment by Thomas A. Burns packs a punch in the first chapter and the tension only increases from there. Natalie McMasters finds herself accused of a crime she didn't commit. While working to prove her innocence, she learns of family secrets which will impact the rest of her life. The tone of this book was eerie and unsettling, dealing with uncomfortable issues that are all too prevalent in our daily news cycle. But no matter how disturbing the subject matter, I could not stop reading. Burns paints a vivid picture of his characters and the dilemmas they face. One twist leads to another which culminates in an ending you won't expect. I'm already waiting for the next book in the series! – Brenda Donelan, Author of the University Mystery Series

The Legacy of the Unborn: A Novel of Lovecraftian Horror (as Silas K. Henderson - 2020)

***** - This is a very well written and engaging book that read like a mix between Sir Arthur Conan Doyle and H.P. Lovecraft. Part detective story, part horror story, the characters were very well developed and the plot intriguing. When I took breaks in my reading, it did so with reluctance and looked forward to when I could pick the book up again. Highly recommended! – Amazon review

***** - Well-crafted characters and a compelling plot. Plenty of action mystery suspense and building tension. First rate Lovecraftian writing, well worth reading. – Amazon Review

Sherlock Holmes and Dr. Watson: Ten Steps from Baker Street
A New Collection of Untold Stories

Also by Thomas A. Burns, Jr.

The Natalie McMasters Mysteries

Stripper! (2018)
Revenge! (2018)
Trafficked! (2019)
Venom! (2019)
Sniper! (2020)
Killers! (20210
Sister! (2022)

Writing as Silas K. Henderson

The Legacy of the Unborn – A Novel of Lovecraftian Horror (2020)

Thomas A. Burns, Jr.

Sherlock Holmes and Dr. Watson: Ten Steps from Baker Street
A New Collection of Untold Stories

Thomas A. Burns, Jr.

Ten Steps from Baker Street

The Wizard of Montague Street © 2023 by Thomas A. Burns, Jr.

The Adventure of the Persistent Pugilist © 2018 by Thomas A. Burns, Jr., appeared in Sherlock Holmes and Doctor Watson: The Early Adventures, Ed. David Marcum. Manchester, NH: Belanger Books.

Christmas at the Red Lion © 2021 by Thomas A. Burns, Jr. appeared in The MX Book of New Sherlock Holmes Stories, Part XXVIII: More Christmas Adventures (1869-1888), Ed. David Marcum. London, UK: MX Publishing.

The Adventure of the Drunken Teetotaller © 2022 by Thomas A. Burns, Jr. appeared in The MX Book of New Sherlock Holmes Stories, Part XXXIV: 2022 Annual (1875-1887), Ed. David Marcum. London, UK: MX Publishing.

The Camberwell Poisoner © 2021 by Thomas A. Burns, Jr. appeared in The Strand Magazine, March-June 2021, 20-34.

Blood and Gunpowder © 2020 by Thomas A. Burns, Jr. appeared in The MX Book of New Sherlock Holmes Stories, Part XX: 2020 Annual (1891-1897), Ed. David Marcum. London, UK: MX Publishing.

A Case of Murder© 2021 by Thomas A. Burns, Jr. appeared in The Nefarious Villains of Sherlock Holmes Sherlock Holmes Stories, Vol. II, Ed. David Marcum. Manchester, NH: Belanger Books.

Another Case of Identity © 2021 by Thomas A. Burns, Jr. appeared in The MX Book of New Sherlock Holmes Stories, Part XXIV: Some More Untold Cases (1895-1903), Ed. David Marcum. London, UK: MX Publishing.

Thomas A. Burns, Jr.

The Horror in King Street © 2019 by Thomas A. Burns, Jr. appeared in The MX Book of New Sherlock Holmes Stories, Part XIV: 2019 Annual, Ed. David Marcum. London, UK: MX Publishing.

The Witch of Ellenby © 2019 by Thomas A. Burns, Jr. appeared in The MX Book of New Sherlock Holmes Stories, Vol XVIII: Whatever Remains…Must Be the Truth (1899-1925), Ed. David Marcum. London, UK: MX Publishing.

Thomas A. Burns, Jr.

Printed in the United States of America

First Printing: March 2023

ISBN-13: 979-8-9872099-2-9 (print)

ISBN- 13: 979-8-9872099-3-6 (e-book)

Dedication

*To the memory of Sir Arthur Conan Doyle, who created
the best and wisest man we ever knew.*

Thomas A. Burns, Jr.

Table of Contents

'From that day to this I have never for an instant regretted the course I took in killing Sherlock. That does not say, however, that because he is dead I should not write about him again if I wanted to, for there is no limit to the number of papers he left behind or the reminiscences in the brain of his biographer.'

Sir Arthur Conan Doyle, A Gaudy Death: Conan Doyle tells the True Story of Sherlock Holmes. An interview of Arthur Conan Doyle in Tit-Bits, 15 December 1900.
'

Thomas A. Burns, Jr.

The Wizard of Montague Street

It was Tuesday, July 3, 1877.

The slender young man exited the park at Russell Square and crossed the road into Montague Street. To save a fare, he'd walked all the way from St. Pancras station, nearly a mile away, toting a carpet bag with his heavy Inverness jammed between the handles. July in London is not an overly hot month, but it was still much too warm for that garment.

At twenty-three years old, Sherlock Holmes had come down from Camford today to realize his life's dream. Here in London, he would become the world's first consulting detective. He would earn his bread and cheese by using his peculiar abilities to advise other investigators regarding the odd, arcane, seemingly insoluble cases they would bring to his door. The fact that he knew next to no one in the city did not trouble him greatly—a current copy of the *Illustrated Police News* would provide him with a plethora of mysteries to investigate, solve and build his reputation. To support him during this uncertain time, he carried a purse containing five gold sovereigns in his trousers pocket.

If I cannot establish myself before these are exhausted, perhaps I have chosen the wrong career.

The west side of Montague Street contained house numbers ascending from 12, so he walked along until he spied a note on the door of number 24. Ascending the stairs, he plucked it off.

> *Mr. Holmes* (it ran),
> *Meet me around back.*
> *R. Potts*

Looking back toward Russell Square, he saw an archway between numbers 20 and 21. He walked back and entered it. The strong scent of horses came to his nostrils and the light ebbed as the sun was obscured by the buildings and a damp chill clasped his skin. He realized he'd entered a mews that ran behind the houses.

A rotund gentleman wearing a soiled, white shirt, a black canvas vest, grey woollen pants and knee-high Wellingtons was waiting halfway down the mews. Approaching him, Holmes took note of his sour expression.

'Halloa! Mr. Potts?'

'Ye'd be Mr. Sherlock Holmes, then? Yer muther wired me to expect youse.'

Holmes extended his hand. 'I am he.'

Ignoring the outstretched hand and pointing to a door at the top of the short flight of stairs, Potts replied, 'I've got yer room ready fer youse. It'll be five bob a week, and I'll have the first two weeks now.'

Holmes took his purse from his pocket, extracted a gold coin and handed it to Potts.

'I've no change fer this, lad.'

'Then make it a month in advance, sir,' said Holmes.

His expression now greatly improved, Potts slid the coin into his vest pocket. He went up the stairs and unlocked the door with a large key. Opening it, he revealed another, much longer staircase that led to the top floor. Handing the key to Holmes, he said, 'I've no wish to do all them stairs. Ye'll find yer digs at the top—it's the only room up there. I'll see youse in a month fer the August rent.'

Potts walked off and Holmes stepped on the first step, closing the door behind him. He immediately opened it again as it had become pitch black inside.

I'll need to leave a candle at the bottom of the stairs to come and go.

He ascended the stairs and opened another door at the top, squinting as the sunlight inside hit him in the eyes. He was looking into a large room, approximately 20' by 20', with windows on all four sides. Obviously a storage attic, it smelled of dust and dead mice, but he reckoned a few good pipefuls of black shag would fix that. The air was hot and close, but he saw that the windows should open (if they weren't swelled shut). The place was furnished with a plain wooden cot, a large table that would do for his chemical apparatus that should arrive from Cambridge later today, a straight back chair and a pot-bellied stove.

At least I won't freeze to death come winter. I wonder if this isn't mother's way of encouraging me to move back home instead of remaining in London. I'll need a sofa, and a couple of easy chairs to entertain clients here, which I hope I can get from a second-hand shop in St. Andrew.

Suddenly, the four pounds Holmes had left seemed a lot less money than it did a few minutes ago.

***

By 6 p.m., Holmes had improved the place greatly—in addition to the aforementioned items, he had secured a sideboard, a roll-top desk with a top that wouldn't come down and a swivel chair to go in front of it. It had lots of drawers and cubbies where he could organize case notes and other writings. After a dinner of pea soup and fried fish purchased on the street, he reclined on his sofa, a foot too short for him, perusing the aforementioned *Illustrated Police News*. Tomorrow, he hoped to find a mattress for the cot. Blankets or a quilt could wait until the cooler weather arrived.

The windows were open wide to let the heat of the day escape. The voices of boys playing a game in the mews below drifted upward—the urban equivalent of crickets in the countryside. Abruptly, the tone turned acrimonious.

Perhaps I'd better see what is going on.

Once downstairs, Holmes saw a group of about a dozen street arabs gathered at the back of the mews. Two of the older lads were bracing each other, circling nose-to-nose, their fists bunched up at their hips. Both of them were dressed in the motley garb of the poor; the larger of the two even wore mismatched shoes. The rest of the group surrounded them, their eager expressions indicative of their anticipation of the commencement of fisticuffs.

'I freed the pris'ners, I'm tellin' ye!' said the bigger boy.

'Nay!' said the other. 'I caught youse before ye could get yer foot in the jail. Game's over. We won!'

'D'youse want a punch in the mush, Cal? Cos youse never did touch me noggin, so there!'

'Dickie 'ere see'd me do it. Didn't ye, Dickie?' The speaker reached into the crowd to drag forth a younger lad, dressed in a clean white collarless shirt, tan corduroy pants and low shoes with brass buckles. Dickie's tight lips and wide eyes suggested that he didn't relish being inserted into a dispute between the older lads—he was likely doomed no matter which side he came down on.

'If you cannot agree, why don't you toss a coin for it?' Holmes said. 'That's a gentleman's solution.'

The two prospective combatants looked at Holmes as if he were the Prince of Wales come down to the mews from Buckingham Palace.

'Watcher care about it, matey?' said the oldest boy, likely the leader of the gang. 'And wot makes ye think the likes o' us would have a coin to toss, anyway?'

Holmes raised his arms above his head, fists clenched, then with a flourish, opened one hand to reveal a shilling.

'Here, catch,' he said, as he whipped his hand forward to toss the coin. The boy reached out to catch it, then looked at Holmes stupidly when he realized there was nothing to catch.

' 'Ere, watcher playin' at?'

Walking forward, Holmes opened both hands to reveal that he had no coin in either one. He stepped up to the leader and reached for his ear, then drew his hand back to reveal a shilling held between his thumb and forefinger. The boy grabbed for it, but Holmes drew his hand back before he could get it, then opened both hands again to show them empty again.

' 'Ere now!' shouted the lad, obviously angry now.

'It's in your pocket, you know,' said Holmes.

The boy's face plainly said he didn't want to look, but he had to. Then his eyes doubled in size as he reached in his pocket and felt the coin.

By this time, Holmes had the entire group enthralled, and the importance of who had won the earlier game dwindled to nadir. He proceeded to treat the crowd to a dazzling display of prestidigitation, producing more coins from thin air, changing pennies into shillings and back again and even dragging a foot-long handkerchief out of one boy's nose.

'Yer a real wizard, sorr' ' one boy said 'How'd youse do that?' So, Holmes sat on his heels to show them how to perform a simple coin vanishing trick. As he proceeded with his instructions, he suddenly reached back to catch a hand that he had felt in the vicinity of his purse, dragging forth a lad of nine or ten wearing filthy clothes and a hat two sizes too large for him.

'What do we have here?' said Holmes.

'Wiggins!' shouted the leader, whose name was Alf. 'That's a foine way t'treat a gennelman who's givin' ye a free magic show!'

Holmes looked down his nose at Alf. 'Do you really think that I didn't see you signal to Wiggins here when you thought I'd be too busy to notice my purse being snatched?'

At least Alf did have the courtesy to look at his feet. 'Ye can't blame a feller for tryin', now can ye?' he said.

***

Over the next two weeks, Holmes spent more and more time with the boys in the mews. He had found that most all of the cases reported in the *Illustrated Police News* were monotonously straightforward, with the guilty party apprehended in the act, or confessing soon thereafter. So, he spent most of his days either in the British Museum, for which admission was free, indulging his many and varied interests and outlining a number of monographs on various subjects, or on long rambling walks throughout the City, committing details about the neighbourhoods he visited to his prodigious memory. However, as gratifying as those activities were, Holmes was still a young man and he missed the camaraderie of peers that he had enjoyed at University. By this time, all of the boys were calling him Wizard because of his skill at sleight-of-hand, which somewhat stroked his vanity, and he found himself looking forward to the time spent with them in the evenings.

Thus it was that he was dismayed upon arriving home on a Monday night to see a Black Maria blocking the archway on Montague Street leading to the mews. He pushed his way past it and found a group of peelers had the terrified boys bunched up against the wall at the end, and a rather large constable was slapping the darbies on Alf. Holmes noted that two boys were missing–Wiggins and Dickie. The police action was being supervised by two men; a fortyish fellow dressed in a frock coat and bow tie, accompanied by a smaller, rat-faced chap in a simple dark suit and a nondescript tie. Holmes approached the ratine fellow, whom he correctly identified as a police Inspector.

'What is the meaning of this?' Holmes asked, not importunely.

'And who might you be, and why should this concern you?' asked the rat-faced chap.

'My name is Sherlock Holmes, Inspector. And whether the actions of the police are lawful or illegitimate should always be of concern to any citizen.' He turned again to the other man. 'Has something happened to Dickie?'

The well-dressed gentleman frowned, regarding Holmes with an expression that questioned the younger man's right to make such an inquiry, then he decided to pose a question of his own. 'What makes you think I would know anything about this action.'

'Other than your propinquity to it, I rather doubt that Scotland Yard would dispatch an Inspector to look into the misfortunes of a common street urchin,' said Holmes.

The inspector cut in, 'You'll address his Lordship with proper respect.'

'Obviously, he's a peer, but since no one has bothered to introduce him, I'm unsure just how he should be addressed,' replied Holmes

The older man drew himself up so he stood tall. 'I am the Right Honourable Robert Thackery, the Lord Aldington. My son Richard has been missing since last evening. I have it on good authority that he has been seen in the company of this lot, and I wish to know if they have anything to do with his absence. I called Inspector Lestrade here to look into it.'

'I dinna know nuthink about it, Mr. 'Olmes,' shouted Alf. 'I swears!'

'A likely tale,' said Lestrade. 'We'll see if you stick to that line when we have you down at the Yard.'

'Mr. 'Olmes, I 'asn't seen Wiggins since yestidday, neither,' said Alf. 'And 'im and Dickie was t'gether when I last seed 'em.'

'Who is this Wiggins?' Lestrade asked.

'Another of the boys who frequent this mews,' Holmes said, 'One who does not have an affluent father to look out for him.'

'Then it must be this Wiggins person who has taken my son!' said Lord Aldington.

'Oh, do stop it!' said Holmes angrily. 'Wiggins is eight years old, the same as your son. Hardly a vicious kidnapper, what?'

'I don't like your tone, sir!' said Lord Aldington.

'I'm sure I don't care,' Holmes replied. 'Your Lordship,' he added.

Lestrade looked at a constable, indicating Holmes. 'Bring this one in, too,' he said.

The constable stepped toward Holmes, but the detective's aquiline glare froze him in his tracks. 'Please do come along, sir,' the policeman said after a moment. 'There's a good gentleman.'

Holmes strode boldly off toward the Black Maria.

***

Several hours later, Holmes and the boys were in Whitehall Place, having just been released from custody. Yellow halos surrounded the gaslights, illuminating the malodourous mist that had drifted from the nearby Thames. The redoubtable Lestrade had insisted on incarcerating Alf, more to placate Lord Aldington than anything else.

'Wot're we gonna do about Alf, Wizard?' said Jem, another of the older boys.

'That's Mr. Wizard to you,' replied Holmes, absently. 'And I don't know if there's anything we can do, other than find out what happened to Wiggins and Dickie. What can you tell me about them?'

'Well, we all knowed Dickie was a toff,' said Jem. 'He brung us vittles from 'ome 'n gave Alf some coin to let 'im 'ang round wit' us.'

'He and Wiggins were close?'

'I guess. Dickie liked to 'elp 'im black boots onna square.'

'I'll wager that went over just grand with his Lordship,' Holmes said sarcastically. 'Which square?'

'That'd be Bedford. By the cabstand.'

'Then the first step will be to talk to the cabmen tomorrow.'

***

Ten Steps from Baker Street

Number nine Bedford Square was a fine Georgian greystone house in the middle of the block on the south side. Sherlock Holmes, wearing his best (and only) set of dress clothes with his college tie, noticed that a fancy four-wheeler was parked in front—his Lordship had a caller.

Perhaps I should wait until the company has departed.

But no, the boys had been gone nearly two days by now, so every moment was precious. Holmes mounted the stoop and stood in front of the white wooden doorframe. He straightened his tie, checked to see that his newly acquired business cards were handy, then raised the door knocker and let it fall.

The door opened to reveal a liveried housemaid. She looked Holmes up and down and a slight wrinkling of her nose told him that he was found wanting.

He proffered his card. 'I would like a few moments of Lord Aldington's time.'

She removed a sterling salver from a side table and held it out. 'I'll see if his Lordship is taking callers.'

After Holmes surrendered his card, she closed the door again, discourteously leaving the up-and-coming detective standing on the porch. Holmes clasped his hands behind his back to wait—the time passed at the pace of a funeral march, as it generally does when one is waiting. He rocked back on his heels and stretched his neck, then turned and surveyed the street. Looking at the four-wheeler again, he noticed the crest on the door—*Or a fess Sable and in chief three torteaux*—the caller was another nobleman, then. He hadn't memorized Boutell, but the detective would retain the design in memory until he could consult him in the reading room of the British Museum later. A slight sound behind him caused him to wheel around in time to face the door again as it opened, once again revealing the disapproving maid.

'What shall I say your visit concerns?'

'It's about Master Richard,' Holmes replied, and the door closed again.

After a longer wait than the first time, the door opened again. 'His Lordship regrets that he is occupied with another matter...' the maid began,

More important than the whereabouts of his missing son?

'... but the Lady Aldington will see you momentarily. Follow me, please.'

She led Holmes to a bright room overlooking the square, which featured ornamental plaster decorations and an oval plaque on the chimney breast engraved with the figure of knight. The chimneypieces were of gleaming white marble decorated with Ionic capitals and coloured marble shafts. Holmes was no stranger to such finery

8

but found it impressive nonetheless. As the maid closed the door behind him without inviting him to sit, he looked up to view a finely ornamented ceiling.

A short time later ,the door opened again and a youngish woman entered, wearing a one-piece white housedress with long sleeves and a high neck, adorned with a chintz pattern, and gave the detective an anxious look.

Apparently, Lord Aldington was not above a little cradle-robbing when he chose a wife.

'I am Winona Thackery. I'm told you have news of my son Richard's whereabouts.'

'I apologize for taking you from your noble caller, my Lady,' Holmes answered, "and I'm sorry that you were misled."

Lady Aldington looked down at the rug. She said, "Lord Banleigh is a family friend. He's come to aid us in finding Richard."

'That is my intention as well. I told your maid that I wished to speak with his lordship about it. Apparently, Richard was in the company of a lad of my acquaintance when he went missing, whom I intend to seek.'

She looked expectant once more. 'You're a policeman, then, Mr. Holmes.'

'No ma'am, I am a consulting detective.' She looked puzzled, but Holmes continued speaking, to forestall questions that he did not want to answer. 'I was hoping that you had a photograph of Richard that you could lend me to aid in my endeavours. I expect that if I am successful in finding my young friend, I might locate your boy as well.'

'I see,' she said, although it was evident in her expression that she did not. She brought her hands upward and removed a gold locket from her neck. 'I had this made when Richard was born,' she said. 'I replace the picture inside every year on his birthday.' She opened it to show Holmes the face of a smiling boy with dark hair whom he immediately recognized as Dickie. Closing it, she handed it to the detective, saying, 'I am putting a great deal of trust in you, a young man whom I do not know, but such is the depth of a mother's love for her son.'

'I shall return it to you along with your son, Madam,' Holmes said, slipping it into a pocket.

At least I sincerely hope that I shall.

'See that you do,' she replied, opening the door to usher Holmes into the hall.

A rumble of footsteps and loud male voices caused Holmes to glance left, where he saw two gentlemen approaching. One was Lord Aldington, and the other was an older man in rich garments, likely Lord Banleigh, the owner of the four-wheeler out front.

'I shall talk to Sir Edmund straightaway,' he was saying, 'and tell him to build a fire under that Lestrade fellow to bring this affair to a successful conclusion.'

Aldington looked up and noticed Holmes.

'You!' he snarled. 'What are you doing here?'

Lady Aldington began, 'Mr. Holmes has come to help…'

Holmes raised his voice to speak over her. 'Your Lordship, I am happy to see you at last. I just wanted to say that the way I spoke to you the other evening was unpardonable, and I wanted to offer my sincerest apology. I can only offer the poor excuse that I was worried about my young friend, as you are for your boy.'

Lord Banleigh regarded Holmes in a peculiar manner– the detective wasn't sure whether his look was one of disdain or apprehensiveness. But he was certain that Aldington's expression was one of contempt.

'Get out!' Aldington grated. 'And darken my doorway no more!'

Holmes glanced at her ladyship: *Please say nothing of the locket,* his eyes said.

She understood–she said naught.

Eschewing the assistance of the maid, the detective found his own way out. Walking to the cabstand on the corner of Bloomsbury Street, he approached a group of three cabbies assembled on the pavement, awaiting a fare.

'Cab, sir?' asked one.

'No.' Holmes withdrew the locket from his pocket. 'I wanted to ask you about a boy who is sometimes a bootblack here, and his mate.' He extended the hand holding the open locket. 'This boy. They seem to have gone missing.'

One of the remaining two cabmen looked away from the detective.

Holmes addressed the diffident cabbie. 'You, sir. Have you seen them?'

'Nossir, I hain't.' The man's tone indicated that Holmes would get no more from him with red-hot tongs.

'Anyone?'

No answer.

Holmes reached into his pocket, secured his purse, and extracted one of his precious remaining sovereigns. Holding it between thumb and forefinger so the gold glinted in the sunlight, he said, 'Are you certain, now? Does anyone know anything that could help me to find these lads?'

The cabbie who had looked away returned his gaze to the coin and licked his lips, but remained reticent. Another, an older fellow, spoke up. 'As much as I'd like to take yer money, sorr, I won't lie t'ye. That bootblack is here sometimes, but not always. I t'ink he hangs out wit' a gang in da mews. T'other boy is Lord Aldington's son. That's all I knows.'

Trying not to allow the disappointment to show on his face, Holmes muttered an oath under his breath as he extended the coin to the man who spoke up. 'Share that with your mates,' he said, then walked back to his digs.

***

Holmes spent the afternoon in his flat, sitting, smoking, and ruminating on the many fates that might have befallen the boys.

That cabbie knows something, and so does Lord Banleigh. But how can I find out what? The cabbie has already stonewalled me, and Banleigh would surely expel me from his home as soon as he laid eyes on me.

In the morning, Holmes went to the British Museum to consult *Burke's Peerage*. He found that Lord Banleigh was Alexander Salton Junior. Salton's father was the recipient of a tiny earldom in Stafford from William IV, and Alexander inherited the title when his father died. It would pass on to his son as well, but Salton was currently unwed.

Unusual that, for a man of thirty-five years.

Walking back to Montague Street, Holmes formulated a plan. It was a poor one at best, but it would have to serve until something better revealed itself. He entered the mews and saw the boys gathered at their accustomed place at the rear, but no sounds of exuberance or horseplay came to his ears. The lot simply stood with gloomy faces as Holmes approached.

'Why so glum, lads?' Holmes said.

'Wot're youse, daft?' cried Cal. 'Alf's in the lockup, Dickie and Wiggins are gone, and da peelers are just waiting fer da rest o' us to put one foot out o' line so's they can put us away too. How're we supposed ta be?'

A rumble of assent arose from the rest of the boys.

'What if I told you that you could help me put all of that right?' asked Holmes. 'Are you game?'

'Owinell's we supposed ta do that?'

'Help me find our lost lambs. Do as I tell you and we'll soon have Wiggins and Dickie back, and Alf, too. I ask you again, are you game?'

'Wot is it dat youse want us to do?' asked Cal.

***

For the next few days, Holmes crouched in his Montague Street attic like a spider in the centre of its web, consuming endless pots of coffee and copious amounts of black shag tobacco, ruminating about the possible fate of the missing young men. Because of the manner in which Lord Banleigh had looked at him during their encounter in Lord Aldington's residence, Holmes suspected that Salton knew something about Dickie's disappearance. He instructed the boys to follow the cabbie and Salton everywhere they went and to report to him at least three times a day. That presented difficulty to some of the lads because they could neither read nor write, but others had developed prodigious memories to compensate for that deficiency. Holmes had suggested that they work in pairs, for safety.

The fledgling detective had spent some of his precious coin on several of Edward Stanton's highly detailed maps of London, which he tacked up on the angled roof of his attic, and he also purchased a set of coloured push pins from the stationer's—red for his Lordship and blue for the cabbie. Each time a pair of boys reported in with the list of places visited by either man, he decorated his maps with pins showing the locations they visited.

For the third day in a row, the cabbie had gone to an address on Rathbone Street—a squalid slum. And Holmes knew the man lived elsewhere. Later, another team reported that Lord Banleigh had visited the same address.

Hmmm! Very interesting indeed!

Holmes was in Rathbone Street in an hour. Dusk was falling, and the sky had clouded over, a fine rain filled the air. The cobblestones glistened orange in the light from the setting sun, accentuating the odours of poverty and deprivation—sour cooking smells intermingling with decaying garbage, and animal and human waste. The buildings here were built of brick during the previous century to provide flats for the middle-class, but the area had currently fallen on hard times—most of the three- and four-storey structures now housed twice as many as originally intended. The few inhabitants out on the street this damp afternoon barely gave Holmes more than a sidelong glance, for he had dressed in his oldest clothing and had a woollen fore-and-aft cap crammed on his head against the weather. He spied a pair of his juvenile aides-de-camp lurking in an alleyway where they could keep a close eye on number 48, the residence of interest to the cabbie and his lordship.

Holmes extracted a flask from his jacket pocket, unscrewed the cap and took a pull, then spat it out so as not to befuddle his senses, pouring the rest down the front of his clothes so he reeked to high heaven of gin. His plan was rudimentary —enter the premises and discover if the boys were there. If someone caught him at it, they would simply assume he was a drunk who had wandered in from the street.

Crossing the road, he opened the door to number 48 and found a dingy, unlit hallway. It was cooler in here and the smells of the street were intensified, making his eyes water. He'd brought no light, so he left the door ajar for the light from outside to trickle in, barely illuminating the hall. The walls had been papered years ago—now the mouldy covering peeled, exposing cracks and holes in the plaster beneath. Doors on either side of the hallway presumably gave access to ground floor flats and another door at the end was adjacent to a flight of dilapidated steps leading up. He paused, not having any reason to choose one way over another until he noted the brightness of the brass knob on the rear door and the scratches on the floor that might indicate it had seen frequent use of late. Sewer smells came welling up as he pulled the door open onto a flight of ramshackle stairs descending to a dank basement.

A lantern hung on a hook just inside the door. Holmes removed it and searched through his pockets for his vesta case, removed a match and struck it on the wall to light it. Holding it high in his right hand, he started down the stairs, grasping the railing with his left.

The river smells became stronger as he went down, the yellow aura of the lantern gradually expanding to reveal more and more of the subterranean chamber—it was strewn with trash, sections of the floor undulating as squealing marked the flight of the resident rats from the encroaching light. Holmes froze for a moment, surveying the floor, his sharp eyes picking out a pathway where someone had walked through the detritus leading from the stairs to a doorway in the opposite wall.

Hoping fervently that the ratine denizens dreaded him more than he feared them, Holmes hopped off the stairs and made his way across the room. The light from his lantern glinted from a padlock hanging from a hasp affixed to the door.

Should I unlock it, or just bash it off, then?

Deciding on caution rather than mayhem, Holmes fished a set of lockpicks from a pocket and had it open in a minute. He pushed the door inward and illuminated a stone room made up as a bed chamber of sorts, holding a bare mattress, a low table next to it and a battered armoire against a wall. A row of wooden boxes about two feet square stood at the base of the opposite wall, metal screens closing off the fronts of them. Behind the screen, his light glanced off dirty white flesh. A boy!

He set his lantern on an upended barrel, and stepped over to the cage, looking for a tool to strike off the lock. A brick from the mess on the floor came to hand, and in a moment the detective was opening the door and kneeling above the naked body of the lad. It was Wiggins, all right, passed out. A faint odour of chloroform suggested the cause. He was filthy and cold, but Holmes did detect a slight rise and fall of his chest.

Still alive, then, thank fortune.

The boy's eyes snapped open, and a snarl appeared on his face as he cocked his arm back to strike, apparently not recognizing his rescuer. The detective had no trouble fending off the feeble blow, yet his heart swelled at the bravery of the lad who attempted to deliver it, fighting to the last.

'It's me, Wiggins!'

'Cor! Wizard?'

As Holmes reached into the cage to take the lad under the armpits, he heard a scraping sound behind him. Wiggins's eyes widened in surprise and fear. Holmes wheeled around to face this new threat, but was at a decided disadvantage kneeling on the floor. The figure of a man loomed over him and a cudgel descended. The detective threw up his arms to block the blow, which might have saved his life. Pain exploded in his forehead and white light flashed before his eyes, then a pall of darkness fell.

***

After Holmes had disappeared inside number 48, the two boys lurking in the alley across the street watched in dismay as a growler pulled up in front of the building, the door opened and the passenger disembarked. Standing on the pavement, he apparently noticed the open door, so he beckoned to the driver, who got down, and the two men went inside.

'Blimey!' said Robbie, the younger of the pair. ''They'll catch the wizard fer sure!'

Stubbing out his cigarette and giving his partner a none-too-gentle poke in the ribs, Callum, the older lad, ordered, 'Go! Tell Jem to wait fer me to report back.'

Robbie ran off into the rain while Cal kept watch. A few minutes later, the door to the house opened again and the men appeared. One bore the limp body of a man over his shoulders, while the other clutched a struggling boy by the arm. The prisoner, whom Cal recognized as Wiggins, was crying for help, but unfortunately, that would do him no good at all in this neighbourhood.

The fellow carrying Holmes loaded him into the four-wheeler, then took Wiggins from his partner, delivering him a savage backhand across the face. Cal heard the crack of the blow in his hiding place across the road. He ached to burst from his hiding place and go to his friend's aid, but he knew he could do nothing against two grown men. Wiggins's yelps ceased, replaced by the muted sound of weeping.

The man thrust the boy into the carriage then followed, shutting the door. The cabbie climbed up to his perch in front, reaching for his whip to start the horse on his way.

As the cab lurched off, Cal made an instant decision. Bending low, he ran across the street, grabbed on to the back of the growler, and hauled himself up on a small platform at the back for carrying luggage, which extended about eighteen inches from the body of the carriage. It had a metal rail that ran round the perimeter as a place to tie off ropes to secure bags. Cal wrapped his hands around the rail and held on for dear life, hoping it was sufficiently strong to hold him if the driver hit a bump hard enough to bounce him off. He crouched low so he wouldn't be seen by the occupants through the small window in the back of the cab.

The cab went north, progressing to wider, more well-travelled streets. Cal was aware that he stuck out like a sore toe riding on the luggage platform, but darkness had fallen and the rain was keeping the crowds down—the few who were braving the streets were too concerned with their own affairs to point out an unwanted passenger to the driver. Pedestrians became scarcer as they made their way into the suburbs, then out into the countryside toward Harrow. Cal was not well-travelled and had only a hazy idea of where he was, but he knew the roads the driver had taken and could get himself back home, he was sure.

After what seemed like days to Cal but was only hours, the cab stopped in front of a gate on the roadside. Cal surmised that the driver would put up his reins in preparation to descend to manage entry, or someone would be waiting to open it— either way, Cal's chances of being seen were excellent, so he hopped off the platform and scurried into the weeds on the opposite side of the road. The driver chose the former option. As he returned to his perch on the growler, Cal debated climbing on again, but the road beyond the gate was a bumpy two-track, so the carriage couldn't go very fast. He decided to follow on foot.

The carriage proceeded about another quarter mile before arriving in a yard with a ramshackle farmhouse on one side and a barn on the other. A loud squealing arose from a pen adjacent to the barn as the carriage entered the yard.

Cal peered through the foliage of a nearby clump of bushes as the driver and the passenger disembarked from the carriage, and a man and a woman came from the house to meet them. The weakly struggling boy was carried into the house by the passenger, while Holmes, still unmoving, was dragged into the barn by the couple from the house. Cal had to wait nearly fifteen minutes before they emerged again and re-entered the farm house.

***

Holmes came back to the world with a searing pain in his shoulders that burned along a line to his spine, ran upwards into his neck and down his legs. His arms were fully extended and loops of rope around his wrists suspended him in mid-air. It was pitch black, but the draughts flowing around him told him that the walls of his prison were open to the outside. He could breathe only with difficulty--the redolence of straw and animal waste filled his nostrils (pigs, if he was not mistaken)—he was in a barn! His ankles were tied together, with his toes barely in contact with a surface—if he extended them, he could raise himself slightly to make it easier to breathe. He noticed that the thing beneath his feet wobbled slightly when he touched it with his toes. He had to be careful not to tip it over, for he would be in a really bad way if it wasn't there.

His mouth was full of something—cloth, he thought, held in by a strip of material tied behind his neck. He couldn't even scream for help! Someone had surely put him in a fine pickle.

My career as a consulting detective may be over before it has properly begun!

He heard a scraping noise, followed by approaching footsteps, then a voice said, 'Cor, Wizard! Yer in a pretty kettle of fish now, aintcha?'

Holmes's heart leapt as he recognized the voice. Cal!

'I'll get youse down from there. It'll take a few minutes, tho.'

***

16

It was so dark in the barn that Cal couldn't even make out Holmes's features. He could discern that the detective hung by ropes tied to a beam that ran between two posts. A small barrel sat beneath his bound feet. The only way that the boy could figure to free the trapped man was to shinny up a post and crawl across the beam to where the rope was tied, and cut it with the clasp knife that he carried. However, he'd have to cut the ropes one at a time, and when the first one released, all of Holmes's weight would suddenly be thrust hard on the other bound arm, possibly putting the shoulder out of joint. That would certainly render the detective useless as a partner to help rescue Wiggins.

Cal rolled the barrel from beneath Holmes's feet and the detective's body sagged further toward the floor as he struggled futilely against the ropes. The boy stood on the barrel and reached up to remove the cloth round his mouth. Holmes spat out the gag in his mouth and croaked, 'Barrel... can't breathe...'

Cal hopped off the cask and rolled it back so Holmes could get his feet on it once more. The detective straightened up and greedily sucked in air until he was able to speak once more.

'People who did this... must have ladder,' Holmes said. 'Find it.'

After a protracted search, Cal stumbled across the ladder in a stall in another room next to a second stall containing a horse. He dragged it over to where Holmes hung.

'Put the top against the beam, between my hands,' said Holmes. 'That's right. Now cut the rope on my feet, and get them on a rung.'

Once Cal had done that, Holmes was able to take the weight from his arms, and the agile street boy could scamper up the pole and free Holmes's right wrist. The ladder rocked precariously as the detective struggled to maintain his balance, but it did not tip over. Cal reached across to cut the rope around Holmes's other wrist, and this time the ladder did tumble sidewise, but it had the fortunate effect of breaking the detective's fall.

Holmes sat on the floor for nearly five minutes, rubbing the life back into his limbs, before arduously regaining his feet.

'I'm afraid I may be of little use if it comes to a fight,' he said.

'Mebee we should just run,' Cal replied. 'They don't know yer loose yet.'

But they still have poor Wiggins, don't they?' said Holmes. Cal nodded. 'Who knows what they might do with him, especially if the miscreants found out I've escaped them.'

'There's nuthin fer it then but to go in and get him,' allowed Cal.

Holmes stepped to the barn door and peered outside. 'D__n! The growler is gone! It will be a long walk back to London.'

'We've got a hoss,' the boy suggested.

Holmes looked sourly at the old swaybacked plug of a plough horse. 'I suppose he could be ridden, but I'll wager that he hasn't run in years. A child could overtake him.'

'Well, I'll have to just not let 'em hear me when I go inside.'

Holmes thought for a moment. 'Perhaps a diversion would help.'

'Can you think of one?'

Looking about the old barn, Holmes answered, 'As a matter of fact, I can.'

***

Cal crept up the ramshackle stairs in the farmhouse, carefully stepping on the sides of the treads near the wall so they didn't creak. He'd searched the downstairs rooms to no avail and since the house had no basement, an upstairs bedroom was the only place that Wiggins could be. He had no light, but a pale moon shone through a window at the end of a hall that ran to the left from the top of the steps, revealing two doors facing each other halfway down. Cal assumed that the farmer and his wife slept in one of the rooms, so Wiggins would likely be in the other. He looked about for a place to hide until Holmes had done his part. All he could find was a trunk under the window. He sidled down to it—it wasn't locked. The musty odour that rolled out when he opened it nearly took his breath away. It was full of old blankets, cloaks and other household rags. Having no place to put the stuff if he removed it, he closed it again and pushed the entire chest forward away from the wall far enough to crouch behind it. It was a poor hiding place, but he hoped that the farm couple would have other things on their minds when they exited their bedroom and would fail to notice him.

He didn't have long to wait. The sky outside the window assumed an orange glow, the smell of smoke came to his nostrils, and a cry rang out from below.

'Fire! Fire!'

Thirty seconds passed, and the door on the right burst open. The farmer tumbled out bare-chested, struggling to get his arms into his galluses, the old lady in her nightgown close behind. They tore straight for the stairs, never even glancing Cal's way. As soon as they disappeared, Cal ran to the closed door on the opposite side of

18

the hall and grabbed the doorknob. Locked! He pushed on the door and found it as solid as the oak tree it was made from. He muttered imprecations as he vainly tried to think of a way to get inside. Then he heard the sobs coming from the open door behind him.

Wheeling around, he dashed into the couple's bedroom. The furnishings were black silhouettes in the scant moonlight that filtered in through the room's only window, but the crying seemed to come from the foot of the bed. He blundered over there and found a wooden cage.

'Wiggins?'

'Who's there?'

'It's Cal.'

'Cal! Get me out of here!' Another voice spoke up. 'Me too!'

'Dickie! Is that you?'

Cal fumbled around and found the latch on the cage door, but it was held shut with a padlock. He yanked on the bars and found the door too difficult to break, so he cast about looking for something to bust the lock. A fireplace across from the bed was cold in July, but a poker stood in a rack adjacent to it. He grabbed it, jammed the point in the hasp of the lock, threw all of his weight on it, levering it against the body of the cage. The wood crackled as the entire latch mechanism separated from the door. Seconds later, two bare-bummed boys were free.

'C'mon mates, let's go!' Cal cried. There was no time to find the boys' clothes. Getting them covered would have to wait until they were out of danger.

They stumbled down the stairs and out the front door. The air was filled with frantic squeals and the yard was lit by the orange glow of the blazing fire in the barn. The farmer and his wife were dodging panicked pigs while frantically trying to beat the conflagration out with tarpaulins, never giving the boys as much as a glance. Cal ordered Wiggins and Dickie to link hands, then led them round to the back of the house where Holmes awaited with the old plough horse. The detective hoisted the boys up on the animal's back, took hold of the rope round his neck and coaxed him off into the brush.

***

Lady Aldington fainted dead away in her sitting room at the sight of Sherlock Holmes carrying her sleeping son in his arms. His Lordship was summoned from his club, and when he arrived at home, he promptly sent the butler to wire Scotland Yard to arrest Holmes for kidnapping his son. However, by the time Lestrade arrived, Dickie had awakened and convinced his father who the actual culprit was.

***

Lestrade banged on the door of an elegant Mayfair townhouse and showed his warrant card to the butler who answered. Holmes and Lord Aldington stood behind him on the stoop.

'I'll see if his lordship is taking callers.'

'He'll see me,' the inspector said, pushing past him.

Aldington led the way to an upstairs study. Lestrade lay a hand on his shoulder as he reached for the doorknob. 'Better allow me, my lord.'

The inspector threw open the door and the three men entered. Alexander Salton, Lord Banleigh, tipped over a tray table containing his brandy as he jumped to his feet.

'What is the meaning of this!'

'My Lord, I'm afraid you'll have to come with me,' said Lestrade.

'And why must I do that?' sneered the peer.

Before Lestrade could reply, Holmes declared with satisfaction, 'Because he's arresting you for kidnapping children, you blackguard!'

***

Suicide of a Peer of the Realm

The body of the Rt. Hon. Alexander Salton, the 2nd Earl of Banleigh, was found this morning in his Mayfair townhouse by his major domo, Mr. Rupert Headstone. The cause of death was apparently a bullet wound to the left temple. A pistol was found lying close to the corpse, and identified as belonging to Lord Banleigh. The Illustrated Police News has previously reported on this shameful affair. Banleigh was implicated as the ringleader of a scheme to kidnap homeless boys from

20

the streets of London and sell them to the owners of rural establishments as unpaid servants.

Banleigh's downfall came due to the admirable efforts of Insp. G. Lestrade of Scotland Yard, after the peer had engineered the kidnapping of Master Richard Thackery, the minor son of the Rt. Honorable Robt. Thackery, Lord Aldington, ostensibly a friend of Banleigh's. In addition, Mr. Elvin Carmichael, a cab driver, Mr. Dudley Johnston, and Sir Frederick Stokes, whom Banleigh knew from the Bagatelle Card Club, were also allegedly involved in the scheme. Mr. and Mrs. Bennett Howell, farmers from Harrow who allegedly offered the boys for sale to other agrarians, gave evidence against Banleigh in police court, which resulted in his being bound over to the grand jury in the Assizes, who in turn issued a true bill of indictment against him. Her Majesty the Queen was in the process of appointing a Lord High Steward so that Banleigh could be tried at an upcoming session of the House of Lords when word of his demise reached the palace...

***

The article in the *The Illustrated Police News* that he had been reading aloud to the boys in the Mews continued on, but Holmes folded the paper and put it down by his side because he realized he was losing his audience. Alf, who had been released from gaol with apologies from Lord Aldington, was present, as was Cal, his second. Cal was the hero of the hour, after Holmes had told the boys of his exploits in rescuing himself and Wiggins. Wiggins was present as well but much subdued—Holmes felt sure the boy could get past the horrible things he'd experienced if he had the support of his friends, which the detective intended to see to. Absent was Dickie, the young Master Thackery, whose father had shipped him off to public school, deciding that his son had had quite enough of life on the streets, even though it was another peer who had victimized him.

'Cor, Wizard!' said Alf, 'they don't even give youse credit fer bringin' the b_____s to heel!'

'I asked them not to,' Holmes said. 'I don't care whether the public knows of my role in this affair or not, as long as Inspector Lestrade realizes that he's in my debt. And it won't hurt my fledgling career to have a peer of the realm beholden to me, either.'

Holmes paused, looking over the bright young faces arrayed before him. 'I promise you boys this,' he said, 'wherever I go in this endeavour of mine, you shall be at my side. Together we can accomplish much, moreso than we ever could separately. You lads are the ghosts of the City. You can go everywhere, see everything, overhear everyone. You shall become my unofficial police force. My methods and my intellect, coupled with your inimitable character and daring-do, can bring justice to rich and poor alike. Eh, Wiggins?'

Wiggins raised his head and met Holmes's smile with a forced one of his own. 'Whatever you say, Wizard.'

'That's Mr. Holmes, to you,' said the detective.

The Adventure of the Persistent Pugilist

After the singular and baffling affair at Lauriston Gardens, I had an occasion to reconsider my association with Sherlock Holmes, of whom I had learned was employed as a consulting detective and assistant to Scotland Yard. Holmes was gracious enough to allow me to participate in the investigation and observe his methods, and he brought the perpetrator to heel in our very sitting room at 221b Baker Street. Whilst the investigation was in progress, I experienced a thrilling reintroduction to an active lifestyle, which I had eschewed since my return as a convalescent from Afghanistan, and I must say that I found it most invigorating. However, I had not

reckoned with the subsequent sequalae that such exertions would bring.

Thus, it was on Monday, March 7 of 1881, I awoke in a bed of pain in the wee hours of the morning, my wounded shoulder throbbing as if that Jezail bullet I received at Maiwand was still in place, with aches in every joint, and a debilitating headache as well. I tried to roll over and retreat once more to the blissful solace of sleep, but that simply was not to be. I dragged myself into the sitting room. It was a mild night, so the windows overlooking Baker Street were thrown open wide. Of course, Holmes was not present—doubtless he was snug in his bed. I went to the sideboard and poured myself a stiff whisky, followed by a splash of soda from the gasogene. Then I sank into a comfortable chair to sip my drink and reflect on the probable reason for my sudden infirmity.

I have told elsewhere of my misadventures as an Army surgeon in Afghanistan and India. I had first-hand knowledge of the damage that enteric fever could do to a body, but during the thrills of last week's chase, I had forgotten that my Army doctors had informed me that my recovery was apt to be protracted, and that I should refrain from sustained physical activity and mental strain for many months. But I had been feeling so much better of late that I neglected the doctors' prescriptions. Now, I was likely paying for my recent lack of attention to my health.

The whisky worked its magic however, and in a little while I was feeling nearly human again, when suddenly there arose a commotion at the downstairs door.

I struggled out of the soft chair and went to the window, where I beheld a street Arab, pounding on our door.

'I say!' I shouted from the window. 'What is the meaning of this?'

'Doctor Watson?', the lad yelled. 'Mr. 'Olmes wants youse to meet 'im at Davies Street and Brooks Mews!'

I was incredulous. 'What? At this infernal hour?'

' 'E sez 'e needs youse, Doctor. He told me to say to youse, "Come at once!"'

The unbridled cheek of the fellow! Come at once? Really? It was an open question whether I would even be able to dress myself, never mind hieing off all over London to satisfy Holmes' peremptory demand.

The boy was lingering at the door, so I tossed him a tanner for his trouble. My earlier pains had ameliorated somewhat, but I was still by no means in the pink. The thought of struggling into my clothes and venturing into the street to find a cab at this hour was disagreeable, to say the least. I flopped back into my chair.

Then the pangs of guilt began to assail me. Perhaps Holmes was in trouble, and had no one else to turn to for aid. One of the things that had attracted us as to share the same abode was that neither of us had family in the City. And Holmes had told me how much he appreciated my assistance with the murders of Drebber and Stangerson, even though I thought my contribution to the solution was minimal, if not non-existent.

The long and the short of it was that, fifteen minutes later, I found myself walking toward Marylebone Road, a major thoroughfare, where I would be much more likely to find a cab at this hour than in Baker Street. Brooks Mews off Davies Street was only about a mile away towards the centre city, but walking such a distance in my present condition was out of the question. I was in luck—I found a cabbie in Marylebone Road who was either starving or an incontrovertible optimist, who agreed to take me to Holmes.

The ride was a rapid one, clattering through London's empty thoroughfares. Davies Street was just off Grosvenor Square, one of the toniest areas in all of London. As I exited the hansom in the yellow glow of the gas lamps, I noticed a group of men huddled just inside the mews, seemingly studying the pavement with rapt attention. Two of them were constables, recognisable by their tall helmets, and one was shining a bullseye lantern into the mews. I also thought I recognized that ferret-like fellow Inspector Lestrade, who had visited Holmes several times at 221b. I handed the cabbie one and six and approached the group, then I saw that another man kneeling on the cobblestones a little way beyond them. It was Sherlock Holmes, intensively examining the prostrate form of a man.

'Here now!' exclaimed Lestrade as I neared, moving to block my access to the scene. Holmes turned his head and saw me.

'Watson!' he cried, springing to his feet, 'How very good of you to come, old fellow!'

Lestrade moved aside to allow me to pass.

Holmes' obvious delectation at my presence went a long way towards expunging my earlier rancour about his peremptory summons. 'What has happened here?' I inquired.

'That is what I trust you can help me to ascertain,' said Holmes.

I looked down at the unfortunate chap splayed out on the pavement, obviously dead. He was a man in his prime, about Holmes' size, and his frock coat, waistcoat and ascot identified him as a gentleman, as did the crumpled Bowler hat lying just a few feet away from him. The dishevelled state of his clothing, coupled with the bruises and dried blood on his face, indicated that he had taken a terrific beating.

'What would you like me to do?' I asked Holmes.

'Please examine this gentleman, and tell me what you think was the cause of his demise.'

I began to kneel, then asked, 'I should have thought you had already done so.'

'I have, but I am not a medical man. I want to see if your deductions agree with those of mine.'

I sank to the pavement and began my examination with the chap's face. 'He was battered while alive,' I said, 'as indicated by the extensive bruising.' I tried to close his staring eyes with my thumb and met some resistance. 'He seems to be in the early stages of *rigor mortis*, which would indicate that he died approximately two hours ago.' I wiggled his jaw to be certain. Noticing the dried blood in his blond hair, I raised his head from the cobblestones, and found a considerable depression in the back of his skull. 'This head trauma likely killed him, but I don't understand how he could have suffered such a deeply depressed fracture like this by hitting his head on level pavement.' I saw that Holmes was smiling at me now. 'I really cannot tell you any more without a proper autopsy.'

'That's very good, Watson, and it agrees with my observations and deductions perfectly. Constable, would you be so good as to hand me your lantern?' Holmes played the beam around in the mews, then out toward Davies Street. He continued, 'In addition to the excellent reason that Watson stated, it is obvious that the fellow did not fall here, as indicated by the position of his hat off to one side. Also, the hat would not be in such a disreputable state if it had simply fallen from his head. Someone picked it up, crushed it, and threw it where it now lies. And consider his jacket, bunched up behind him, as it would be if he was dragged by his feet.' Looking directly at Lestrade, he accused, 'Had you and your army not rushed into the mews before inspecting the pavement, we could doubtless follow the marks left when the victim was dragged to his present location, to ascertain the place at which the beating actually occurred. However, that should not prove to be an insurmountable difficulty.' Holmes moved back towards Davies Street, the beam of the lantern dancing before him as a herald. He held out his arm when the rest of us attempted to follow. 'Hold, gentlemen. Let us not make the same mistake twice.' Holmes walked a little way toward Brook Street whilst scanning the ground. 'Ha! Here is where our unfortunate pugilist met his doom!

Watson, come forth!' He shined the lantern on a crimson splash on the kerbstone, then handed it to me. 'Stand fast, all of you. The fight took place in the street. Watson, follow me with your light!'

Holmes whipped out a glass from his pocket and dropped to his knees, crawling about on the cobblestones like a child at play. I could see nothing special about the areas he scrutinized, but given the plethora of grunts, groans and ejaculations he uttered, he must have been learning much. Finally, he rose to his feet again. 'All right, Lestrade. You and your men may approach.' When the policemen arrived, Holmes clasped his hands behind his back and began lecturing them as if in a university hall.

'This was no common robbery, gentlemen, even though no valuables were found on the victim. My examination of the street revealed that two men engaged in fisticuffs there, and it is no difficult deduction that our man in the alley lost the match, likely when he was struck and fell to be mortally wounded by yon kerbstone.'

'Then the assailant drug his lordship into the mews to get the body out of sight,' offered Lestrade.

'His lordship?' I asked. 'Then you know who he is?'

'Yes,' said Holmes. 'The miscreants did an exceedingly poor job of searching the body. They left his calling cards in the inside pocket of his frock coat. He was Sir Aubrey Strongheart, Lord Redthorne, a sitting member of the House of Lords.'

It suddenly became clear why Lestrade had summoned Holmes to assist in the investigation.

'What do you mean, the miscreants?' asked Lestrade. 'I thought you said there was only two men that was involved in the fight?'

'That is correct, Inspector. But as many as five men, one of whom was the assailant, participated in dragging the unfortunate peer into the mews.'

'Then what were the other four doing while the fight was in progress,' I asked.

'Due to the disturbance of the signs in the mews by the police, there is no clear indication,' Holmes replied, 'but it is probably a safe assumption that they were watching from just inside.' Holmes pauses, then goes on, 'And there is one other confounding factor.'

'Which is?' I ask.

'Lord Redthorne has all of the characteristics of an accomplished boxer.' Holmes said. 'His ears are thickened, his nose and hands show signs that they had been broken in the past, and he has more missing teeth than I would expect for a man of his age.'

'Well, if he was a boxer, then how in Hades did he get beaten so badly?' asked Lestrade.

'Elementary, Inspector. The other fellow was the better fighter.' said Holmes.

***

In Baker Street, the morning sun was peeping over the rooftops, but the cobblestones were still enveloped in a cool shadow when we finally returned. Lestrade had summoned a police wagon to convey the hapless Sir Aubrey to the morgue, then instructed Holmes and I to go home. But rest was not in the cards for us. Our landlady, Mrs. Hudson, apparently heard us arrive, and delivered a fine, full English breakfast to our rooms before we scarcely had time to settle in. We were immersed in the midst of it when there came a rap upon the door, which quickly opened to admit Lestrade.

'I was just going by to see Lady Redthorne, and I wondered if you gents would care to come along,' he asked.

'Have a spot of breakfast first, Inspector,' said Holmes. 'To paraphrase Balthasar, bringing bad news may be your job, but there's no need to be in a rush about it.'

'It's the part of my job I care for the least, Mr. Holmes, and that's no lie,' the Inspector said.

So, it was about an hour later we found ourselves in Grosvenor Street, not far from Brooks Mews, seeking admittance to a venerable Georgian townhouse, Sir Aubrey's residence. A maidservant opened the door, and conveyed Lestrade's card to the lady of the house. She returned with the message that Lady Redthorne would see us, and conducted us to a parlour with broad windows overlooking the street, now bustling with early matutinal traffic. Shortly thereafter, Lady Redthorne appeared, resplendent in a purple and white morning dress with a broad skirt, however, with her hair still down.

There is no need to recount in detail the delivery of our sad message to Her Ladyship. Lestrade prevailed upon me for the duty, because as a doctor, I've had to do this sort of thing much more often than I would have liked. First comes the disbelief, then the grief emerges, and finally, the reluctant acceptance that a loved one will be seen no more. I must say that Lady Redthorne admirably controlled her emotions when she heard, although I was sure that would last only until our departure. She even had the equanimity to offer us coffee, which we politely declined.

Sherlock Holmes addressed her. 'My Lady,' he asked, 'did His Lordship have any enemies?'

She looked at Inspector Lestrade before answering, as if to ascertain that this brash young fellow did indeed have the authority to question her. When Lestrade nodded, she replied, 'Not really. Oh, there were a few in the Lords with whom he disagreed politically, but none of them would resort to physical violence against him.'

'Do you know where he was last evening?'

'Not precisely, but I would guess either at a boxing match or at his club. I'm sure someone there would know.'

'And his club was...'

'Lockerman's, in Saint James Street.'

'He was fond of prize-fighting?'

'Oh heavens, yes!', she exclaimed. 'You could almost say he was obsessed with it. He attended matches all over London, sometimes three or four a week.'

'And he was a boxer himself?'

'He was. He trained at the West London Boxing Club in the Strand.'

'Was he an accomplished pugilist?'

'He liked to think so. He won a few small purses at matches in the boxing clubs in the City, but the larger ones eluded him, likely because those matches drew the best fighters.' She paused, shaking her head. 'But I just cannot believe he would have fallen prey to a street tough, or even a gang of them. He was a better fighter than that.'

'Did he wager on boxing matches?' I asked.

She gave me a peculiar look, but answered, 'Of course he did, mostly at Lockerman's.'

'Do you know if he habitually took the same route home from Lockerman's every night?' Holmes asked.

'I don't know, but it wouldn't surprise me. Aubrey liked his little routines.' She suddenly stopped speaking, and her gaze rose to the ceiling.

'You've remembered something that might help us?' Holmes essayed.

'Possibly. I'm sorry to tell you that my husband had a most singular habit of challenging beggars and passers-by to fisticuffs.'

'Really!' I exclaimed.

'He wouldn't give a penny to a mendicant unless the man would fight him for it. But if the fellow gave him a good show, he would reward him handsomely.' She smiled. 'A few months ago, Aubrey came home with a glorious black eye. "Lucky shot from a fellow begging in the Haymarket! Gave him a guinea for his trouble", he told me.' She pulled a handkerchief from her bodice and dabbed at an errant tear running down her cheek. 'Silly old fool!'

After Holmes confirmed with Lestrade that the Inspector had no other questions for Lady Redthorne, we took our leave. On the street, Holmes said to me, 'Watson, you're looking a bit peaked. Why don't you go back to Baker Street and get some rest?'

'I say, Holmes, I'm fine...'

'I have a little investigating to do, best accomplished alone, old boy. If it would suit you, you can accompany me to Lockerman's this evening.'

'Rather!' I replied. Truth be told, I was feeling a little under the weather, and didn't not want to again find myself in a state where I was useless.

***

Upon returning to Baker Street for the second time that morning, I was surely beginning to feel the effects of my nocturnal excursion. I took to my bed and managed a few hours' slumber, arising in mid-afternoon. I rang Mrs. Hudson for tea, and the dear lady, probably taking note that I had gone without luncheon, included some biscuits and tea sandwiches on the tray. After such fortification, I picked up a new book by that excellent author Wilkie Collins to while away the remainder of the afternoon.

Abruptly, I heard heavy footsteps on the stairs, not at all like Holmes' rapid tread, so I braced myself for a knock upon the door. However, it did not come. Instead, the door sprang open and a most singular, disreputable-looking chap invaded the flat.

He was tall, a tatterdemalion in mismatched garments—a filthy brown jacket over a bright blue waistcoat, a white cotton shirt, burgundy knickers and hideous red-and-white striped knee socks, carrying a dirty tan cloth sack on his shoulder. And he affected the most curious headgear—a hat with a short, pointed brim in front that ballooned out in the rear like a cancerous growth, hanging halfway down his back. The blood came to my face as I sprang up in outrage against this untoward invasion of my home.

'See here, my good man, you cannot just waltz into a private residence...'

'Youse got any trash needs collectin', Guvnor?'

'I should say not! Take yourself back downstairs, go to the servant's entrance, and discuss it with the landlady!'

The fellow screwed up his disfigured face into a scowl, wheeled around and took two steps toward the door, then turned back to face me, removing his enormous hat.

'I must say that you are deucedly unkind to the tradespeople, Watson,' Sherlock Holmes said.

My knees became weak, and I collapsed backwards, falling heavily into my chair.

'Watson!' exclaimed Holmes, rushing to take me by the hands. 'I had no idea my little charade would affect you so! Please accept my humble apology.'

I was chagrined as well, displaying such pathetic weakness to my friend. 'I'm sorry too, Holmes. It's just that I'm not as strong as I would prefer to be, as yet.'

'And I should have realised that.' He stepped to the whisky cabinet to prepare a fortifying libation for me.

'Whatever are you doing in that outlandish attire?'

'Impersonating a venerable London dustman, old boy.'

'But why?'

'Most of our class know the dustman as the chap who visits our homes to carry away our trash. But many do not realize that he is also a tradesman, engaging in buying and selling the second-hand merchandise that he collects in his travels. Given that Brooks Mews and Davies Street is a rather genteel neighbourhood, I suspected that Sir Aubrey's assailant was not native to the area, and may have left something of himself behind. Thus, I was happy when I was able to purchase these from a dustman who serves that area.' He reached into his shoulder bag and withdrew another set of tattered clothing—trousers, shirt and coat. 'The dustman who had these said he collected them not far from Brooks Mews. While I cannot say for certain that our unknown aggressor wore them, I think it likely.' He held up the shirt, indicating some brownish spots. 'I am sure my reagent will show these to be bloodstains,' he said. Throwing the shirt and coat on the sofa, he unrolled the trousers and held the waistband to his own waist. Several inches of cloth ran out over his shoes. 'He was a large man, and as indicated by Sir Aubrey's condition, and a proficient boxer. In fact, I suspect he was a professional prize-fighter.'

'What is your next step?' I asked him.

'As I alluded earlier, I think a visit to Lockerman's is in order. That is, if you feel up to it.'

His remark stung, even though I knew he did not mean it in a deprecatory way. D__n my infirmities!

***

Lockerman's was a gentleman's club in St. James Street, situated in a grey stone building constructed early in this century. Unlike in many other such establishments, its members did not ascribe to a particular political stance, but rather were united by a love of gaming in all of its varied forms. Cards, backgammon, wagering on sporting contests and races were all engaged in. As non-members were generally required to be accompanied by a member to be granted admittance, Holmes prevailed upon Lestrade to accompany us, so his police credentials could open the doors.

We were admitted by a liveried manservant, who conducted us to the Club Secretary, Mr. Wystan York. York, a thickset man in his 40's, was attired in full evening dress and seemed to look down his nose at us, who were not. Holmes appeared not to notice.

After introductions were made, Holmes addressed him, 'Please convey my condolences to the members concerning the death of Sir Aubrey Strongheart. We came here with the hope of meeting some of his friends, who might shed light on some of his predilections, thus providing insight into this sad affair.'

'I really do not see how we can help you Mr. Holmes, even though it would be our fondest wish to do so,' responded York. 'It is my understanding that Sir Aubrey was waylaid by ruffians on his way home last night.'

'It may have been meant to appear so, Mr. York, but there are unresolved issues that a discussion with some of His Lordship's acquaintances might elucidate.'

At York's frown, Lestrade interjected, 'Scotland Yard would be grateful for any assistance the members could give us, sir.'

'Oh, very well,' said York. Puckering his lips, he told us, 'I suppose that Sir Aubrey's best mates were the Punters. I will ask them if they will meet with you in the Visitor's Lounge.'

'The Punters?' I inquired. 'What a curious sobriquet.'

'Just a group of fellows linked by similar interests,' said York dismissively. 'Walters will conduct you to the visitor's lounge.'

The Punters proved to be a motley band of gentlemen of similar age to Holmes and myself, causing me to wonder how Sir Aubrey, at least two decades older, came to be associated with them. The lot of them reeked with alcohol. Seeing them, I came to understand York's demeanour when discussing them.

'I was hoping that you could tell me of Sir Aubrey's personality and habits,' said Holmes, 'which might explain how he came to be targeted.'

'Oh, Aubs was young at heart, y'know' said Dinky Peckham, a moustachioed, blond fellow attired in an outlandish grey plaid suit and pink waistcoat. 'He found many of the older members much, much too stodgy for his tastes.'

'Rawther!' agreed Fido Drinkwater, who affected a brown long coat with broad, velvet lapels over a chequered vest and a polka-dotted ascot. 'Said keeping our company made him feel like a kid again, he did.'

The other two Punters were Reggie Searles, a burly, morose man with a large, bulbous nose and a square jaw, who wore unorthodox garments similar to the other two, but a size too small for him, and Braddey Bathgate, a short chap with a black moustache and a triangular beard, who eschewed jackets and waistcoats altogether. He was clad in black trousers, and a billowy black shirt with a high collar. He wore a remarkable gold medallion around his neck, comprising interlocking triangles with an Egyptian ankh in the centre.

'Did Sir Aubrey habitually follow the same route home from the club each evening?' Holmes asked.

'Yes,' said Bathgate.

'No,' said Peckham simultaneously.

Holmes raised an inquiring eyebrow. 'Which is it, gentlemen?'

Tossing a bad eye at Bathgate, Peckham continued, 'That is, I'm told he didn't.'

Bathgate said, 'Aubs had a lot of little 'abits. Way he fixed 'is pipe, that sort of thing. Said that a gentleman should 'ave order in his life. Never cared much for it, myself.'

I'll bet you didn't, I thought.

Looking at Searles, Holmes asked, 'Did you ever box with him? How good of a fighter was he?'

'Yeah, I fought 'im,' Searles replied. 'Once.'

'Beat you into the canvas too, didn't he?' Drinkwater chortled, earning a glare from Searles.

'I wouldn't say so,' rejoined Searles. 'He won all right, but I got my licks in too.'

'Laid you right out like a piece of meat, he did,' Drinkwater said.

'All in good fun, was it?' asked Holmes.

'Sure! Why wouldn't it be?' said Searles. 'What are you inferrin'?

'I'm not implying anything, Mr. Searles.' Holmes hesitated, then he asked, 'How many opponents would you think would be necessary to take Sir Aubrey down?'

'Now that would depend on the opponents, wouldn't it,' said Peckham.

'An astute observation, Mr. Peckham,' said Holmes. 'I was thinking along similar lines myself.'

'What do you mean?' asked Peckham.

'Just that it's hard to believe Sir Aubrey would be beaten so badly by random street toughs.'

Now the Punters were trading surreptitious glances. It was obvious even to me that something was being concealed here.

The room abruptly became quiet. It seemed that the Punters had mentally informed each other that silence was the order of the day.

'Very well,' said Holmes, abruptly. 'Lestrade, I think we've learned all that we're going to.'

We parted from Lestrade in front of the club, engaging separate cabs to Scotland Yard and Baker Street, respectively. As we rode through the streets, I turned to Holmes and said, 'It was them, wasn't it?

'Oh yes,' said Holmes. 'They didn't do it themselves, of course. They likely hired it out. But now, I must prove it.'

'How will you do that?'

'By finding the man who pounded Sir Aubrey into the cobblestones,' said Holmes.

***

Still feeling the effects of my exertions on this case, I slept late on Tuesday morning. Holmes had already breakfasted and was gone when I arose. I rang for breakfast and occupied myself with the papers for a while, and then turned back to Collins' excellent novel. Thus it was that I was feeling quite fit and relaxed when Holmes made his appearance close to supper time. He was dressed in rough clothes, but unlike yesterday, his face was his own, and by the expression on it, I knew that he hadn't any luck.

'I noticed in the paper this morning that the Belgian violinist Leopold Auer is playing at Willis's tonight,' he said incongruously. 'His playing is said to lack fire, but his technique is reportedly impeccable. Let us go and hear him for ourselves.'

I am not nearly as fond of the violin as Holmes is, but it was obvious that he needed someone to commiserate with about his lack of success, so I agreed to accompany him. Since Mrs. Hudson already had supper on, we chose to dine at home, but we still had plenty of time to don our evening dress and make the 8 p.m. performance in King Street.

All I can say about the performance is that I found that I preferred Holmes's playing to Auer's, which did indeed lack the emotion that my companion was able to evoke from the instrument. I told him so as we were exiting the venue, and he responded, 'My blushes, Watson!' However, I could tell that he was pleased by my remark.

Once we were on the street, Holmes said, 'It is still early, Watson, and it seems that we have much competition for cabs. Are you up for a walk across the square to the Red Lion for a pint?'

It was a mild evening, with a gentle breeze blowing from the east, which carried much of the ever-present effluvial miasma away from the City. Just right for a brisk walk.

'That would suit me down to the ground,' I told him.

So, we made our way into St. James's Square, intending to cut across the gardens to Duke of York Street. As we approached the statue of King Edward, a man stepped out of the bushes into the path, blocking our way. He was a very large fellow, and he stood balanced on the balls of his feet with his arms at his waist, his fists clenched.

'Yer Sherlock 'Olmes, ain'tcha,' he grated.

'I am. And who do I have the dubious honour of addressing?'

'Never you mind,' the man said. 'I'm 'ere t'tell ye t'quit meddlin' in things that don't concern ye.'

'This is most gratifying,' said Holmes. 'I have spent the entire day searching in vain for you, and now, here you are.'

'What do ye mean?'

'I mean that Inspector Lestrade of Scotland Yard would be delighted to have a conversation with you about the death of Sir Aubrey Strongheart.'

'I guess that means I have t'teach ye t'mind yer business,' the bruiser said, raising his fists in front of his face, and stalking towards us.

'Stay out of this, Watson,' Holmes said, handing me his topper and his stick, then taking a similar stance before advancing to meet the brute.

I wished mightily for my British Bull Dog, which was safely ensconced in my bureau at home, because it was totally inappropriate to carry it when in evening dress, and besides, I had no reason to think I would even need a revolver tonight. Holmes had told me previously that he had done considerable boxing while at university, but the ruffian advancing upon him must have weighed at least fifteen stone and was two heads taller, giving him a tremendous advantage in reach. I feared for the worst, and contemplated defying Holmes's injunction by making this fight two on one.

The big man stepped up and threw a jab that Holmes easily ducked, then a second and a third, which he similarly avoided. I could see that each fighter was taking the measure of the other. Suddenly, the giant uncorked a wicked roundhouse! Holmes let it whistle over his head, then dived inside, blocked a left uppercut, and landed several strong blows to the chest and the ribs. He worked his way to right, still punching, forcing his opponent to turn the same way to prevent Holmes from slipping behind him. His arms were so long that he couldn't effectively punch while Holmes was inside, but he could and did grab my friend by the shoulder and thrust him away, staggering him. Holmes just kept dancing backwards until he regained his footing.

'Is that all ye got?', the big man taunted, but I thought I detected a slight hitch in his step as he advanced.

Holmes did not reply. He went in again, ducking the jab and feinting, then inside once more, smashing a wicked right, followed by a crashing left to the ribs. Unfortunately, this time, the ensuing uppercut connected, knocking Holmes backward several feet and spilling him to the ground. I dropped Holmes' cane and hat and gripped my own stick tightly, ready to wade in and batter the colossus before he could reach the supine Holmes. But Holmes came up in a crouch like a Rugby player and rushed the giant, catching him just above the knees and taking him to the ground. Holmes smashed a hard right into the brute's face before rolling away and regaining his feet.

'Oi, below the belt, that's not fair!', the big man growled as he rose, blood running freely from his nose. He took his boxing stance once more.

Now the two fighters circled warily, each imbued with a healthy respect for the prowess of the other, seeking an opening. Suddenly the big man rushed and Holmes went to meet him, but sidestepped at the last second, letting the behemoth run by. Holmes pivoted like a ballet dancer and drove two hard rights into the man's back just above the belt line. Kidney punches! The giant's mouth opened in agony and he went to one knee, his arms outstretched like a supplicant at an altar. Seeing my chance, I stepped in and with both arms, brought the knob of my stick crashing down on his head. I heard the stout wood crack, then the titan was splayed across the pavement.

Holmes glared at me with fury in his eyes. 'I told you to stay out of this!' he snarled. 'I would have bested him!'

'This was no contest with rules,' I responded, panting. 'This was a battle. In battle, you seize whatever opportunities you have.'

My injured shoulder was burning like someone was thrusting a hot poker into the joint, and my breathing became ever more rapid, coming in fits and starts. I could feel the blood draining from my head as the air rippled grey in front of my eyes, then my knees abruptly buckled and everything went black.

***

When I regained consciousness, I found myself in my own bed in Baker Street. I tried to rise, but a cool hand pressed my forehead, pushing me back into bed. 'Nae, Doctor,' Mrs Hudson said. 'Tak' some time to find yersel' afore ye try t'rise. I'll bring Mister Holmes.'

I did as she said, because my abortive attempt had left me as weak as a child. I lay there a few moments until the door opened, and Holmes entered the room.

'Watson! Thank God! How are you, old man?'

'I've been better,' I admitted. I struggled to sit up again, but failed. 'Could you help me to sit up, please?'

Holmes came to my side and pushed me forward, placing a couple of pillows behind me as a prop. After ensuring that I was stable, he settled in the armchair next to my bed.

'Firstly,' he said, 'I must humbly apologise for snapping at you last evening. The only excuse I can offer is that my blood was up, and it is a poor one.'

'Perfectly understandable, old boy. And I do believe that you would have beaten that ruffian, but you may have been severely injured in the process. I simply could not have that.' I took a breath, then asked, 'So you have Sir Aubrey's murderer?'

'I think so, but unfortunately, we do not know for sure. That was a mighty blow you struck with that fine ash stick of yours, and the recipient of it has not yet awakened.' Holmes hesitated, then, 'Perhaps he will not ever awaken.'

I was immediately saddened. Even a soldier despairs when he must take a life.

Holmes, noticing my dismay, continued, 'You were right to do what you did. Even Lestrade has said so, and he said he will speak with the Crown prosecutors on your behalf. If the fellow regains consciousness, I have no proof it was he who beat Sir Aubrey unless he confesses. And even if he does, I am afraid that the actual instigators will go free.'

'You mean the Punters.' Holmes nodded.

'I feel sure it was they who engaged our boxer to fight Sir Aubrey. Remember, there was evidence that several men were in the mews that night, most probably at the time that the fight was going on, watching it.'

'But what motive would they have to murder Sir Aubrey?'

'None, I think.'

'What?'

'I suspect the entire incident was meant to be a joke,' Holmes said. 'The Punters obviously knew of Sir Aubrey's predilection for challenging street beggars, so they paid a professional prize fighter to dress as one and ask Sir Aubrey for alms as he returned home. What a surprise he'd have when he received the beating of his life! But no one imagined that he would be knocked down and crack his skull on a kerbstone. They were doubtless frantic when they realised what had happened, so they dragged his body into the mews, rifled his pockets to make it look like a robbery, and decamped.'

'So, they're not actually guilty of murder?'

'They would certainly not be if they had summoned help. Sir Aubrey may have even lived for a time after the injury, and perhaps he could have been rescued if in hospital. But when they chose to conceal the incident, they moved into the realm of paying for a homicide. Unfortunately, without the testimony of the prize-fighter, I cannot put them in that alley. And even if he testifies, it is his word against theirs. I am certain that the Punters would alibi each other.'

'So, what are you going to do?'

'I don't know. It is quite a three-pipe problem. Ask me in the morning.'

Holmes left to summon Mrs. Hudson to bring me tea and a bowl of milk toast. When I protested the insipid fare, she promised me a proper breakfast tomorrow. 'I have some lovely mutton kidneys on ice in the kitchen,' she told me.

***

38

I woke with the sun on Wednesday. Most of my symptoms had abated, but that changed when I stepped from my bedroom into the sitting room, into a purple haze of tobacco smoke that burned my eyes and seared my lungs. I found Holmes in the centre of the room with the furniture pushed back, perched on a cushion like the caterpillar in *Alice in Wonderland* on his mushroom, eyes closed, with his calabash dangling from his lips. My head spinning, I fought my way through the misplaced furniture to the windows overlooking Baker Street and threw them open, allowing God's air to cleanse our dwelling of the noxious fumes.

'Great Scott, Holmes! Are you actually trying to suffocate yourself?'

He opened his eyes and assumed a dour expression. 'I have found through experience that replacing the oxygen in my brain with nicotine stimulates creativity, allowing the solution of impenetrable conundrums.'

'Have you solved this one?'

'I believe so.'

'And what is your solution?'

'You are going to have one of the Punters confess to you,' he said.

***

So, I found myself that evening in Sackville Street near Piccadilly, in front of a fine old townhouse, the residence of Mr. Braddey Bathgate. Holmes had sent that wight a telegram at Lockerman's earlier in the day, which ran,

> *I know what you did to Sir Aubrey. If you will agree to meet with me alone at your residence at eight o'clock tonight, I will tell you how you can escape the consequences. If you chose to inform your associates of this message, I am afraid there is no hope for you.*
>
> *John H. Watson*

After I had read it, I asked Holmes what I should do when I met Bathgate.

'Just ask him to tell you what happened in Davies Street. I am sure he will cooperate.'

Ten Steps from Baker Street

I knocked on Bathgate's door, which swung open at the first impact of my fist. Strange. This was a genteel neighbourhood, but I still would not leave my door unlatched if I lived here. I stepped onto a black and white runner with an interlocking triangular pattern in a gaslit hallway, whose walls were sheathed with a greyish-black damask wall paper, all of which contributed to a dark, sombre atmosphere. As I advanced to a doorway on my right, my eyes were taken by a portrait adjacent to it. A round-faced woman with dark hair, wearing a shapeless black dress, stared out of it into my eyes, and I felt a shiver of dread run down my spine.

I rapped lightly on the door. 'Bathgate!' I called. 'Bathgate! It's Doctor Watson. Are you here?' Receiving no answer, I opened the door, and the smell of incense and old wood enveloped me. I entered the room.

It was a parlour overlooking the street, which was not visible because heavy maroon drapes masked the windows. The room was dark because the gas was low, but I could see that the decor was similar to that in the hallway. Floor-to-ceiling bookcases, interrupted by an open doorway, lined the wall to my left, and a large, carved desk lay at the far end of the room. Behind it, sprawled in a chair, was Bathgate. He was not moving!

As I hurried to him to check the pulse in his neck, I thought I heard a door slam in the rear of the house. I removed the medallion for easier access to the carotid artery, and confirmed that Bathgate was still in the realm of the living. I cast about until I spotted a decanter and glasses on a sideboard. The aroma that drifted up as I filled a glass told me it was brandy. I hurried to Bathgate, and put the glass to his lips. His eyes soon opened and he sputtered, the spirits running down into his beard.

'Man, what has happened to you?'

He grabbed my wrists so strongly that I winced, looking into my eyes with terror in his.

'We did it,' he said. 'We killed him! We thought it would be a lark.'

'What was it you did, Bathgate?'

'We 'ired Livermore to brace Aubs on his way 'ome. Thought it would be fun to see 'im get 'is comeuppance. Never thought the brute was going to murder 'im!'

I did not have to work very hard to worm the story out of him. It was just as Holmes said. The Punters hadn't intended that Sir Aubrey be killed, but they committed a criminal act by trying to cover up what they'd done.

Finally, I asked him the question to which I was not sure I wanted an answer.

'Why are you telling me all of this now?'

He grasped my wrists again and said fervently, 'Because I told 'im I would, Doctor! I told 'im I would, if he wouldn't 'aunt me no more!''

A furious pounding on the door to the street arose. 'This is Constable Warren! Open the door!'

I admitted the Constable, and prompted Bathgate to repeat his story, which he seemed most happy to do. The Constable assured me that he would take the miscreant to Scotland Yard, where Lestrade would see to rounding up the rest of the Punters.

***

I returned to Baker Street to find our sitting room empty. Was Holmes out? I could not imagine he had gone to bed, knowing the errand on which he had dispatched me. I knocked on the door to his bedroom. It opened, and I found myself staring into the smiling face of Sir Aubrey Strongheart!

***

Sometime later, I was ensconced in my chair with a quilt over my legs, a fine Havana and a glass of Holmes' best single malt. 'It's the least I can offer after the shock I gave you, Watson.'

'But it's marvellous, Holmes!' I said. 'How could you so flawlessly assume the identity of Sir Aubrey?'

'I believe I have told you that I have had some little training as an actor. And my performance was hardly flawless. It helped that Sir Aubrey was a public figure, with many images of him available to me so I could get the make-up right. However, I having never met the man, I was unaware of any little mannerisms he might have had, as well as of the timbre of his voice. However, I did not think that my impersonation had to be perfect to fool Mr. Bathgate. That proved to be so.'

'Whatever led you to choose him for this charade?'

'I noted his necklace when we met the Punter's at Lockerman's. It bore the symbol of Madam Blavatsky's Theosophical Society, which indicated that he might be vulnerable to spiritualism. I reasoned that if I could convince him that Sir Aubrey had come back from the other side to exact retribution, he might crack under the pressure. As you observed, I was correct.

'I arrived at Bathgate's townhouse shortly before you did,' Holmes continued, 'and let myself in through the front door. The wire I sent in your name ensured that Bathgate would be home, and given the air about him when we met at Lockerman's, probably inebriated. The look on his face when I found him in his parlour was priceless! I told him in a whispery voice that I would visit him nightly until he confessed to what he and the other Punters had done. He fainted into his chair, so I skedaddled before you arrived.'

'I thought I heard you close the back door on your way out.'

'Doubtless, you did. I met the good Constable Warren on my way home, so I directed him your way.'

I took a long draw on my cigar, followed by a sip of the excellent Islay malt. 'But you took a tremendous risk, Holmes What if Bathgate had seen through your disguise, or worse still, produced a pistol and shot you as a burglar?'

'The risk was a calculated one. Bathgate and the other Punters are cowards, preferring to bedevil a man from the shadows instead of facing him directly, so I was not too worried about bullets. And even if he had seen though my disguise, then he would know indubitably that I was on to them, and they would likely make a mistake that would bring them down.'

'Like they did when they set that unfortunate boxer on us in St. James Square,' I observed. 'I was also glad to learn that our erstwhile assailant had regained consciousness, and that he corroborated Bathgate's confession in every respect.' And I was very relieved that I had not killed the fellow after all. Lestrade assured me that no charges would be forthcoming, as I was simply defending Holmes and myself from a scurrilous attack.

'Precisely. I knew they were shadowing us when we left Baker Street, but I chose to say nothing. They likely went to fetch the prize-fighter to threaten us while we were immersed in Auer's melodies at Willis's. Guilt is a powerful force, Watson,' Holmes continued, 'which has brought many a miscreant low. As the Bard said,

> *"So full of artless jealousy is guilt,*
> *It spills itself in fearing to be spilt."*

Thomas A. Burns, Jr.

Christmas at the Red Lion

The year of 1881 was a singular one for many reasons. First and foremost, it was the year that I first met the man who was to become my best and most trusted friend, Mr. Sherlock Holmes. After agreeing to share lodgings with him in Baker Street, I learned that he was a consulting detective; a profession unique in the world of crime. He graciously allowed me to participate in one of his investigations—the murders of Enoch Drebber and Joseph Stangerson, which occurred last spring. As my physical condition precluded working more than half-time as a physician, Holmes began to call on me for assistance more and more, until 'Watson, get your hat and stick, the game is afoot.' became a familiar refrain.

Now, as Christmas rapidly approached, we had settled into a comfortable relationship, although I sensed that it had become a bit strained of late. Holmes had been injured in a recent case, which limited his mobility. We had originally agreed to share lodgings because neither of us had kith nor kin in England, but while Holmes was largely content to burrow in and hibernate during the Yuletide, I found myself growing melancholy and restless as the holiday neared. Even in Afghanistan, I had my comrades-in-arms to celebrate the Season with. Our landlady, Mrs. Hudson, had informed us that she would leave us a cold supper for Christmas day whilst she was off with relatives, which I counted as a poor substitute for Christmas feasts I'd experienced in past days. When I suggested to Holmes that some modest decoration of our sitting room would not be amiss, he pooh-poohed the idea saying, 'The twenty-fifth of December is just another day.' He thereupon went back to the study of one of those abstruse subjects of which he was so fond, lounging on the sofa amidst a pile of books and papers, which I was sure he was going to set ablaze with his constantly smouldering pipe.

Sitting in my chair, vainly trying to become interested in the morning paper, my heart leapt as I heard our landlady's tread on the stairs, followed by a knock at the door. 'Come in, Mrs Hudson,' I cried. Seeing that she bore a silver tray with a business card, a frisson of joy coursed through me. A client! Surely this would exorcise the demons from my soul. She moved to the sofa and offered the card to Holmes.

Holmes plucked the card from the tray and examined it half-heartedly. After a moment, he said, 'Tell them I'm otherwise engaged, Mrs. Hudson.'

No! 'Surely these people must be in some imminent distress if they wish to consult you this close to Christmas,' I said.

He regarded me with a half-smile, which suggested that I had confirmed a deduction of his. He said to the landlady, 'Oh very well, we'll give Dr. Watson an early Christmas gift. Let's have them.' Mrs. Hudson nodded in acquiescence and went downstairs. Holmes rolled into a sitting position, shuffling his papers off the couch onto the low table in front of it, giving me an accusatory look that spoke volumes; *I'm doing this for you*, it said. 'Bring two chairs near the fire for our guests, he ordered, and I hastened to do his bidding.

In a minute's time the door opened again and the landlady showed a couple into our sitting room. I rose from my chair, but Holmes remained seated. Our gentleman caller was tall and stocky, about thirty years old, wearing a black, double-breasted greatcoat and a fedora against the cold. He had dark hair and a handlebar moustache.

The lady was attractive and somewhat younger, with brown hair peeping beneath a wool hat, a pert nose and red-rimmed eyes. She was clad in a cloth overcoat with fur on the lapels and round the collar.

Mrs. Hudson took their coats and hats. The gentleman offered his hand to me.

'Hugh Jasper,' he said, 'and this is my wife, Trinity.' I took his hand and nodded to his wife; with the overcoat gone, it was quite obvious that she was with child.

'I'm Dr. Watson, and this is Mr. Sherlock Holmes.' Holmes nodded laconically, still not rising to greet his guests. 'Would you care for coffee, chocolate or tea to remedy the morning chill?'

'Anything hot will be welcome,' answered Jasper. I nodded to Mrs. Hudson, and she left the room.

'You'll pardon me for observing that you have an unusual given name, Madam.' I said.

'My father was a churchman, Doctor. All of us children were christened with such names.'

Jasper appeared to be somewhat put out as he addressed the detective. I hoped it was not because of my remark. 'You were recommended to me by Arthur Bathgate, Mr. Holmes.'

'Yes,' said Holmes. 'I handled a trivial matter for him, regarding a less than honest servant. But what has happened to mar the joy of the Season for a watchmaker and his wife?'

As many do when surprised by one of Holmes's deductions, Jasper started. 'However did you know how I make my living, Mr. Holmes?' he asked. 'Did Arthur inform you I was coming to consult you?'

'No, Mr. Jasper. Your squint, your monocle and your long, thin fingers provide ample evidence of your profession. But please be seated and tell me what brings you here on a cold Monday morning?'

Before sitting, Jasper withdrew an envelope from an inside pocket and handed it to me. 'This arrived in the morning post along with our Christmas cards.'

It was addressed to Mr. Hugh Jasper, 41 Great Windmill St., SW1. I handed it over to Holmes, who extracted a folded paper from inside. He sniffed it, made a face, then unfolded it and held it up to the light streaming in the window. Handing the contents to me, he said, 'A typewriter can be as distinctive as handwriting, but that is of help only if one can find the individual machine.'

The note was indeed typewritten. I read:

The child that Trinity Jasper carries is a bastard.

I offered the letter back to Jasper, but he turned his face away as if I held a foul thing. 'It should not be necessary to say that that accusation is a vile canard,' Hugh Jasper averred. 'However, I was prepared to let it go uncontested until I arrived at work this morning.'

'What happened to change your mind?' asked Holmes.

'My employer, Mr. Peter Burkmeier, has a shop in the Strand. He approached me with a note similar to this one, which he said he received in this morning's post. It alleged that I was unhappy with my position in his shop because he paid me insufficiently.'

'Is that true?' Holmes asked. 'What was Mr. Burkmeier's reaction?'

Jasper's eyes dropped to the floor. 'I suppose few workmen feel that they are receiving proper compensation for their efforts. As to his reaction, of course I told Mr. Burkmeier that I was perfectly happy with my situation with him. He seemed to believe me.'

'And to whom, besides your wife of course, have you expressed such displeasure? Any co-workers?' Holmes asked.

'Oh, I don't know!' replied Jasper in an exasperated tone. 'It's not like I go round telling my troubles to every Tom, Dick and Harry I meet in the street. And I do know better than to air my grievances at work.'

A knock came at the door, and I rose to admit Mrs. Hudson, who was bearing a tray containing a silver tea service. She placed it on our dining table and served everyone.

After she had departed, Holmes said, 'I am at a loss Mr. Jasper. What exactly is it that you would have me do for you? Identify who sent these missives? Typically, poison pen writers are erstwhile friends or acquaintances, usually women, who take umbrage with the subject of their persecution, which they assuage by sending their hateful letters. Fortunately, their bile is quickly spent in most cases, and the vitriolic messages cease. In this case, I fail to see much benefit to you from identifying the writer. You couldn't even sue for libel, because one of the allegations is true and the other false one was not publicly communicated. I suggest we wait and see if the campaign is continued.'

Trinity Jasper spoke up for the first time. 'Perhaps Mr. Holmes is right, Hugh. No real damage has occurred.'

'I simply cannot have someone going about saying such awful things about you and our child,' Jasper said.

'But the deed is done.' Holmes said. 'The most that could be gained is informing the writer we are on to her, but even that wouldn't prevent her from making future allegations, especially truthful ones.' Jasper's expression made it evident that he didn't like what he was hearing. Holmes continued, 'Mr. Jasper. Have one of these excellent biscuits and finish your tea. Then go home, and you and your wife make a list of all the people you know, thinking about what, no matter how seemingly inconsequential, you may have done so one of them might choose to respond in this way. However, I'll wager that by the time you have finished, the letters will have stopped and you can enjoy a happy Christmas.'

Hugh Jasper wasn't the only dissatisfied individual that morning. Holmes placed Jasper's letter on the mantlepiece with his unanswered correspondence, then went back to his pipe and his papers after the Jaspers had departed. I was thus left to wallow in my holiday funk once again. I briefly considered a stroll in Regent's Park, but it was much too cold to subject my war wounds to such conditions. I dallied away the rest of the day reading a newly published novel by Wilkie Collins, *The Black Robe*, which I found exceedingly long-winded. It had a rambling plot about a scheming Jesuit seeking to deprive a man of his ancestral home by converting him to Catholicism. I was glad to put it down and retreat to my upstairs bedroom as darkness finally fell.

When I awoke, my fire consisted of only a few dark coals. My bedchamber was damp and chilly, which doubtless accounted for the pain in my wounds and joints. Arising, I lighted a candle and looked out my window. The back yard was shrouded in darkness, but the glass was coated with tiny droplets that swelled and ran into each other as I watched. Knowing there would be no more sleep for me, I donned my dressing gown over my pyjamas and made my way downstairs. As expected, Holmes had not arisen. I put a couple shovels full of coal on the fire and rang for Mrs. Hudson to bring coffee. God bless the good woman, she promised me an early breakfast within half an hour.

The church bells were ringing half-eight when Holmes arose. He went immediately to the sofa and his papers and I rolled my eyes to the ceiling as I contemplated another day like yesterday. Then the downstairs bell sounded, momentarily followed by Mrs. Hudson's rap upon our door. 'Come in!' I cried, and she did, bearing a folded paper on a silver tray, which she immediately offered to Holmes.

'Hah!' he ejaculated. 'The plot thickens!' He flipped the paper to me as he rose and made for his room. 'If your constitution will allow, I would appreciate your assistance this morning.'

It was a wire posted from Soho. It ran:

Scotland Yard here. For God's sake come at once.

H. Jasper

'Obviously dashed off in a great hurry, since he neglects to inform us where 'here' is. I think we can safely assume he's at home in Great Windmill Street. Get dressed, Watson! Our client awaits!'

We threw on our clothes, greatcoats and hats, and Holmes took up his cane on the way out the door. I felt distinctly better as our hansom rattled through the streets, even though the cold drizzle had not abated. Number 41 Great Windmill Street was easily identified, as a constable was posted outside. The Jaspers' rooms were in a four-storey red brick edifice that looked as if it had been built sometime during the previous century. As the officer moved to deny us entry, Holmes mentioned Lestrade's name, and the policeman quickly stepped aside.

Trinity Jasper responded to Holmes's rap upon the door with his cane. 'Mr. Holmes, thank God for you,' she cried. 'That horrible little man wants to take Hugh away!' She led us to the sitting room in which two great windows overlooked the street. Hugh Jasper sat on the sofa while Lestrade loomed over him like an owl over a mouse. Trinity ran to her husband's side, taking his hand as she sat next to him.

'What has Mr. Jasper purportedly done to deserve your undivided attention, Lestrade?' Holmes asked.

Jasper spoke first. 'The Inspector thinks that I burned my employer's place of business. But I assure you Mr. Holmes, I did not!'

Lestrade took up the tale. 'Somebody threw a paraffin bomb through the window of Mr. Burkmeier's shop in the Strand during the wee hours this morning, Mr. Holmes. This gent here claims he was in bed with his missus at the time, which we both know ain't no alibi at all. And he tells me he can't think of anyone else with a grudge against his boss who would do such a thing.'

49

'But that's where I was!' cried Jasper, his wife nodding vigorously. I was at the Red Lion until closing last night, then I came home to Trinee and we went right to bed.'

'And why, pray tell, are you so sure Mr. Jasper did the deed, Inspector?' Holmes asked. 'Surely anyone can throw a bottle of paraffin through a window. Is there something else that makes you suspect that my client is to blame?'

'If he's innocent, why did he engage you, Mr. Holmes?' Lestrade answered pointedly.

'Mr. Jasper, may I reveal the details of our engagement to the Inspector?' Holmes asked. Jasper nodded, and Holmes told him about the letter that Jasper had received. 'I suspect you may have gotten a similar communication, Lestrade?'

Lestrade looked at the floor as he said, 'We did receive a letter at Scotland Yard in the first post, which accused Mr. Jasper because he thought Mr. Burkmeier was treating him unfairly.'

'Typewritten and unsigned, I'll wager.' Lestrade nodded. 'I don't suppose you have it with you?' The Inspector produced the missive from his coat pocket. Holmes retrieved from his pocket the letter that Jasper had brought to Baker Street yesterday, and compared the two. 'Look here, Lestrade. See the notch on the top of the lowercase *e*, and how the bow of the capital *J* is flattened on the bottom? It's very likely these two letters were produced by the same machine. Don't you agree this suggests someone else attacked Mr. Burkmeier's establishment and is trying to put the blame on Mr. Jasper?'

'That's a possibility, Mr. Holmes. It's no good sayin' it ain't. But it's also possible Mr. Jasper engineered this whole scheme to deflect suspicion from himself.'

Holmes's face indicated what he thought of Lestrade's suggestion, but he wisely didn't say so. Instead, he said, 'I'll take the responsibility that Mr. Jasper keeps himself available to you if you have further questions for him. Surely you don't have to separate him from Mrs. Jasper at Christmastime, especially given her delicate condition?'

'Well, if you'll be responsible for him...' Lestrade said.

'Very well, then,' replied Holmes. Mrs. Jasper sprang up and raised her arms to embrace Holmes, but he caught her wrists and lowered them to her sides, shaking his head. Lestrade departed after warning our client to remain in the city until further notice.

After the inspector had gone, Holmes addressed Jasper. 'Tell me, sir, do you spend considerable time at the Red Lion?'

The client looked at Holmes with indignation. 'I do fancy a gill or two after a long day at work, Mr. Holmes, if it's any of your business.'

'Oh, I assure you it most definitely is my business, sir. You wouldn't have told any of your fellow drinkers there that you were dissatisfied with your remuneration from Mr. Burkmeier, would you?' Jasper didn't answer Holmes, but he didn't have to. His face told the tale. 'If you don't mind,' Holmes continued, 'I would ask you to avoid the Red Lion this evening.'

'And why should I do that?'

'Because I would like to visit the establishment myself, and I don't want you to interfere with what I'm trying to do.'

Again, Jasper's face revealed that he didn't like it, but Trinity spoke up. 'Please Hugh, it's just for one night. I can even go up early and bring you some beer to have here.' Jasper nodded his assent.

Back on the street, we found that our cab was gone since we did not ask the driver to remain, and a light rain was still soaking the cobblestones. Looking north, I spotted the Red Lion on the corner of Archer Street, dark and empty at this hour of the morning. We walked toward Shaftsbury Street and Piccadilly Circus to find another hansom. My leg began to throb almost immediately, and Holmes seemed to fare little better. Abruptly he stopped, and poked at something with his stick; I looked down and saw that it was just a dead pigeon, its feathers darkened from the dirty water flowing in the gutter. The detective raised his head and looked about, then extended his cane to point to another bird lying against the side of a building. 'Curious,' he said. He stooped and picked up something from the pavement, which he placed in a piece of paper that he folded and put in his pocket.

I was rapidly becoming cold, damp and ill-tempered, and had no interest whatever in the local fauna. 'Let us be off to Baker Street Holmes, where we can have a late breakfast and some of Mrs. Hudson's excellent coffee.'

'Be off, then,' he said, and we went on our way.

Several cabs were immediately available when we arrived in Piccadilly Circus. By this time, my leg was throbbing, so I boarded one, but Holmes directed the cabbie to wait. 'Indulge me for a moment Watson, if you will.' He moved off to the west along Piccadilly. When he returned in a couple of minutes, he gave the cabbie an address in the Strand instead of Baker Street.

'Mr. Burkmeier's watch shop,' Holmes replied, no doubt seeing my sour expression. 'I don't expect to learn much there, but it's best to leave no stone unturned.'

51

Ten Steps from Baker Street

Sadly, Holmes's prediction proved correct. Onlookers crowded the area in front of the establishment even in the rain, drawn to the tragedy as flies to a corpse, which made the shop easy to locate. The storefront was nothing but a burnt-out shell, with ugly black streaks running up the outside of the stone building that housed it. It was a mercy that the entire neighbourhood did not go up. Holmes shook his head and did not even bother to get out of the cab. Then, to my surprise, instead of directing the cabbie homeward, Holmes gave him an address in Rathbone Place. When I inquired as to why, his cryptic response was, 'You'll see.'

Rathbone Place proved to be a seedy area filled with dilapidated tenements built in the previous century. After directing me to wait in the cab, Holmes hopped out and disappeared inside one of them. In a few minutes, he returned with a bulky parcel wrapped in brown paper.

In response to my inquiry, Holmes said, 'I have found it useful to maintain several boltholes around the city where I can go during an investigation if I wish to remain inconspicuous. In addition to some non-perishable foodstuffs and a place to sleep, I maintain some useful accoutrements for various disguises there. It would hardly do to turn up at the Red Lion this evening in gentleman's garb if we want to gain the confidence of working-class drinkers, so I have secured us more appropriate clothing.'

We waited a couple of hours after the sun went down to strike out for the Red Lion. Holmes had provided a pair of wool trousers, a collarless, long-sleeved white shirt, a wool scarf and a driver's coat for me, while he dressed in a pullover atop a pair of plaid trousers and two sack coats against the cold. We scuffed up our own shoes, and two flat caps completed our outfits. All of our garments were ill-fitting and none too clean, ensuring that we'd fit in well with the working-class crowd at the Red Lion.

When I asked him what he hoped to accomplish on our foray this evening, he said, 'I'm nearly certain that the writer of these hateful missives is well-acquainted with our client, and what better place to become so than the local pub. Our purpose is to meet the Jasper's neighbours and find out what's been transpiring in the area of late. Has anyone else been receiving poison pen letters? But we must be circumspect; if we give the locals the impression that we're spying, they'll shut up like clams on the beach.'

We walked to Marylebone Road for a hansom to Piccadilly Circus. 'I'd prefer to have the driver drop us further from the Red Lion than that,' said Holmes, 'but I fear that neither of us is up to a longer walk on such a cold evening.' Indeed, the temperature hung just above freezing and snow flurries were beginning to swirl around us as we embarked on our night's adventure. By the time we alighted, the snow was beginning to adhere to the cobblestones, and I wished I had brought a stick as Holmes had done, but mine were much too fine and would clash with my workingman's outfit.

As we turned the corner from Shaftsbury Road, the Red Lion, which occupied the corner of Great Windmill Street and Archer Street across from Ham Yard, was a glowing blue and gold beacon of comfort amidst the whirling snowflakes. Indeed, there is nothing that bespeaks *home* to an Englishman more than a good old pub; I know it was what I missed most whilst in Afghanistan. The public house is as much of a symbol of England as St. George's cross, rare roast beef with Yorkshire pudding, and the White Cliffs of Dover. It is a place where class distinctions fade and camaraderie reigns, where a cabman and a gentleman may converse on equal terms; a place where a man's thoughts and actions are determined solely by himself; not by his wife, his employer, his minister or some government functionary. As Holmes pressed the brass latch on the heavy oak door and pushed it open, the warm beery effluvium that inundated us actually brought tears to my eyes—I now knew what the prodigal son felt upon returning to the bosom of his loving family.

Two huge gas chandeliers provided ample light. We passed a parlour on the right as we entered, furnished with stools and small round tables that could hold pints of beer and plates of bread, cheese and onions. Beyond it, an L-shaped oaken bar ran the length of the room with the bottom of the L extending into the parlour; a mound of sawdust lay beneath the brass rail at its base, where a drinker could conveniently rest his foot. There was a row of candles in front of the mirror behind the bar, whose top was festooned with garlands of crimson-berried holly in honour of the Season, and a sprig of mistletoe dangled from an overhead beam near the centre of the great the room. On the left, a brown-painted wooden bench sat next to the windows looking out on Great Windmill Street, providing ample seating for drinkers weary of standing. The custom was mostly male, though there was one woman acting as barmaid whom I thought to be the landlord's wife, as well as three other ladies whose profession was much older, I fancied. Even though the pub had opened only a quarter of an hour ago, nearly two dozen people now occupied it.

We shouldered our way through the throng and elbowed up to the bar ('Watcher self, matey!'), where Holmes ordered two pints of the best. The landlord plied the large white china handle of the beer engine, filling two mugs held in one ham-sized hand before plopping them down in front of us. 'That'll be a tanner, gents,' he said, and Holmes laboriously counted out three pence in payment for his. The landlord looked to me for the remainder, and I scowled at Holmes as I paid.

53

Ten Steps from Baker Street

Because both of us had game legs, we moved to the side parlour to see if we could find a table. We were in luck; two chairs were open. As we settled in, a nearby man handed Holmes a hat saying, 'The refuge over at Ham Yard is collectin' fer the holiday banquet at the Leicester Soup Kitchen.' Both of us tossed in a penny each and passed the hat along. Everyone dug into their pockets to give what they could in the spirit of Christmas until the hat came to a chap in the corner, who held up both hands as if he were warding off evil when it was offered to him. He was a singular-looking fellow, a giant of nearly twenty stone from the look of him; a top hat hovered over his long, fat face, which resembled nothing but a swollen old boot. He was dressed rather better than the rest of the customers, in a maroon frock coat and shiny black trousers.

'C'mon, Horseface, you've got more brass than any of us!' a drinker jibed, only he didn't refer to the gentleman as *Horseface*, but rather something more profane that rhymed with it. 'If youse don't pony up,' said another, 'we won't let youse play Father Christmas on Saturday night.' That comment evoked a round of derisive laughter, which caused the redoubtable Horseface to spring up suddenly, tipping his drink over as well as a couple of the others'. 'Oi mate, yer payin' fer that!' shouted an outraged lush, but the big man ignored him as he parted the crowd like the Red Sea on his way out the door, muttering curse as he went.

'A cheerful fellow,' said Holmes to no one in particular.

'Aye, 'e 's a rum 'un, Mr. Throckburton is,' agreed a patron. 'Thinks 'e's a toff 'e does, don't know why 'e 'angs around wit' our lot.'

Holmes crooked a finger, and I leaned in close. 'Let's split up, old man, cover more ground. Remember, be circumspect.' Holmes arose and moved toward the great room, leaving the table to me. Another chap slid into the vacant chair, saying, ' 'Aven't seen you 'ere before, matey. Now, d'ye follow football?' I said that I did, and we were soon embroiled in a spirited discussion about the recent defeat of Kensington by St. Patrick's Rovers at Turnham Green. Later, the talk turned to the railway tragedy in the Finsbury Park tunnel in North London last Saturday.

'If it was me was in charge,' averred one worthy, 'I'd 'ang that signalman up in Piccadilly Circus by 'is short 'airs.'

'Gan wit' yer!' said another. 'Don't blame the poor hunks of a signalman; 'e's just a workin' stiff like us. Them tracks ain't enough fer all them trains that runs on 'em, and the bluidy gov'ment won't come up wit' the brass to build more.'

Oftentimes it seemed as if things would come to blows, but somehow, magically, that never transpired. Before I knew it, time was called and I was shaking hands with all of my new friends prior to meeting Holmes out on the street.

'Well, what have you discovered?' asked Holmes as we hustled off in search of a cab.

'Other than that Kensington is poorly coached and the budget for the Underground is in sore need of an increase, not much,' I told him.

'Perhaps you should be a bit less circumspect next time, Watson.' Holmes said, not unkindly.

'And what have you learned?' I asked him.

'That the Jaspers were not the first people in the neighbourhood to receive poison pen letters. Last spring, a family moved out of the area after a man was accused of a questionable relationship with his stepdaughter. That's further evidence that our miscreant is a local.'

By the time we arrived back at Baker Street, three pints of beer and two treks through the snow had me totally fagged.

'I shall do some more investigating on my own tomorrow, Watson,' said Holmes. 'Given your delicate condition, you had best take the day to recover.'

I must confess that I felt somewhat annoyed by Holmes's solicitude, but I realized that he was correct. Overall, I was much stronger than I had been earlier this year, however the effects of my trials in Afghanistan still weighed upon me. I slept in until ten the following morning, waking to find blue skies outside my window and last night's snow but a frosty memory. Mrs. Hudson informed me that Holmes had departed before the sun rose, again clad in workingman's clothes. I lingered over breakfast, reading the *Morning Post* and Mr. Dickens's *Daily News* cover to cover, before falling asleep again in my chair over Verne's *Giant Raft*. I had not been awake but fifteen minutes when Holmes returned, just as the sun was going down.

'Well, how did it go?' I asked him.

'I've been shadowing our client's wife, Trinity Jasper, as she went about her daily chores. It appears that someone else is also interested in her peregrinations.'

'Who, pray tell.'

'That is unclear, although I have my suspicions. I noticed a four-wheeler, it's windows heavily curtained, ambling along in her tracks. When I approached it closely enough to see the number plate, I found it didn't have one. However, either the driver or the passenger must have noticed my interest, because it suddenly sped away.'

Holmes continued, 'I also heard a rumour on the street that the fire-bombing in the Strand was contracted, but no one seems to know by whom. Tomorrow, I shall cast my net wider.'

I rang the landlady for supper whilst Homes repaired to his room to eradicate all vestiges of the labourer from his person. We were just lighting post-prandial pipes after a leisurely meal when we heard the front bell, followed by rapid footsteps on the stairs. Our door burst open without even a knock and Inspector Lestrade stood on the threshold.

'I thought you'd want to know,' he said. 'Your client Hugh Jasper was waylaid by a gang of toughs on his way home from the Red Lion. He's been rushed to Barts.'

Holmes's expression was incredulous. 'What? Of course! The pigeons!' He looked to me. 'Get your hat and coat Watson. We're off to Bart's.'

Lestrade had a four-wheeler waiting downstairs, anticipating that Holmes would want to be away as soon as he heard the news. We clattered off for a quick trip because the streets were largely empty due to the cold. On our arrival, we found our client in a ward, unconscious. Mrs. Jasper was there, her face a portrait of anguish as she sat by his bedside, holding his hand.

Holmes approached her. 'Madam, I am so sorry,' he said. 'I should have foreseen this.'

How could you have? I thought.

'It was not your fault, Mr. Holmes,' she said.

'Would you mind terribly moving aside, so Dr. Watson could examine your husband?'

She complied. A bandage on Jasper's forehead concealed a nasty gash which was doubtless responsible for his present state. He had other bruises and abrasions on his face, arms and legs, but these looked to be mostly superficial and would cause nothing more than some aches and pains for a day or two. I said as much to Holmes.

'How serious is the head wound?' Holmes asked.

I piloted him away from his wife, who had returned to her husband's side, before answering. 'It's hard to say. It's likely he hit a kerbstone when he fell. It could be life-threatening if the skull is fractured, or he could awaken in the morning with nothing more than a headache. The next twenty-four hours should tell the tale.'

Holmes entreated Mrs. Jasper to go home, but she refused. 'I don't want him awakening all alone in a strange place,' she said. I told her that it was likely he wouldn't awaken for several hours, but she was adamant.

'Very well,' said Holmes. 'But if you decide to leave, I want you to send for me so I may accompany you. Your tormentor seems to have dangerously escalated his campaign. I don't want you injured as well.'

'I will, Mr. Holmes', she promised.

***

On the morning of December 22nd, I rose at dawn to find an icy fog hanging over the city. As she said she would, Mrs. Jasper had sent Holmes a message the previous night when she was ready to return home, and he had escorted her without incident. We had just settled down to breakfast when Mrs Hudson admitted a lad of twelve or thirteen, clad in layers of ill-fitting garments to protect him against the cold.

'Ah, Wiggins!' Holmes greeted him. 'You have my thanks and Mrs. Hudson's for obeying my wishes that you leave your comrades behind on these visits.' Wiggins was the leader of a gang of street arabs dubbed by Holmes as *the Baker Street division of the detective police force*, who often assisted him when information had to be gleaned from the streets. 'You will have heard of the arson attack in the Strand?'

Wiggins nodded. 'Yes, Mr. 'Olmes.'

'Rumour has it that it was bought and paid for. And there was a second attack on a gentleman in Great Windmill Street last evening, which also may have been contractual. I want you and your minions to see if you can discover who the perpetrators were.' Holmes removed a bag of coins from his pockets. 'The pay scale is as usual; a shilling a day, with a crown for the individual who discovers what I want to know. If you can discover who hired this business done as well, there's a sovereign in it for you.' The boy's eyes widened at that—a sovereign was more money than he saw in months.

'Time is of the essence,' Holmes continued. 'Report to me every morning whether you have results or not.' He handed the money to Wiggins, who said, 'Aye-aye, sir,' then turned on his heel and dashed out of the room.

'If he brings such energy to his future endeavours, that boy cannot help but rise above his station,' said Holmes. 'Now there is nothing to do but wait. Fortunately, I have a little monograph in preparation that requires my attention.'

A couple of hours later we received another visit from Mrs. Jasper. 'I am on my way to hospital to sit with my husband,' she said. 'I received this in the first post today and thought you should see it right away.' She held out an envelope to Holmes, who took it and removed a sheet of paper.

Opening it, he said, 'Hmmm. Same typewriter.' He read aloud.

> *You are free now. Your lying husband got what he deserved. I will come to you soon.*

'What does that mean—I will come to you soon?' asked the lady, her voice trembling.

'It means that I will dismiss your bodyguard and be traveling to Barts with you, and that I will see you safely home when you are ready,' Holmes said. 'Watson, please remain here and take the report from Wiggins should he return.'

After Holmes and Mrs. Jasper had departed, I tried in vain to interest myself in my newspapers and books, to no avail. The poison pen writer's last message indicated that the case had taken an ominous turn, and I feared for my friend's safety, as well as the lady's.

It was sunset before Holmes returned. I inquired of our client's health.

'Much the same,' said Holmes. 'The doctors do not know when, or even if, he will awaken.'

'If a good and a poor outcome are equally probable, we must maintain a positive outlook,' I said.

'Good old Watson!' said Holmes. 'If optimism was a remedy, you could work miracles.'

'Sometimes it is, old man, sometimes it is.'

***

It was Friday morning, the twenty third of December, before Wiggins graced us with his presence again. He stood before Holmes with his hat in his hands, a dejected expression, looking at the floor—a clear indication that he and his mates had been unsuccessful.

'I don't expect miracles, Master Wiggins. Perhaps you should just tell the lads to give it another day,' Holmes said.

The boy continued to study the carpet. 'I don't think that will do much good, Mr. 'Olmes. They already done their best.'

Holmes looked at Wiggins with an odd expression. 'I'm sure they have,' he said. He hesitated, then continued, 'Come, Wiggins. What's really the matter?'

'Ain't nuthin' the matter, Sir. We just failed youse, that's all.'

Holmes was silent for a moment more, then, 'I don't believe that you did fail me. I think that you succeeded. It was some of your mates that attacked Mr. Jasper, wasn't it, Wiggins? And who threw the paraffin bomb?'

Now Wiggins gazed straight at Holmes, fear shining in his eyes. 'How do you know that?' His voice shook.

'Aside from his head wound, which he likely received when he fell, the rest of Mr. Jaspers's injuries are superficial, consistent with the theory that he was waylaid by a group of young boys. Who were they Wiggins? Anyone in my employ?'

'I ain't no snitch,' Wiggins said.

Holmes seemed to consider carefully before speaking. 'All right then. If you won't reveal who the perpetrators were, how about the person who hired them? He's not one of your mates too, is he?'

'Naw, he ain't.' said Wiggins. 'But I don't know 'is name. All I knows is that 'e lives at the Albany.'

The Albany was an exclusive set of bachelor apartments not far from Piccadilly Circus.

'Can you describe him?'

'I ain't never seed 'im. I just know that he pays some of the lads to do little jobs fer 'im, like you do.'

'But I don't pay you to break the law, do I, Wiggins?'

'Nossir.'

'Very well. You tell your mates that if Scotland Yard and I have to come looking for them, we will find them, you know. We can't have them burning down buildings and attacking people in the streets. When we do find them, they will suffer the full penalties prescribed by the law. Of course, if they were to turn themselves into me, perhaps some arrangement could be made...'

'I'll tell 'em, Mr. 'Olmes.' Holmes held out a coin. 'And youse don't need to pay me. I didn't do nuthin' fer youse.'

After Wiggins departed, I asked Holmes, 'So now what will you do?'

'Go to the Albany, of course,' he said. 'And I have a pretty good idea who I'm going to find there.'

Ten Steps from Baker Street

***

It was Christmas Eve, and snow was falling in earnest as I walked up Great Windmill Street towards the Red Lion. After returning from his sojourn to the Albany, Holmes had spent the balance of the day playing with his chemicals or scraping on his fiddle. When I remonstrated that he was no longer working on the case, he told me he had done all that was necessary. He directed me to travel to the Red Lion by myself on Christmas Eve, saying he would join me later in the evening. The drinkers in front of the place milled about as they waited for admittance. Just as I walked up, Pete the landlord threw the door wide and the crowd surged inside. Chaos ensued for a while as everyone converged on the bar, simultaneously shouting orders, and Pete plied the handles of the beer engine as fast as he could, sometimes holding as many as four mugs in one hand, until all had been served. An alcoholic yeasty fragrance soon filled the air. Out of the corner of my eye, I caught a glimpse of Lestrade in the crowd, a gill in hand, showing no indication of his profession.

Because I had my back to the door as I endeavoured to garner my pint, I hadn't seen Throckburton enter. However, when I went to the front parlour he was in his usual place, taking service of his libation from the barmaid. I took a seat nearby and waited for the night's performance to begin.

It was not long before the front door opened and Holmes entered, clad in the foppish finery of a workingman masquerading as a toff, with whom but Trinity Jasper on one arm and his cane hanging from the other. Her hair was done up high with jewels twinkling between the strands and a green garland around her brow, and she was resplendent in Christmas attire; a floor length crushed velvet skirt in emerald green with a matching hooded top, worn over a white blouse with a ruffled front under a red tartan vest—she resembled anything but a wife disconsolate over her husband in hospital. The festive couple approached a table and Holmes glared at the occupants, who immediately rose to offer the fine lady and her escort a seat. The barmaid came and took their order, returning quickly with a pint for Holmes and a bottle of stout for the lady.

I took an opportunity to glance at Throckburton—that worthy sat like a statue, glaring at the pair with obvious venom.

Holmes drained a quarter of his glass with a generous swig and banged it down on the table.

'Cor!' he hollered. 'Wot sort o' a pub is this? Ain't ye got no music on Christmas Eve?'

In short order one man brought out a squeezebox and another a fiddle, and they struck up *God Rest Ye Merry Gentlemen.* The crowd eagerly joined in singing, with Holmes's vibrant baritone soaring above all. *Hark the Herald Angels Sing* and *Good King Wenceslas* quickly followed. When the musicians segued into a lusty rendition of *Landlord Fill the Flowing Bowl*, Holmes stood and took Mrs. Jasper by the hand, pulling her into a gay dance. Several other enterprising wights snatched up the ladies of the evening and joined the fun, while the barmaid retreated to safety next to her husband behind the bar. Holmes still had his cane hanging from an arm, but as he danced, his leg showed little sign of infirmity. When the song was done, Holmes steered Mrs. Jasper under the mistletoe, puckered his lips and leaned forward to perform the traditional Christmas ritual.

'Fer the love of God, no!' bellowed Throckburton, springing up and overturning another table full of drinks. Enraged, he charged Holmes, who spun Mrs. Jasper behind him, and stabbed at the big man's diaphragm with his cane. Throckburton grabbed the stick with both hands, intending to pull it out of Holmes's grasp, but Holmes slapped his hand down on Throckburton's, locking his thumb to the stick, and rotated it up and around, carrying his attacker's arm with it and spilling him onto the floor.

'Not so easy when you're not hiding behind a poison pen, is it now?' Holmes taunted.

'Ye should of listened!' Throckburton yelled at Mrs. Jasper as he struggled to his feet. 'I would have taken you away from that lout. 'E isn't worthy of ye!'

Wary now, the giant threw a right at Holmes, his left ready to block the cane if Holmes swung it at his head, but the detective slapped the punch away with his arm and brought the stick up between Throckburton's legs instead, simultaneously stomping down on his foot, pinning it to the floor. Holmes then twisted the cane against the immobilized leg, buckling both of his adversary's knees. There was an audible snap as Throckburton tumbled to the floor once again. This time he didn't rise—rather he sat there bawling like a baby, both hands clasped around his ruined knee. He gave Lestrade no trouble as the inspector clapped the darbies on, but a couple of constables had to be summoned to carry the big man from the premises.

***

Ten Steps from Baker Street

I sat back in my chair, removed my napkin from around my neck and sighed. Holmes and I had just finished Mrs. Hudson's cold Christmas supper, and what a fine feast it was! She had provided us with oysters, a cold salad of potatoes, beets, celery and eggs, and a whole turkey with cranberries. We could not even touch the plum pudding with whisky sauce.

Holmes had a wire from Lestrade earlier that evening. After using Throckburton's statements during the fight at the Red Lion to secure a warrant, a search of his rooms at the Albany had turned up a typewriter that proved to be a perfect match to the one that produced the poison pen letters. Additionally, by touting Holmes's unparalleled abilities as a detective, Wiggins had convinced the boys who had fallen under Throckburton's spell to come forward and identify him as the man who hired them to bomb Mr. Burkmeier's shop, and to waylay Hugh Jasper.

'I have a friend in a high position in the government who can doubtless convince the crown prosecutor to accept a punishment other than prison for the lads,' Holmes said. 'A year or two at sea should serve nicely. On the other hand, Mr. Harrison Throckburton has many years of walking the wheel to look forward to.'

'When did you know it was Throckburton who sent the poison pen letters?'

'I suspected that the writer was from the Jaspers' neighbourhood from the beginning. I had an inkling that he or she might be dangerous when I saw the dead pigeons in Great Windmill Street on leaving our clients' flat that first day. One dead pigeon is happenstance, two coincidence, but I saw no less than sixteen on our walk from the Jasper residence to Piccadilly Circus. When I left you there to go a little further west, I found more. A wire to Dr. Swithers at the British Museum confirmed that no avian pestilence was currently rampaging throughout London, so why so many dead birds? The answer was obvious—someone was poisoning them. A test of the corn I picked from the pavement confirmed that hypothesis; it contained a fair amount of arsenic. Cruelty to animals has been linked to all sorts of criminal behaviour, so I stored the hypothesis in my brain-attic that those birds just might be victims of our writer.

'It was Throckburton's outburst at the Red Lion Wednesday night that caused me to suspect him. He had all the characteristics of a poison pen; unattractive, petty, and egotistical; the only contraindication was his sex. Women comprise the majority of poison pen writers, however, the attack on the watchmaker's shop strongly suggested a man might be implicated.

'After Wiggins told me about the involvement of his mates and that the man who hired them lived at the Albany, all it took was a look at the post boxes in the lobby to confirm that one H. Throckburton was a resident there. I could see him in my mind's eye, strolling from the Albany to the Red Lion, a pocketful of poisoned corn, scattering death in his wake.'

I interrupted. 'Why would he choose the Red Lion as a place to imbibe if he thought everyone there was beneath him?

'He was slumming, Watson. His sort craves an atmosphere in which he can consider himself superior to everyone around him. I was certain that the boys would identify him as their employer; less so that their accusation would carry enough weight to convince the crown prosecutor because of the social distance between them and Throckburton. I needed more—I needed that typewriter, which I was sure I would find in his flat.'

'So you convinced Trinity Jasper to aid you with that charade at the Red Lion,' I finished for him.

'Once I explained the situation to her, she was only too happy to do so. I felt sure that the vile letters were motivated by unrequited lust, and that Throckburton now harboured the insane notion that she might be attainable to him with her husband out of the picture. Incidentally, I had a wire from Mrs. Jasper a while ago that her husband had awakened for a few moments earlier today, which his doctors consider a very encouraging sign. Anyway, I was sure that seeing her with another man who was not himself would provoke a strong reaction from Throckburton. You saw that I was not mistaken.'

'Indeed I did.' Knowing Holmes's views about women in general, and seeing his behaviour with Trinity Jasper at the pub, I couldn't resist adding, 'It's a shame that she is taken. You two certainly made an attractive couple.'

Holmes cocked an eyebrow at me. 'I have noted that you evidence a definite strain of pawky humour, Watson. I expect that someday, I will lose you to a wife; your expression upon seeing the solicitude that Mrs. Jasper showed to her husband in hospital left no doubt in that regard. Now, it is a peculiarity of many who covet the married state that they expect that everyone else would also be better off married, but I can assure you there are no nuptials in my future. For every happy marriage that you can show me, I can show you one plagued by infidelity, thievery or murder.'

'But don't you think that the joy of the Season would be enhanced by the presence of family?'

'For some yes, and for you, certainly, but not I. My work is all I need.'

I looked at the small fir tree on the sideboard, hung with gaily coloured bits of paper and cotton wool, which Holmes had finally allowed me to bring into our rooms in honour of Christmas. Even with my good friend beside me, the lack of a family wore heavily on my heart. I only hoped that, for his sake, Holmes was speaking truly.

The Adventure of the Drunken Teetotaller

It was a snowy winter's night, in 1895, I think, when Holmes and I were ensconced in Baker Street. A cheery fire burned in the grate, and Holmes had grown bored with updating his indices—a never-ending occupation. In order to distract him from the task, which I knew could continue all night, I lowered the copy of Lloyd's Weekly that I had been perusing, and addressed him. 'I have just finished an interesting article about the contradiction that our era embodies,' I said. 'The writer specifically refers to the spectacular increase of wealth and power that the Empire has enjoyed during

these last few decades, and contrasts it with the disreputable state of the poor and the working classes.'

'That is no contradiction,' replied Holmes. 'Everything has a rational explanation. The cognoscente who penned that piece has doubtless advanced a specious argument for his position, which would inevitably lead to his labelling his conclusion as a contradiction. He obviously does not consider the premise that the state of the individual and the state of the empire may be mutually exclusive. A spiritualist employs a similar strategy. When attempting to explicate so-called paranormal phenomena, the spiritualist constructs his argument so that a contradiction inevitably occurs. To resolve it, he must resort to a supernatural explanation.'

'Surely you oversimplify. This world is not only stranger than we know; it is stranger than we can know.'

'If I believed that, I should immediately close my consulting detective business and retire to Sussex to keep bees,' asserted Holmes. 'I reiterate—contradictions do not exist. If you encounter one, always return to the premises you began with. Invariably, you will find that one or more of them are in error.' He paused to apply a vespa to his calabash, puffing until it was drawing to his satisfaction. 'I applied this principle to solve one of the more interesting cases I encountered. You were not involved; it occurred whilst you were not residing at 221b, in 1883, I think. It was an apparent contradiction that induced me to accept it.'

'And that contradiction was?'

'In my case notes, I refer to it as the tragedy of the drunken teetotaller. Would you care to hear about it?'

I felt sure that Holmes had discerned what I was doing when I initiated our conversation, and simply could not resist outmanoeuvring me, but here was a chance I simply could not ignore. 'Of course,' I said.

'Then pour us a couple of brandies and I'll tell you the tale.'

I did as he asked and settled back in my chair.

'It was a Monday as I recall, in late July of 1883. I was in Stratford, attending the appearance of Virginia Matsford in the West Ham police court, who was accused of poisoning her children for the insurance money...'

***

Matsford was bound over to the Crown Court, and afterwards, removed from the police court for transfer to Newgate Prison to await trial in the Old Bailey.

The unseasonably cold and rainy weather did not discourage a crowd of about 1,000 from gathering outside; they had apparently heard of the heinous nature of Matsford's crime. Holmes had joined them, his collar turned up and his fedora pulled down to remain anonymous, and careful to remain on the periphery in case the mob became ugly. Sure enough, unruliness erupted when the prisoner was brought out, flanked by four burly officers who conducted her to an awaiting police van in front of the building. The mob surged forward, trying to remove her from the carriage to exact rough justice. Holmes took particular notice of an individual at the forefront of the throng, who shouted loudly, 'Let's have her out of there, then!' He was half staggering and slurring his words as if consummately inebriated. The horde likely would have followed his instructions, except for a dozen constables who suddenly stormed out of the building, plying their truncheons with abandon, driving back the mob and arresting several of the rascals, the vociferous fellow among them. The rest had to give way or be trampled as the van clattered off, then they dispersed as the object of their wrath was no longer in propinquity.

Two days later, London was still atypically cold and rainy. Holmes barely noticed the weather unless it impacted his work, but he did have the sitting room windows closed and a fire smouldering in the grate. He was at breakfast when the bell rang downstairs, followed by footsteps on the stairs. A gentle knock came on the door.

'Come in, Mrs. Hudson.'

The door opened and the good lady entered, carrying a silver salver. 'It's a lady, sir,' she said. 'I informed her that you'd still be eatin' your breakfast, but she insists she must see you right away.' She offered the tray to Holmes.

He picked up the calling card on its surface. *Mrs. Thomas Berry,* it read.

'Show her up, Mrs. Hudson,' Holmes said. 'If she's out so early, perhaps she's had no breakfast either.'

The landlady sniffed. 'Very good, sir,' she answered, and left the room.

Holmes rose as Mrs. Hudson returned in a moment with Mrs. Berry. The visitor was a large woman, just an inch or two shorter than Holmes, with strawberry blond hair in a bun and ringlets dangling round her ears. She affected a grey tight morning dress of the type she would wear to receive a visitor in her own home, with wide black stripes and a black ruffled collar and cuffs. Doubtless, Watson would have found her fetching. However, her face was drawn and her eyes tinged with red.

Holmes greeted her. 'Good morning, Madam. Your husband must have gotten himself into serious trouble for you to come all the way from Stratford to see me in such beastly weather. Pray sit down, and tell me about it. Will you have some breakfast?'

'No thank you, sir. I couldn't eat a bite.' Suddenly, she started. 'How did you know I travelled here from Stratford?'

'A cup of this most excellent coffee then,' Holmes entreated, pouring her one. 'I was in Stratford myself only the other day. You likely picked up the petals of the dahlias and cornflowers that I see adhering to your boots when you walked past the flower seller outside Stratford station. Was your husband involved in the fracas in front of the West Ham police court on Monday?

Mrs. Berry had a look on her face akin to wonderment and apprehension all at once. 'How did you know it was my husband in trouble?'

'For whom else would you come, madam? Pray tell me what difficulties he has gotten himself into. And be sure to omit no detail, however inconsequential it may seem to you.'

She picked up the cup and sipped the strong black brew, and some colour came back into her cheeks. 'My husband Thomas is a solicitor who sometimes works in the West Ham police court. He often assists his clients in the courtroom of the magistrate, Mr. Ian Harris. He had a case there Monday morning.' A glistening tear swelled at the corner of an eye, then she took another sip of the coffee to fortify herself before she could continue. 'On Monday afternoon, Thomas was arrested for drunk and disorderly. They… they told me he allegedly tried to remove a woman in custody from a police van!'

'It was no mere allegation, ma'am. I was there and I observed it myself. Your husband appeared to be thoroughly intoxicated.'

Her face fell, but she continued on, gamely. 'Yesterday, Thomas appeared before the magistrate, Ian Harris. He was convicted of being drunk and disorderly, and Harris sentenced him to three weeks' hard labour. But the drunken man you saw couldn't have been Thomas, Mr. Holmes. He's a teetotaller; he's been active in the temperance movement for most of his adulthood.'

'I take it that witnesses who testified in court identified him as the man who tried to remove the prisoner from the van?'

She nodded.

'You'll pardon my saying so, Mrs. Berry, but it wouldn't be the first time a husband has lied to his wife about his vices.'

'No! Not my Thomas, Mr. Holmes.' She paused, the tears welling up in earnest now.

Holmes reached forward and took her hand. 'There, there, madam. Surely this is no great tragedy. The worst of it is that Mr. Berry will have three weeks' discomfort as a present from a petty tyrant.'

'No, Mr. Holmes, I fear not. My Thomas has a bad heart. I fear that being put to hard labour for that time could actually kill him.'

'I am truly sympathetic to your plight, madam. But I must tell you again, I was at the West Ham Police Court during the incident in question. I saw your husband try to free the prisoner, exhorting others to assist him. He certainly appeared to be grossly inebriated.'

'If it were my Thomas you saw, Mr. Holmes, then he must have been out of his mind for some other reason. He would never touch alcohol, I tell you.' She paused to wipe her eyes, then went on. 'You should know that I am not Thomas Berry's first wife. His Lily was killed two decades ago when a drunken drayman ran her down with his cart in a busy street. After that, Thomas vowed he would never drink again, joined a teetotaller's society and has worked tirelessly ever since to have beverage alcohol banned throughout the kingdom.'

Holmes rose to retrieve his morning pipe from the mantle, giving Mrs. Berry a questioning rise of his eyebrows. 'May I smoke?'

She nodded.

He plucked a coal from the fire with the tongs and got his briar going. When it was drawing to his satisfaction, he sat and asked, 'I take it there was bad blood between your husband and this magistrate? Three weeks hard labour is a severe sentence.'

'Possibly. Thomas has told me that Magistrate Harris has a reputation for austerity around the court.'

Holmes considered. He had often said to Watson that it is a capital mistake to theorize before all the data have been gathered. Had he been doing that? After observing the donnybrook in the square Monday afternoon, he thought that it was a certainty that the man who had tried to get to Virginia Matsford was very drunk; if it were Thomas Berry, the probability that he had broken his vow was high. But there was no firm evidence that this truly was the case.

Ten Steps from Baker Street

'All right, Mrs. Berry, I'll see what I can do.' Holmes said. 'But you must realize that the overturning of a Magistrate's sentence is no small order. I shall have to find new and compelling evidence to present to Mr. Harris, and even then, he may elect to have your husband remain where he is.'

'You must tell him that even if Thomas did as it appeared, drunkenness should not be punishable with a death sentence.'

'I certainly shall do that, Madam. Perhaps, you would know where your husband was taken to serve his sentence?' Holmes knew that most prisoners sentenced in the West Ham Court served their sentences at the nearby Pentonville Prison, but there were exceptions.

'They told me that he was taken to Pentonville, Mr. Holmes. They won't let me in to visit him, though.'

After Mrs. Berry had departed, Holmes found his telegraph pad amongst the clutter in the sitting room, scribbled for a few moments, then rang for the page. Inspector Lestrade owed him several favours for giving the Scotland Yard detective sole credit for the solutions of a few important cases; now it was time to call a marker due. After handing his missive off to the lad, Holmes retired to his bedroom to dress. A response was waiting for him when he returned to the sitting room.

He caught a cab to Scotland Yard, and asked the cabbie to wait whilst he went inside. He soon returned and directed the cabbie to Pentonville prison.

Her Majesty's prison at Pentonville occupied an area of about six acres in the north London district of Islington. It was constructed as a so-called 'Model Prison', intended to remedy the deficiencies of older institutions such as Newgate, by enforcing a silent system of incarceration akin to that found in a monastery. Each prisoner occupied his own sparsely furnished cell, whose heavy stone walls muffled sound and added to the cloistered atmosphere inside. Such construction was supposed to promote penitence and introspection in the inmates, which was considered a key component of rehabilitation. The inmates were expected to remain silent except in a case of dire emergency. Penalties for noncompliance were severe.

Holmes's cab drew up before a wide square gatehouse with portculli on all four sides, rearing high above a curtain wall that encircled the entire prison. The detective asked his cabbie to remain, alighted and presented a letter to a guard, who conducted him through the gatehouse to a horizontal corridor that ran between two-storey administrative buildings on either side. Holmes turned neither right nor left, exiting

70

the corridor through a door in its centre into a walled courtyard in front of the main building.

Holmes's escort led him across the courtyard and passed him off to another lackey, who brought the detective to the governor's office, which occupied a nexus of four wings containing four floors each. The wings radiated from the rear of the central building like the struts of an open fan, and comprised the prison's living quarters. Holmes found the governor waiting in the internal gallery outside his office, a convenient vantage point from which he could survey the entire prison from a central location.

The governor perused the letter that Holmes gave him, then handed it back, saying, 'You may visit the prisoner Berry. He is currently at his labour in the basement. You must realize that the time he spends talking to you will count against him in terms of the completion of his required tasks to earn his meals.'

'Were you not informed that Mr. Berry has a heart condition that would preclude hard labour?' Holmes asked.

'Indeed, I was. That is why I had Mr. Berry examined by the doctor upon admission. It was determined that he was unsuited to the treadmill, so he has been assigned to the crank instead.'

'Hardly an adequate substitute,' said Holmes.

'That is your opinion sir,' said the governor with a tone of finality. He addressed Holmes's consort. 'Otis, take this gentleman to see prisoner Berry.'

Otis, the guard, led Holmes downstairs into the basement, a dank and cheerless place that stank of mould and stale water. Cells opened on either side of a corridor; the guard conducted Holmes halfway down before stopping at an iron door. He plied a key and opened the door onto a clammy little room. Filtered daylight entering from a window near the ceiling, illuminating a man struggling to turn a crank protruding from a black metal box on a pedestal near the wall. A small meter mounted on the side of the box contained numbered wheels that advanced with each rotation of the crank. Holmes knew that turning the crank forced a series of paddles through sand inside the box, performing no useful work. Moreover, the tension of the handle could be adjusted, making it more difficult to operate the crank.

The only other furniture in the room was a three-legged stool which was too short to sit on while working, and a chamber pot with no cover. The fellow's breathing rasped like a crosscut saw across a log as he struggled to raise the handle upright, then push it downwards again.

'Mr. Thomas Berry?' said Holmes.

The man stopped working and turned to face the detective. His countenance radiated death; his mouth hung open as he struggled for air, streams of drool ran down his chin and his skin was an unhealthy shade of cyan. 'Who are you who comes to see my misery?' he asked.

'I am Sherlock Holmes. I'm here at your wife's behest.'

Berry broke into tears. 'Oh, dear little Sheila! Shall I ever see her again?'

'Perhaps you shall, sir. We must talk.' Holmes turned to the guard. 'A little time alone with my client, if you please, Otis.'

Otis clearly did not want to honour the request, but Sherlock Holmes was a man difficult to say no to. Otis stepped outside and pushed the door to; seconds later, the key clattered in the lock.

Holmes indicated the stool. 'Sit down and rest, Mr. Berry, while we talk.'

'I dare not, sir. I must turn this terrible handle 3,000 times before supper if I wish to be fed.'

Holmes took Berry by the shoulder and pulled him away from the infernal machine. 'Sit, sir, and let me work for you for a while.' He removed his coat and jacket and handed them to Berry, then began to spin the crank much faster than the prisoner could ever hope to. However, even Holmes, a strong young man, found the task challenging.

'I must understand your actions on Monday last, which led you to this place,' Holmes said.

'There isn't much to tell,' Berry replied. 'I had a case that morning in Mr. Harris's court.'

'Did you win?' asked Holmes.

'No, but I should have done. I informed Magistrate Harris that I would be appealing his decision to the Crown Court.'

'You've done that before.' It was not a question.

'Yes, three times. Harris was overturned in each case.'

'So, you went to lunch and had a pint or two to celebrate?'

As knackered as he was, Berry still managed to look insulted. 'I did no such thing! I had lunch at the King of Prussia public house to be sure, but I touched no alcohol. I have taken a vow of abstinence.'

'With whom did you lunch?'

'My fellow solicitors Roger Starling and Howard Livingstone.'

'Did they consume any alcohol?'

'No. They know my feelings, and choose not to indulge in my presence.'

'What was your lunch?'

'I had a delightful steak and mushroom pie.' He hesitated, then, 'It was the last I have eaten before being brought here.'

'What about your companions?'

'Let me see... I think Livingstone had the pie as well, and Starling a ploughman's lunch.'

'Tell me about what happened later in the square.'

Berry assumed a frantic expression. 'That's just it, Mr. Holmes! I don't know! They tell me I had done outrageous things, called witnesses in court who confirmed it. But I don't remember anything!'

'Do you remember leaving the King of Prussia?'

'Yes. I had another appearance before Harris that afternoon, and I remember thinking that it wasn't going to go well because of our difficulties that morning.'

'Did you feel ill after lunch?'

'A little, sir, as if what I had didn't quite agree with my stomach. But I don't remember feeling really in distress. The three of us arrived back at the Police Court and I bade goodbye to my comrades. That's the last thing I remember before waking up in jail Tuesday morning.' His face fell. 'I was absolutely flummoxed when they recited the list of things they claimed I had done in court.'

By this time, Holmes's arms and shoulders were aching from turning the crank. He stopped and looked at the counter—barely a hundred turns since he'd begun, and poor Berry needed thousands to receive his dinner.

Holmes retrieved his garments and donned them. 'Mr. Berry, I promise I will exert my best efforts to have you out of here as quickly as I can. I suggest you defy your jailers and turn that crank as slowly as you can. It will take you much longer to die of starvation than of heart failure.' He banged on the door with a clenched fist. 'Guard! I am ready!'

Otis apparently thought it amusing to make Holmes wait a further ten minutes before releasing him. The detective said nothing about the delay, knowing it was a battle he couldn't win. 'Please take me back to the governor,' Holmes asked the guard.

Once in the presence of the great man again, Holmes expostulated, 'I really must protest your treatment of my client in the strongest terms. The man is clearly not sufficiently healthy for the crank. Surely it is within your power to find an alternative.

He could be assigned to pick oakum, make nets or engage in some other trade for the benefit of all.'

'Are you a physician, sir?' the governor asked.

'No.'

'A surgeon, then, or a nurse?'

'No, I am not.'

'No formal medical training at all,' the Governor observed, shaking his head. 'Yet you presume to instruct me about the treatment of my convicts.'

Holmes surely missed his Watson now. It took every bit of willpower he possessed not to smash the fellow's nose with his fist, flat against his face. But his joining Berry here in prison would benefit no one.

Outside, the sky was painted dark grey with clouds and a cold rain fell in sheets. Weather appropriate to the events of the day, Holmes thought. However, lunchtime was approaching. He mounted his cab. 'The King of Prussia public house, Stratford,' he said to the driver.

Twenty minutes after leaving Pentonville Prison, Holmes's cab rattled over the River Lea on the ancient Bow Bridge, into Stratford. Stratford was a town in East London, a ward of the parish of West Ham that was eventually subsumed into the metropolis. Its marshy plains, inundated by the Lea, proved an ideal site for the many manufacturing enterprises that sprang up after the railroad came about forty years ago, after dangerous and noxious industries were banned from metropolitan London. Currently, Stratford served as a manufacturing hub for medicines, chemicals, and processed foods, among other goods. Holmes's cab juddered past the elaborate Italianate town hall at the junction of Broadway and High Street, whose cupola and weathervane towered 100 feet above the pavement. The King of Prussia public house occupied the lower floor of a grey-fronted building from the previous century just up the road, across the street from the West Ham Police Court. Holmes alighted and paid off his driver, as he intended to take the train back to London when he was finished here this evening.

As Holmes approached the pub, a sign on the pedimented door between two bay windows informed him that the proprietor was one G. Demeris. A Greek name, Holmes thought. He knew that the Greeks had a long and distinguished history in London, dating back to the Tudor era. Many of London's Greek citizens were of humble origin; sailors from the myriad ships who docked at the port. In 1820, reprisals by the hated Turks against Greeks living in the Ottoman Empire forced many middle-

and upper-class citizens to flee their oppressors; many ended up in London where they were able to take up their lives again. It was not odd to see a Greek as a business owner now—some of the more prominent London Greeks had even assimilated into the upper middle class.

A warm, beery aroma wafted over Holmes as he opened the door to the public room and pushed inside. The warmth from the kitchen immediately seeped into his bones, driving out the chill imbued in them by the cold rain. He was in a large room that occupied most of the ground floor, full of tables and chairs. A bar to his right ran from front to back, behind it was a pass-through to an open kitchen on which plates of food rested, awaiting conveyance to the diners who ordered them. At the rear of the room, a staircase running from right to left gave access to an upper floor; doubtless the domain of the proprietor.

The place was still three quarters full with the lunch crowd, but a table near the bar adjacent to a bay window was clearing, so Holmes took it. A serving wench noticed him immediately and approached.

'What'll it be, ducks?'

'A pint of your best, please. What are you serving for luncheon?'

'Steak and mushroom pie is our specialty.'

'That will be fine.'

The girl brought the beer immediately. Holmes took a long draught and found it hoppy, bitter, but well-bodied; it was doubtless brewed on the premises. The tingle that suffused his muscles alerted him that it was also quite strong, but it would take much more than a pint of beer to get him into the condition that he observed in Berry during the affray outside the police court. The steak and mushroom pie arrived in its own ramekin in due course, steam rising from the top and a rich brown gravy bubbling round the circumference of the crust.

Holmes ate slowly, not only because the food was very hot, but also to allow the crowd to diminish, as he hoped to have a word with the landlord. He found the pie delicious and filling, and it extirpated the remains of the chill from his body.

Finally, he finished, and waved at the waitress to come and remove his dishes. When she arrived, he inquired, 'Can you ask the landlord to step over here for a bit?'

A look of suspicion appeared on her face. 'Why? Did I do something wrong? Was the food not to yer likin'?

'On the contrary. Your service has been exemplary and the food more than satisfactory. I just wish to pay my respects.'

Her apprehensive aspect transformed into a smile. 'Oh! I'll let him know.' A pause, and a coy look. 'My name's Annie, by the way.'

'Thank you, Annie.' She scurried off.

A few minutes later, the landlord approached. He was a tall, grey-haired man in his sixties with a handlebar moustache and a definite Hellenic cast to his features. 'You wish to see me, sir?'

'Yes, Mr. Demeris. Sit down, if you please. Firstly, I wanted to compliment you on a most excellently prepared steak and mushroom pie.'

'Thank you so much, sir. It is an old family recipe for *kreatopita,* adapted to suit my new home here in England.'

'I wonder if I could speak to you about one of your patrons? Are you acquainted with Mr. Thomas Berry?'

'*Nai fysika*! Yes, of course! He comes in for lunch, two, t'ree times a week.'

'Do you remember if he came in this week?'

'*Nai.* He was here on Monday, with two friends.'

'Do you remember what he had for lunch?'

Demeris gazed through the bay window into the street. 'Let me t'ink... Ah! I have it! He had a dish of *moussaka,* I t'ink.'

'Did he drink any alcohol?'

'Oh yes, Mr. Berry, he likes my beer very much! He had a pint or two. And a little glass of whisky, I t'ink, to drive off the cold.'

'Hmm. Very interesting.'

'If that will be all, sir, I must return to my kitchen now.'

'Yes, of course. Thank you.'

Holmes watched Demeris as he rose and retreated to safety behind the bar. He was nearly certain that the innkeeper had lied, and moreover, that the man was terrified. But Holmes only had the word of Berry to support his conclusion. He decided to visit the police court to gather more evidence.

The rain had abated when Holmes exited the pub, but patches of dark clouds still peppered the blue sky, promising more precipitation. Holmes was happy to be able to walk to the old court house across the square without a further soaking.

The London Police Courts were an institution unique in the European criminal justice system. Established at the end of the eighteenth century to preserve the public order after the Gordon Riots, the courts were available to all; both the police or a common citizen could seek a summons from a magistrate against someone. The magistrates themselves were paid a handsome annual stipend for their service in order to allow them to preserve their independence and remain unbiased. Even though a magistrate could convict and set punishment only for misdemeanours and certain minor felonies, his judicial power was nevertheless sweeping; he was largely unsupervised and difficult to question or reverse. A solicitor could appeal a magistrate's decision to the Crown Court, but the process was lengthy, so, as in Thomas Berry's situation, it often provided inadequate requital.

However, many magistrates did much more for the public than simply render judgments. The best of them intervened pro-actively in disputes of all sorts; with family, with neighbours, with tradesmen and even with the police. Sometimes they even interceded in the lives of their predominantly working-class clients, originating summonses, dispensing advice and even charity from court slush funds established for that very purpose, all in the name of encouraging the common man to look to the law for redress and protection instead of fearing it as an oppressor.

After inquiring of some of the people in the halls, Holmes found Roger Starling in the solicitor's lounge, organizing his notes from today's cases.

'You've only just caught me here, you know,' said Starling. 'I'm off for London and won't return until next week.'

'Then I am fortunate indeed,' said Holmes. 'I have agreed to assist Thomas Berry with his current difficulty, and I was wondering if you could provide any insight about his behaviour on Monday last.'

'I'm whacked,' said Starling. 'I had lunch with Berry and Howard Livingstone that day, and I saw nothing to suggest he'd get himself into such a kettle of fish.'

'He wasn't drinking at lunch?'

'Tommy Berry? Drinking? Good Lord, man, who told you that? Berry was the most obdurate teetotaller I ever laid eyes on. He'd sooner sip a cup of boiling lead as drink a beer with his luncheon.'

'Did he seem all right when you left him?'

'Now that you mention it, he was a little green around the gills, as if his repast did not agree with him.'

'Was there anything wrong with his meal?'

'He didn't say there was. Livingstone had the same thing, the steak and mushroom pie, as I remember, and he was fine. I had the ploughman's lunch myself—can't stomach bloody mushrooms, you know.'

'Is Mr. Livingstone here today?'

'Yes. He's arguing a case before Magistrate Harris, poor devil. Involves a young maidservant who is suing her master for her wages after she was dismissed. She claims the old man behaved inappropriately towards her, let her go without paying her when she protested. Livingstone should be here before long.'

'How does an unpaid maidservant afford the services of a solicitor?'

'Some of the fellows have formed an association to provide *pro bono* services to the poor who end up in court.' He hesitated. 'They shouldn't have to; it's the magistrate's job to look out for them after all, but Harris doesn't always do that.'

'I assume Thomas Berry is a part of that.'

'He started it, sir, and roped the rest into it.'

'Including you?'

'No sir. I know better than to antagonize a magistrate.'

'Is Harris's behaviour why Livingstone is a poor devil?'

Starling looked right and left as if to assure he wouldn't be overheard. 'Harris runs his court with an iron fist. He's usually made his mind up very early in the game, according to his own view of things, and it's right difficult to change. But mind you, most of the time, he takes the correct decision.'

'Did Mr. Berry have trouble with Harris?'

Starling gave a barky laugh through his nose. 'You might say so,' he averred. 'Went after the magistrate tooth and nail, he did, even when it was clear that his cause was lost. Even took Harris to the Crown prosecutor a few times, for failure to follow proper legal procedures.'

'I assume Harris took exception to that.'

'Let's just say there's no love lost between the two of 'em. And Harris took Tommy's establishment of his little legal aid society as a direct affront to his authority. Couldn't do a thing about it, though.'

Holmes thanked Starling for his time and went over to Harris's courtroom, where Livingstone was arguing. He pushed the double doors open, and the smell of ancient books and unwashed humanity rolled over him. The public gallery was nearly empty; apparently only a few had chosen to spend their Wednesday afternoon viewing the police court proceedings. A plainly dressed young woman stood in the witness box, being interrogated by Harris himself, a stocky, black-robed fellow with a boxer's nose who sat behind a bar on a raised platform at the rear of the courtroom. Two solicitors occupied adjacent tables facing the magistrate and his witness; a well-dressed older gentleman, apparently the defendant, sat next to one of them while the other was by himself. The defendant was extremely tall and thin, with the protruding forehead characteristic of the scholar. He was clean-shaven, pale, and appeared older than he actually was, Holmes thought, chiefly due to his eyes, which were deeply recessed in his head. He was stooped over the table when Holmes entered, studying a paper, but he looked up, staring at the detective with his sunken eyes in a curiously reptilian fashion. Holmes felt a cold frisson run from his feet to his face, as if someone had stepped on his grave.

Harris questioned the witness. 'You say that the defendant's behaviour towards you was inappropriate. How so?'

' 'E follered me into the bedroom, your worship...'

Harris cut her off short. 'And whose bedroom was it that he followed you into, Miss Darcy?'

'Why, it was 'is bedroom, sorr, but then 'ee...'

Again, an interruption. 'So, you're telling me that it was inappropriate for the defendant to be in his own bedroom in his own house?'

'Why no, sorr! But 'e pushed me against the bed, and 'e put 'is 'ands on me...'

'Perhaps he was only attempting to get you to leave his bedroom so he could attend to private matters.'

The lone solicitor rose and addressed the court. 'Sir, if you would please to allow Miss Darcy to give her evidence in her own way...' Holmes assumed that this worthy was Howard Livingstone.

Harris spitted the solicitor with a glare. 'It seems that cheeky behaviour is going round today,' he said. 'Your client presumes to tell a man what to do in his own home, and now you tell me how to conduct myself in my own courtroom.' He turned back to the woman who was now shivering in the witness box. 'It seems that your employer did exactly right when he sacked you, Miss Darcy. Moreover, I find that you have wasted this court's time with your frivolous suit. Therefore, I'm sending you the women's house of correction in Brixton Hill for a week, so you may ruminate upon the error of your ways. Perhaps you'll act differently towards your master in your next position, assuming that you are so fortunate as to secure one.' He slammed his gavel down on the block. 'Constable! Take this witness into custody and see that she is duly processed.'

'Your worship, I must protest!' Livingstone shouted, but Harris paid him no mind as he rose.

Miss Darcy screamed, 'No, please don't take me!' as the burly constable seized her wrists and led her struggling from the witness box.

The defendant turned to survey the courtroom, a broad smile on his face. Holmes felt that frigid spasm again as the man's eyes met his, and he smiled even more widely.

Harris moved toward a door behind his bench, and the usher intoned 'All rise!' The magistrate turned and exited the courtroom.

Holmes waited until the defendant and his solicitor left the courtroom, then wended his way through the outgoing crowd to approach Livingstone at the solicitor's table. The lawyer stood there with both hands flat upon its surface, staring at the portal through which his erstwhile client had disappeared, as if he quite didn't know what had happened.

Holmes introduced himself. Upon questioning, the solicitor confirmed the information that Starling gave Holmes in every particular.

'So, you think that Harris sentenced Berry to such a harsh penalty because of Berry's disrespect for him?' asked Holmes.

'I'm sure of it,' said Livingstone. 'And the timing of it was awful.'

'How so?'

'Tommy told me a few days ago that, after talking to the young woman who was just removed from here, he'd recently found out something about Harris that would really take him down a peg or two. Wouldn't say what it was, though. He said he was going to confront Harris about it soon.'

At that piece of information, Holmes pursed his lips. 'Tell me, was Starling present when Berry told you that?'

Livingstone looked at the ceiling for a moment then said, 'Why yes, now that you mention it.'

'How is Starling's relationship with the magistrate?'

'Better than mine and Tommy's,' Livingstone answered. 'Roger's always saying that we're hurting ourselves by antagonizing Harris. But how can we not, when he does things like he just did?'

'Did you speak to the maid about what she may have told Mr. Berry?'

'Yes, but she was terrified. Told me she just wanted her wages so she could leave London and go home.'

He went silent for a moment, then continued. 'Unlike Miss Darcy, Thomas Berry actually committed the crime for which he was sentenced. I think there's little chance of having him released before his time is up.'

'Harris could do it,' Holmes said.

'Certainly! A magistrate can do almost anything. But I think there's very little chance that he will do it.'

'We shall have to see about that,' Holmes said. 'Thank you for your time, Mr. Livingstone.'

'Good luck,' Livingstone said, as Holmes walked away.

Holmes went back into the corridor and inquired about the location of Harris's chambers. Soon he was knocking at the magistrate's door.

'Come in.'

Holmes opened the door upon an office filled with bookshelves, and tables that held as fine a collection of Chinese memorabilia as he'd ever seen. Harris sat at a massive desk in front of a window looking out over West Ham Lane, his black robe hanging on the back of his chair. He wore a fine tweed suit that looked as if it had come from Savile Row, and a gold ring with a large ruby glinted on his right hand. He was engaged in paging through a pile of legal documents.

'Mr. Harris, my name is Sherlock Holmes. I am a consulting detective.'

'What do you want?' the magistrate answered brusquely, not even bothering to look up for the papers he was reading.

'I've come to talk with you about Thomas Berry. In particular, about the effect that the hard labour you sentenced him to is having on his health.'

Now Harris looked up, a half sneer upon his face. 'And why, pray tell, should that be a concern of mine?'

'Because it's becoming increasingly likely that Mr. Berry will not survive his sentence. You did not intend that he should suffer capital punishment for drunkenness, did you?'

'I did not intend anything, Sir. I merely sentenced him to what I thought was an appropriate term for the infraction he committed. Actually, I may have done him a favour. I could have easily remanded him to the Crown Prosecutor to face charges of obstructing the police, for which I'm sure he would have received much harsher punishment.'

By now it was apparent to Holmes that he was flogging a dead horse; still, he felt the need to press on.

'If your worship cannot see his way clear to releasing Mr. Berry, perhaps you could rescind the hard labour, or ask that the prison put Mr. Berry to some task that won't have such an adverse impact on him.'

81

'The purpose of punishment is to have an adverse impact upon an individual, so they'll think twice before committing a subsequent crime.'

Holmes hesitated, then he took the plunge. 'Mr. Harris, I have evidence that Mr Berry was not drunk when he interfered with the police. I believe he was suffering from food poisoning. If that were true, then he would not be responsible for his actions.'

Holmes thought he saw Harris's jaw drop and his eyes briefly widen, but then his expression became a sneer once more. 'Balderdash! What evidence have you?'

Holmes explained that Berry was a lifelong teetotaller, and had become ill after his lunch of steak and mushroom pie. 'If Thomas Berry drank no alcohol, as he averred, then he must have been poisoned. And some poisons can mimic the effects of drunkenness. Mushrooms, for example.'

'If that were the case, we'd have had a major outbreak,' said Harris. 'Steak and mushroom pie is a speciality of the King of Pru. Nearly everyone in the place would have been sick.' His eyes narrowed. 'Or are you saying that Berry was deliberately poisoned?'

'I believe that is a possibility, Mr. Harris.'

Harris gave Holmes a look of pure venom, and the detective wondered if he had gone too far. The magistrate could issue a summons to Holmes here and now, and he'd be in prison with Berry this evening. That would do neither of them any good. Then Harris smiled, and Holmes shivered inwardly.

'I'll tell you what, Mr. Consulting Detective. You bring me evidence that what you say is true, and I'll release Mr. Berry. I'll give you until Monday, at which time I will issue a summons for you, for attempting to interfere with the legal activities of the Police Court. Now get out of here.' He returned to perusing his documents.

As he walked through the courthouse, Holmes found himself quivering, not from fear but from anger. Harris was exactly the sort of person who had inspired him to take up the mantle of a consulting detective in the first place; someone who thought he could run roughshod over anybody he chose to. He silently vowed that he would see Thomas Berry safely out of Pentonville Prison, even if he had to strong arm Magistrate Harris to do it.

Holmes returned to The King of Pru. It was suppertime; the food aroma made Holmes salivate, but he was not here for dinner. The detective took a seat at the bar and ordered a pint. He spotted Demeris coming out of the kitchen, inspecting the plates of food lined up on the pass-through before they went out to the customers. Holmes just sat there, watching the publican's every move. Demeris would notice him soon enough. His goal: make the Greek nervous.

At first, Demeris did not notice the detective, but it was like Holmes was shooting rays of heat from his eyes. Finally, the Greek glanced in Holmes's direction, meeting that hawklike stare. He turned away, going about his business once more. But he couldn't help himself—he looked back again and Holmes still had him on the spit. He averted his gaze once more, then straightened up as if he'd made a decision. He approached Holmes. 'Can I help you, sir?'

'Tell me why you poisoned Thomas Berry.'

The look in the Greek's eyes was all the evidence Holmes needed. Fear!

'I... I did no such thing,' Demeris stammered. Unsuccessfully, he tried to mask his apprehension with indignation. 'I'm afraid I'll have to ask you to leave the premises, sir.'

'Or what?' Holmes said, his voice dripping with contempt. 'You'll call a constable? I think that's the last thing you want to do, Mr. Demeris.' An innocent man *would* call a constable, Holmes knew.

'Enjoy your beer then. It's the last one you'll be served.' The publican retreated to the far end of the bar.

Holmes was now certain that Demeris was involved. He was also certain that the Greek would never admit his guilt. He was petrified, and Holmes did not think it was himself that the landlord feared. It was whomever was behind the poisoning of Thomas Berry.

***

A few minutes before midnight, in the alley behind the King of Pru, a cloaked figure bent over a door, manipulating a pair of lockpicks with freezing fingers. The rain had returned with a vengeance, and all was blackness. Holmes had brought a dark lantern with him, but he dared not risk a light while still outside, so he had to work solely by feel. He inserted his right-angled pick, feeling for the lever inside; ah, he had it! Switching the pick to his left hand, he exerted slight pressure upward, taking care not to allow the pick to slide off the lever. Now he inserted a second probe beneath the first one, feeling for the deadbolt. Once he had it, he turned the second pick slowly to the right, all the while maintaining the upward pressure with the first one. A satisfying click seemed as loud as a gunshot, but the lock was open. Holmes swiftly removed the probes and stowed them in a pocket of his Inverness.

He pushed the door open and slid inside, closing it behind him, but taking care that it remained unlocked in case he had to affect a quick exit. Black silhouettes of hanging pots and pans informed him that he was in the kitchen. He was sure that this would not be where he would find that which he sought, if it was present at all.

He moved silently into the public room. The gate that separated the area behind the bar from the dining area was open—was someone here? Holmes froze and listened carefully; all he heard was the rain softly pattering on the bay windows and the haunting creaks of an old building in the gusty wind. He reached inside his cloak and came out with a vespa and a small dark lantern. He struck the match on a table top and lit the lantern; a bolt of yellow light burst forth. Careful to keep it away from the windows, he played the light about until he located the staircase to the first floor. He zigzagged his way between the tables to its base, where he stopped and listened intently again. He heard nothing, but an innate sense told him that someone was there. He briefly considered aborting the mission, but he knew that if he was to free Berry, he must find evidence. He crept slowly up the stairs, keeping his light low and stepping only on the edges of the treads.

The first floor comprised one large room that had been outfitted as an office. A large dormer containing a window ten shades blacker than the dark room loomed over the square. The bullseye picked out bookcases, filing cabinets; a desk with a man in a chair behind it, slumped over, unmoving! Holmes swallowed to remove his heart from his throat, then stepped over to the body. It was George Demeris, of course.

The publican's left cheek lay on the desk, his eyes bulging, his tongue protruding, a leather belt wrapped tightly round his throat. The yellow light illuminated his battered nose, and dried blood clung to his cheeks. A closer examination revealed strawberry petechiae on his face, leaving no doubt to the manner of death—strangulation.

Small, irregular brownish objects were scattered around on the desktop. Holmes noticed an open strongbox to one side, the key still in the lock. He picked up one of the leathery brown objects and smelt it—a mushroom! Inside the strongbox were two leather pouches, both apparently empty. He picked each one up and shook it to make sure. One was indeed empty, but a few more mushroom fragments fell out of the other. Holmes swept up a small handful and put them back in the pouch, stowing it in a pocket.

No one locks an empty pouch in a strongbox—what had the other bag contained? It must have been gold, Holmes realized. The bag likely held the pub-keeper's nest egg.

Holmes quickly went through Demeris's pockets but found nothing; no wallet, no watch, no keychain. Apparently, the killer had picked him clean. So, was this a robbery gone bad, or something more sinister? Though Holmes had no direct evidence, he suspected the latter. He suddenly realized that the absence of a keychain explained why the downstairs door was locked when he arrived—the murderer must have taken Demeris's keys and locked it behind him when he left. Did he arrive with Demeris? That would mean the killer was someone the Greek knew. Unlikely, Holmes thought. One does not bring company when he raids his hidden strong box. Did the murderer arrive after Demeris, who went downstairs to let him in? No again. Surely Demeris would have closed up and rehidden the strongbox before doing so. Did the fellow get in the same way as Holmes had done? He must have, and locked the door behind him. A professional, then.

And what was Demeris doing with the strongbox in the middle of the night? Getting ready to bolt, Holmes realized. It was clear then, that Demeris had poisoned Berry, in all probability by slipping some of the mushrooms now in Holmes's possession into Berry's lunch. Likely, the detective's incursion into the pub at dinnertime had convinced the Greek that Holmes suspected him, and sufficiently unnerved him so that he thought flight was in order.

But why poison the solicitor at all? Demeris could not have foreseen the events of that afternoon, which led to Berry's incarceration. Did he intend to kill Berry, or to just make him sick? Pieces of the puzzle were still missing.

Holmes dropped to his knees, shining the bullseye on the carpet, minutely examining the fibres. He rose and went round the desk toward the dormer and inspected the floor there, then, directing the light away from the window, he stepped up and scrutinized the glass. Fortuitously, the waning moon peeped out as a crack split the clouds, and Holmes extended a finger toward a minute crack in a windowpane. He returned to the body, shining the beam on the floor again. He reached down and plucked something from the rug, and held it in the light. A small hank of brown hair; the blood on the bottom indicated that it had been pulled out by the roots. The detective stood, stepped back a bit, placed his hands on the belt gripping Demeris's neck. Finally, he examined the Greek's hands, then smiled, as if a hypothesis had been confirmed.

85

Abruptly, a thump from downstairs, then a man's voice. 'Mr. Demeris! It's Constable Pritchard! Are you here?'

Holmes's hands leapt away from the belt as if it was white-hot. The constable had probably noticed the unlocked door while on patrol and was checking to see that the premises were secure. Holmes saw his career as a consulting detective vanishing in a puff of smoke if he was found here with burglar's tools and the landlord's corpse!

The constable's voice again, louder this time. 'Mr. Demeris! Are you up there?' The fellow was at the base of the stairs!

A tread creaked as the constable put his weight on it, coming up. Holmes glanced frantically about. Nowhere to hide!

He extinguished the bullseye lantern and sat it on the desk. It was much too hot to put back in his cloak. No matter; Scotland Yard would never trace it to him. He stepped round the desk, bent his head and charged the dormer, smashing though the multipaned window and onto the roof above the square. He rolled to the edge, clutching it with fingers made strong by years of violin playing. He pushed off the edge, hanging so the fifteen-foot drop to the street became seven feet, and let go. The shock ran from his ankles to his teeth as he hit the rain-drenched pavement and fell to his knees.

The shriek of the constable's whistle resounded through the square as Holmes scampered to his feet and dashed into the night. 'Oi! Stop! Murder! Bloody murder!'

Once he'd disappeared into the darkness, all of Scotland Yard's finest would never catch Sherlock Holmes.

***

Friday morning, the weather had finally broken. White clouds scudded across an achingly blue sky driven by a fresh wind from the Thames. The warmth of the sun promised an excellent day.

Sherlock Holmes sat in Harris's courtroom as the night charges commenced; the first order of business each morning. They comprised the relatively minor offences that occurred last night; loitering, drunken brawls, petty thefts, etc...

Holmes wore a Van Dyke with a pince-nez perched on the end of his nose; he was clad in a long-sleeved white shirt with a collar and no necktie, under an ochre tattersall vest. He held a notebook in his left hand in which he scrawled periodically as the proceedings continued. When Harris entered the courtroom to the usher's cry of 'Oyez, oyez!' and surveyed the spectators, he did not give Holmes a second glance. The detective was present because he thought it a good bet that last night's perpetrator might end up here this morning if he spent some of that ill-gotten gold on a night's revelry; if he did not, the detective could always browse the police sheets for viable candidates, which contained the results of past cases that came before the magistrate.

The parade of wrongdoers seemed to be uniformly impoverished, and most were well-known to Harris. Many were of the fair sex, most of them arrested for loitering, some for abusive language aimed at passers-by and two for pickpocketing. Harris dealt with them expeditiously. The loiters were fined and paid surprisingly swiftly, the harridans were consigned to Brixton Hill for a week and the thieves referred to the Crown Court for more severe punishment.

Holmes perked up as the usher brought a man before the magistrate. He was about six foot two; the right height, Holmes thought; slender and wiry, and dressed roughly in a canvas jacket over an open-collared work shirt. Holmes noted in passing he used a knotted rope to hold up his trousers. His brown hair was a dirty, unkempt mop atop his head, and dried blood mottled his hairline and his cheeks. Somewhat astonishingly, he seemed quite chipper, given his surroundings.

Harris knew him. 'Good morning, Cyril,' he said. 'What brings you to my courtroom this fine day?'

'Mr. Edwards is charged with disturbin' the peace, yer worship,' the usher said. 'He engaged in a brawl wit' another gent in the street outside the Barkin' Dog this mornin'.'

'And where is this other gent,' Harris asked.

' 'E's in hospital, sorr,' said Edwards. 'I'm rightly sorry about that, but I was just defendin' mesel' from a scurrilous attack.'

'I am sure you were, Cyril,' said Harris. 'But you know that I cannot have you turning up here like this every morning. So here is my final warning—if I see you again, it's hard labour at Pentonville for you. Do you understand?'

Edwards now stood with bowed head in the classic pose of the penitent. 'Yes, yer worship, I surely do. And thankee for another chance.'

The usher led Edwards out, and after a moment, Holmes followed.

The usher left Edwards in the corridor and returned to the courtroom. Edwards lost no time in heading for the front door and out on the square with Holmes on his heels. He turned south on High Street and walked briskly, crossing the river on the bridge and turning into the neighbourhood by the gas works. He entered a tenement, and Holmes waited a moment before following him inside. He heard Edwards on the stairs as he entered the darkened lobby and crept up behind the man, arriving at the top of the stairs in time to see him entering a flat. Holmes drew his revolver from his pocket and followed him inside, knocking Edwards to the floor as he pushed the door inwards.

Edwards, on his back, extended his hands upward, fingers splayed to ward off his attacker. 'Oi, mate! Go easy! I got nuthin' fer yer!'

'Oh yes you do, Cyril,' said Holmes. 'You murdered George Demeris last night, and I am here to see that you hang for it! Shall I tell you how you did it?'

'I never...'

'You scooped up some pebbles from the square and threw them against the dormer window, then went to the front door where Demeris let you in. You followed him up to his office, taking your belt from your pocket as you went, where you'd already placed it for easy access. When you arrived upstairs, you looped the belt over his head, but he managed to turn himself round and grab your hair, yanking out a thatch by the roots, so you let go of the belt and smashed in his nose with your fist. He fell against his desk, and you got hold of the belt again, turning him round so he faced the desk while you choked the life out of him. Why you left the belt behind when you were finished I cannot tell; perhaps it was because the glint of gold from the desktop so excited you that you could not wait to scoop it into your pockets.'

Cyril stared unbelievingly at Holmes. 'Where wuz yer hidin' to see all that?'

Holmes levelled his revolver so it pointed between the man's eye's, which were as big as saucers. 'Never mind. Show me the gold, Cyril. Show it to me!'

As if an unseen force governed his movements, Edwards slowly reached into his pocket and came out with a handful of sovereigns. ' 'Ere, yer worship. Ye can 'av it all, if ye'll only let me be...'

Holmes dashed the coins out of the killer's hand; they went spinning and ringing across the floor. 'There's only one way out for you, man! Tell me who ordered you to kill Demeris!'

The level of fear on Edwards's face intensified tenfold. 'I can't! It's not just me I have to worry about. Me Mum and me Da are still with us. He'd go after them too!'

Holmes continued to cajole Edwards, promising to protect his family, all to no avail. Finally, he spat, 'Pah! I'm done with you! We both know it was Magistrate Harris—that's why he went so lightly on you this morning in court.' Holmes produced a pair of handcuffs from a pocket and shackled Edwards to a gas pipe. 'There will be a constable up here shortly to collect you, Mr. Edwards.'

Holmes left the villain pleading and struggling, and sent an anonymous note about where to find him to Scotland Yard by post, being sure to mention the thatch of hair on the carpet in Demeris's office. He then repaired back to Baker Street to change clothes.

***

Magistrate Ian Harris heard his last case of the day at 3:50 p.m. on Friday afternoon. He had sentenced a second-hand clothes dealer to six weeks hard labour in Pentonville for stealing a purse containing 11s., 6d. in coins from a woman shopkeeper. He shook his head. If he had it his way he'd have had the man hanged; he knew that the prison sentence would have no real effect and he'd likely see the vagabond here again in a few months for a similar offence. This would go on and on until the fellow either seriously injured or killed someone, at which time he could be dealt with properly.

A knock came on the door.

'Come in!' intoned Harris.

It was the page, with the four o'clock post. He had one envelope for the magistrate. It was of fine, cream-coloured vellum, carried no stamp and was sealed with wax. Harris rose from his chair to accept the letter from the page. He noted the elaborate coat-of-arms embossed in the upper left-hand corner, which matched the one pressed into the seal. A tremor ran through him as he retrieved a letter-opener, slit the envelope and extracted a single sheet of heavy paper, folded in thirds. He unfolded and read the elaborate copperplate script. His hand opened involuntarily, and the letter fluttered to the floor. White as a fish's belly, he collapsed into his chair.

***

At six o'clock, Sherlock Holmes and Sheila Berry stood on the pavement outside the gatehouse at Pentonville Prison, next to the four-wheeler that had conveyed them there. Holmes was greatly uncomfortable, as Mrs. Berry was clinging to him as she would to a life-preserver in a stormy sea, staring into the impenetrable black depths of the structure. She gave a little start as she noticed motion within, then released Holmes and ran forward as her husband emerged into the moonlight, supported by a guard.

Sobbing, she threw her arms round his neck as the guard released him, and Holmes stepped up to help conduct him to the waiting brougham.

With Holmes supporting him on one side and his wife on the other, Thomas Berry took a couple of halting steps. He stopped, and Holmes felt the solicitor's entire body go rigid as he exhaled a rattling breath. He became nothing but dead weight and Holmes had no choice but to allow him to slide to the ground.

***

'The poor fellow was as dead as a doornail, Watson, but at least he saw the light of freedom before he succumbed.'

I held my empty snifter up to the firelight and contemplated a refill; prudence won out, as I knew I'd regret it in the morning. I set the glass down on the side table, and looked at Holmes. 'You went to Mycroft, of course.'

'Yes,' said Holmes. 'Once it became clear to me that Edwards would actually rather risk hanging for murder than betray Harris, I had to take a step back and reconsider my original objective—to free Thomas Berry from his captivity. Besides, it was dubious whether testimony from the likes of Cyril Edwards would convince a Crown Court justice to indict a colleague anyway. So, I went to my brother and told him the entire sorry tale.'

I don't suppose you're going to tell me whom it was that wrote that letter to Harris?'

'It's enough to say that it was someone very high in the British government who owed Mycroft a favour. And it meant that I now owed my brother one in turn.' Holmes looked glum. 'He has yet to collect.'

There was something else I just had to know. 'Was that the first time you had laid eyes on Professor Moriarty?'

Holmes smiled ruefully. 'Yes, it was. It was interesting—I think both of us somehow realized that our lives were to be inextricably entwined from that moment on. Of course, I did not know at the time that the professor was the one behind all of it.'

'I assume that George Demeris poisoned Berry on Harris's orders. But why would he want to make Berry seem drunk?'

'The mushroom that Demeris employed, the fly agric *Aminita muscaria*, often causes confusion, hallucinations, and erratic behaviour. The onset of symptoms is typically half an hour to an hour and a half after ingestion, and they reach their most severe in about three hours. In other words, just at the time that Thomas Berry would be in court. If that had happened, Harris not only could have jailed Berry, he could have applied to have his right to practice removed, permanently eliminating a thorn from his side. And I'm sure that the magistrate would have also enjoyed inflicting the professional humiliation. However, mycotoxins are known for their notoriously varied effects on individuals; the poison hit Berry hard and early so he was no doubt hallucinating before he even returned to court, whilst the demonstration against Virginia Matsford was in full swing.'

'And what of Harris? Did he ever receive his comeuppance?'

'Ah ha! That, Watson, is another tale...'

The Camberwell Poisoner

My good friend Sherlock Holmes has sometimes accused me of choosing those cases of his that I consider for publication based on their potential as good stories, instead of as demonstrations of the singular methods for practical criminology that he has pioneered. I must admit that, as a writer for the popular press, I am often guilty as charged. However, I think that even Holmes would agree that the affair of the poisonings in Camberwell had both academic and sensational aspects, and thus is a good choice to put before the general public.

My notes inform me that the case began on a wild, tempestuous night in mid-October, 1887. Just last week we had snow on the streets of London, and now, a gale had blown in from the Atlantic; the wind howled amongst the dormered rooves of Baker Street, and the rain pelted the windows like grapeshot. Holmes had been scraping on his violin for hours, filling our sitting room with the low, sonorous chord progressions that he favoured for introspection, while I wandered the wilds of Africa, immersed in Henry Rider Haggard's new novel, *She*. Lowering my book to rest my eyes, I reflected that I was grateful indeed for our warm and cozy home on such a night, and that my companion currently had no case that would require us to venture into the storm.

Holmes removed his violin from beneath his chin, resting it on his bended knee. 'Would you like me to play some of those music hall ditties of which you are so fond, as a favour for your indulgence of my own musical choices this evening?'

'Only if you wish,' I replied. 'Your playing has captured the mood of the weather perfectly.'

Holmes wiped the rosin from his Stradivarius with a cloth and laid it gently in its case. 'I think I shall treat myself to a brandy-soda before retiring. May I make one for you as well? Hello! We have a visitor!'

A rumble of footsteps on the stairs was followed by the abrupt breach of our sitting-room door as a young man burst into the room. Tall and gangly, he was clad in a tan canvas coat, a red-and-white striped scarf and a top hat that looked as if he'd found it in the trash. Rivulets streamed from his clothes, soaking the carpet.

'Wiggins!' Holmes cried. He continued in a more normal tone, 'To avoid Mrs. Hudson's wrath, I won't ask you to sit.'

I stepped to the cellarette and poured Wiggins a brandy—the lad was sopping and looked as if he was freezing. He took it and drank it down like so much milk.

'What can I do for you at this hour?' asked Holmes

'I 'aven't come fer youse, Mr. 'Olmes. I've come fer Doctor Watson.'

'For me? What on earth is the matter?'

'It's Billy, Doctor. 'E's awful sick. You gotta come and see to 'im.'

Billy was obviously one of the group of street urchins that Holmes referred to as his Baker Street Irregulars, with Wiggins as its leader.

'Where can I find this Billy?' I asked.

'Ee's in Sultan Street, in South'rk,' Wiggins said. 'I've got a cab downstairs. I'll take youse. Please come quickly, Doctor.'

Ten Steps from Baker Street

It only required a few moments for me to fetch my heavy wool overcoat and cap, my stick and my Gladstone from my room. Upon my return, I found Holmes waiting with a bullseye lantern in hand.

'You may need this, old fellow,' he said, handing it to me. 'And you may wish to take your revolver as well. Sultan Street is one of the worst rookeries in all of London. It can be a most dangerous place at any time, and especially this hour. Do keep your wits about you.'

I went to the desk and removed my Webley Bulldog from the drawer, placing it in my overcoat pocket. I turned to Wiggins. 'I am at your service,' I said.

'It seems that my particular talents will not be required in this instance,' Holmes said. I shall anxiously await your return.'

'Don't wait up for me,' I told him. 'I have no idea at what time I will be finished. I shall give you my report in the morning.'

I followed Wiggins to the ground floor where Mrs. Hudson cast us an evil look as she mopped up the water that Wiggins had brought in with him. Another torrent blew into the vestibule as he opened the door, and I accompanied him into the downpour. Luckily it was only a few yards to the waiting cab, so I remained relatively dry upon entering it. I banged on the roof with my stick; the driver opened the hatch and water cascaded inside. 'Sultan Street, Southwark,' I commanded. The hatch snapped shut and the cab was off with a lurch.

I began to question Wiggins as to Billy's condition, to obtain some clarity about what I might be facing, but Wiggins could only say that the boy was very sick.

After a twenty-minute ride, the cab halted. Wiggins sprang out, looked around, then shouted to the cabbie, 'Oi mate! This ain't Sultan Street.'

'Yer right,' the cabbie replied. 'It's Avenue Street, and it's as far as I go.'

I followed Wiggins out on to the cobblestones. Multi-story buildings loomed in the rain and darkness like towering cliffs in a Gothic novel. The wind had abated somewhat, but water still fell in sheets.

I addressed the cabbie. 'I say, old man, surely you're not going to make us go on foot in such beastly weather.'

'It ain't worth me life to go in there at this hour,' the cabbie replied.

Seeing that the fellow was adamant, I asked him to wait. 'Here is a crown, and there will be a guinea for you if you are here when we return.' I wasn't sure that even the promise of gold would induce the man to remain, but I had to try.

Wiggins led the way down a narrow areaway between two buildings, as black as the Styx, into the back court that was Sultan Street. The dank foetor of human waste and garbage welled out of the basement of a windowless tenement, and I had to stop and wrest control of my stomach before proceeding. I followed Wiggins into the structure, and we lighted the lantern in the vestibule. We heard scuttling, and the strong, white beam revealed crumbling plaster walls and a wooden floor with an ankle-breaking hole just a few feet in front of me. Wiggins proceeded up a ramshackle staircase, instinctively avoiding broken steps that might have caused him to come tumbling down; I was glad for the lantern's light, which enabled me to follow in his footsteps.

My old wound was throbbing by the time we reached the third floor, where Wiggins waved me through a doorway. Inside was a 10-by-10-foot room in which half a dozen boys sprawled on three filthy mattresses, obviously scavenged from the streets. I sneezed loudly as the mustiness and the stink of body odour invaded my sinuses, along with the scent of a wood fire smouldering in a metal box in a corner, vented outside through a hole in the wall. I wondered that the dilapidated wooden tenement hadn't caught fire!

Wiggins pointed out Billy, lying on a straw tick in another corner, his frail form concealed under a moth-eaten blanket. The stark beam of the bullseye lantern revealed him to be of tender age, nine or ten, no more. His elbows and knees were bent, and he lay in a relaxed foetal position. I handed the lantern to Wiggins with instructions to keep the light on the boy, then I gently touched the lad's forehead with two fingers. His skin was hot to the touch, and all of his muscles instantly constricted into a seizure. My first thought was tetanus; if that was what ailed him, the poor child was likely doomed. Then I remembered that tetanic seizures didn't usually involve the entire body.

I turned down the blanket, and I spied something lying not far from his face—a round, brown orb, a little larger than the end of my thumb. I picked it up, and sniffed it—chocolate! A bite had been taken from one side. I asked Wiggins to move the light around. There, on the floor! Another one, and another! I took those as well, wrapped them in a handkerchief and put them in my Gladstone.

I looked around at the other boys in the room, who had gathered behind me and were anxiously watching me minister to their friend.

'Have any of you eaten any chocolates today?' I asked.

95

'No sir,' one boy said. The others nodded. I surmised that they were truthful, because none of them seemed ill.

'Well, if you value your lives, don't eat any chocolates you may find in here after we're gone.'

I ran Billy's symptoms through my mind again. Evidence of a fever, seizures triggered by a touch. He had eaten part of one chocolate, and possibly others. Could he have been poisoned? I knew of only one toxin that would produce such symptoms. Strychnine!

I turned to Wiggins. 'Can you find some water?' I asked.

Wiggins departed, returning in a few minutes with some in an old tobacco tin.

I sniffed it—it did not smell stagnant. 'Where did you get this?'

'It's rainwater, Doctor. It's still rainin' pitchforks outside.'

I was relieved that he didn't take it from a cistern or other standing water source. I removed a bottle of chloroform from my bag, soaked a piece of gauze, and held it to Billy's nose. His muscles constricted again at my touch, but after a minute they relaxed as the chloroform did its work. Then I tore off a piece of the blanket, poured some of the water on it, and bathed his filthy face and forehead.

'We must move quickly while the anaesthetic remains effective,' I said 'Wiggins, carry Billy to our cab. We shall transport him to Guy's Hospital in St. Thomas Street.' I hoped to God that my offer of a guinea had induced that cabbie to remain.

I never saw a happier sight in my life than that hansom, standing in the rain on Avenue Street. The cabbie looked askance as we loaded Billy inside, but gold silenced any complaint he might have. Since the cab would hold only two, I instructed Wiggins to remain here. 'Come to Baker Street tomorrow and I'll give you a report on Billy's condition.' I boarded the cab and ordered the driver to take us to Guy's.

In a short time, we rattled beneath the cast iron archway into the forecourt of the great hospital. I gave Billy another dose of chloroform before slinging him over my shoulder and carrying him inside.

'I have a boy here who needs immediate attention for strychnine intoxication!' I shouted. A white-clad orderly appeared and took Billy from me, whisking him off into the bowels of the hospital. I had to sign a paper agreeing to be responsible for the cost of his treatment, which I was only too glad to do.

I took a seat in the anteroom to await news about my charge. In about an hour, a doctor approached me.

'Doctor, your quick action may have saved that boy's life.' I released a breath that I did not realize that I was holding. The physician continued, 'You know as in many things of a medical nature, the first twenty-four hours are the most critical, but right now, the lad is resting comfortably. You may as well go home—there is no more you can do here tonight.'

The rain was finally abating as I walked from the hospital to Borough High Street, where I was fortunate enough to find a cab at such an early hour. The church bells were ringing six o'clock as I pulled up in front of 221b. I removed my sodden overcoat in the vestibule, and trudged upstairs, bone-tired. Naturally, Holmes had gone to bed as any sane person would have done. I took the chocolates from my bag, then wrapped them in a piece of paper and put them in the drawer of the table that held Holmes's chemical apparatus. Finally, I took my sore body off to bed.

When my eyes opened again, sunlight was streaming through my bedroom window. I had a dull, throbbing ache in my sinuses, which I recognized from my Army days; the result of too little sleep following a prolonged period of wakefulness. I rose and donned my dressing gown, then went downstairs to the sitting room.

Holmes was sitting in his chair reading *The Police Gazette*, which he immediately lowered as I entered the room. 'Finally,' he said.

I cocked an eyebrow. 'If you're referring to the time of my rising, I'll have you know I went to bed just five hours ago.'

'Quite.'

I'd seen this before. Holmes could become unbelievably testy when someone had news he wanted to hear. Well, two could play at that game. I deliberately rang for breakfast and settled myself at the table without answering him.

'Well? Out with it! How is Billy?'

'I'm unsure,' I answered. 'I delivered him to Guy's at two this morning. I believe he was suffering from strychnine poisoning.'

'Strychnine! And where would he have gotten into that, pray tell?'

'Look in the top drawer of your chemistry bench.' He did so, immediately spotting my handkerchief. As he unwrapped the candies, I said, 'I found those near Billy's bed.'

Holmes sniffed the candies and grunted noncommittally before pushing them back into the drawer. He closed and locked it, then removed his dressing gown prior to donning his coat and hat.

'Where are you going?' I asked.

'Out, to get the supplies I will need for a strychnine analysis. I could have saved hours if you had simply left me a note, you know.'

Ruefully, I realized that he was spot on, but I would not give him the satisfaction of admitting it.

I was in a much better frame of mind when he returned, having disposed of most of a pot of Mrs. Hudson's excellent coffee and a pair of kippers. Holmes seemed to have forgotten our altercation as well, humming to himself as he set up his bench for the analysis.

I sent a note to Guy's by the first afternoon post, inquiring about Billy's condition. The reply came in the second post; he was hanging on, but not out of the woods as yet. Wiggins came by a bit later as I had asked, and I gave him the report. 'And remind the other boys at Sultan Street not to eat any chocolates they may find lying about.'

'I'll tell the lads,' Wiggins said.

I briefly wondered what was to become of Billy even if he did survive; strychnine intoxication can have long-lasting effects, which would not be mitigated by life on the streets.

It was nearing suppertime when Holmes announced that his analysis was complete. 'The filling of that chocolate contained enough strychnine to kill several grown men,' he said. 'That may have been fortunate—perhaps the bitter flavour of the toxin was off-putting after a single bite, contributing to Billy's survival. I've also analysed the chocolate itself. The cocoa, fat and sugar content indicates a French formulation. Will you hand me Mr. Kelly's book from my shelf, please?' He riffled through the pages for a few moments. 'Ha! Monsieur Gaston Nazaire is a chocolatier in Camberwell Green, not far from Sultan Street. I think a little excursion is in order.'

'Won't the shop be closed at this hour?' I asked.

Holmes flipped a few more pages in Kelly's. 'I can find no residential address for M. Nazaire in any street near the shop. Perhaps he lives above it. We shall see.'

As the weather had taken a turn for the better, we walked the few short blocks to Dorset Square to find a cab to Southwark. Gaston Nazaire's chocolate shop was just across from Camberwell Green, a picturesque park bounded by a wrought-iron fence, green hedges, and ringed with glowing gas lamps. Approaching the glass door, I noticed the shade was lowered and a sign reading '*Closed*' dangled in the centre of the glass.

Indicating the first-floor windows, Holmes said, 'Obviously, M. Nazaire resides upstairs. He pounded on the door frame. 'Halloa, Gaston Nazaire! It is Sherlock Holmes and Doctor Watson.' There was no response.

'Perhaps he's out, having a bit of supper,' I said, ruefully realizing that I'd not had mine yet.

'Possibly,' agreed Holmes. 'Let us wait and see if he comes home.' We repaired across the road to a bench on the green, where we had a clear view of the shop.

Not long afterwards, a young woman arrived; twentyish, dressed in a grey sweater over a cream-coloured blouse and a long, dark skirt. She wore a shawl on her head; she was obviously a working girl. She halted at the chocolate shop door and withdrew a key from a pocket. Holmes plucked my coat and hissed, 'Watson, come on.' Crossing the street, he raised his voice to address the girl. 'Oh Miss! Might we have a word?' She turned to face us, a look of alarum on her winsome features, understandable because she was being accosted by two strange men in the night time. Holmes continued, 'You needn't worry. I am Sherlock Holmes, the consulting detective, and I would like to ask you about Monsieur Nazaire.'

By now we had reached the kerb on her side of the street. 'What do you want with my betrothed?' she asked with a quiver in her voice.

'Your betrothed is Gaston Nazaire?' Holmes asked.

'Yes. I clerked for him. We fell in love, and he asked me to marry him just last week. Of course, I said yes.'

'We wish him no ill,' Holmes reassured her. 'We merely want to speak with him. He does not appear to be in.'

'He should be,' the girl said. 'It's not unusual for him to have the shop open at this time in the evening.'

'What is your name, lass?' I asked.

I am Honora Kimball,' she answered, 'but most call me Nonnie.'

'May we come inside, Nonnie?' Holmes asked.

She hesitated, still unsure, then looked at me and decided. 'Yes,' she said.

We entered the shop, and the aromas of sugar and chocolate immediately made my mouth water and my stomach growl. However, another, earthier odour that I could not immediately identify lurked beneath the sweetness. We occupied a rectangular room about ten by fifteen feet, with stark, white walls and several glass-fronted cases arranged in a U-shape before us. Piles of chocolates of all shapes and sizes were heaped on silver trays in the cabinets.

Ten Steps from Baker Street

I looked at my companion. His nostrils twitched, then he said, 'Watson, please keep Nonnie in this room for a moment.' He went behind the cases to a partially open door in the rear wall, and went inside. In a moment, he stood in the doorway again, and said, 'Watson, please take the young lady outside.'

'What's wrong?' Nonnie said. 'Is it Gaston? Is he hurt?' I had a hand on her shoulder, but she tore away from me and ran toward Holmes, who gathered her up in both arms in an attempt to keep her from the back room. However, she'd apparently seen enough. 'Oh my God!' she screamed, then collapsed in Holmes's arms.

'Watson, please take her. And please fetch a constable.'

I did as Holmes asked. As we left the shop, the poor girl was crying, 'He's dead, he's dead, oh my God, my sweet Gaston is dead!'

A crowd had gathered in front of the shop; I noticed a matronly woman among them. 'Could you please see to this young lady?' I asked her, and she immediately came forward to comfort Nonnie. 'Go for a constable,' I told another man; watched him run off, then I went back inside the shop and into the rear room.

Holmes was surveying the body of one whom I assumed was Gaston Nazaire, hanging from a rope tied to an exposed beam. He had apparently affixed a noose around his neck and simply fallen over backwards so it closed off the airway. His face was mottled blue with the petechial haemorrhaging characteristic of strangulation, and his tongue protruded like a dark grey slug.

'His was not an easy death, Watson. Partial suspension hangings are the most common in suicides and usually always messy. The marks on the floor from his heels indicate that he struggled, but it is no simple matter to get to one's feet while one is strangling. Doubtless we shall find fibres from the rope under his fingernails, as he futilely endeavoured to loosen it.'

'Do you think this could be murder?' I asked.

'I strongly doubt it,' Holmes answered. 'It is extremely hard to murder someone by hanging unless it's done by at least two people. I see no evidence of multiple individuals in this room.'

Holmes began a meticulous search. The back room of the shop had been outfitted as a kitchen, apparently in which Nazaire crafted his candies. Plucking a white box from a carton, Holmes returned to the front of the shop and began taking samples from each tray of chocolates in the cases.

When he finished, he returned to the kitchen. He took his glass from a pocket, and began a painstaking examination of the baseboards. 'Ha!' he exclaimed, 'Scatology indicates that Monsieur Nazaire apparently had a mouse problem.' He began opening cupboards. 'Here 'tis!' he said holding up a clear bottle with a loop embedded in the cork. The label read '*Strychnine sulphate*'.

'Surely you're not suggesting that the man poisoned his own wares?' I said.

'I suggest nothing,' Holmes replied. 'I merely remark.'

Holmes turned his search to the countertops. 'What's this, now?' He held up an envelope.

'It's made of cream-coloured stock, about four inches by six, and the rather thick paper is of the type used to send a formal note,' Holmes opined. 'Beyond the obvious facts that this was addressed by a woman who knew the decedent fairly well, and who was depressed and emotionally repressed with an unstable personality, I can tell little else.

'How do you know all that from one word scrawled on an envelope?' I asked incredulously.

'Surely even you can see that the script is feminine, Watson. Because the envelope is addressed to the recipient with his last name only, we can conclude that the sender had some acquaintance with him. I have made a little study of hand-writing and personality traits, which I hope to publish as a monograph one day. The severe back slant indicates repressed emotions, the dropping baseline depression, possibly due to a tragic loss, and hook on the letter 'z' that drops below the baseline is a classic shape known as the felon's claw, found in the handwriting of many violent criminals. At the very least, it implies a highly unstable personality.'

I had a flash of inspiration. 'Where there is an envelope, surely there should be a letter,' I said. 'Where is it?'

'Capital, Watson! We'll make a detective of you yet!' Holmes began casting about the room again. He opened the door of a squat, pot-bellied stove in the corner. 'I was sure I smelt smoke earlier,' he said, showing me fingertips blackened with ash. 'I fear we shall never know the contents of the letter.'

'Why would the man burn a letter, then take his life?' I asked.

'I can think of at least six reasons,' said Holmes.

A clatter in the front of the shop announced the arrival of the law. The constable surveyed the situation, then went outside and blew his whistle to summon his fellows, dispatching one to Scotland Yard for an Inspector. 'I'm detaining you until he arrives,' the constable told us, 'as he will surely wish to ascertain what you know about the matter.'

Holmes's expression told me that he chafed under the restriction, but there was little he could do until the inspector arrived. While we waited, Holmes asked Nonnie to write her name on a slip of paper, which he then compared with the envelope. The writing was completely different.

About an hour later, we were gratified to see that the inspector assigned was our friend, Lestrade. He quickly granted us permission to return to Baker Street upon Holmes's assurance that he would share the results of his investigation with him on the morrow.

Upon our arrival at 221b, Holmes immediately began setting up to analyse the chocolates he had taken from Nazaire's shop, while I rang Mrs. Hudson for a cold supper.

'I have no time to waste taking sustenance, Watson. It is going to be a long night for me, I'm afraid. You may as well retire after your supper.'

As I was short on sleep after my exertions of last evening, I followed his suggestion.

When I came downstairs the following morning, my nose was instantly assaulted by the noxious vapours from Holmes's nocturnal endeavours. I rang for coffee before asking him what he had found.

'My findings are troubling indeed, Watson,' he answered. 'I have ascertained that only a few of the chocolates from the case were poisoned.'

'Why should that trouble you? I should think it would be good news.'

'It troubles me because it indicates that Billy likely did not steal the chocolates he ate. It is much more probable that someone gave them to him.'

A chill seeped into my bones. 'What sort of monster gives poisoned chocolates to a child?' I asked.

'The sort that we must apprehend as quickly as possible,' said Holmes. He took up a blank telegraph pad and scratched out a message, then exchanged his laboratory coat for a jacket. 'I am going to inform Lestrade of my findings. I am also going to wire Guy's for a report on Billy's condition. I shall return soon,' he said, then departed.

Despite the coolness of the weather, I opened the windows to clear the stench from our rooms, so that I might enjoy my coffee while I waited for Holmes's return. He was back in fifteen minutes.

'You will be gratified to know that your efforts were not in vain, Watson. Guy's answered my wire to tell me that Billy is awake and able to speak. Get your hat and coat. We're off.'

I sorrowfully considered the silver covered dish on the table, then moved to follow his instructions. Breakfast would have to wait.

The day was bright, cool and crisp, and the trip to Southwark was short; only twenty minutes. We alighted from our cab in the hospital forecourt, then inquired at the desk for Billy's location. The receptionist called for an orderly to show us the way to the ward.

The ward was a cavernous chamber with twenty-foot ceilings, filled with the clean scents of carbolic and alcohol. It contained about a dozen patients, one of them Billy, sitting up in bed with a tray in front of him containing the remains of his breakfast. We approached and introduced ourselves.

'Yer the gent that saved me, ain'tcha?' Billy asked.

'Yes,' I replied.

'Thank'ee, guvnor.' I reflected that this thanks from a street urchin was worth more than the gold I got from a paying patient.

'Now Billy,' began Holmes, 'we wish to ascertain how you came by that chocolate you had. Did someone give it to you?'

'Yessir,' said Billy. 'It was a lady.'

'Can you describe her?'

'Well, it was loike this. I was beggin' on Camberwell Road, by t'church...'

'Emanuel Church?' Holmes interrupted.

Billy looked annoyed. 'That's the one. I saw this swell lady who looked loike a soft touch.'

'Why did you think that?' I asked him.

'Oh I dunno,' he said. 'Y'can just tell. She 'ad on fine rags, and a fur 'round 'er neck. One o' them kind wif t'heads and eyes still on. I tried to nick 'er for a bob, but she said she 'adn't any. But she took three candies out o' 'er purse and give 'em t'me.'

'Can you provide a more precise description of her?' asked Holmes.

'Well, she was normal.' Billy said. 'A swell, fer sure.'

'What colour was her hair? Her eyes?'

'I couldn't see 'er eyes. 'Er hair was brown.'

Billy, you just described half of the women in London, I thought.

'But I fink she was playin' wif me,' Billy said. 'Them was the worst chocolates I ever 'et!'

On the way out of the ward, a nurse stopped us. 'Are you aware that Billy will be discharged later today?', she asked.

While I was gratified to hear that he was doing so well, this was disheartening news. Surely the lad couldn't go back to Sultan Street. I asked her at what time he must leave, and she told me half eleven. I surmised that the hospital did not want to feed him another meal.

'Perhaps you can prevail upon Mrs. Hudson to watch over the lad for a bit, so he can convalesce properly,' Holmes said, reading my thoughts.

'We can but try,' I answered.

After hearing Billy's sad story, our landlady said she'd be only too glad to look after him for a few days while he healed. I fetched him from Guy's, then I spent the rest of the day helping her get him settled. When I finally returned upstairs, I found that Holmes had gone out again.

As I was having supper, I heard footsteps on the stairs, and the door to the sitting room opened. A man in overalls and a dark wool shirt, wearing a flat cap, entered. I had to look twice to make sure it was Holmes. He removed his cap and tossed it at the coat tree; it hit the hook but did not stick, falling to the floor instead. 'Thus is the tale of my day,' said Holmes.

'I take it you had no luck,' I said.

'Brilliant deduction, Watson,' Holmes said unkindly. 'What else would be expected with the meagre description of the poisoner that I have?'

'Sit down and eat something, old man,' I said. 'You'll feel better.'

'I don't want to feel better,' Holmes raged petulantly, slamming his hand on the top of mantle. 'Do you know that five more poisonings have been reported in Camberwell today, all likely stemming from Nazaire's shop before it was closed down? I wish to remain in extreme discomfort until this wretch, this poisoner of children, is brought to heel!' He retired to his bedroom, slamming the door, presumably to remove his make-up.

The atmosphere in our rooms was tense for the rest of the evening. I retired early, so I did not have to further subject myself to Holmes's silent brooding.

He was gone again when I arose the following morning. After breakfast, I went downstairs to assess Billy's progress. He remained weak, and appeared frustrated that he could not stay out of bed for any length of time without being overcome by fatigue. I reassured him that he would be a little better every day, but I privately worried about what was to become of him when he was finally well.

Holmes returned shortly after luncheon, in the same disguise as he had affected last night.

'It's no use, Watson,' he said. 'The streets of Camberwell teem with the *hoi polloi*. One cannot make bricks without clay. Unfortunately, the price of more clay in this case may well be lives.'

Sadly, Holmes's words proved prophetic. At mid-afternoon. Lestrade burst into our rooms. One look at his face told the tale.

'There have been additional poisonings,' he said. 'Five more so far. They could not have come from Nazaire's shop, for that has been shut down.'

'The symptoms are consistent with strychnine poisoning, Lestrade?' asked Holmes. The inspector nodded. 'Where have they occurred? Pray, be specific.'

'All over bloody Camberwell,' Lestrade replied. 'All Souls, St. Giles, The Green, Denmark Hill. I have my officers canvassing to attempt to determine the sources, but Scotland Yard does not have the facilities to test all of the foodstuffs in each victim's home.' He hesitated, then went on. 'And a few of the victims have received letters, as well.'

Holmes's eyebrow went up. 'What kind of letters?'

'Hateful, they are. Accusing the recipients of all sorts of vile things.'

'Our poisoner has a poison pen as well,' Holmes observed sardonically. 'Capital! Do all the letter recipients show signs of strychnine poisoning?'

'No,' Lestrade said, 'No. Only some do.'

'So, all of these poisonings are not random,' Holmes observed. 'She must be delivering tainted goods to some of the victims herself. I could test the foodstuffs for strychnine,' he mused, 'but it would be a great deal of work and it may not be necessary. I think it's safe to assume that the sources of the random poisonings are close to the victim's homes. Have the addresses of anyone showing symptoms and anyone who has received a poison pen letter sent here to me at once, Inspector, as well as the letters and their envelopes.'

'But we must identify the businesses selling the poisoned goods, so we can shut them down,' Lestrade said.

Holmes spit the rat-faced detective with a glare. 'You would employ me as a mere technician, would you? Tell your superiors to hire a private chemist! Wouldn't you rather I identified this scoundrel so you can remove her from the streets entirely? I rather think the damage will be done long before anyone could complete the analyses, at any rate.'

'Would you like to visit the crime scenes? Talk to the victims who can speak?' Lestrade asked.

'No, Inspector,' Holmes replied. 'The crime scenes themselves and the victims will have little to tell me. What is important here is not who is being victimized. It's where the incidents are occurring.'

He snatched up a sheet of paper and a pen, scrawling a message.

'Have this placed in all of the papers sold in Camberwell, Lestrade.'

I looked at it over the inspector's shoulder.

> Anyone who has received an anonymous letter containing scurrilous accusations or slanders, [it ran], please deliver same, along with the envelope, to S. Holmes at 221b Baker Street, W. A fee of 1 crown shall be paid for each letter, and your anonymity assured.

Holmes took up his coat and hat and moved toward the door.

'You're off to Camberwell again?' I asked.

'No, to Edward Stanford's in Long Acre.'

'What on earth for?'

'Ordinance survey maps of Camberwell and vicinity,' he said. The walls shook as the door slammed behind him.

Holmes returned within the hour with rolled maps under his arm. He pushed the furniture in the sitting room against the walls and spread his maps out on the floor, anchoring the corners with books. In the meantime, Lestrade had sent up the first batch of addresses and poison pen letters, which had also been posted from various locations in Southwark. By this time, the number of people showing symptoms of strychnine poisoning had increased to nine.

'Our foe is cagey, Watson. She attempts to hide her tracks in her peregrinations. But I shall have her soon.'

Holmes compared a few of the poison pen letters to the envelope found at the chocolate shop. 'Ha! The handwriting is the same. And the prevalence of felon's claws in these missives is truly terrifying.'

He fell to his hands and knees and began marking the locations of the victim's homes and the locations indicated by the postmarks on the ordinance survey maps, employing different coloured pencils depending upon whether a poisoning was random, deliberate, or just a letter had been received.

When he had finished, he burst out, 'Confound it! Not enough data yet! And three more dead!'

The tide of material ebbed by dinner time, and nothing more came in that evening. Holmes paced the floor like a caged wolf, muttering imprecations. I am ashamed to say that I again retreated to my room with a book to escape.

The next day, all was quiet until the church bells rang eleven, then the ominous messages from Scotland Yard began arriving once more, and poor Mrs. Hudson was kept busy running up and down the stairs to deliver poison pen letters from people who had knocked on our door. Holmes dutifully entered information from each on his maps, then perched on the edge of his seat, quivering like a snake about to strike, as he impatiently waited for the next bit of information to arrive.

Late that afternoon he gave an exuberant shout, then snatched up a ruler and began measuring distances between various points on the maps, which he entered into a table on a chalk board he'd brought up from the basement. He scribbled diverse equations next to each line of the table, solved them in turn, then it was back to his maps again, employing a pin, a piece of string and a pencil to inscribe overlapping circles on the parchment.

Finally, he exclaimed 'I have you, you rogue!' laying his finger on a point on the map where the circles intersected.

The northern end of Denmark Hill.

Ten Steps from Baker Street

***

A cool October breeze countered the warmth of the morning sun on my face as I snapped the reins on the back of the horse pulling our covered wagon. Beside me sat Billy, dressed in his usual urchin's rags, and beside him Holmes, wearing similar attire. The old mare in front of me barely noticed the touch of the leather; she was a Tinker's horse and cared not a fig about my urgings to move faster.

Holmes cried 'Tools, knives, we can fix anythin'' as our wagon plodded along. Billy was silent, his eyes roving the crowd on the sidewalks, looking for a familiar face.

Even though Holmes's geographical analysis had pinpointed the area where the poisoner probably resided, it encompassed a number of blocks along Denmark Hill, an area that contained literally hundreds of residents. He saw no way to positively identify the poisoner without having someone who knew her to do it. While Billy was improving daily, by no means was he up to walking the streets of Camberwell all day long. So, Holmes had hit upon the stratagem of disguising himself as a tinker, one of the many itinerants who travelled along the streets of London in their covered wagons, offering their goods and services to the population at large. Such men often employed young boys as assistants.

'But even if he's riding in a wagon all day, it's possible that Billy may still experience *sequalae* from his intoxication,' I argued. 'What will you do then, Holmes? You are not a doctor.'

'But you are, Watson,' Holmes observed. 'You'll just have to come along.'

So it was that I found myself clad in rags and a large floppy hat, a mixture of dirt and greasepaint coating my face, driving a stinky old nag along a London thoroughfare.

'There!' exclaimed Billy. Holmes reached across to slap the boy's arm down as he attempted to raise it to point at the woman he ostensibly recognized.

'Describe her,' Holmes said.

'She's the one in the purple dress, with the big a.., I mean, wit' the bustle in t'back.' Mrs. Hudson had been working on Billy's word choices all week.

'I see her,' said Holmes.

I did too, among the crowd, walking purposefully toward a bake shop.

108

'Pull up,' Holmes ordered me, and I complied. 'Billy, remain here. Watson, come with me.'

We hopped down from the wagon and hurried over to the shop, peering through the plate glass window. The woman was standing to one side, next to a tray of tea biscuits on a counter.

'There!' exclaimed Holmes, as the woman's hand dipped into the voluminous purse she carried, then moved toward the tray of biscuits. Holmes fished inside his jacket for the police whistle he wore on a lanyard underneath it, and blew a long, shrill blast. Then he burst through the door of the bakery, rushing up to the woman and grabbing her wrist as she attempted to put something on the tray.

Her other hand strayed into her purse again, and came out clutching an ice pick, which she directed toward Holmes's ribs. Not knowing what else to do, I balled my right hand into a fist and hit her on the point of her jaw before she could stab my friend. She went limp as a fish in his grasp.

A few months later, myself, Holmes and Lestrade were in Baker Street. We had just finished one of Mrs. Hudson's fine suppers of Scotch pie, tatties and gravy, and were tucking into bowls of cranachan with raisins. We were celebrating the end of the Camberwell poisoning case, with the conviction of Clara Eddins at the Old Bailey that afternoon. The jury had imposed a death sentence.

'A murderer who selects his victims at random is the most difficult to identify,' said Holmes. 'Mrs. Eddins was a sad case. 'Once a respectable lady, she went completely off the rails after the death of her husband two years ago. She noticed Gaston Nazaire when she patronized his shop, formed an attachment to him that he in no way encouraged, and convinced herself that they would be married. When she learned that he was going to wed his clerk, Nonnie, instead, she became further unhinged, and she decided to ruin him by poisoning his wares.'

'So, she sent him a note to tell him what she had done?' I asked.

'That is what I surmise, although I cannot prove it,' Holmes replied. 'The poor man apparently realized that he was finished in his profession; even though it was not his fault, the public would never buy his chocolates again if it became common knowledge that tainted candy originated from his shop.'

'Perhaps you can explain how you were able to locate so precisely the area where Mrs. Eddins lived?', I asked

'It is a little method of geographical analysis on which I have been working for some time,' said Holmes. 'It is based on the idea that all data are not equally valuable;

in this case, some locations had a greater likelihood of being near to the perpetrator's base of operations than others.'

'How so?' I prompted.

'For example, Mrs. Eddins had to be acquainted with those to whom she sent letters, so those people were more likely to reside near to her, while she would likely range farther afield to plant her noxious sweets to be picked up by random individuals. Those estimates could be weighted mathematically, and would be inversely proportional to the diameter of a circle that indicated the likelihood that the poisoner's base of operations was in a given area. Once enough data points were plotted, a reasonable location for it could be derived. I placed it within a quarter-mile radius in Denmark Hill, and that proved to be where she kept her residence for the last twenty years.'

'I had no idea you were so mathematically gifted, Holmes,' I said.

'I had an excellent maths tutor,' he replied.

'But what drove her to wholesale poisoning, and to write the poison pen letters?' asked Lestrade.

'Perhaps it was the death of Nazaire, whom she had convinced herself that she loved, or the realization of what she had done to innocents that caused her to become completely deranged,' Holmes said. 'The tone of the poison pen letters indicated paranoia; she was convinced that others were responsible for her ills, so she felt completely justified in striking back. Her barrister presented evidence in court that insanity ran in her family, but the jury was apparently unimpressed.'

'She's responsible for the poisoning of thirty-one people and the deaths of fifteen, and it's thanks be to the Almighty that it wasn't more,' Lestrade said. 'Hangin's too good for her.'

'I disagree, Inspector,' I said. 'While her crimes were indeed heinous, she was not responsible for her actions. Our legal system must come to grips with mental illness sooner or later.'

'I agree, Watson,' Holmes said. 'That's why I've asked an acquaintance of mine in the British government to speak to the home secretary about commutation of her sentence.'

I looked at Lestrade. 'And if you think that's a mercy, Lestrade, you've never been inside of one of London's asylums.'

A knock came on the door. 'Come in, Mrs. Hudson,' Holmes said.

Our landlady entered, come to remove our supper dishes. She addressed Holmes and me. 'Billy's got something to show ye,' she said, turning to regard the open door. 'Ye can come in now,' she called.

Billy entered and stood before us, resplendent in his new, blue uniform with its double row of brass buttons running down the front and his tight-fitting pillbox hat, of which he was obviously self-conscious. In his new position as the page of 221b Baker Street, he would never have to go back to the Sultan Street rookery again.

At least one good thing had come out of this sad affair.

Blood and Gunpowder

May 4, 1893

I sit at my desk in my Kensington study, wallowing in my grief, as the howling wind drives the cold rain into my windows like tiny pieces of grapeshot. Just last week, my poor Mary's illness reached its climax, and now I will see her no more until Our Lord returns her to me at His Last Judgment. My grief is doubly poignant this day, because it was two years ago that I lost my other dear friend, Sherlock Holmes, the best and wisest man I have ever known, at the hands of the despicable Professor Moriarty. After Mary's death, the pastor told me not to remember her in sickness, but in health,

dwelling upon her charm, her vivacity and the joys of our brief life together. I suspect the same should hold true for Holmes. So, to assuage my sorrow, I choose to take up my pen to chronicle one of our last adventures together, which, had I but known it at the time, was a harbinger of the great tragedy to come.

It was in late April of 1891, in Holmes' sitting room in Baker Street, that he told me of a meeting with the professor some weeks earlier, when the latter had essayed to induce my friend to cease his inquiries into Moriarty's machinations. Of course, Holmes refused, preferring to risk death rather than allow the brand of evil personified by Moriarty to run rampant. Holmes recounted Moriarty's words to him at that fateful meeting.

'You crossed my path on the 4th of January...' said Moriarty.

I well remember where I was on New Year's Day of that year, and that it was I who summoned Holmes to that minacious encounter.

***

It was a clammy cold day on a beach about a mile from Sangatte, France, where I was engaged in an onerous duty indeed. The son of an old school chum, Kendrick Wood Jr., had accepted a challenge to a pistol duel, which had arisen, as many do, over drink and cards. Young Kenny Wood was engaged in a rubber of whist at the Bagatelle Card Club, imbibing heavily and consequently losing badly, when he had the uncommonly poor judgment to publicly accuse his opponents of cheating. Unfortunately, one of them was the noted journalist and duellist Isadora Persano. A challenge was swiftly issued and accepted. Since duelling has been illegal in England since 1840, and the prosecution of those who cause injury or death during a duel is the rule rather than the exception, the combatants chose France as the venue for their dispute, because the French take a much more tolerant view of defending one's honour than we Britons do.

As an enlightened modern gentleman, I find the practice of duelling abhorrent, and normally, I would have no part in one. However, my friend Kend asked me to be the attending physician at the affair.

'There's no one on earth with whom I would be more comfortable entrusting the life of my only son, Watson,' he said.

How could a decent man refuse such a request? Even Mary understood why I must be away on New Year's Day.

So it was that I found myself loitering on the sand at Sangatte, where stark white clouds outlined in gold, backlit by the morning sun, loomed above the meadows of Pas de Calais, the salty freshness of the sea tangy in the air. The Woods, Kend and Kenny, Kenny's second Tommy Babcock, and Persano's second Huston Sipes all waited with me for the arrival of Persano on the field of honour, so the shameful affair could commence.

After some fifteen minutes, Persano had still not made his appearance.

'Watson,' Kend called, 'perhaps, since you are the only neutral on the field, you might go to Persano's tent to find out what is keeping him.'

Two tawny pole marquee tents, erected to shelter the combatants from the weather as they made their preparations for the duel, were situated on the other side of the dune from the field of honour. I made my way to Persano's, stopping outside of the closed flap. Uncomfortable with the idea of simply walking into to another man's tent, I raised my voice, 'Persano, it's Dr. Watson. Everyone is waiting for you, old man. Do you require assistance?'

No answer. Heaving a sigh, I drew aside the flap and entered.

Persano was sitting in a canvas chair beside a folding table, staring intently at something that he held in his right hand.

'I say, Persano! Everyone is ready and waiting on the beach. Are you coming?' With all my heart, I hoped he would say no—that he had decided to call the whole thing off.

He did not respond. It did not seem that he heard me. He still stared fixedly at whatever he was holding.

I stepped up behind him, placing a hand on his shoulder. The object he was holding appeared to be a match box. I could not see what it contained. But I could see that the hand that held the box was covered in blood! I shook him, calling 'Persano! Are you ill?'

As he turned his head to look at me, I saw a red stream trickling lazily from his right ear. When his face came into view, I was horrified to see blood running from his eyes, his nose, and his lips, as well!

'Persano! You're bleeding, man! What the devil is wrong with you?'

114

Persano dropped the matchbox onto the sand, and the contents were ejected and bounced along the ground. He brought a bandaged hand to his face, smearing the blood from his nose across his cheek. He looked at his hand stupidly for a moment, then his eyes glowed, and he broke into a smile. His teeth were tinged with pink, with blood red lines between them.

'So I am, so I am! But at least, I taught a lesson to that upstart who accused me of being a cheat.' He began to laugh in a low, measured tone, and the sound of it chilled me to the bone. *He's mad!* I thought. *He thinks the duel is done!*

'I'm a doctor,' I told him. 'I can help you. Come and lie down, let me examine you.' I reached to take his hands.

He batted my hands aside and attempted to rise, but his knees crumpled so he sprawled onto the ground, face first. With difficulty, I rolled the journalist over. He lips worked; he was trying to speak! I lowered my ear to his mouth. I heard what sounded like 'Courtier... Paris...' he began to cough, and I hurriedly raised my head lest he spit blood on my face. His mouth was half-open, blood bubbling from his lips as he wheezed and gasped for air. Suddenly, his eyes assumed that fixed gaze that I knew all too well, and his last earthly breath rasped from his lungs, spewing a cloud of tiny red droplets into the air, which settled back onto his face. I did not need my medical training to tell me that Isadora Persano was stone, cold dead.

Since there was nothing more I or anyone else could do for him, I looked to see what had held his rapt attention in his final moments. A small brownish ball lay in the dirt, its surface festooned with fine, minuscule spines. Closer examination revealed it as some kind of worm, all coiled up into a ball.

Picking it up, I hurriedly dropped it again as a sharp, stinging pain lanced into my thumb. A couple of the spines had embedded themselves in my flesh. Cursing, I retrieved my pocket knife and arduously extracted them. Ruby droplets welled where they had been, and I thrust the hurt finger into my mouth. When I withdrew the digit, I noticed that it still bled. Since the wound was minor, I dismissed it from my mind and hurried to inform my companions about what had transpired.

Coming over the dune, I looked down upon the beach where everyone waited to carry out their sad duties. Kend Woods stood facing his son, his hands on the boy's shoulders, talking to him earnestly. Sipes was ten yards away, his back to the father and son, staring out to sea, assumedly to give them privacy during this difficult time. Joy rose in my heart, due to the news I was about to convey.

'Halloa!' I shouted. 'There will be no duel this day!'

'No duel?' Kend Woods said. 'What do you mean? Has Persano come to his senses?'

'Hardly,' I said. 'He is dead.'

'What mischief is this?' Sipes said, approaching us. 'What has happened?'

I described the scene in Persano's tent, leaving out the details of his madness, and of the worm.

'Why, this is marvellous news,' Kend said.

'A man is dead!' said Sipes.

'Yes, he is,' said Kend, 'and he is not my boy.' Sipes glared at him, coals of fire glowing in his eyes.

'We'd best report this to the police in Calais,' I said. 'Sipes, you can contact those in London who need to know.'

We gathered the things from the beach necessary for the conduct of the duel—the pistols, balls and powder, my medical kit. The tents and their contents we would have to leave for later. We walked back to the road where the broughams we had hired awaited us. The drivers congregated, the smoke from their vile French cigarettes forming a heavy cloud in the air.

'*Tu connais le gendarmerie du Caliais*?' I asked them.

'*Oui.*' One replied.

'*Emmenez nous la.*' I ordered.

We boarded the carriages and set off.

The *Gendarmarie du Pas de Calais* was a three-story white stone edifice with a dark grey slate roof. The drivers pulled the carriages up to the front door, and we all went inside. I had nearly exhausted my meagre French in telling the drivers to bring us here, so I asked the Sergeant, 'Is there anyone here who speaks English? We wish to report a death.'

After a short wait, a short gentleman in an impeccable grey suit and waistcoat, a monocle dangling from a chain on his vest, arrived. ' I am Inspector René Lefébure,' he said with a heavy French accent. 'What is this death you have to report?' He herded the lot of us into his office. He seemed out of sorts with having to deal with this affair at such an early hour, and his demeanour did not improve when he discovered we had come to France to engage in a duel. 'You will pardon me for saying it, but you should do your killing in your own country, English.'

He quizzed us minutely about the circumstances of the duel - what was the insult, who were the participants. When he learned that one of the duellists was the dead man, he said, 'So this gentleman expired before the duel could commence? *Mais bien sur,* that was very convenient for the other participant, no?'

The upshot of the interview was that he arrested both of the Woods for suspicion of murder. 'I must hurry the investigation to get to the bottom of things, as you say.' I thought that he would have liked to arrest myself, Babcock and Sipes as well, but he could not come up with sufficient justification, given our limited roles in the affair.

My protestations for naught, we took our leave, but not before I asked the location of the nearest telegraph office, where I sent a wire to Sherlock Holmes. 'Come at once,' it said. I had a difficult time writing it without dripping blood on the form, because of my d___d finger.

***

The wind off the channel that rattled the window glass woke me from a troubled sleep at *Auberge du Fenetres sur Mer*, in Calais. My thumb was still bleeding at bedtime, so I wrapped it in gauze before retiring. My eyes darted to it immediately. I saw a small, crimson spot on the surface of the gauze. It was obvious that the needles that pricked me contained some substance that interfered with the clotting of the blood. A shiver ran through me—was I to suffer the same horrible death as Persano?

As I contemplated unwrapping my injured thumb, fearful of what I might find, a knock came on my door.

'Watson! It is I, Holmes. Open the door.'

The sound of his voice was like a stiff drink of mellow brandy, warming my stomach and spreading to my extremities. I pulled on my trousers, for I had no nightshirt or dressing gown, and admitted my friend.

'Your message was urgent, so I caught the first ferry from Dover... Hello, man! What the devil is wrong with your hand?'

I told Holmes how I received the injury, as I unwrapped the bandage with much trepidation. When I had it fully undone, I was relieved to see that the wounds were finally beginning to clot.

'Get dressed, old fellow, and allow me to buy your breakfast for you downstairs. You can tell me everything over *croissants* and coffee, and pray omit no detail, however trivial it may seem.'

Holmes was aware of my mission here before I departed London, so I did not dwell upon that. I began my tale at the time I went to Persano's tent. Leaving his food untouched, Holmes sat with his elbows on the table and his chin resting in his hands, taking in every nuance of my story. When I had finished, he asked, 'Is the tent still present on the beach?'

'We did not take it down, so it should be.'

'Capital!' he exclaimed. 'We must examine it at once!'

We went to the local stable, where the duelling party had hired drivers the previous day and found a fellow with a dogcart, who was willing to take us out there. As was usual during the early stages of an investigation, Holmes was taciturn—I knew better than to ask him for speculation in advance of facts. I simply hunkered down in my Fedora and greatcoat to get as much protection from the stiff wind as possible.

Arriving at the duel site, we found the tent still up, but the flap was open and Persano's corpse had been removed, presumably by the *gendarmes*. Holmes made a sound indicating his disgust as he entered, presumably because of the disturbance to the scene that the local constables had caused.

'We must search thoroughly,' he said, 'for there might yet be some piece of evidence that the French police failed to destroy.'

I remembered the cryptic phrase that Persano has spoken to me just before he died, so I told Holmes about it. 'But I do not see how it might be helpful. There must be a thousand courtiers in Paris.'

Holmes' only response was a noncommittal grunt.

A short search turned up the matchbox that had held the worm. We continued to explore the tent, looking for the infernal creature that had caused me such grief. I finally found it among the ground litter, and Holmes teased it into the box with the tip of his penknife.

We went outside where the light was better, and Holmes employed his glass to discern the fine details of the worm. 'I have never seen its like,' he said finally. 'I am no naturalist, but I think it resembles some sort of caterpillar.' He closed the box, and put it in the pocket of his greatcoat along with his glass. 'It appears, Watson, that the trail in France has grown cold. I think London may hold answers for us, however.'

Modern transportation is a marvellous thing. Prior to 1820, no passenger ferry service across the English Channel even existed—one had to arrange private passage. But now, in 1890, the crossing from Dover to Calais was made thrice daily, in the incredible time of ninety minutes. It took us nearly that long to travel by dogcart from Sangatte back to the ferry terminal, with a brief stop at the *auberge* to pick up my valise and pay the cheque. However, we were still able to secure a cabin for the afternoon crossing. The train to London awaited us when we arrived in Dover. We departed Sangatte around noontime, and we were back in Baker Street in time for Mrs. Hudson to provide us a cold supper.

'Your experience with the worm leads me to believe that Persano was deliberately poisoned by person or persons unknown,' Holmes opined. 'You know how I despise theorizing without facts or evidence, yet some amount of speculation is necessary in their absence if we are to make a start on this crime. Let us assume that it was some journalistic activity on Persano's part that made him a target for a murderer. If that is the case, we must ascertain what that activity entailed.'

'And how do you propose to go about that,' I asked, playing the foil for Holmes' acumen.

'How does a *soupçon* of burglary strike you as an end to your repast?'

'Persano's flat?'

'But of course.'

Holmes consulted the London street directory from his shelves to establish that Persano occupied rooms in Farringdon Street in St. Andrews. We passed a few hours in desultory activities, myself with a copy of the novel *Micah Clarke* sent to me by my literary agent, and Holmes with some samples of cigar ash, the characteristics of which he was considering adding to his monograph on the subject.

Finally, as the bells of St. Marylebone struck eleven, Holmes rose from his work and said, 'All good folk should be going to their beds at this hour, so it is time for lawbreakers to go about their nefarious business.'

To be circumspect, we had our cab drop us in Fleet Street, then walked the short distance to Persano's lodgings. We had to pick our way through some pavement work to reach his door, which was difficult for me in the darkness because my leg pained me, but I managed. Holmes made quick work of the lock on the front door while I watched, then we were inside. The plan of the residence was much the same as 221b—the landlord's apartment on the ground floor and Persano's digs on the first. The stairs stayed mercifully quiet as we ascended, and the lock on the dead journalist's door gave Holmes no more trouble than the one downstairs had. Once inside, we lit a bullseye lantern that Holmes had brought, the light from which had only a small chance of being observed from the street.

Persano's digs comprised just two rooms—a spacious sitting room made less so because it was crammed with tables, bookshelves and a massive roll-top desk. Open volumes and papers lay scattered on every flat space—finally, I had the misfortune to encounter someone even more disorderly than Holmes.

Holmes stood, shaking his head. 'Nothing is ever easy,' he said, surveying the effluvia. 'I think that the desk will afford the best chance of discovering something of interest.'

The roll-top was closed and locked, so the detective employed his picks for the third time. My heart skipped a beat as it clattered noisily when he raised it. The white beam of the lantern showed a myriad of small drawers in the back, and piles of folders littered the writing surface.

'Why don't you go through the desk drawers, Watson, while I examine the contents of these folders?' Holmes suggested. He cast the light about until he found a candle, which he lit from a match from a box in his pocket before handing it to me. He grabbed an armload of folders and carried them to a nearby table in order to give me room for my work.

Beginning with the topmost one on the left, I opened each of the small drawers in turn, examining the contents in a cursory manner. I suspected that Holmes had assigned me this task just to keep me busy while he went through Persano's papers. The contents of the drawers comprised the deadwood that a man accumulates after long stay in one place—writing instruments, clips, business cards, etc. I did discover an ornately carved, pearl-handled, double-barrelled pistol that fit in the palm of my hand—unfortunately, it had not protected its owner from an untimely demise. Another drawer yielded a diverse collection of matchboxes. I mentioned it to Holmes, but received no answer. Fine.

I tried to open the first drawer on the right in the pedestal, but it stuck, so I closed the roll top and tried again, after hearing the metallic sound of the pedestal lock as it disengaged. This time the drawer slid out easily. I was just about to reach inside when I caught a glimpse of something in the candlelight that sent a chill up my spine.

'Holmes,' I said quietly. 'There is something here that you should see.'

Holmes approached the desk and directed the lantern beam inside. There, in stark relief in the white light, a bristling tan mass about the size of a cricket ball resided. Worms!

Shuddering, I said, 'If the candle had not revealed those infernal things, I would have reached into that drawer...'

'Which is doubtless what Persano did, sealing his doom.'

'That is likely the source of the worm in Persano's matchbox,' Holmes opined.

'But why would he carry the thing all the way to France with him? To a duel, of all things?'

'Eliminate the impossible, Watson. He had no use for the worm at the duel. He was not going to throw it at his opponent. Therefore, he had use for it elsewhere.'

And where would that be?'

'Paris. He planned to travel to Paris after the duel was over. A skilled duellist such as Persano would have expected to win, of course.'

'He was going to Paris to see a courtier?' I asked, puzzled.

'No, Watson. He was going there to see *Monsieur* Courtier.' He paused, then extended his hand, holding a piece of paper. 'This note informs me that M. Courtier is a noted toxicologist at the Université de Paris known for his work with haemolytic toxins, whom Persano identified after he realized he'd been poisoned,' Holmes went on. 'He was hoping that Courtier would know how to help him. He took a single caterpillar along to France with him to show it to Courtier.'

'Persano showed amazing resilience after he jammed his hand into that ball of worms,' I said. 'It's amazing that he survived long enough to go to Paris to duel. Why would he even go if he was in such condition? Why didn't he just destroy the caterpillar ball in his desk? I would have stomped the thing into paste on the carpet.'

'You must realize, Watson, that Persano had to be a cold fish to be a renowned duelist,' Holmes lectured. 'When he realized his wound wouldn't stop bleeding, he immediately employed his skills as a researcher to identify someone who might help. He didn't cancel the duel, because that would brand him as a coward. He wasn't expecting a catastrophic, systemic response from his wound.'

I shuddered. 'It's a wonder I survived,' I said. 'I must have received a much smaller dose of venom from the single worm.'

'I found something else as well,' Holmes said, extending another scrap of paper. It was about three inches by four, and looked like it had been torn from a pocket notebook. The following symbols were scrawled on it in pencil ink:

'What is this codswallop?' I inquired.

'It is Isaac Pitman's shorthand,' Holmes replied. 'It is not surprising that a journalist would be familiar with it.'

I knew he was just waiting for me to ask. 'And I suppose you can decipher it?'

With a satisfied expression, he said, 'It says, Porlock, Ten Bells, Spitalfields, 8 p.m., December 27. T

I was familiar with the Ten Bells, a public house over a century old in the East End, from our investigation of the horrific events of the fall of 1888. 'I know that name. Porlock.,' I said.

'You should. You encountered it during the affair at Birlstone two years ago. Almost to the day, in fact.'

I remembered, and it seemed if the room had suddenly grown much colder.

'Professor Moriarty! Is he involved in this?'

'I have cautioned you previously that it is a capital mistake to theorize in advance of facts,' he said. 'However, that is certainly a possibility.' He hesitated, then continued, 'I have also told you that Porlock defied me ever to trace him among the teeming millions of this great city. To date, I have found no reason to endeavour to do that. That seems to no longer be the case.'

'What do you intend to do?' I asked him.

He smiled thinly. 'Finish searching poor Persano's papers to ascertain a motive for his murder, if I can. Then, if your good wife will allow it, I would be most gratified if you would accompany me to the Ten Bells tomorrow evening.'

The following day at my practice was a busy one, as the ailments that people had put off investigating during the Yuletide once again became important considerations. When the last patient had departed, I nipped outside to the jewellers, where I was fortunate to find an inexpensive cameo brooch. I placed the box in my pocket and hurried home for dinner. After the meal, I presented the trinket to Mary. Of course, she was delighted—cameos were her favourite—but she regarded me with a jaundiced eye.

'I know that we have spent little time together since I returned from France,' I said. 'I thought that this small bauble might make up for it a bit.'

She raised an eyebrow. 'And...?'

She knew me too well. 'And Holmes has asked me to accompany him on another excursion this evening.'

She glowered, but I could see the corners of her mouth twitching, so I waited for her smile. I knew her well also, you see. It eventually blossomed, and she said, 'Oh, you're a child! Be off with you, on your adventure. Don't be too late!'

That is one reason why I loved her so much.

Holmes was hovering impatiently when I arrived in Baker Street, already downstairs with a cab waiting. We both were dressed in somewhat rough garb, as to not stand out in Spitalfields. Spitalfields, more particularly, Dorset Street, had a reputation as the most notorious rookery in London and was certainly not a place where a gentleman would go after dark unless he desired less than savoury entertainment. The Ten Bells was only a short distance from Dorset Street, directly across from the Spitalfields Market. In the daytime, the presence of the market made the area more or less safe, but after dark, one travelled there at one's peril.

Light from the pub, in a fine old three-storey building, brightly illuminated the adjacent area, but murky shadows loomed just a few feet away. It was a bit warmer this evening than it had been for a few days, but the warmth brought the fog, which was settling over the City like a shroud. We disembarked from the hansom in the lighted area and Holmes paid the driver, who then clattered off as if he could not wait to be away.

We passed between the two Corinthian columns at the entry to the pub and Holmes pushed open the double doors. The odours of beer and humanity greeted us as we entered the public room. The place was fairly full, with most of the scattered tables occupied by men of the rougher sort, while ladies of a similar type circulated among them, plying their wares. We elbowed our way into the crowd at the bar, drawing some irritated glances, but no one was sufficiently roused to start an altercation, thank goodness. The publican, clad in a derby hat, tan waistcoat and a shirt that was once white, asked, 'Wot'll it be, gents?'

'Porlock,' replied Holmes.

A flicker of annoyance passed over the man's features, quickly replaced by puzzlement.

'We only 'as our own brew 'ere, gents. Ye wants fancy bottles, the Strand is over that way.' He pointed toward the exit.

'Tell Porlock that Mr. Smithson is here to see him,' Holmes said. 'And give us two pints of your strongest while we wait.'

'That'll be the XXXX,' the barman said., picking up a dubiously clean mug and exercising the tap handle. 'And ye'll wait till the cows come home. Oi never knew no

Porlock.' He slapped down two brimming mugs in front of us. 'That'll be fourpence, gents.'

Holmes paid him, and we retired to a table in a corner.

'The barkeep is lying of course,' Holmes said after sipping his ale. 'I expected no less. I must follow him after he closes for the evening, and that will be much easier if I am alone. Go back to your Mary after we've finished these.'

I must confess that I was a bit miffed with him. 'If you knew you'd be stonewalled and would have to follow someone, why did you bring me along?'

He smiled. 'Because I wanted to drink an ale with my old friend this evening,' he said, and I was ashamed.

We left the pub together, and Holmes walked with me to the edge of Spitalfields, where the chances of finding a cruising cab were much improved. 'Come to Baker Street after dinner tomorrow,' said Holmes, 'and I'll tell you the tale of my evening's adventures.' I climbed into the cab and watched him vanish into the fog as we clattered off.

The following day, January 4, 1891, was Sunday. As was our custom, Mary and I attended church, then spent a leisurely afternoon at home, which culminated in a cold supper. I broached the subject of my going out after dinner and Mary said, 'I have been feeling tired of late, John, so I would not be the best company this evening at any rate. Go and see your friend.'

So, it was about 7:30 p.m. when I arrived at Baker Street. I entered and found Holmes taking his ease on the sofa with a glass of whisky and soda. He offered me the same, and I quickly assented, saying, 'Don't get up. I know where everything is. May I freshen yours?'

After I was ensconced in Holmes' chair, he told me of his adventures after I left him in Spitalfields.

'You are aware that I have several places around the City to which I may repair to equip myself with the accoutrements necessary to conduct various clandestine activities,' he said. I established one of these in Whitechapel, near Spitalfields, when I was hunting Saucy Jack, and I went there to procure some beggars' rags. Thus clad, I returned to Commercial Street before closing time and availed myself of the shelter of the Old Market to keep watch on the Ten Bells.

'The publican appeared wary when he exited, but seeing nothing he did not expect, his circumspection soon turned to insouciance. I followed him for a few blocks and he approached a corner building. He looked about carefully, but of course, he did not notice me, then he removed a brick from a stanchion and placed something inside. He replaced the brick and hurried on his way. I saw no need to follow him any longer.'

Holmes sipped his whisky-soda appreciatively, and continued. 'Not long thereafter, an urchin arrived and removed the message from the cache. I followed him to a toy shop in Regent Street, which was closed at that hour, of course, where he slipped the envelope he'd gotten from the mail drop into a postal slot in the door.

'Well, there was nothing for it but to wait it out for the rest of the evening. When the shopkeeper arrived after breakfast, he made no motion to retrieve anything from the floor after opening the door, so it was no difficult deduction that the message had disappeared. Now that part of Regent Street has no back yards, so it was evident that the person who took the note must have entered from a nearby building, possibly through the sewers. I quickly retreated to another nearby lair, where I keep a number of reference books. A quick check of Kelly's Postal Directory revealed that one F. Porlock resided at No. 10 Kingly Street, just behind Regent Street. I was a bit chagrined to realize that I could have found my man just by combing the city directories, but of course, that search would have consumed many days, so it was comforting that the means I had chosen yielded results much more quickly.

'You may imagine the good Mr. Porlock's discomfort when he found me at his door. He is an older gentleman, fifty or so, well-dressed with a prominent nose and the broad brow of the scholar. There is nothing about him to indicate that he's the lackey of a criminal mastermind. Naturally, he feigned ignorance when I mentioned Persano's untimely demise, but when I threatened to inform his master of his duplicity, he gave me a name.'

'And that name is?' I asked.

'Courtland Dodd.'

'Who is Courtland Dodd?'

Holmes tossed off the last of his drink, then swung his long legs off the sofa prior to standing. Untying the cords of his mouse grey dressing gown, he said, 'You will meet him in just a few minutes. I sent him a wire earlier, telling him that I know all about the Persano murder.' He turned toward his bedroom door, saying, 'I must assume more formal attire before our guest arrives.'

As Holmes reappeared, now dressed in sack coat, trousers, collar and necktie, I heard the downstairs bell, announcing our visitor. A moment later, there was a knock on the door.

'Come in, Mrs. Hudson,' said Holmes.

The door opened and the landlady said, 'Mr. Courtland Dodd to see you, sir.'

'Send him up, dear lady.'

In a moment, Dodd arrived, dressed in a similar fashion to Holmes and I, carrying a cane and a briefcase. Mrs. Hudson had relieved him of his coat and hat downstairs.

Holmes plucked his evening briar from the mantle, took up the Persian slipper and began filling it. 'Good evening, Dr. Dodd. So good of you to come. My condolences on the death of your wife. You have been in Brazil, I perceive.'

Dodd, having placed his briefcase and cane on the sofa, was in the act of withdrawing something from his pocket as Holmes spoke. He assumed an irritated expression and said, 'You've been prying into my affairs? How dare you?'

'Not at all, sir. The bulge in your jacket pocket tells me your profession, and the groove on your left ring finger from an absent wedding band informs me of your recent bereavement. And that is a fine walking stick of Brazilian cherry and silver, if I am not mistaken. I can also see you've fallen on hard times since your wife passed, and have been under a great deal of stress.'

Unlike many who have been treated to one of Holmes' little demonstrations, Dodd made no further remarks about the veracity of his deductions. Instead, he fished in his pocket again and withdrew a piece of paper, shaking it open so I could see that it was a telegraph form.

'I would like to know what the meaning of this is, my good man,' he said, obviously trying to control the tone and the volume of his voice.

'I think that should be quite evident, Doctor.' Before Dodd could reply, Holmes turned to me, saying, 'Watson, would you please go downstairs and tell Mrs. Hudson to send up tea for three.'

Downstairs? 'But Holmes...'

'Please, Watson. There's a good fellow.'

Trying to refrain from shaking my head, I went to the door and out to the stairs. Two rings on Mrs. Hudson's bell meant *Bring tea*, followed by a number of additional rings to indicate that more persons than Holmes would be served. He obviously wanted me out of the room, so I went to do as he asked.

When I returned in a few minutes, I entered a scene of chaos!

Holmes stood in his bedroom door, a bull pup levelled at Dodd, who was on the sofa. The doctor was clutching his right hand with his left, and blood was running from the former onto the wrist of the latter. I noticed the Persian slipper was now on the floor, with tobacco strewn around it, and a pair of tongs lying nearby. And there was something else, a round, tan mass about the size of a cricket ball...

'You fiend!' Dodd said to Holmes. 'You have killed me!'

Holmes lowered his pistol and placed it in the pocket of his jacket.

'You have no one to blame but yourself for your fate, Doctor,' Holmes said. 'After watching me fill my pipe, you were going to plant that noxious thing in the slipper to ambush me the next time I wanted a smoke.' Dodd shook his head, but Holmes accused, 'I saw you do it from my bedroom. It is not my fault that your surprise when I suddenly reappeared to catch you in the act, caused you to wound yourself. It's obvious from the splashes of mud on your shoes and gaiters that you've been in Farringdon Street recently. It also provides further evidence of your wife's passing, because I'm certain she would not have let you go out in such a state.' Pointing to the ball of worms on the floor, Holmes continued, 'And that is ample proof that it was you who murdered Isadora Persano. What I want to know is why?'

Dodd glared up at Holmes from his seat on the sofa. 'I am a dead man walking, Mr. Holmes. I once saw a Brazilian Indian die from a sting less severe than this one in only two days, blood pouring from every orifice. I have no wish to leave this earth in that manner. If I do as you ask, will you release me so that I might take my own life in a more humane fashion?'

Holmes looked at me, and after a moment, I nodded. 'Nothing good would be served by turning this wretch over to the authorities.'

'We'll see, Doctor, but if I find you're lying to me...' Holmes cautioned.

'I have no reason to do that, now,' Dodd said. 'Might I trouble you for a whisky before I begin?'

I gave him a glass with three fingers of single malt, and he took a sip before beginning.

'Some months ago, I had an elderly patient who had a tumour. It was killing her slowly and painfully. Her daughter was caring for her while she wasted away, and it was putting a strain on her marriage. So, I took it upon myself to end the old woman's suffering without informing her daughter. I knew it was for the best for everyone involved.'

As a doctor I was horrified by Dodd's confession, but I said nothing.

'For some weeks after the incident, everything was as usual, but then I received a letter in the morning post. It was unsigned, but it informed me that someone was aware of what I had done, and if I did not perform a service for that individual, to be designated at some future date, rumours of my misdeed would be communicated to the woman's family and spread among the medical community. True or not, a scandal such as that could end a physician's career, as well as open him up to investigation by the Crown Prosecutor. So, I waited with great trepidation to see what would be required of me to prevent it.

'About a month later, a similar missive arrived. It contained a door key, an address on Farringdon Street, and it directed me to end the life of the person who lived there in the first-floor rooms. It said that if I did this, no more would be asked of me, and that my secret would be safe.' He took another sip of his drink, then put the glass down on the low table in front of him so that he could spread his hands in supplication. 'What could I do, gentlemen?'

This time I could not help myself. 'You could have acted ethically, abiding by your oath, and reported all of this to the authorities.'

'Says a man who has never found himself in a similar situation,' Dodd retorted. He emptied his glass and held it out for more, but Holmes shook his head.

'Finish your tale, Doctor,' he said. 'Then you may have another.'

'I am somewhat of an amateur naturalist and, as you've deuced, Mr. Holmes, I spent about a decade in Brazil when I was young and foolish, caring for the natives there to fund my scientific studies. I became aware of the venomous caterpillars when I had to attend to the unfortunate Indian whom I mentioned previously. I immediately saw the medical applications of such a potent haemolysin, so I brought a crop of the caterpillars with me when I returned to England. The moths are quite simple to rear, requiring only vegetable matter for food and water, so I was able to observe the morphology and development time of the eggs, the larval instars, the pupae and the adults. I have documented all of it in a monograph that will be released upon my death.'

'Why wait until your death to publish?' I asked.

'Because I had some difficulties with the medical applications. Some of the patients on whom I tried my preparations did not fare too well. I had heard that that oaf, Courtier, was working on a similar product in Paris, and I had no wish to give him any assistance. I wanted my product to be the first on the market.'

'So, you chose these worms to carry out the execution of Persano,' Holmes prompted.

'They're not worms, they're caterpillars. No one but my dear wife was aware that I possessed these creatures, so I knew I had a means to dispose of the unwanted Mr. Persano that would prove baffling to the police.'

My blood lay static in my veins like immobile ice. How could someone who had dedicated his life to ministering to the sick and injured condemn a man to such a cruel and callous death?

I noticed that Holmes had produced the Webley from his jacket and was pointing it at Dodd again. 'Go downstairs and summon a constable, would you Watson, so he may remove this vermin from my home.'

'No!' Dodd shouted. 'You said that you would release me...'

'I said that I would see, then I heard your tale. I only give you the same fate you bestowed on another.'

Dodd's face hardened, and he leapt up to rush Holmes, even with the loaded revolver trained on him. But Holmes, understanding what Dodd wanted, did not fire. When the charging doctor neared him, he stepped nimbly aside and lashed out with the heavy gun, catching Dodd on the temple, and sending him sprawling unconscious on the on the floor.

'Go see to that constable, Doctor,' he said grimly. 'I like not the smell in this room.'

The next few days were busy ones. Holmes and I went to the Inner Temple to swear out a statement to gain release of the Woods from the French jail, then to Holmes' brother Mycroft to facilitate its transmittal to the *gendarmes*.

Scotland Yard told us that Dodd died the day after he was arrested. His death was not easy.

Holmes had left Persano's apartment with a sheaf of papers under his arm. He informed me that they were notes, written in Pitman's shorthand, for a story about a new crime boss who was currently establishing himself in London. No names were named, but Holmes was sure it referred to Professor Moriarty.

'Thus, we have the motive for the murder of Persano,' said Holmes. 'He did not name the sources for many of his facts, probably keeping them in his head, so it would be useless to turn the notes over to the press. Doubtless the Professor has his sources there as well, so it would just put someone else life in jeopardy. Holmes' eyes flashed fire as he continued, 'I swear to you, Watson, that I will not rest until this pestilence is eradicated from our land, even if it costs my very life!'

I did not realize at the time how prophetic his words were.

A Case of Murder

I can think of no adventure that I shared with my friend Mr. Sherlock Holmes that had a more dramatic opening than the sad affair that occurred in the summer of 1894. The weather in London was glorious that day, sunny and seventy degrees. Holmes and I were in our Baker Street sitting room with all of the windows open, allowing the balmy breeze to purge the last remnants of stale tobacco smoke and acrid chemical odours from our home. Looking outside, I noticed that many residents were taking advantage of the unusually beautiful weather, and I resolved to attempt to lure Holmes out for a sojourn in Regent's Park after luncheon.

Ten Steps from Baker Street

The crowd in the street below made way for a cab approaching from the south. It came to a halt in front of our door and a well-dressed woman alighted. She wore a high-necked summer dress and matching bonnet, carried a parasol in her right hand, and a two-handled bag dangled from her arm. As the cab drove off, she looked apprehensively up at our window and my heart fell—a prospective client would ruin any chance of an afternoon stroll. She gave a slight nod, apparently having made up her mind, and moved toward our doorstep. Abruptly, a man in a workman's jacket with a flat cap pulled low stepped up beside her, put a pistol to the back of her head, and pulled the trigger before I could so much as cry out a warning. She collapsed onto the pavement as he shoved the gun back under his jacket. He reached down and wrestled her bag from her limp arm, then fled in the direction of Marylebone Road and Regent's Park. The entire incident consumed less than ten seconds.

Both Holmes and I froze momentarily. 'He shot her!' I exclaimed, and grabbing my bag, I ran to the stairs, with Holmes only a step behind.

Arriving on the pavement, I shouted to Holmes, 'He ran north, toward the park! He was wearing a grey coat and a flat cap. Go!' Holmes ran in that direction, blowing a police whistle. I hollered at the crowd surrounding the stricken woman, 'I'm a doctor. Let me through!'

They obediently moved aside. I regarded the victim, who was lying on the cobblestones with her limbs at the odd angles usually associated with death, and a rapidly spreading dark red pool flowing from beneath her head. My heart went cold. Reflexively, I reached down to check the carotid pulse, but I knew what I would find. It was absent.

A constable ran up, dispersing the crowd further, and after taking my report about the incident, sent for a wagon from the mortuary and requested an inspector from Scotland Yard. By this time Holmes had returned, shaking his head. He had not succeeded in catching the murderer.

After giving his name to the P.C., Holmes knelt and performed an examination of the victim. She looked to be a dark-haired woman in her forties. He looked at her hands and her boots, then took a lens from his pocket to minutely examine her clothing. Because the killer had made off with her bag, Holmes could find nothing to identify her.

As we trudged up the stairs to our rooms, Holmes said, 'By God, Watson, this will not stand! I will not have prospective clients shot down in the street for coming to consult me!'

The inspector proved to be Stanley Hopkins, whom Holmes had often referred to as one of the best of the Scotland Yarders. He was an intelligent fellow of thirty or so who resembled a retired soldier more than a policeman. We gave him the few facts that we had, and Holmes promised to keep him apprised of anything we might learn.

After he had gone, Holmes retrieved his telegraph pad and wrote out a message. He tore it from the pad and handed it to me, then rang for the page. It ran:

If the cab driver who picked up a woman in Mayfair and delivered her to Baker Street on the 18th will report to 221b Baker Street, he will find it to his advantage.

'I assume you are going to tell me how you know that the poor woman came here from Mayfair,' I said.

'I have told you that I have made a study of local soils; it was the mud on her boots that informed me. Additionally, the lady's fine garments, her gold wedding ring and her hands unblemished due to a lack of manual labour indicate that she was well-to-do, so she could afford such an affluent neighbourhood.' Taking up his pad a second time, Holmes wrote a similar message about witnesses to the shooting. 'I suppose it is too much to hope for that someone got a close enough look at the shooter to describe him. Unfortunately, when an incident such as this one occurs, most people's eyes travel straight to the victim.'

There was a knock on the door. Holmes opened it to reveal the page. He handed the boy both of the messages and sufficient funds to place them in today's editions of every evening paper in London.

After the lad had gone, Holmes said, 'And now we wait.'

***

It was not until the following morning that Holmes's advertisement bore fruit. I was awake early, unable to sleep because the heavy rain last night had caused my old injuries to flare up. As I poured my coffee the downstairs bell rang, and a minute later Mrs. Hudson entered to announce a Mr. Johnnie Winter, who was clad in a dripping oilskin and holding a copy of last night's Evening Standard.

I confess that I took a modicum of evil satisfaction in knocking Holmes up to talk with him.

'I didna see yer advertisement until late last evenin',' the fellow said, 'so I waited till this mornin' to come by.'

'That's all right,' said Holmes. 'Do you have the address of the woman you picked up in Mayfair yesterday?'

'No, guvnor. She hailed me from the end of the street.' Holmes's face fell. 'But it was in Great Stanhope Street where I found her,' said the cabman, and Holmes brightened considerably again.

To our housekeeper's displeasure, we had a hurried breakfast, then dressed for the short trip to Mayfair. Holmes offered Mr. Winter a cup of coffee and some toast if he would wait to take us to the place where he picked up his fare yesterday. Thankfully, the rain was abating as we stepped outside.

Blue sky peeped between the rapidly absconding clouds as we arrived at the head of Great Stanhope Street, adjacent to Hyde Park. Luckily, the street was a short one, stretching only a hundred yards and containing about a dozen Georgian townhouses.

'Best we begin knocking on doors, then,' I said.

'Oh, I think we can be a bit more precise than that,' said Holmes, pointing to an area where the pavement had been torn up. 'The mud on our victim's shoes doubtless came from there.' He mounted the steps to No. 10, the townhouse nearest the mudhole, and worked the brass doorknocker.

In a moment, the door opened to reveal a woman dressed in livery; a long grey dress with a high neck, white apron and white bonnet.

'May I help you, sirs?'

Holmes produced his card. 'We'd like to speak with the lady of the house.'

She took the card and read it; her expression became worried. 'Mrs. Gabriel is not in.'

'How long has she been gone?' Holmes inquired, and apprehension curled her features.

'Since yesterday mornin',' she said. 'Has something happened to the missus?'

'Is Mr. Gabriel here?' I asked.

'Nossir, he ain't here, neither.'

'May we come in, please?' Holmes asked. The housekeeper retreated, beckoning us into a cramped vestibule with a white tile floor, which opened up into a larger hallway done in white with gold trim. 'Is there somewhere we can talk?' Holmes prodded, and she led us into a drawing room that had a large window looking out on Great Stanhope Street. I had to step around some toy soldiers scattered on the floor as I entered.

The drawing room was very much a man's chambre, evoking a medieval air. A long trestle table ran down its centre, and an ornate marble fireplace pierced the opposite wall, with two richly upholstered wingback chairs flanking it. A ragdoll occupied one of the chairs, its legs splayed out in front. A large gun case fronted with bevelled glass doors stood against the wall opposite the doorway through which we entered the room, with a liquor cabinet containing a wine rack nearby.

The housekeeper, clearly ill at ease, asked, 'May I bring you some coffee, gentlemen?'

'No thank you,' said Holmes. He indicated one of the wingback chairs. 'I think you should be seated, Madam. I may be the bearer of disturbing news.'

'Is there something wrong with Mrs. Gabriel?' The housekeeper asked as she sat.

'To whom do I have pleasure of speaking?' inquired Holmes.

'I'm Addy, sir.'

'I am Sherlock Holmes, a consulting detective in Baker Street, and this is my colleague Dr. Watson. It seems that your mistress came to consult me yesterday morning.'

'Then you know where she is?' She sounded hopeful.

'Possibly. Your mistress is in her forties, with dark hair?' Addy nodded. 'When you last saw her, she was wearing a checked promenade dress with a black satin collar and a feathered hat?'

'Yessir.' Again, the nervous expression. 'But you would know that if you had spoken with her.'

Holmes opened his mouth to speak, but I interrupted. 'Holmes. Allow me.'

He looked at me sharply. 'Quite.' he said.

I took Addy's hand and knelt in front of her to bring our eyes to a level. She knew what I was going to tell her; I was sure of it, but she would not believe it until she heard. 'Addy, I am sorry I must tell you that your mistress has passed away.'

She gave a little whine, and her blue eyes brimmed with tears. She sucked in her breath; she was going to be brave.

'What happened to her, Doctor?'

'I am afraid she was attacked in the street.'

Addy's eyes widened and her mouth popped open like a fish out of water. Now, her expression belied terror. 'But who...?'

'That is what we are attempting to ascertain,' said Holmes. 'Did Mrs. Gabriel tell you she was going to visit me?'

Addy looked at the ceiling. 'Nossir,' she said.

'Where is Mr. Gabriel?' Holmes asked.

'He never returned from his trip.'

'What trip?' asked Holmes

'He travels twice a month for his firm. He's usually gone for four or five days.'

'What firm?'

'He never told me,' Addy said, 'He isn't dead, too, is he?' she asked.

'I don't know,' Holmes replied, 'but I do not believe so.' He paused, then, 'Would you tell the children what's happened?'

'It might be better if it doesn't come from a stranger,' I added.

Addy's face plainly said she did not want to, but she responded, 'I will if you think it best. Shall I do it now?'

'Yes, please,' said Holmes. 'And I should like to speak with them when you've finished.'

'What is going to become of them?' Addy asked.

'Can you stay on until arrangements are made?' Holmes asked.

'I shall have to be paid,' said Addy.

'Of course.'

'Then I shall go and tell them now. I'll bring them when I've finished.'

While we waited for Addy to return with the children, Holmes busied himself looking about the drawing room. He wandered to the fireplace and inspected the mantle. Removing his glass from a pocket, he peered at the top. 'There was something here earlier. A photograph, I think.' He then went to the gun case, opened it, and removed a fowling piece. 'Hmm. A Purdy. New too, it seems. Probably never fired.' He replaced it in the rack, then closed the door. Noticing that a lower drawer was partially opened; he opened it fully, then closed it again. Finally, he meandered to the sideboard and took a bottle of claret from the wine rack. He glanced at the label, wrinkled his brow, then returned the bottle to its place.

We waited another ten minutes before Holmes said, 'It's taking her an awfully long time,' before striding out of the room and up the stairs. I quickly followed him. We found ourselves in an upper hallway with closed doors on both sides, and another stairway at the end. It was still and quiet.

Holmes looked at me with a sombre expression. 'Watson, we have been properly had.' We hurried down the rear stairs, emerging into a kitchen. A door, partially open, led to a yard in back. Holmes said. 'Oh, well done, Miss Addy!

A servant's staircase gave access to the basement. Holmes said, 'Watson, wait here,' and vanished. He was back in a trice. 'Addy's room is empty. She's absconded.'

'But why?' I asked.

'Apparently she did not believe me when I said that she would be paid,' Holmes said.

I could not help myself. 'Disgraceful! What sort of person would desert a child whose parent had been killed?' Holmes had no answer for me.

We went back upstairs and began opening doors, and we found the master bedroom at the rear of the townhouse. Holmes quietly opened the next door in line, looked inside, then closed it with a finger to his lips. 'It's the little girl,' he said. 'Let us wake the boy first.'

A room on the opposite side of the hall proved to be his. Entering, I looked down on him, sleeping the sleep of the innocent, and understood that we were about to destroy his world. He was a strapping, brown-haired lad a little over five feet in height, with a build that suggested that he might become a rugby union fullback one day. I gently touched his shoulder, rousing him. His eyes opened, and for a moment he did not comprehend there were strangers in his room. Then disquiet showed in his eyes. 'Who're you?' he said.

'I am Dr. Watson. What is your name, lad?'

'I'm Jerry. Jerry Worthington.'

'I thought your surname was Gabriel.' I said.

'That's my stepda's name.' A pause. 'Where's Ma?'

'She's not here right now,' Holmes said.

'Then where's Addy?'

'She's not here either.'

The boy addressed Holmes, standing at the foot of his bed. 'Who're you?'

'Sherlock Holmes.'

Jerry's eyes got big. 'Cor! Yer the gent from the Strand, ain'tcha?'

Holmes cast me a scathing glance. 'Yes. That is I,' he admitted.

'Whatcha doon at our house?'

There is no easy way to break the news of the death of a loved one to a person, and it's much, much worse with a child. Even the meanest of children evidence an irrepressible hope, and it makes one feel dirty somehow, when it falls to one to take that away from them. 'I have some bad news Jerry,' I said 'It's about your mum.'

He looked into my eyes, and he knew. His lower lip trembled, then his face hardened—he was a young man, after all, and he would not cry in front of strangers, and certainly not in front of a hero from the Strand.

'Somethin' happened to 'er.' It wasn't a question. 'She ain't comin' back, is she?'

I shook my head.

'What was it?' he asked.

I wanted to spare him as much of the detail as possible. 'Someone killed her,' I said.

'D'ye know who?'

'Not yet,' said Holmes. 'But I will have him. I promise you that.'

Jerry smiled at Holmes's words. 'I read about youse. I know y'will.' Then he asked, 'What about Addy?'

'She's gone too, Jerry,' Holmes replied with as much kindness as he could muster. 'She's left you.'

'So, what's gonna happen to me and Lindee?' A flash of trepidation appeared in his eyes.

'Is there anyone we can contact to take care of you? An aunt? A grandparent?' I asked him.

'Nossir. It was just me, Lindee and Ma before Mr. Gabriel came along.' He paused. 'We won't have to go to the workhouse, will we?'

My gorge rose in disgust that he even asked such a question. 'No,' I said adamantly. 'That will not happen.' Holmes looked at me strangely.

'Does Lindee know, yet?' asked Jerry.

'No,' I told him. 'We woke you first.'

He sat on the side of his bed in his pyjamas, looking very much a little boy. Then he raised his eyes to us. 'Better let me tell 'er. She should hear it from family.'

Holmes nodded. 'Of course, my lad. I'll need you to do it now, then the two of you dress and come downstairs. I have some questions for you.'

The boy rose and donned a robe hanging from a bedpost. Then he walked to the hallway, to go to his baby sister. From the rear, he looked like an old man.

***

After we arrived downstairs, Holmes said, 'Watson, could you make some tea, find something for the children to eat and bring it here?'

'Of course, old man.' I went to the kitchen to see what I could scrounge.

I returned in fifteen minutes with the tea, and some bread, butter and jam. Not an elaborate breakfast, but sufficient, provided we could get the children to eat any.

They were in the drawing room. Both children were formally dressed, Jerry in a jacket, knickers, knee socks and Oxfords, his sister Belinda, a petite seven-year-old with straw-coloured hair and blue eyes, in a blue frock, socks and pumps. As to be expected, both were morose while sitting at table, staring listlessly at the cups of milky tea we had provided.

'When I asked you to dress, I did not expect church clothes,' said Holmes.

'You're comp'ny. You dress for comp'ny,' the boy said.

'My error,' said Holmes. 'Quite correct.' He paused, then, 'I have wired a friend of mine, Mrs. Hudson, to come here and be with you until we can make other arrangements,' said Holmes. 'Now I must ask you some questions, which I hope will allow me to find the man who hurt your mum, so I can bring him to justice.'

'Like y'do in the Strand,' Jeremy said.

Holmes smiled, despite himself.

'There was a photograph on the mantlepiece, which is now absent.' Holmes said. 'What can you tell me about it?'

'It was a picture of us kids with Ma and Mr. Gabriel,' said Jerry. 'He had it made when he married Ma.'

'When did you last see it?'

'T'other day,' Jerry said.

I saw Holmes's eyes narrow. I knew he was being patient. 'Before your stepfather left, or afterwards?'

'It was before,' Jerry said.

'Can you describe your stepfather for me?'

'He's a regular gent,' Jerry said. 'Not too tall, not too short.'

'Do you know his age?'

'About forty, I think.'

'And his hair? His eyes?'

'His hair's like mine. And I think his eyes are grey.'

'Do you know where he works?'

'He said in Fenchurch Street. I don't know fer who.'

'How does he treat you?' I asked. 'Is he a good Da?'

'He's all right. He brings us things when he comes back from his trips.'

139

'What sorts of things?' Holmes asked.

'Oh, chocolates, mostly.'

'He brought me a dolly once,' Lindee said.

Holmes indicated the rag doll that he was now holding. 'That one?'

'Nossir. She's in my room, in her case. She's a lookin' at doll, not playin' with doll, Ma said.'

Holmes raised an eyebrow at me. 'Watson? There's a good fellow.'

I sighed and went upstairs to Lindee's room. The doll was in its display case in a prominent place on top of Lindee's highboy, well out of her reach. It was a delicate thing of porcelain bisque, dressed in a vibrant deep blue gown with white lace trim. Odd to give it to a young child, I thought. I removed it from the case, stand and all, and brought it down to Holmes, who had the children telling stories about their day-to-day lives in Mayfair. Lives that were about to change drastically, I thought.

'Does she have a name?' I asked Lindee as I set it down next to Holmes.

'Our stepda said she was Cosette,' Lindee said.

'Tell me Lindee, did Mr. Gabriel bring you this doll before or after he and your Ma were married?'

Lindee appeared to be puzzled by the question, but Jerry said, 'It was before, I'm pretty sure.'

Holmes said nothing in reply, but he assumed an air of satisfaction, as if a deduction had been confirmed.

Mrs Hudson soon arrived, and Holmes did not have to work very hard to prevail upon her to mind the children. 'Hopefully it will only be for a day or so, until I can make some arrangements,' he said.

After Mrs. Hudson took Jerry and Lindee into the kitchen, Holmes said, 'Come Watson, help me to look for information about the family's finances, and to see if there is a last will and testament, or information about a family solicitor.' We began in the study, and before long we had found deposit receipts from a bank in Regent Street. 'Let us go and talk to the banker,' Holmes said. 'If sufficient finances are available, I am willing to assume guardianship of the children.'

Holmes' statement surprised me somewhat. 'How would you ever fit children into your life?' I asked.

'I did not say I would take them to live with me. But I would undertake to find them a situation in which they would be properly reared, and monitor their care to ensure they were well-treated.'

I saw this was simply another example of the bigness of the man, like his employment of the street Arabs of London to assist in his investigations, among other good works.

The plight of the orphan in London is a well-known issue which has been a bone of contention for a long time. Poor laws in England date back to medieval times, when they mandated various punishments for those whose poverty was deemed the result of idleness. A modern reform was implemented in 1834, when the current system of parish unions and workhouses was created to reduce the burden on the rate payers, who were largely middle-class property owners. Conditions in workhouses were made deliberately harsh so the impoverished would avoid them except as a last resort; these circumstances were admirably documented and condemned by reformers such as Dickens, Trollope, and Mayhew, among others. However, a child who was an orphan had no choice but to become a ward of the parish union, and had no option but a workhouse unless a benefactor undertook to find other accommodations. Foundling hospitals and orphanages existed, but were often overcrowded and inaccessible. Siblings were almost always separated because of the difficulties inherent in having both sexes under the same roof. Should an orphan be fortunate enough to reach majority, he was cast out on the street to survive as best he could.

We met the bank manager Mr. Harmon Struthers at Hopkinson and Co., and he was initially reticent about disclosing the financial details of a client until he heard my companion's name. He then told us that all of the accounts had been emptied several weeks ago.

'Did Mr. Gabriel do that?' Holmes asked.

'Nossir. It was the Missus. Took it all in cash, she did.'

'Didn't you think that unusual?'

'Aye, but she told me that some friends of her husband's were undertaking a new banking venture and that he was desirous of aiding them,' Struthers said. The banker also confirmed that the house on Great Stanhope Street was mortgaged, with payments made through funds from other investments periodically deposited with Hopkinson and Co. 'Doubtless the Gabriels will make arrangements with their new financiers to cover that,' Struthers said.

After we had returned to Baker Street, Holmes began going through newspapers from previous days. 'Ah ha!' he exclaimed. 'I knew I had seen this, though there was no connection for me at the time.' He handed me a copy of *The Evening Standard* dated Friday, July 6, indicating an advertisement on the front page:

Missing [it ran] on the morning of the sixth of this month, a gentleman named James Montgomery Gabriel, who failed to return from a scheduled business trip. About 5'8'; stocky, pale complexion, black hair, balding in the centre. When last seen, wearing black frock-coat, plaid waistcoat, dark tweed trousers black boots with dark gaiters. Come to No. 10 Great Stanhope Street with information for reward.'

The anger in Holmes's voice was palpable as he said, 'This wretch murdered a woman who loved him and left her children destitute. I will have him if it is the last thing that I do.' He took up a sketch pad and charcoal and began to draw. In fifteen minutes' time, he showed me a rendition of Addy the housekeeper.

'Why are you so concerned with the housekeeper?' I inquired.

'Have you asked yourself how the murderer knew to be lurking outside of our door when Mrs. Gabriel arrived?' Holmes asked.

The light dawned. 'The housekeeper! She told him that the lady was coming to visit us.'

'Precisely.'

'So, she knows where he is.'

'Or was,' corrected Holmes. 'I suspect that dear Addy is also a victim of this charlatan. He likely told her that they would run off together and live happily ever after. I intend to spend as many days as necessary in tracking her down.'

'But if the murderer has victimized her as well, Addy won't know where he is, either.'

'That's all right. I know with whom we're dealing, and where to find him.'

I just stared at him, totally nonplussed. Finally, I asked, 'How?'

'Never mind.'

'And you know where he is?' I asked unbelievingly.

Holmes nodded.

'Then why don't you just have him arrested?'

'I have told you before, dear Doctor, that knowing a thing and proving it are two very different things. The children could identify him as their stepfather, but a child's testimony always carries less weight than an adult's. I need Addy's as well. He paused. 'And I have an important task for you to do tomorrow.'

'And that is?'

'I want you to go to Lambeth, and see the Reverend Vernon Charlesworth at the Stockwell Orphanage. I handled a matter of no little sensitivity for him some years ago, and he owes me a favour. Let us see what he can do to help a couple of orphans.'

'Of course. And what will you be doing?'

He waved the sketch at me. 'I'll drop this off at the engraver's in the morning. By Thursday, I'll have the Baker Street Division of the detective police force canvassing the city for Miss Addy. Then, I will keep watch on our miscreant to ensure he doesn't fly the coop before we brace him.'

I rose early the next morning for an early breakfast, then to put on full morning dress; I wanted to impress the Reverend Charlesworth with the gravity of my plea as much as possible. It lacked only a few minutes until nine when I walked out of 221b and up to Marylebone Road to find a cab. The five-mile ride to Stockwell was a pleasant one despite my serious mission, past Buckingham Place and across the busy Thames on Vauxhall Bridge, arriving at Stockwell Orphanage a little before ten.

The Stockwell Orphanage was founded in the borough of Lambeth in 1867 by the philanthropist Charles Spurgeon. Initially, it was built to house orphaned boys, but a girls' wing was erected ten years later—this was one reason Holmes chose to investigate it as a home for the Worthington children. The Reverend Vernon Charlesworth became its headmaster in 1869, and still held the post to this day. My cab drew up into a spacious courtyard surrounded by gabled brick buildings. Upon leaving the hansom, I noted a number of well-fed boys and girls who were happily playing in the fine summer weather. Unlike residents of other orphanages, these children did not wear distinctive uniforms, but were simply dressed as individuals, lending them an air of normalcy. I hailed one of the boys: 'You lad! Where might I find the Reverend Charlesworth?'

'I'll take you to him, sir,' he said.

He led me inside, and I was happy to see that the accommodations were clean and sunny. We passed a large chapel with pews on either side and classrooms in which well-behaved children were being instructed by their masters. The dormitories were spacious, all of the beds were made and each occupant had a trunk for their possessions at the foot. Finally, I was ushered into an office where the Reverend Charlesworth rose to greet me. He was a great bear of a man in his fifties with thinning brown hair, a full beard and a ready smile.

'Good morning, Dr. Watson,' he said. 'I had a telegram from Holmes last evening telling me to expect you. How may I be of service?'

143

Ten Steps from Baker Street

I told him the sad tale of the Worthington children. 'Holmes hoped that places might be found for them here, so that, while not living together, brother and sister might still be in proximity to see each other from time to time.' His face fell, and I knew that my entreaty was to be in vain.

'This facility was originally constructed to hold 500 children,' he said, 'but now we have nearly twice that many, and a long list of those waiting for admittance.'

'Having seen what you do here, I can completely understand that,' I said. 'You are to be commended for the level of care you extend to these children, whom the rest of society would simply see as outcasts.'

I knew that my expression was despondent as well, for now I had no idea where we were to find a home for these waifs. Charlesworth looked at the floor, obviously troubled, then raised his eyes to mine once more.

'Mr. Holmes assisted me in a situation which could have easily led to the ruin of my reputation and my life,' he said, 'and he would take no payment for doing so, saying that the work was its own reward. He was right about that, for there is no nobler reward in this world than doing God's work. To that end, my wife and I foster a number of orphans in our own home—two more will not strain our resources to the breaking point, I think. We will take on these unfortunate children, Doctor. Just give us a few days to make things ready for them.'

I was amazed at the magnanimity of this great man, as well as the way in which the effects of Holmes' work seemed to extend far beyond the simple solution to a client's problem, like ripples from a pebble cast in a pond. I thanked Reverend Charlesworth effusively before leaving, and rode back to Baker Street with joy in my heart. I knew that nothing would ever replace the mother that the children had lost, but at least they'd remain together and not subject to the horrors of the workhouse.

***

The next few days were uneventful as far as the case was concerned. Holmes had pocket-sized prints made from his sketch of Addy and passed them out to his Baker Street Irregulars, the group of street urchins who served as his eyes and ears among London's teeming masses. He paid each of them a shilling a day, with the promise of a sovereign to the one who located the elusive Addy. Holmes himself was up at first light each day, assuming the disguise of a dustman who could prowl the streets invisibly. When I asked him where he was off to, he neatly evaded my question before departing.

Saturday dawned. It was five days ago that the unfortunate Mrs. Gabriel was shot down in the street before our home. Breakfast was a tense affair, with Holmes, wearing his mouse grey dressing gown with his face made up as the dustman's, bolting down some dry toast and coffee. A clatter on the stairs caused his eyes to light up, and a smile bloomed on his face. A young man burst into our rooms, followed closely by a much smaller lad.

'Mr. Holmes! Davy here has found her, in the Charing Cross Hotel!' He handed Holmes a slip of paper. 'Here is her room number.'

'Excellent work, Wiggins!' cried Holmes. Moving to his desk, he extracted a coin purse from a drawer and retrieved a sovereign, which he presented to the boy Davy, whose eyes became as large as dinner plates. It may have been the first gold coin he had ever held in his hands.

'I'll need twenty-two shillin's more t'pay the rest of the lads,' said Wiggins, and Holmes duly counted out the money. When the two had departed, Holmes turned to me and said, 'Get dressed quickly Watson, and let us lay hands on Miss Addy before she has a chance to elude us again.' It was not long before we were clattering off for the great railway terminus and hotel overlooking the Thames Embankment.

Addy's room was on an upper floor, so my game leg was appropriately throbbing by the time we stepped from the staircase. As we walked down the hall to the room, a door opened and a woman dressed for the street in a skirt, jacket and broad hat, holding a valise, came out—it was Addy! She saw and recognized us and gave a little yelp, then began running towards the exit at the other end of the corridor. Holmes sprinted after her while I hobbled along behind. He caught up to her and scooped her up in his arms like a new husband preparing to carry his bride across the threshold, saying, 'Get her valise, Watson.' Holmes carried her, kicking and screaming, back into her room and unceremoniously dumped her upon the bed. I followed with the valise, shutting the door behind me.

Demonstrating a vocabulary that was most unladylike, Addy threatened us with arrest if we did not release her forthwith.

Holmes countered, 'You must know by now that your lover isn't coming, Addy. And you've run out of funds, haven't you, and are uncertain where to go next? Perhaps back home to Nottinghamshire, if they'll have you. But by telling that wretch that his wife was going to consult me, which resulted in her death, you've opened yourself to a charge of accessory to murder. You may even be charged as a co-conspirator, which could mean the noose.'

Addy's eyes grew wide and her mouth popped open at the word *murder*. 'I never knew he was going to kill her!' she said, tears streaming down her cheeks. 'I swear it!'

Holmes replied, 'I believe you, but what I believe does not matter. All that does matter is that he did in fact kill her. Your only hope is to throw yourself upon the mercy of the court. That will be greatly facilitated if you assist me in bringing this foul murderer to justice.'

'What would you have me do?' she said resignedly.

'Come with me to arrest him. Identify him to the police.'

'Oh my God! If I do that, he'll surely murder me too!'

Seeking to calm her distress, I told her, 'He can't hurt you if he's under arrest and in jail.'

She stopped crying at that, but her face still told me that she was not keen about incriminating her erstwhile lover.

Holmes's expression hardened. 'You must and you will do this thing, woman! This fiend has left two young children without their mother!'

Addy's expression brightened. 'The children!' she said. 'You don't need me. They can identify him as their stepfather.'

'Yes, and they will,' Holmes agreed disgustedly. 'But as an adult, your word will carry more weight with the court.' Her face fell again.

'All right,' Addy replied. 'When shall we do this?'

'Right now,' said Holmes. 'We shall go by Scotland Yard to pick up an officer, then brace the hyena in his den.'

The three of us repaired downstairs to the lobby. At Holmes's direction, I asked the concierge to summon a four-wheeler while he dispatched a wire.

We rode to Scotland Yard where Inspector Stanley Hopkins and a constable awaited us. After the two had boarded the conveyance, Holmes said to the driver, 'Take us to number 31 Lyon Place in Camberwell.'

I remembered hearing that address before, but now I was unsure to whom it belonged.

In about twenty minutes, we arrived in front of a modern townhouse, not far from Denmark Hill. Leaving the constable in the cab, the rest of us went to the door, where Holmes plied the brass knocker.

In a moment, the door opened to reveal a large woman in a plain housedress and a scarf. To my surprise, I recognized her; she was a former client, Miss Mary Sutherland. 'Mr. Holmes! What are you doing here?' She asked.

'I've come to see your stepfather, Mr. James Windibank, Miss Sutherland.'

'My stepfather!' She paused, obviously puzzled. 'I'll ask him if he's taking callers.'

Displaying his badge, Hopkins said in peremptory tone, 'He'll see us, Miss. I am Inspector Hopkins of Scotland Yard.'

Miss Sutherland's eyes widened. 'Of course sirs, do please come in. Mr. Windibank is in the drawing room with my mother, his wife.'

As we followed Miss Sutherland through the house, my mind was awhirl. How the devil had Holmes hit upon Mr. James Windibank as the villain of this piece? True, Windibank had proved himself a reprobate when he deceived his stepdaughter, Miss Sutherland, that he was a suitor named Mr. Hosmer Angel, desirous of marrying her, then deserting her at the altar, all to preserve some income he had from an inheritance of hers that he would lose were she to wed. She had come to Holmes to help her locate the errant Mr. Angel, whom she believed had met with foul play. While despicable, Windibank's actions were not illegal, so Holmes had to let him go. The detective had elected not to inform Miss Sutherland of Windibank's deception because he was convinced that the lady would not believe him, as she was totally enamoured of Mr. Angel; besides, she still would have to reside with Windibank and her mother, because she did not have sufficient funds to strike out on her own.

We arrived at a closed door and Miss Sutherland knocked before easing it open and entering a large sunlit drawing room that fronted the street. A man and a woman occupied two tallback armchairs in front of a fireplace, with cups and saucers balanced on their knees, and a small table holding a coffee service between them. Upon noticing us, Windibank sprang up, tipping his coffee onto the floor. 'You!' he shouted. 'What is the meaning of this?'

Miss Sutherland, who was in the act of retrieving her father's fallen cup, looked at him with a surprised expression. 'I didn't know that you knew Mr. Holmes, Father,' she said.

'Oh, he knows me, all right,' Holmes said. 'We met at the conclusion of that little problem you brought me seven years ago.'

But it wasn't Holmes that Windibank was looking at. He was staring at Addy.

'Hello, James,' she said.

In an instant, Windibank's expression went from one of astonishment to one of puzzlement. 'Do I know you?' he asked her. 'I am sure I do not.'

'Oh!' Addy exclaimed, bringing a hand to cover her mouth.

'It really won't do, Mr. Windibank,' said Holmes. 'In addition to the children whom you left penniless, there are doubtless others who can identify you as Mr. James Gabriel of Great Stanhope Street. It will just take a bit of looking to find them.'

Mrs. Windibank spoke in a quavering voice. 'Who are these people, James? What do they mean?'

Windibank extracted a handkerchief from a pocket and wiped his sweating brow.

'Mr. Sherlock Holmes is a busybody of some little renown in the city, Esther, largely due to the efforts of a mediocre writer who has chronicled some of his exploits in the popular press. He has uncovered a little indiscretion of mine, and has come here in the hope of profiting from it.'

'What 'little indiscretion'?' Mrs Sutherland asked, her tone strained.

'I'm afraid that I must make a clean breast of it,' he said to his wife. 'I am ashamed to tell you that for a little while, I was carrying on with a woman in Mayfair. It began as a harmless friendship, as I was trying to comfort her on the loss of her husband, but then it went too far. Due to her perilous emotional state, I was loath to break it off, but as I sank more deeply into it, I realised that I was doing a great disservice not only to her, but also to you, the love of my life. So, I finally did break it off.' He employed the handkerchief again, to wipe a tear from his cheek. Indicating Holmes, he continued, 'This... man!... found out about it and threatened to tell you and Mary if I refused to pay him extortion. I told him I would not be bled, and now he has come here to drive a wedge between us.' He took his wife's hand and sank to one knee before her. Looking soulfully into her eyes, he cooed, 'My dear, can you ever forgive me?'

Mrs. Windibank's features went from stone to velvet in a flash. 'My poor James!' she said.

I couldn't believe the absolute cheek of the devil! I had to speak up. 'Madam, your husband is a callous murderer! He shot a helpless woman down in the street to avoid exposure as a bigamist!'

Windibank gave me a look of pure hatred. 'Why would I do such a stupid thing as that, sir? The penalties for bigamy are often nominal, if the offender can provide a justification.' Turning back to his wife, he said earnestly, 'You see, Esther? You see to what lengths they will go to destroy me? You must be strong. After they take me, you must call our solicitor and tell him what's happened.' He squeezed his wife's hand in both of his. 'As long as I know you love me, I can bear anything!'

His wife's expression hardened again, but this time in resolution. 'Don't worry, my darling. We will fight them to the bitter end!'

'Perhaps you are correct, Mr. Windibank,' said Holmes. 'Perhaps you will be able to beat a charge of murder in the Assizes, if a test of your clothing of my own devising does not indicate that you fired a gun while wearing it. But your reputation in this city will be irreparably ruined, especially when it's revealed that you left the Worthington children penniless.'

'That will not matter to me as long as I have Esther's love,' Windibank sneered. 'Besides, the money was mine.'

Through all of this, Miss Sutherland was thoroughly nonplussed. Addy stood glaring at the man who had deceived her; who had quite possibly taken from her that which she could never regain. She reached into her purse and withdrew something that flashed silver in the light from the window. As Hopkins leapt to stop her, her hand belched flame and smoke, and a crimson rose sprang into being on Windibank's breast. She screamed with pain as her hand opened and the little gun dropped to the floor. Too late, Holmes grabbed her wrist and Hopkins wrapped both arms around her from behind, wrestling her to the carpet. Mary Sutherland looked horrified at what had happened. I hurried to Windibank, who lay supine in front of his shrieking wife. It required only a glance to tell me that this vile man would never stand trial for his crimes.

***

Later that evening, after finishing the excellent supper that Mrs. Hudson had provided, Holmes, Hopkins and I sat in Baker Street; the policeman and I with fine Cuban cigars and Holmes with his meerschaum; the three of us with snifters of Napoleon brandy given to Holmes by a grateful French government.

'There is one thing I would like to know, Holmes,' I said. 'After you saw that advertisement that Mrs. Gabriel placed in the Standard, you said you knew whom we sought. How could you know? That description could have fit a thousand men.'

'True enough,' Holmes agreed. 'But it only fit one who worked in Fenchurch Street—I found several bottles of claret from the wine importers Westhouse and Marbank in the Gabriel residence, and the doll that Lindee had was clearly French.

You'll remember that James Windibank was a buyer for that firm, and took periodic trips across the Channel.'

'I didn't,' I said, 'but you remembered such details from a case that occurred seven years ago?' It was more of an expression of astonishment than a question.

'Of course,' Holmes said. He continued, 'This case is a perfect example of how so-called trivial offenses can ultimately lead to tragedy. When I first encountered Mr. Windibank, I said he was a cold-blooded scoundrel who would commit further crimes and end his days on the gallows. I erred only in the means of his departure from this mortal coil. I count it as a personal failure that two children will grow up without their parents, and that a foolish woman may end her life at the end of a noose because of him. And I also count it as a personal failure that I did not realise that Miss Addy had taken a gun from the cabinet in the drawing room, too. When I saw that a drawer had been opened, I assumed that the cabinet was the source of the weapon that Windibank used to shoot Mrs. Gabriel in Baker Street, which was likely at the bottom of the Thames.'

'But whatever drove Windibank to the end of shooting his bigamous wife?' I asked. 'Surely he could have found a less violent means of dealing with her.'

'I think it was pure panic, Watson. He was undoubtedly poleaxed when I revealed him as Hosmer Angel seven years ago, and he realised that he escaped retribution that time by the skin of his nose. When he heard my name again in connection with Mrs. Gabriel, he simply snapped. He told us that the penalties for bigamy are strictly nominal, but a perusal of the *Illustrated Police News* will reveal that is not always the case. Some magistrates have been known to impose hard labour.' The detective shook his head. 'Much tragedy would have been avoided if I had been able to bring that rogue to heel the first time.'

'You cannot blame yourself, Holmes,' I said. 'The law is the law.'

'Dr. Watson is correct,' Hopkins agreed. 'It is the policeman's curse; for every miscreant we remove from society, another takes his place. And the courts do not always impose the penalties that we would wish them to. It does not mean that the job is not worth doing.'

'I know it,' said Holmes, 'but that does not prevent me from deploring it. At least I was finally able to tell Miss Sutherland who the elusive Mr. Hosmer Angel really was. After seeing her stepfather's perfidy first-hand, she had no difficulty believing me.'

'What of the Worthington children, Holmes? Will the funds that Windibank absconded with ever be restored to them?'

'Reverend Charlesworth, as the children's guardian, has instituted proceedings to that end,' Holmes replied. 'Whether or not it will come to pass is now a matter for solicitors and judges, unfortunately.' He took a deep breath, and sighed. 'Sometimes I yearn for the power of an absolute monarch, who does not mind the law, because he is the law.'

'But many of those monarchs used that authority for ill, not good,' I countered. 'That's why limits were imposed on such power.'

'True enough, Watson, but I'd like to think that I am more enlightened than they were,' said Holmes. 'However, the late Mr. Windibank is a perfect example of what can happen to a man when he feels he is responsible only to himself.'

I said, 'I don't think I've ever met a man with a greater sense of responsibility to his fellows than you, Holmes.'

'I concur,' agreed Hopkins.

'My blushes, gentlemen!' Holmes exclaimed. 'I simply follow the maxim of Phillip Stanhope, the fourth Earl of Chesterfield, for whom Great Stanhope Street was likely named. 'Aim at perfection in everything, though in most things it is unattainable,' he said. 'However, they who aim at it, and persevere, will come much nearer to it than those whose laziness and despondency make them give it up as unattainable.''

Another Case of Identity

Since our auspicious meeting in 1881, I have accompanied my friend, Mr. Sherlock Holmes, during his investigations of hundreds of cases, only a small number of which I have chosen to chronicle, and only a fraction of those have eventually been published. There are many reasons why my narrative of a particular case may never become part of the public record. A case might be too politically sensitive, such as the mission that Holmes had carried out for the royal family of Holland, or that matter of supreme importance to the French government. Some of our adventures are frankly too sordid to conform to current publication standards; the repulsive story of the red leech comes to mind in this regard. Publication of the record of a particular case might serve to bring unwanted publicity to innocents, or spark a libel suit; for example, the affair of the Abbey School, in which the Duke of Greyminster was so deeply involved. Sometimes I find myself in disagreement with my literary agent about the public appeal of a tale, and, hard to believe as it may be, a few of my stories have been refused outright by a publisher; The Adventure of the Middle-aged Bachelor and the two Loquacious Women falls into the latter category. And finally, there are stories for which the world is simply not, nor may ever be prepared, such as The Adventure of the Giant Rat of Sumatra.

Holmes, of course, is the final arbiter of whether the record of a given case may be published. I have been known to argue with him if he said no, but as his historiographer, I must always honour his wishes. However, I feel that some of his exploits are worth recording even though they may reside in my battered tin dispatch box for the rest of my days. So far, Holmes has refused to allow the publication of an account of the death of Reginald Balfour. When I asked him for a reason, he said, 'There is another who shares complicity in this affair, Watson, and I'd rather he not be aware of what I know of it at the present time.'

So it was that Holmes and I found ourselves in Baker Street on Monday morning, May 11, 1896, yet another dry and sunny day. Over Mrs. Hudson's excellent breakfast of coffee and kippers, I was perusing The Daily Mail, a brand new paper which had just begun publication the previous week.

'Good Lord, Holmes!' I remarked. 'Yorkshire set a record for the County Championship by accumulating an innings total of 887 against Warwickshire last Friday! Remarkable, what?'

Ten Steps from Baker Street

I knew Holmes found my comments about sporting events tedious, but frankly, I was hoping that the minor annoyance might prompt him into speaking, of which he had done quite little for several days. He sprawled on the sofa in his mouse grey gown, his pipe full of yesterday's dottles between his lips, in a brown study since wrapping up his last case—he did not find the missing child in time. He did manage to prove that the lad's absence was not the result of kidnapping, as his parents feared, but that provided them cold comfort at best.

A tap at the door, then our landlady entered, partially closing the door behind her. 'You must get up, Mr. Holmes. You have a distinguished visitor.'

'Send him away, woman!' Holmes exploded. 'I am of no use to anyone!'

'It is the Duke of Brownley, sir, and I am afraid that he will not be put off. Oh my! He has followed me upstairs...'

The door sprang open, and a white-haired gentlemen burst into our rooms. Tall and stylish in full morning dress, he had a disconsolate expression and pallid complexion; an obvious indication that he was overwrought. Having heard Holmes's last comment, he said, 'If you are as useless as that idiot Hopkins, then I am truly a woe-begotten wretch. I have just lost my only son, sir, and I suspect foul play. Will you not agree to hear me out?'

The phrase 'lost my only son' apparently gained Holmes' attention. He sat up, smoothed his disarranged hair, and replied, 'I must apologise, your Grace, for my state of dress. I was not expecting visitors.'

'Nonsense, man!', the Duke ejaculated. 'How else should you be dressed at this hour, in your own home?'

I said, 'Mrs Hudson, take the Duke's hat and stick. Sit down your Grace, and let me pour you some of this excellent coffee. Will you take a bit of breakfast? It may calm your nerves.'

'I thank you for your kind offer, sir,' the Duke answered, taking the high-backed chair. 'but I am much too distraught to take refreshment.'

'Some whisky, then? I think we can excuse the early hour.'

The Duke acquiesced, and I poured him a tot of Holmes's best single malt, then a cup of coffee for the detective. The Duke tasted the whisky, and I saw a little colour come back into his cheeks.

Now, sir,' said Holmes, 'tell us your sad tale. And omit no detail, however unimportant it may seem.'

The Duke began, 'I am Fitzhugh Balfour, the Duke of Brownley. My son, Reginald, arrived at Brownley Manor, my estate, on the night of Friday, May 8, 1896, just before bedtime. He was sweating heavily, complaining of nausea and abdominal pain. He collapsed in the vestibule, saying 'The b—ch has poisoned me!'

Holmes interrupted, 'Do you have any idea of whom he spoke, your Grace?'

The Duke looked annoyed at the inquiry. 'No sir, I do not, or I would have mentioned it.'

'Sorry. Pray continue your most interesting narrative.'

'Reggie was put to bed in his old room with his former governess, Roberta, to watch over him. The only further words he uttered before he passed away during a seizure early on Saturday morning were "Dr. Warren, Harley Street". We sent a wire to this Dr. Warren forthwith, summoning him to Bromley Manor, but received a note in return that the telegram could not be delivered because the Doctor was not in residence.'

'What time was the wire sent?' asked Holmes.

Again, the Duke scowled. 'I sent the page to the telegraph office in the village before sunrise. He had to knock the operator out of bed to have him send it.'

'And I take it that your son was under the care of this Doctor Warren?' Holmes asked.

'If he was, I didn't know of it,' said the Duke. 'These constant inquiries of yours are distracting, Mr. Holmes.'

'I apologise, your Grace, but the truth often lurks in the most inconsequential of things.'

'Rather,' said the Duke. He took a sip of whisky, then continued, 'Later that morning, we contacted Scotland Yard. An Inspector Stanley Hopkins came to Brownley Manor, but after I told him what had transpired, he said only that he would look into it, but he saw no evidence that Reggie's death was not simply due to illness.'

'Was there anything other than your son's earlier statement that suggested to you that the inspector was incorrect?' I asked the Duke.

'Poppycock!' he snarled. 'Boy was a top oarsman for Westminster, never sick a day in his life!'

'Tell me more about Reginald,' said Holmes. 'What sort of chap was he? Did he have a position? What were his interests? Who were his friends?'

155

'He didn't require a position,' the Duke said in a condescending tone. 'I gave him an ample allowance. Does no harm for a fellow to take a few years after University, decide his course in life.'

Wouldn't it be grand if all of us had that opportunity, I thought.

'So, what were his diversions?' asked Holmes.

'He resided at the townhouse in Cavendish Square. Spent a lot of time at his club. The Nonpareil.' A tony gaming club.

Holmes asked, 'And how were his debts?'

Now the Duke's expression became extremely frosty. 'I'm sure I do not take your meaning, Mr. Holmes. I informed Reggie some time ago that if he was going to play at cards, he must absolutely manage any losses from his allowance. He never gave me any indication that he was not doing so.'

'With whom did he play cards?'

'I neither know nor care.'

'How about female friends?' Holmes inquired. 'Enemies?'

'He hasn't got any of either!' the Duke exploded. 'Mr. Holmes! I came to consult you because that fool Hopkins gave me the distinct impression that Scotland Yard is going to sweep Reggie's death under the rug. Now will you take this assignment or will you not?'

'Again, I must beg your pardon, Duke,' said Holmes in a deferential tone. 'I will aid you to the best of my meagre abilities. If your son was poisoned, there must be a reason that someone would do that. I must ask such questions in order to ascertain one. Where is Reggie's body now?'

'Hopkins sent a wagon to take Reggie to the city mortuary for examination later on Saturday morning. I was not happy about that, but I suppose it was necessary to get this mess sorted. He said that he would inform me when the body would be released for burial.'

'I shall consult the medical examiner at Bart's, then pay a visit to you at Brownley Manor later this morning,' Holmes told the Duke. 'I shall want to speak to this Roberta, and to your page.'

'I shall see that they are available,' answered his Grace.

'Then, of course, I must visit the Nonpareil, and also try to locate the elusive Dr. Warren. After that, we shall see.' Holmes regarded the Duke with a sympathetic expression. 'Your Grace, you must prepare yourself for the possibility that your son did in fact die from a disease.'

'If you tell me that you have good evidence that Reggie's claim that he was poisoned was unfounded after a thorough investigation, I will accept your word,' the Duke said. 'You do come highly recommended, Mr. Holmes. And it would be a comfort to know that he did not die from foul play.'

I could sense the immense grief beneath the Duke's matter-of-fact tone. I have dealt with parents who lost children on hundreds of occasions, but have never become accustomed to it. I think I would get out of practice if I did.

After his Grace had departed, Holmes turned to me. 'If you have nothing better to occupy yourself with today, Watson, I would much appreciate your company. Your medical expertise might prove invaluable in this case.'

'It does appear that the young man expired because of some fatal malady,' I said.

'Yes,' said Holmes, 'but mark you what I have said about theorizing in the absence of data. Let us give the Duke his money's worth, even if this be merely a low tragedy.'

Holmes rang for the page and dispatched him to find a cab whilst we changed into morning dress—we were going to call on a duke later this day. The ride to Smithfield was protracted, as there was considerable congestion on Oxford Street, so it was nearly eleven before we debarked in front of Bart's. Holmes led the way to the mortuary, where he was well-known, so it was not long before we were gazing at the corpse of the unfortunate Reggie Balfour. The boy looked serene in death, and much younger than his twenty-five years. Dr. Eames, the medical examiner, was in attendance.

'Have you formed an opinion about the cause of death?' Holmes asked the Doctor.

'I found marked haemorrhage in the mucosal membranes of the gastrointestinal system, which was consistent with what I was told of the patient's complaints, and which could be indicative of any number of conditions,' the medical examiner said. 'I also found systemic organ damage.'

'Then he could have been poisoned?' Holmes asked.

'Yes, but the signs are not definitive,' said the Doctor. 'Enteric fever, food poisoning or other intestinal maladies will also exhibit such signs.'

'But those things are not uniformly fatal,' I said, 'and if they are, suffering may be protracted before death occurs.' I knew this first-hand from my own battle with enteric fever after Maiwand.

'That's correct,' said the Doctor.

'There have been no other reports of such diseases in the City?' Holmes asked.

'Now that you mention it, I had one other with similar signs.' the Doctor said.

157

'Whom?' asked Holmes.

'He was a scullion, employed at the Criterion.' The Criterion was a tony restaurant in Piccadilly, where Holmes and I occasionally dined.

'Most curious,' Holmes observed. 'No other cases linked to the restaurant?' I knew what Holmes was considering—food poisoning.

'No, it seemed to be an isolated incident,' Eames said.

There was no point in conducting my own examination after a full autopsy had been carried out, so we repaired back to our cab, giving the driver an order to go to Charing Cross Station, where we boarded a train for the village of Brownley.

We crossed the Thames and had a fine view of Battersea Park to the west, then a pleasant ride to Brownley, about half an hour south of London.

On arrival, we were informed by the ticket agent that Brownley Manor was approximately half a mile from the station, along the one long street that comprised the greatest part of the town. No cabs were in evidence, but it was a fine sunny day, so we decided to walk to the Duke's estate. It was peaceful to be here after the hustle and bustle of the capital, yet the poignant reason for our visit weighed heavily on my mind.

After passing out of the village proper, we came to a side road shaded by overarching oaks, which the ticket agent had told us was the approach to Brownley Manor. As we emerged from the leafy tunnel, the scent of spring flowers hung heavy in the air, and the bulk of the manor house reared up before us—a three-storey red brick mansion with stone dressings, which dated from the late 18th century. It featured tall arched windows on the first floor, a slate roof lined with dormers flanking a gabled entry on either side, and four fine brick chimneys spaced equally along its length—a residence fit for a duke, indeed. We proceeded up a short brick stairway between meticulously trimmed rectangular yew hedges, and a heavy oaken door with gleaming brass fittings swung silently open at our approach.

'Obviously, someone at the station called ahead of our arrival,' Holmes muttered.

A liveried butler took Holmes' card and conducted us to a sitting room with lofty, painted ceilings and a majestic brick fireplace. In only a few minutes, the Duke entered.

'What have you ascertained so far?' he asked Holmes in a brusque tone.

Holmes informed him of the medical examiner's findings. He asked, 'Now that you've had time to reflect, are you sure you have no idea of the identity of the woman to whom your son referred?'

'None whatsoever,' averred the Duke. 'If Reggie was keeping company with a woman, he did not see fit to share that information with me.'

'I wonder if you have a recent photograph of Reggie that I might borrow for a while,' Holmes asked.

'No sir. If I want pictures of family members, I'll commission a portrait,' said the Duke.

Holmes spent a fruitless half hour interrogating the page, and Roberta the housemaid, but got no further clarity regarding the cause of the unfortunate Reggie's demise.

'I suppose our next step is to return to London and attempt to speak with this Doctor Warren,' Holmes said dejectedly. I dearly hoped that this case was not doomed to become another failure, following so closely on the heels of the affair of the missing boy last week.

The Duke had not seen fit to offer us luncheon, so I was famished by the time we returned to the railway station. I prevailed upon Holmes to allow me to procure box meals from an adjacent public house. As I have observed in other accounts of Holmes' adventures, he is wont to go without sustenance for days when on a case, especially when things are not going well. I was determined not to allow this during this investigation.

Once back in London, we secured a cab outside Victoria Station, and Holmes directed the driver to Dr. Warren's Harley Street office. We found the following note tacked to the locked front door.

Dr. Malachy Warren has been called away on urgent business (it ran) and the date of his return is undetermined at this time. The following physicians and surgeons have indicated that they will see Dr. Warren's patients who have urgent needs:

Dr. Moore Agar 6 Harley Street
Dr. Arthur Ainstree 35 Harley Street
Mr. Ronald Atkinson, Surgeon, St. Mary's Hosp.

'So, it seems that Dr. Warren has decamped for the duration,' observed Holmes. 'I wonder what the good Doctor is so fearful of?'

We returned to Baker Street. While changing from our morning dress to less formal attire, Holmes dispatched a wire to Stanley Hopkins at Scotland Yard, asking the inspector to join us for dinner. Mrs. Hudson was a bit miffed at the short notice, but finally allowed that she could stretch tonight's menu to accommodate another diner.

Holmes' motives for involving Hopkins became clear at the table. Over a fine meal of boiled gigot of mutton with neeps and tatties, he assured the young policeman that he had no desire to step on his toes.

'By George,' said Hopkins, 'after all the assistance you've given to me, Mr. Holmes, and seeking no credit for yourself, I shouldn't care if you'd tread on them with hobnails. But I must tell you that I've not been able to find any evidence that the poor chap didn't die of a sudden illness.'

'Nor have we, sir, but I've promised the Duke that we'd leave no stone unturned. That is why I'd like you to accompany us to the Nonpareil Club this evening. As we are not members, we'll need your badge to gain admittance.'

'And what do you hope to discover there?'

'I want to talk to Reginald Balfour's mates to see if a motive for his alleged murder can be ascertained,' said Holmes. 'Also, the Duke tells me that he has no knowledge of his son's female friends. It's difficult to believe that a gentleman of that age hasn't got any.'

Because a hansom cab is a bit of a tight squeeze for three large men, Holmes hired a brougham for the trip to Pall Mall. St. James's Street is a broad thoroughfare wide enough to accommodate carriages three abreast and lined with fine Georgian townhouses that house some of London's most exclusive clubs, including the Thatched House Club, the Conservative Club, Boodle's, the Devonshire Club, and of course, the Nonpareil Card Club. After Hopkins displayed his badge, we were met in the foyer by the night manager, a Mr. Edwin Newsome, who conducted us to his office. On the way, we passed through a corridor, one wall of which was lined with framed drawings and photographs.

'Your members, I presume,' Holmes said to Newsome.

'Yes,' he replied. 'This display represents a venerable tradition of the Nonpareil. Upon acceptance, a new member sits for his photograph, which will be displayed here in perpetuity, along with his coat of arms or family crest.'

'Ordered by date of admittance, I see,' observed Holmes.

'Of course. That way, we don't have to rearrange everything when a new member is admitted.'

Holmes abruptly froze, staring intently at one of the photos. I came up behind him to see which one interested him so. It was a double picture with a comely young man above, with a high forehead and aquiline features, looking off into the distance instead of at the camera, as if he was uncomfortable having his picture made. Beneath was a family crest done in red and white. A brass plaque on the bottom of the frame noted:

Dr. Malachy Warren, b. 1847, member 1882.

'

Fascinating,' said Holmes.

'What?' I said. 'That he's been a member for 14 years?'

He turned to look at me disbelievingly. 'You don't see it?'

'See what?' I said, perplexed.

'Never mind.' He turned and followed Newsome into his office. Typical.

After Holmes had informed the manager of the reason for our visit, Newsome said, 'Of course, Mr. Holmes. Mr. Balfour's loss was a blow to all of us. I'm sure his comrades would be glad to speak with you about him.'

'With whom did he spend most of his time?' Holmes asked.

'Mr. Balfour was very fond of whist,' the manager said. 'He was part of a regular foursome that comprised Mr. Bertie Greene, Mr. Rupert Bennington-Smythe and Count Negretto Sylvius.'

I could see Holmes's head twitch at that last name. 'Which was Balfour's partner?' Holmes asked.

'Mr. Greene,' said Newsome.

'I should like to speak with each of them,' said Holmes. 'Greene first, then Bennington-Smythe, and Count Sylvius, last, if he doesn't mind.'

A few moments later, Newsome ushered Bertie Greene into the office, then departed. Greene was a young chap about Reggie Balfour's age. He had curly brown hair and broad features and he was dressed in a grey-plaid towncoat that hung loosely on his scrawny frame, black trousers with a white shirt and black tie. He appeared somewhat nervous in the presence of Holmes and a Scotland Yard Inspector—Holmes's name had become quite well-known by now, since I'd been chronicling his cases.

'Sit down, Mr. Greene,' Holmes said. 'You have nothing to fear from us. We're simply looking into Mr. Balfour's last days at his father's request.'

Greene seemed insulted by Holmes's remarks. 'I'm not afraid,' he said. 'Just discommoded. We were having a rubber, and I was winning.'

'For a change?' Holmes asked.

Greene suddenly looked guilty. 'Well, yes,' he said. 'How did you know?'

'If I had a tailor who cut a bespoke towncoat that poorly, I should certainly hold him accountable,' said Holmes. 'I assume you had it made in better times, and haven't had it altered due to lack of funds. Just how much do you owe Bennington-Smythe and Sylvius?'

'Two hundred thirty-eight pounds and five shillings,' Greene answered. 'And I don't owe Bennington-Smythe anything. The Count takes care of that part of it.'

Holmes took his gold cigarette case from an inner pocket and flipped it open, extracted one, and held it out to Greene. His hand trembled as he reached for one. 'Take two,' Holmes told him. Then, 'The Count is graciously allowing you to make payments to him? With interest, I suppose?'

'He doesn't charge me any,' Greene said. 'He advances me the coin so I can keep playing, and when I win, like I am tonight, he deducts it from what I owe him.'

'What a generous fellow!' said Holmes. 'But I'll wager that you must make regular payments as well, correct? Weekly?'

'Once a month. He says it's good for my character, and it keeps me from getting into him too deeply.'

'And it also keeps you at fighting weight,' Holmes observed. 'He's looking out for your well-being, the Count.'

'He says that he likes to play whist,' Greene said. 'If he won all the time and didn't give a fellow a break, no one would play with him.'

'And that would be a tragedy, indeed,' finished Holmes. 'I think I've learned all that I need to know from you, Mr. Greene. I also think we can dispense with an interview of Mr. Bennington-Smythe. Would you please ask the Count if he would be so kind to grace us with his presence?'

Once again Greene regarded Holmes fearfully, as if he wondered if he'd told too much. 'You won't...'

'Run along, Mr. Greene,' Holmes said. 'A piece of advice. Mortgage all that you own, impose upon your family and friends if you must, but get yourself out from under the Count's thumb, and don't get back underneath it again. You won't regret it. That's all.'

Greene turned and slinked out of the door. When he'd gone, I asked Holmes, 'And just who is this Count Sylvius? A peer?'

'He has a reputation as a big-game hunter. But he's a womanizer, a cad and an all-round rotter,' Holmes said. 'He's been within the spectrum of my awareness for some years now. And his title, if real at all, is certainly not British. Possibly Italian. Now that I'm cognisant that he's involved in this affair, I certainly suspect foul play in young Balfour's death.'

'I agree, Mr. Holmes,' said Hopkins. 'The yard has had rumours of this Count Sylvius, but nothing actionable, as yet.'

'He prefers to have others do his dirty work,' Holmes said. A tap on the door. 'But hush, gentlemen. Here he is now.'

The office door opened and the Count entered. He was a huge, dark-skinned fellow of southern Italian aspect, dressed in the continental fashion in tails with velvet lapels, white waistcoat and black tie. He wore a huge black moustache under a large beaky nose and sported a monocle that he probably didn't need, dangling on his chest. He favoured us with a thin-lipped smile as he made a little bow, then he stepped straight up to Holmes and extended his hand.

'I am so pleased to make your acquaintance, Mr. Holmes.' His voice had just a hint of an Italian accent. 'I have heard much of you, even in Rome.'

Holmes seemed not to see the proffered hand. He motioned to the chair that Greene had just quitted. 'I have heard much of you as well, Count.'

The Count favoured us with an oily smile as he sat. 'I hope it was all flattering.'

'Hardly,' Holmes said. 'I am here to discuss with you anything that you might know of the demise of young Reginald Balfour. I am told you played cards with him.'

'Yes, that is true. Such a pity. Reggie was a fine young man.'

'I assume he owed you money?'

'On the contrary, Mr. Holmes, Reggie and I were square. He paid his debts to me in a regular manner.'

'The Duke must provide him a generous allowance.'

'Yes, that must be so.'

'I wonder if you could tell me of Reggie's other acquaintances. Female friends, perhaps?'

'Not to my knowledge. Reggie seemed entirely dedicated to whist. He even talked about playing professionally one day, although I must say, I don't think that he possessed the necessary acumen.'

Holmes reached again for his cigarette case, but the Count stopped him. 'Please,' he said, extracting his own black and gold case from his jacket, 'you must try one of mine. Balkan Sobranies. The Latakia gives them quite a unique flavour.'

'I prefer my Virginias,' said Holmes, offering his case to Hopkins and myself. Neither of us took one. The Count produced a cigarette holder and fixed his cigarette to the end, then a lighter. Holmes did allow the Count to give him a light. 'Do you know whether Reggie had much to do with Dr. Malachy Warren?' he inquired.

The Count assumed a peculiar grin. 'Oh, I would say that the two of them were certainly acquainted, but I couldn't tell you the nature of their assignation.' It seemed to me that he was implying something more, but I could not fathom what.

'So they kept regular company?' Holmes pressed.

'I'm sure I don't know,' replied the Count.

Holmes paused, considering, then asked, 'And what was your relationship with the good Doctor?'

The Count's grin blossomed into a broad smile. 'We spoke to each other on occasion, Mr. Holmes, as fellow club members will do. That was the extent of it.'

I could not help but feel that the fellow was lying through his teeth, but I couldn't imagine why.

'Is that all, Mr. Holmes?' The Count asked. 'My partners are anxiously waiting for me, so that we may resume our game.'

'Yes Count, that will be all. You'll hear from me if we need to resume our conversation.'

'I look forward to that hour,' the Count said. He rose, touched his right forefinger to his eyebrow in a mock salute to the three of us, then departed.

'There goes a very dangerous man,' said Hopkins.

'Indubitably,' Holmes agreed. 'Only God knows the sins he's responsible for, although I am aware of a few.'

'Care to share them with Scotland Yard?' asked the inspector.

'When I have evidence, certainly,' replied Holmes.

'Do you think he's responsible for Reggie's death?' I asked Holmes.

'Leaving aside for the moment the question of means,' began Holmes, 'I can discern no motive for Count Sylvius to want Reggie out of the way. The boy was a golden goose for him, and apparently, much more assiduous in paying his debts than the hapless Greene, if the Count is to be believed.'

'So where do we go from here?' I asked.

'Baker Street,' replied Holmes. 'I must be off early in the morning.'

'To do what?' I asked.

'To locate the evanescent Dr. Warren.'

We went to find Newsome, to thank him for his accommodation. 'No thanks necessary,' the club manager averred. 'I only hope you can shed some light on Reggie's tragic demise.'

'By the way,' said Holmes, 'would it be possible for me to borrow Reggie's photo from the corridor? I assure you, it will be returned.'

'By all means,' said Newsome.

When we arrived back at our digs, the bells of St. Marylebone's were just chiming ten. Holmes went straight to bed after knocking up the page and sending him off with a wire, but I, knowing that sleep would be a rare commodity this night, poured a stiff brandy and sat in my chair to muse over this puzzling case, if even a crime had been done! We had no evidence that poor Balfour's death was anything other than natural. Holmes now seemed convinced that the minatory Count Sylvius was somehow involved, but the man seemed to simply have no reason to want Reggie out of the way. After a bit, I could feel the Cognac doing its work, so I made my way upstairs to bed.

True to his word, Holmes was absent when I came downstairs at eight forty-five. The morning papers were on the table, so I rang for coffee and breakfast. I reached for *The Daily Mail*, but spied an open book beneath it—a copy of Who's Who. I perused the page that presented itself and found the following entry:

> **WARREN, Malachy Bernas**, *MD Univ. of Edinburgh 1871; F.R.C.P. (Lond.) 1886: 74th Regt of Foot, India, 1871; HM 66th, Afghanistan, 1879: Returned to England 1881, entered private practice: Address 29 Harley Street, W*

It was not unusual for a doctor to be transferred from the regiment that he had originally joined, according to the needs of the service. If Warren was with the 66th in 1879, he was likely at Maiwand in 1880! I strained to remember. After that disastrous battle and my wounding, I met many doctors in the course of my treatment. Was Dr.

Warren one of them? I tried to summon up his features from the photograph at the club last evening.

It was near eleven when Holmes returned. 'I have had an interesting morning, Watson,' he said. 'I see that you have had a chance to review Dr. Warren's Who's Who entry. Do you remember at all meeting him during or after Maiwand?'

'Yes,' I replied. 'I do seem to remember encountering a young man who looked like him, who helped care for me during that awful bout with enteric fever. He was unusually solicitous of my comfort—army doctors can be a cold lot.' A pause. 'I found it interesting that the entry contains no information about Warren's life before he entered medical school.'

'It contains only that which Warren wanted,' said Holmes. 'The information was gleaned from a questionnaire provided by the good Doctor himself.' Holmes should know, having his own entry in Who's Who.

'I spent a fruitful morning at the War Office in Cumberland House,' he continued. 'With a bit of prodding from brother Mycroft, they were able to tell me why a healthy army doctor was returned so abruptly to England in 1881.' He smiled, making me wait for it, then, 'Doctor Warren was denied promotion due to excessive gambling, or more likely, because he owed the wrong people and had trouble paying.'

'And yet he joins a gaming club after he returns to London,' I observed. 'He doesn't seem to have the best judgment, does he?'

'No, he doesn't,' agreed Holmes. 'What would you say to a little stroll over to Harley Street after lunch?'

After an excellent luncheon of fresh fish provided by our landlady, Holmes and I set out for Harley Street, just a few blocks east. It was glorious spring day, with a slight breeze from the northeast clearing away much of the objectionable street scents. If Warren still had not returned to his office, I resolved to ask Holmes if he cared to take in nearby Regent's Park. As we approached no. 29, I was gratified to see that the notice was still on the door. Holmes stopped in front of the steps and gave a low whistle. A ragamuffin suddenly appeared from a nearby stairwell leading to a basement.

'All quiet, Sam?' asked Holmes.

'Yessir. Nobody's come in or out.'

Holmes fished in his pocket for a crown, which he flipped to the lad. 'Good job. The surveillance is over. See that you pay the others.'

166

As the boy ran off, Holmes brought out a ring of keys. It only required three or four tries before he had the door open and beckoned me inside. Passers-by on Harley Street paid us no mind—we could have been a pair of residents entering our home.

Holmes closed the door and I inhaled the familiar scents of a doctor's office—hints of iodine and carbolic mingled with lemon wax. We were in a hallway tiled in a black-and-white motif, with closed doors right, left and to the rear, and a broad, polished staircase rising to the first floor.

I regarded Holmes questioningly. 'How is it that you have Warren's keys?'

He favoured me with a deprecating smile. 'I observed Warren's locks the last time we were here,' he said, 'and earlier this morning, I visited a locksmith whom I once rescued from the dock. He was kind enough to provide me with a set of skeleton keys.'

'These would be Warren's examining rooms, surgery and office,' Holmes continued, 'with the living quarters upstairs. I think it more likely that clews to the Doctor's present whereabouts will be found in the latter location.'

We ascended the stairs, and Holmes had to ply his skeleton keys once more to unlock the door at the apex. As he opened it, an odour of tobacco and food with an underlying sweetness of flowers or perfume wafted out from the rooms beyond. We entered a large salon that featured painted azure walls with vertical white stencilling in a diamonded pattern, ivory-upholstered furniture and a marble fireplace. Three broad windows curtained in blue and white looked out over Harley Street. Holmes went straight to his work, opening drawers and cabinets, presumably searching for anything that might give an indication of where Warren might be.

'Why don't you look about in the other rooms, Watson?' Holmes said, indicating a doorway across from the one to the stairs.

I opened it and found myself in a hallway, again with doors left and right, and a staircase to a second floor at the end. I opened a door to a bedroom that was decidedly masculine, done in dark wood and leather and smelling of sweat and whisky. A second door led to a larger bedroom decorated with a feminine flair—again in blue and white, with lace doilies and throws covering white-painted furnishings with gold trim. A vanity topped with a mirrored triptych occupied one wall with a large white wardrobe on another. I opened the latter and found a dozen men's suits hanging in a row. In the bottom were several pair of men's shoes and boots, and a cardboard box. I picked it up. Southall's towels? The drawers of a nearby bureau contained yet more haberdashery. I was beginning to come to an unsettling conclusion.

I went back to the salon where I found Holmes at the liquor cabinet, holding a bottle of amber liquid up to the light streaming in through the windows.

'Holmes,' I said, 'I believe that Dr. Warren is a woman! And there is a man living here as well.' I told him about the bedrooms that I found.

'Yes, Watson,' replied Holmes. 'I realized that as soon as I saw her picture at the Nonpareil Club. The absence of an Adam's apple is quite diagnostic. Come here and look at this.'

I approached and he turned the bottle that he was holding so I could see the red-and-white label.

> *Craigshall*
> *Single Malt Scotch Whisky*
> *Made with Meticulous Care in our Lowlands Distillery*
> *Aged in Oak 16 Years*

Beneath the words, a familiar family crest was displayed—the same as the one beneath Warren's picture at the club!

'Now I think I have a good notion of where Dr. Warren might be,' Holmes said.

'There's another floor above us,' I pointed out.

'Yes,' he replied. 'We might as well take a look for thoroughness's sake.'

Once again Holmes had to use his keys on the door at the top of the stairs. Pushing it open, we entered an attic room with a low ceiling, dark because insufficient light was admitted through the narrow stained glass windows. A sweet solvent aroma, not unlike that which pervaded our rooms in Baker Street on occasion, tickled my nostrils. Sure enough, in the low light I could see the silhouettes of flasks, condensers and other chemical laboratory equipment, occupying two long tables in the centre of the room.

'Apparently Dr. Warren and I share an avocation,' said Holmes.

Holmes approached a desk in a corner, while I surveyed the chemical equipment. Due to my long association with Holmes, I was able to ascertain that the equipment necessary to carry out an extraction has been erected on one bench. I found a beaker half full of dried beans, tan mottled with brown, and an open notebook nearby. I picked up the latter, hoping to find out what the experimenter had been doing.

I raised my voice. 'Holmes? Are you familiar with a process known as a Stillmark extraction?'

'Watson,' Holmes voice was low, and cold as ice. 'Put that book on the bench, and get away from there. We must leave immediately.'

I did as he asked. As I approached him, I could see that his face was livid, and he had an expression that I'd seldom seen on his countenance. Fear.

'Holmes, what's the matter? What's got you spooked, old man?'

'Lectins, Watson. Lectins. Stillmark carried out an aqueous extraction of the castor bean in 1888, and isolated an extremely toxic product. I fear that we might have become exposed to it here.'

He ushered me out of the door and down the stairs, continuing all the way to the ground floor and out on to Harley Street, where he began walking south at a brisk pace. I had to trot to keep up.

'Holmes! Where are you going in such a hurry?'

'To the Argyll Baths off Regent Street,' he said.

After entering the baths, we went into the dressing room to disrobe, and Holmes told the attendant, 'Please do not touch these garments. Bring a laundry sack so that we may place them inside, then have them burned. We will eschew the warm room and go directly to the bathing pool.'

Once at the pool, Holmes said, 'Immerse yourself Watson, and scrub every inch of you. Your life depends on your cleanliness.'

When we were bathed to his satisfaction, I asked if we might go to one of the warm rooms to dry off, as I was chilled to the bone from the cold bath, and my shoulder was throbbing.

'No Watson, in this case I think it better for our pores to remain shut. The next day or two will tell us whether we left Warren's laboratory in time.'

That was the last he would say on the matter. He sent a wire to Baker Street for fresh clothes.

Afghanistan had taught me the futility of agonising over that about which I could do nothing. I resolved to put the possibility of exposure to the back of my mind, and hope for the best.

We were back in Baker Street just before supper time. Holmes dispatched a pair of wires, one to Hopkins and the other to the Scottish Records Office in Edinburgh.

'Prepare yourself for an excursion, old boy,' he said to me. 'The Flying Scotsman leaves Charing Cross at 10 a.m. tomorrow.'

'And why, pray tell, are we going to Scotland?' I asked.

'To beard the lioness in her den.'

Ten Steps from Baker Street

Given Holmes' comments of yesterday, I was grateful to see the light of day on Wednesday morning. I had asked him once more about the substance that we may have been exposed to, and he said, 'Don't fret about it, Watson. If we've received a lethal dose, there's nothing anyone can do. Best not to waste one's life worrying about losing it.'

Holmes indicated that our trip to Scotland would only consume a day or two, so I packed a single valise, and carried my Norfolk jacket and my Fedora in case of chilly weather up north. We boarded the Flying Scotsman and were whisked away precisely on time for the nine-hour trip—the fastest way to Scotland from London. Upon our arrival in the Scottish capital, we booked a room at the Royal Hotel, where a package from the Records Office awaited Holmes. After perusing the contents, he arranged for a carriage to take us south in the morning.

Under other circumstances, our morning ride would have been delightful. The Lowlands south of Edinburgh is a sprawling, sparsely forested, verdant land of cultivated fields and sheep pastures, impossibly green during the early spring lambing season. A Scot myself, even though I had no more family here and had not been back in decades, I felt a vague yearning for the land of my birth. I suppose that is natural.

After approximately two hours, we entered the village of Craigshall, whose narrow streets and grey stone buildings evoked an earlier, simpler time. The air was redolent with peat smoke, likely the product of our destination, a towering granite castle on a lofty hill above the town. After passing through tall wrought iron gates, we made not for the castle which housed the distillery, but instead for a gabled cottage of stone and white-painted clapboard, cozily nestled into a hollow at the base of the hill.

We disembarked from the carriage, and Holmes bade the driver to wait, then led the way along a stone path, up to a stout wooden door rimmed with beds in which purple crocuses and yellow narcissus bloomed. He rapped sharply on the door with his stick. After a moment, it was opened by a white-haired gentleman in a black jacket, white shirt, bow tie and tartan kilt.

Holmes held out his card. 'I wish to speak with Miss Minerva Warrender,' he said. 'She's expectin' ye, Mr. Holmes.'

We entered into a well-appointed sitting room, but the Doctor was not there. The butler led the way toward the rear of the house, into another, larger room with an oval dining table of dark wood flanking a grey stone fireplace, in which ashes still smouldered against the morning chill. Miss Warrender, still in male attire—jacket, waistcoat and trousers—sat at the far end. She had a cigarette in a holder in her mouth, and she reached up and removed it with a slender hand when she saw us. A large gold ring clinked against the cut glass ashtray as she laid it down.

'Thank ye, Alasdair,' she said. Her voice was a strong contralto with a slight Scottish burr, which could have belonged to a man or a woman. 'Welcome tae my home, gentlemen. Please be seated. May I offer you some refreshment?'

'Given the reason of our visit, we politely decline,' said Holmes.

'I understand. But be assured that I would nae pollute the noble elixir of which my family was so justly proud, with a noxious substance. Bring the Century Cask, Alasdair.'

The butler nodded almost imperceptibly, then vanished. Holmes addressed Miss Warrender. 'I thought you might return with us to Edinburgh, where you would surrender yourself to the police for the murders of James Blackfriar, a scullion, and Reginald Balfour, the Duke of Brownley's only son.'

'I am mightily sorry about the scullion, Mr. Holmes. His death was quite unintentional.'

'It happened because you had the unutterably poor judgment to poison Mr. Balfour in a restaurant. Surely you knew the risk with a toxin so potent.'

'I did nae think Reggie would be daft enough tae accept a drink from me in my home,' she said. So, I suggested the Criterion as a suitable neutral ground to discuss our arrangement.' She looked down at the table top. 'Reggie did nae finish his wine,' she said.

'And the scullion's colleagues informed me that boy was in the habit of draining the dregs before washing the wine glasses,' Holmes replied. 'It was likely the only way in which he would ever sample a vintage so fine.'

Miss Warrender still studied the tabletop. 'As I said, I regret that. It was unintentional.'

'You also put your neighbours and others at risk when you isolated such a deadly poison in your laboratory.' Holmes chided.

'Please g'ie me some credit for professional competence, Mr. Holmes. I planned to remain in that house after Reggie Balfour was eliminated, as I thought that would be the end o' my worries. Alasdair and I scrubbed the laboratory thoroughly when the procedure was finished.'

She looked up suddenly, staring Holmes right in the eyes. 'But I'm nae sorry for Reggie. He would hae bled me dry before he ruined me.'

'He discovered your secret,' Holmes said.

'Yes. I do nae know how he did. Previously at the club, he never gave any indication that anything was amiss, yet he came to me one evening and revealed that he knew all.'

I turned at a slight disturbance behind me. Alasdair had entered, bearing a large silver tray that held a small cask with a spigot on the end, and four balloon glasses. He carried it past Holmes and I and set it on the table beside Miss Warrender.

'Gentlemen, I assure ye that this cask has nae been breached except for that tap, in over a hundred years,' she said. She picked up one of the snifters and held it under the spigot, opening the valve and letting the liquid inside trickle down the side of the glass. A sweet, peaty aroma suffused the room, causing my mouth to water. She closed the tap and swirled the umber liquid around in the glass, where it coated the inside like a syrup.

She offered the snifter to Alasdair, who accepted it with one of his miniscule bows.

'Are ye sure, gentlemen? 'Ye'll hae only this chance to sample a single malt so auld and fine as this one.'

I turned to the detective. 'What was it you said to me yesterday, Holmes? Best not to waste one's life fretting about losing it?'

'A touch, Watson, a distinct touch!' To the Doctor, 'I am certain that you would not poison your faithful old retainer, Miss Warrender. Go ahead. Pour two for us.'

After the glasses had been distributed, smelt, sipped and enjoyed, Miss Warrender said, 'Mr. Holmes, will ye not hear my sad tale before ye bear me away to Edinburgh and the dock?'

'It will make no difference to your fate, Madam, but you are free to tell it whilst we enjoy this fine brew.'

'I was born in this very house,' she began, 'one of twins. The other was my brother, Malachy. Our da had him tabbed to take over the family business, but one day, when we were eight, ma fell ill and we despaired of her life. The village doctor was called, and after many days labour, he saved her. After that, nothing would do but for Malachy to become a doctor. That boy was the apple of his father's eye, so he was prepared for the university at Edinburgh. For me, a suitable match would be found when I came of age.'

She paused for a sip of the noble old whisky, then resumed her tale.

'All was well in Craig's Hall until that terrible autumn of '64. A plague of fever tore through the Lowlands, and when it was done, Da, Mum, and Malachy were among

172

its victims. Only Alasdair and I remained. It was then I decided that I'd nae become a shepherd's wife. If my brother could nae realize his dream of becoming a doctor, I would do it for him. He and Da had already started the process for admittance to Edinburgh. Malachy and I looked very much alike—peas in a pod, Mum used to call us—so it was nae great feat to dress as him, and finish the examinations. I went up to Edinburgh in his place in '67 and never looked back.

'After matriculating, I joined the army. An army doctor has much more privacy than most, so it was not too difficult to keep up the deception unless someone saw me disrobed, of which I was very careful. I would hae made the army my life, but I became close to a fellow officer and foolishly told him my secret. He agreed to keep it only if I would agree to leave the service.'

'Your docket at the War Department says you were denied promotion due to excessive gambling,' Holmes told her.

'Well, it had to say something if the actual reason was nae given. But my discharge turned out to be a blessing. I went into private practise, specializing in women's medicine, and I was very successful. Even though my patients were nae aware of my true sex, they seemed to find in me a kindred spirit. In a surprisingly short time, I was able to purchase the Harley Street practise that I have now.'

'I brought Alasdair down to serve me after I returned to England, and we led a peaceful and fulfilling life. I loved my work, found diversion at my club, and did all of the things as a man that, as a lowly woman, I would never have been allowed to do.'

'And Reggie Balfour would have ruined all that for you,' said Holmes.

'Yes,' she agreed. 'When he first came to me, it was money he wanted. Reggie was an uncommonly poor whist player and had racked up considerable debt at the club. But money was something I had much of, due to the success of my practise and the annual stipend I received from the distillery. But then Reggie demanded that which I was unwilling to give to him.'

'Of course, he did,' said Holmes.

'Oh, I am an adult, Mr. Holmes, and a woman does have her needs. If it would have been but once, I could have borne it, but it was again, and again, and he finally demanded things to which nae man has any right. So, I determined to be rid of him.'

'You mention needs. I take it you had other gentlemen friends from time to time?' asked Holmes.

'Yes, Mr. Holmes, I did. What of it?'

'I mean only that one of them may have been the source of Reggie's information about you.'

'I cannae imagine that. I was very careful whom I told, and I did so only after long acquaintance. None of them would betray me!'

'Not even Count Sylvius?'

Now Miss Warrender wore an expression like that of a deer ringed by a pack of hounds. 'Not Negretto. Especially not Negretto. He even talked of taking me back to his homeland if I ever tired of my vocation, where we could live openly as man and wife. Why would he do such a thing?'

'Because Reggie owed the Count money that he could not pay. It would amuse one such as him to have that money come from you, by proxy as it were.'

'He would never!' she uttered. Her tone told us she did not believe her own words.

'He would, and he did, Miss Warrender,' Holmes said, not unkindly.

She sat quietly for a moment, contemplating the amber liquid in the glass before her. Then she placed her hand above it, squeezing the ring on her right hand with the fingers of her left. The top of the ring popped open and something within fell into the glass.

'No!' I cried, and sprang to my feet, but before I could stop her, she drained the glass and hurled it into the fireplace, where it shattered into a million shards. On the contrary, Holmes sat quietly, a melancholy expression on his face.

'I regret to tell you that I will nae be accompanying you to Edinburgh after all, Mr. Holmes. Surely you would nae deny a poor woman's request to spend her last hours in her ancestral home?'

***

Several days later, we found ourselves back in London. We paid the Duke of Brownley a visit earlier that day, at which time Holmes had told the nobleman that it was clear that his son had died of a sudden illness. True to his word, the Duke did not demur. Holmes accepted his fee from the Duke, but on the way back to Baker Street, we stopped by a church in the East End, where he folded the £50 notes one by one, and stuffed them into the poor box.

'No good could come from informing the Duke that his son was a blaggard, Watson, and I had no proof but a dead woman's word. His father was much more apt to accept the lie that I told him and take comfort in it, but I surely have no wish to profit from it.'

As a courtesy, Holmes asked Hopkins to come for dinner at Baker Street, to provide him the details of Reginald Balfour's murder.

'A sad tale, Mr. Holmes,' Hopkins said when Holmes had done, 'but a cautionary one. It's never a good thing for one to try to become something they are not.'

'But indeed, my dear Hopkins, one may never know truly what one is, until one becomes it.'

'Now a woman must know that she is a woman, and a man that he is a man,' Hopkins replied. 'Everyone must know their place.'

'Must they?' asked Holmes. 'Difficulty arises when one is denied that which they desire because of arbitrary societal strictures. Miss Warrender wished to become a physician to honour her beloved brother's memory, but as a woman at the time, she was not allowed to do that. Currently we have a school of medicine for women here in London, where Miss Warrender may well have been able to realize her life's purpose, had it existed but a few years earlier.'

'That doesn't excuse her for wanton murder, though,' said Hopkins.

'Doesn't it?' asked Holmes. 'True, she would have had to have been held to account for the death of the innocent, an unfortunate accident arising from poor judgment. But her judgment had undoubtedly deteriorated due to the indignities that a scoundrel inflicted on her, indignities that no one should have to bear. I could argue that she killed Reginald Balfour in self-defence.'

'I have a question,' I said. 'How did you know that Count Sylvius and Miss Warrender had been lovers?'

'Based on the Count's demeanour at our interview, I thought it likely,' Holmes said. 'Of course, I had no proof, but Miss Warrender confirmed it.' Holmes turned the spigot on a familiar cask that sat on the sideboard behind him, which the lady had given him in gratitude for honouring her last request, and allowed a dram to drizzle into his glass. Swirling it round, he said, 'Count Sylvius will pay someday, for what he has done to an essentially good woman. I can promise you that, Watson.'

The Horror in King Street

As a general rule, I take great pleasure in writing these chronicles of the cases of my good friend and companion Mr. Sherlock Holmes, but not this one. As soon as I have finished writing it, I will carry it straight to the bank of Cox and Co. at Charing Cross and bury it in the depths of my battered tin dispatch box where it will never again see the light of day. The other parties who were officially involved

in the affair, Inspector Athelney Jones and his superiors at the Metropolitan Police Force, are of a similar sentiment. Writing this account is purely cathartic—I am trying to make sense of that which makes no sense, but merely serves to illustrate the depths of depravity to which so-called civilized men can sink. No good purpose will be served by putting the facts of the case before the public, but perhaps the act of thrusting the manuscript into the dispatch box will erase my memories of the horror. I hope it will be so.

It was early in the evening of Saturday, January 30 in the year 1897, a week to the day since Holmes and I had brought the matter of the Abbey Grange to a satisfactory conclusion. The weather was still frigid. Baker Street was well-nigh deserted except for the hansom cab which bore me home from an afternoon of billiards with Thurston at my club. A peculiar tranquillity that often accompanies very cold weather embraced the city, muting all but the most propinquant sounds such as the tattoo of the carriage horse's hooves, which were perversely magnified in the chilled air. The cab came to a halt across from 221B and I steeled myself against the anticipated blast of cold, then shoved the door open and slid out on to the cobblestones. My feet nearly went from under me as the soles of my boots contacted the street rime and I had to grab the door of the cab for support lest I find myself sprawled on the pavement. When I had righted myself, I handed the driver a florin and waved him away when he essayed to make change—he deserved a few extra pence for simply being out in such weather.

I was making for the door of my lodgings with the help of my stick when a woman suddenly emerged from an adjacent doorway, blocking my path. She was youngish, probably in her twenties, but the grime and syphilitic sores on her face revealed her to be of lower class, likely a prostitute. A dirty, brown, hooded woollen cloak shielded her from the freezing cold and she was shod in heavy, lace-up boots. What was her likes doing in this genteel neighbourhood? I moved to avoid her but she shifted in tandem to oppose me. Her voluminous skirts fluttered and the face of a ragamuffin peered out from their folds. Now all of my nerves became instantly alert—it was a common ploy for some low-class women to use their children as accomplices for robbery. The urchin would rush out from under the woman's clothes and grasp the victim around the knees, taking scurrilous advantage of the natural reluctance of a gentleman to harm a child, while the parent rifled his pockets for a purse, a watch or jewellery. I brandished my stick at the pair, shouting, 'Away with you riff-raff, or I shall call for a constable!'

The woman replied, 'Oh, please don't do that, Mr. 'Olmes! Not after I've come all this way to see ye.'

Of course. What else would such a woman be doing in Baker Street but desiring to consult my famous companion?

'I am not Mr. Holmes. I am Dr. Watson.' I hesitated, then continued, 'And you must come upstairs out of this beastly cold.' I unlocked the door to the flat and held it for her, then preceded her up the stairs. Once in the sitting room, I turned up the gas and bade her and the boy to sit. 'Why did you linger outside with a child in this terrible weather, Madam?' I asked her. 'Did Mrs. Hudson refuse to let you in?' Our landlady should have known better than that, given all of the strange characters who have visited Holmes in these rooms over the years.

She gave a short dry cough. 'Oh no, sir. I could see that yer rooms was dark, like nobody wasn't 'ere. So I waited for Mr 'Olmes to come 'ome.' She certainly had the Cockney's proclivity for the double negative and disrespect for the letter *H*.

During this conversation, the child simply stood next to his mother, clutching her skirts. Now he began coughing as well, more severely than his mother. My blood went cold. I had heard that particular dry cough many times, and it never boded well.

'What is your name, lad?' He looked at the floor.

'Come on! Tell the gennleman your name.'

The boy mumbled words that I could barely hear, then began that dry, hacking cough again.

'We calls 'im Lit'l Cedric,' she said, 'On account of 'is father is a Cedric too.'

'Madam, I don't wish to alarm you, but have you and the boy ever been assessed for consumption?'

'Yes, doctor, we 'ave. We've both got it,' she said matter-of-factly.

Consumption was a scourge of poverty and ran rampant among the lower classes in London. It was almost always mortal in one so young. Treatment was painful and problematic. An infected lung was collapsed by injecting air into the chest cavity and increasing the pressure. The treatment deprived the bacillus of life-giving air, which sometimes eradicated it. Long term rest in a sanatorium was also effective, but sadly out of the reach of people such as these.

178

I heard a clatter on the stairs and the door to the flat opened to admit Sherlock Holmes, still in full morning dress. 'I say, Watson, that sometimes my brother Mycroft can be such a pompous ass… Hello! We have visitors.'

I began to introduce our guests, when I realized to my chagrin that I hadn't even asked the woman her name. My concern for hers and her boy's condition had superseded formal niceties.

'That's all right, Doctor, I can klat for meself. I'm Mabel Copley, but folk call me Rosey.'

'Pleased,' said Holmes. 'I can see Madam, that you are the wife of a costermonger, reside in or near the Haymarket, a consumptive and that you are recently bereaved. I also perceive that you have not as yet resorted to that ancient profession taken up by so many of your sisters.'

'All of that is as urt as lepsog, Mr. 'Olmes, but I do not see how you have come to know it.'

'Simplicity itself, Madam. Your familiarity with back slang labels you a costermonger and anyone with more than a passing acquaintance with London knows that members of that profession make their home in or near the Haymarket. I am sure that Doctor Watson has already discussed your medical condition with you after hearing that cough, and the state of your eyes provides ample evidence of your recent grief. The fact that you care enough for your missing husband to retain your wedding ring is a good indication that you have not yet forsaken your marriage vows.'

'And 'ow did ye know I am missing me Ced?'

'Why your boy is here with you, so who else would you grieve for but his father?'

'Yer fegir as nair, Mr. 'Olmes. It's ta help me find me Ced that I've come t'ye for. And I can pay ye!' She reached into the folds of her cloak and produced a leather money bag the size of a cricket ball, swinging it by the drawstring.

'Before we discuss remuneration, Mrs. Copley, pray give me the facts of the case so I may decide if I can be of aid to you. And I'm sure Dr. Watson will appreciate it if you eschew, …er' avoid the back slang.'

'I'll try, Mr. 'Olmes, but it's become an 'abit, ye know. What would ye like t'know?'

'When did your Ced go missing? What were the circumstances?'

'Me Ced is a coster and sells in the 'Aymarket, as ye've guessed.' I saw Holmes wince at the word *guessed*. 'Times is been 'ard of late 'cause winter is no time t'find veg t'sell. Poor Ced 'as been sellin' shif from the Thames, but so many is doin' the same it's 'ard to make a yennep. We knowed Lit'l Cedric is sick and we been trying to get 'im in the work 'ouse, but they want papers and neither me nor Ced 'as much letters. Ced swore 'e would raise enow gelt to get Lit'l Cedrick a cure. Two days ago, 'e come 'ome wit' a proper toff, an 'e gimme a sack wit' an 'unnert guineas to pay for treatment for Lit'l Cedric. Then 'e said that 'e'd 'ave to go away with the gennleman for a while. I thot e'd 'av t'do summat agin the law to get that much yenom. Ced seemed real sad when he left, like I was never gonna see 'im a'gin on this airth. And I ain't seen 'im since. Ye gotta he'p me find 'im, Mr. 'Olmes! 'E's all I got!'

I couldn't believe my ears. 'You have a hundred guineas in that bag?' That was more money than many a poor woman saw in her entire lifetime.

She clutched the bag fiercely to her breast. 'I do that, and I'll gi'e ye summat, if ye'll 'elp me find me Ced, Mr. 'Olmes.'

'Your problem is not without singular features of interest, Mrs. Copley. Now, about this toff. Had you ever seen him before in the vicinity of the Haymarket?'

'No, Mr. 'Olmes, but there's so many folk comes to the 'Aymarket that I wouldn't notice 'im if'n 'e did.'

'Would you recognize him if you saw him again?'

'I b'lieve so.'

Holmes fetched a sketch pad from the shelf, along with a piece of drawing charcoal and a soft rubber eraser from a drawer, then bade Mrs. Copley to sit on the sofa and took his place next to her. 'Now, did this toff have a narrow face like mine, or a broad one like Dr. Watson's?'

'More like yers, I fink.'

Holmes drew a wide ellipse on the paper with the charcoal.

'Now, his nose, was it angular like mine, or broad like Watson's?' Thus, he prompted Mrs. Copley for over an hour about each of the man's features, deftly wielding the charcoal and the eraser according to her instructions, to construct on paper the face of the man she remembered.

Finally, she exclaimed, 'Well, I never! That's 'im Mr. 'Olmes, that's 'im! By Gawd, yer a magician, y'are!'

'My grandmother was a Vernet,' Holmes said smugly, 'so I have some small skill as an artist.'

I peered over Holmes's shoulder to view the visage of a youngish fellow with a fine head of hair that framed a cruel-looking face with narrow lips and beady eyes.

'Do you know the fellow, Watson?'

'Can't say as I do.'

'Well, this sketch should bring us much forrader in locating the chap. My dear Mrs. Copley, please allow me the privilege of having you and your son to dine with Watson and I before you return home on this frosty night. I'm sure Mrs. Hudson can accommodate all of us.'

She brandished the money bag like a weapon. 'I can pay fer it, Mr. 'Olmes.'

'I know you can, but this evening you are a guest in my home. Please do me the honour of accepting my hospitality.'

Mrs. Hudson did indeed accommodate us with a fine mutton stew that had been simmering on the back of the stove all day, with bread, pickles and the redoubtable Double Gloucester known as Cotswold, which had been supplemented with onions and chives. Little Cedric's eyes became as wide as saucers when Mrs. Hudson placed his very own egg custard tart before him after dinner. However, conversation at the table was subdued, with Mrs. Copley continually lamenting the loss of her husband.

After we had seen the pair off into the freezing darkness, secure in the knowledge that they were fuelled against the cold for one night at least, Holmes turned to me and said, 'Watson, I'm off in the morning for the Haymarket to see if I can locate our elusive toff.'

'I have an errand as well, Holmes. I'm going to Gray's Inn Road to the Royal Free Hospital to see if I can find a place there for Little Cedric. I fear he will not last the winter if I cannot.'

Holmes had already departed by the time I arose on Sunday morning to the pealing of the bells of St. Cyprian's in Glentworth Street nearby. I would not be in attendance that morning, but I was secure in the knowledge that I would be doing the Lord's work that day.

William Marsden's Royal Free Hospital was the only institution in London that provided proper medical care to the indigent on a regular basis, and as one might expect, it was generally difficult or impossible to secure a place there because of the multitude that sought its services, even though yet another new wing was opened only two years ago. I did not know if I could obtain treatment for Little Cedric there, but I knew that I would not be able to sleep at night lest I tried. Alas, it was as I feared; despite much cajoling and pleading, I came away empty-handed, largely because the treatment for consumption was so protracted. One doctor did offer to collapse the lung *pro bono* but I feared that would do little good without a proper place for the boy to rest and recuperate.

Ten Steps from Baker Street

Darkness was already falling by the time I returned to Baker Street in early evening. As I approached the door to the flat, my ears were assailed by the cry of 'Freessh Fish!', and I turned to see a man in a battered coat and hat approaching, wearing a wooden tray over his shoulders that had several fish tails protruding from it at all angles.

The fish stink nearly overwhelmed me as he stopped a few feet away.

'Buy some fish, guvna? Fresh from de Thames dis mornin', they are.'

'If you'll go 'round to the back gate, Holmes, I'll bring your dressing gown down to you so you can leave those reeking vestments in the yard.'

He straightened up and said, 'Very well, Watson. I suppose I can't go on fooling you with my disguises forever. I will accept your kind offer, and provide these fellows to Mrs. Hudson for our dinner, because they have remained surprisingly fresh in this beastly cold.'

After Holmes had disrobed and scrubbed the fishiness from his body, we sat around the table in our rooms, sipping whisky-sodas and trading tales of our respective, dismal endeavours.

'The Haymarket costermonger community is a close-knit group and most of its members are acquainted with each other, so I had to convince a fellow whom I had kept out of the dock for burglary to claim me as a poor cousin from the provinces. I was still the subject of some rancour however, because as Mrs Copley implied, times are hard for the costers in winter, and I therefore represented just one more mouth for limited resources to feed. I was unsuccessful in identifying our toff, although a couple of fellows admitted seeing him about. However, I did hear a rumour about a posting in the agony column concerning money to be had if a poor man was willing to work for it. Ha! That will be Billy now, with the papers. Come in!'

The door opened to admit our page Billy, staggering under the load of London's Sunday papers, a prodigious lot indeed. Holmes told him to put them on the table but I intervened, because there would surely be no room for our dinner if he did so. He put them on the sofa instead.

'It is well that you said so Watson, as I neglected to tell you we are having a guest for dinner. I've asked Langdale Pike, my old school chum, to drop by.'

Langdale Pike was a gossip-monger who published columns in several of the city's more disreputable rags. Holmes found him an invaluable source about the goings-on in so-called polite society, but I didn't like the fellow at all. Pike was languorous to the point of disconsolateness—I suspected he was no stranger to the opium pipe and I did not care for Holmes to spend much time in his company, given my friend's predilections in that direction. He usually dressed in what he referred to as 'the latest fashions', but which seemed to be outlandishly bad taste to me, and he had an annoying habit of peering at people who spoke to him through a monocle which I doubt that he needed. Pike arrived just as Mrs. Hudson was bringing Holmes' late charges in as covered dishes.

'Thanks awfully, Holmes,' he said when Holmes offered him a plate, 'but I never eat fish unless it's fresh caught from the sea. A fish from the Thames may have eaten someone I once knew, y'know. I will have one of those whisky-sodas though, just to keep you gentlemen company while you dine.'

Holmes poured a tot of single-malt into a glass, followed it with a spritz from the gasogene and handed it to Pike, who took it to the sofa and proceeded to sprawl himself out on the stacks of papers there.

Since Mrs. Hudson had dinner on the table, we made desultory conversation while eating, helped along by Pike's tendency to jump randomly from one subject to another with no apparent stimulus. The Thames fish proved surprisingly palatable, although Pike's ill-timed earlier comment kept resurfacing in my mind. When the plates were cleared, the brandy poured and the cigars lit, Holmes got down to the purpose of Pike's visit.

'I have a drawing of a fellow who may be important in one of my cases, Langdale. I'd like you to look at it and tell me if you recognize him. However, if you do, I must ask you to make no allusion of this in your columns until I authorize it.'

Pike assumed an affronted demeanour. 'You wound me, Holmes. When have I ever betrayed your confidence?'

'Well, there was that time when we were at University...'

'Is that the picture you have in your hand?'

Holmes unrolled the sketch and held it out to Pike, who didn't even take it.

'Whyn't you give me something difficult to do? That is a picture of Shrevvy Anston-Smythe.'

'That is a name with which I am not familiar,' said Holmes.

'I don't wonder. Shreeve, as they call him, is the fifth son of a fourth son and no one who is anyone, although I'll bet he'd like to be.'

'So how do you know him?'

'Because he's a hanger-on of someone a bit more famous.' Pike looked at us expectantly, waiting for someone to ask him.

Holmes obliged. 'Who?'

'Teddy Grenville.'

'Grenville. Now there is a noble name. Watson, I'll trouble you for my Burke's from the shelf.' Holmes riffled through the great tome until he found the proper page. 'Here 'tis. Richard Grenville, 6th Duke of Hereford. Eldest son is also Richard. Ha! Teddy is a fourth son too, it seems. Joined the Hereford Regiment of Foot—of course he did. Saw service in Africa. Now Watson, I'll trouble you again for my index. The G-box, please.'

I retrieved the box of Holmes' criminal index that contained the miscreants whose names began with the letter G.

Holmes flipped through the cards. 'Hmm. The G's are not nearly as eminent as the M's, but here's Gaston, the assassin, Gates, the poisoner and Gilhooley the Irish bomber. And of course, Mr. Teddy Grenville. Seems he was accused of luring a young woman of a fine family into a compromising position last year. It seems that the patriarchs of the two families were able to come to a satisfactory arrangement, doubtless involving a sum of money from the Duke, sufficient to recompense the girl's father for the loss of her virtue. And young Grenville's name has been mentioned in other scandals as well.' Holmes looked at our guest. 'Anything to add, Pike?'

'Only that there's been a rumour that Master Teddy's been recruiting young rakes into a new social club he's forming.'

I raised my eyebrows at that. 'A social club? For fourth sons?'

'Apparently. Rumour has it that they've already conducted some fairly scandalous *soirees*. Teddy seems to think he's the reincarnation of Sir Francis Dashwood.'

'I'm not familiar with the name,' I said.

'You shouldn't be,' said Holmes. 'Sir Francis Dashwood was a well-known scalawag in the last century who formed an association known by various names, one of which was the Hell-fire Club, because of the impious activities that the members engaged in. While ostensibly of a religious nature, the organisation seemed to largely be an excuse to conduct orgies. There were allegations that some of the women involved had not consented to participate, but nothing was ever proven. It seems Master Teddy's group has a similar disposition.'

'But why would such men give a large sum of money to a costermonger to take care of his sick son?' I asked.

'That is the question we must answer, Watson,' Holmes replied. 'They obviously wanted something from the fellow. We have to determine what that was.'

***

I was roused from sleep by a rude hand shaking me by the shoulder. I opened my eyes to see Holmes' angular face wreathed in shadows from the light of the candle in his other hand.

'Holmes! What is it?'

'It's murder, Watson! Murder most foul! And I am an ass!'

I quickly dressed then found myself in a hansom cab. The clip-clop of the horse's hooves echoed from the buildings in the frigid dawn as Holmes and I made for a sordid alley off of the Haymarket, where Scotland Yard Inspector Athelney Jones presided over a corpse.

The alley in question was too narrow for the cab to enter, so the driver stopped in front of the uniformed constable that marked its location and Holmes led the way as we walked in single-file along the side of the alley closest to the wall of the adjacent building. He directed the yellow beam of the bullseye lantern he carried toward the cobblestones in the middle of the passage, and I heard him mutter something about 'a herd of elephants' under his breath. We soon identified the pachyderms at fault—two men standing in an undersized courtyard formed where the alley opened out at the end. Another constable was stationed there, along with a large stout man wearing a tan greatcoat, a woollen toque with earflaps and a yellow scarf wound tightly around his lower face so that only a pair of small black eyes could be seen surveying the tragedy. Even though I couldn't see his face, I identified the man as Inspector Athelney Jones of Scotland Yard by his girth alone.

The beam of Holmes' lantern illuminated a heap of rags laying in a pool of blood—a closer looked revealed the body of a woman among the cloths, lying face down. She was also clad in a hat and scarf against the cold. Holmes reached down and turned her face to the light. Although her features looked different in death, there was no doubt that the woman was Mabel Copley.

Jones was obviously surprised at our arrival. 'Mr. 'Olmes! 'Ow did you 'ear of this?'

'I have my methods, Inspector.' In this case, those methods doubtless comprised a few well-placed agents at Scotland Yard.

'Hmmph,' Jones snorted. 'Well we'll be needin' none of yer theories 'ere, Mr. 'Olmes. It's as plain as a pikestaff wot's 'appened. The gel tried to get out o' the wind by walkin' down this alley, when she was waylaid by robbers. She should 'av known better t'keep t'the main streets at so late an 'our.'

Holmes shined his lantern about as Jones was speaking. 'You may be correct, Inspector. It seems that she entered the alley from the Haymarket and got only this far before she was struck down. If you and the constable hadn't obliterated her tracks in the rime on your way in here, I might have been able to determine whether she knew that she was pursued and the height of her assailant.' Holmes shined his light again upon the unfortunate Mrs. Copley, then said, 'Watson, be a good fellow and hold this light for me. Constable, help me turn her over.'

I took the lantern and shined it on the body as he requested. The constable looked at Jones, who nodded reluctantly, then did as Holmes asked. Holmes squatted down next to the corpse and began undoing her clothes.

''Ere, now!' said Jones. 'Can't that wait until we get 'er back to the morgue?'

Not pausing in his work, Holmes said over his shoulder, 'No Inspector Jones, it cannot wait. I am not accompanying the body to the morgue.'

By this time, he had the woman's outer garments opened and was attacking the buttons on her blouse. He spread that apart and began on the under-bodice. When he had that opened he said, 'Constable, help me pick her up so I can get these clothes off her.'

The constable raised the upper part of her torso off the pavement, getting his hands full of blood in the process while Holmes slid her clothing off so she was naked to the waist.

'Hold her a moment, constable. Watson, shine your light on her back. Ha! Here is the blow that did her in, I'll be bound.' He pointed to a vertical gash about five inches long just beneath her left shoulder. 'Severed the pulmonary artery, from the look of it. She wouldn't have been conscious long. This killing was done with a curious blade, much broader in the middle than at the tip. Just look at difference in the size of the stab wounds, which depends on their depth.' Indeed, it looked as if the killer had indulged in a frenzy of stabbing after she went down, with numerous wounds covering her back. Lay her back down, constable.'

Holmes began going through her clothing, also getting much blood on his hands. 'It is not here, Watson,' he said. 'The bounder has taken his money back.'

'What money?' said Jones. Holmes ignored him.

'I'm afraid that is all we're going to glean from the crime scene,' said Holmes. 'Inspector, you can take her now.'

186

'Well thanks awfully,' said Jones sarcastically.

'Watson, it is imperative we locate Little Cedric as soon as possible,' said Holmes. 'He is now likely an orphan.'

The dawn sky was blushed with crimson as we followed the alley back out to the Haymarket. The lamplighter was extinguishing the flames in the lamps that ran down the centre of the broad boulevard as a few optimistic costermongers already circulated with carts or trays of fish. Holmes retrieved a half-crown from a pocket and began making inquiries, and it was not long before he returned triumphant. He bade me follow him to a vile back court off the Haymarket not far from the murder scene, which was strewn with garbage and nondescript urban effluvia. For once I was grateful for the cold, for it supressed the odour of the decaying trash. We made our way to a basement door, which Holmes pushed open, and we entered a disgusting little black room that reeked of peat smoke and excrement. We found Little Cedric sleeping the sleep of the innocent under a pile of filthy blankets on a pallet next to a stove vented out a broken window. He woke as I picked him up but went back to sleep with his head on my shoulder after I shushed him.

Holmes went off to find a hansom and returned in it. As he exited the cab, he said, 'Watson, the boy is in your charge. Find him a place where he will receive proper care. I have something else to do.'

Finding him a place where he would receive proper care was obviously much easier to say than to do. The orphanages of London were horribly overcrowded, which was the reason that so many children without families lived on the streets. Nevertheless, I had to try. On our arrival back at Baker Street, I asked the cabman to wait, knocked up Mrs. Hudson and delivered Little Cedric into her care. Then I got back into the cab and asked the driver to take me to the London Foundling Hospital in Guilford Street, which had been founded by the sea captain and philanthropist Thomas Coram. The hospital originally accepted only infants, but the problem of homeless orphans in London was so acute that the policy was changed to accept illegitimate children as old as twelve. Most of the children were not housed there, rather places were found for them in the provinces where they could be raised to an age at which they could be apprenticed and repay some of the expenses of their rearing. By and large it was a good system, as the child, now an adult, came out of the apprenticeship with a trade.

My initial experience at the Foundling Hospital was much like that at the Royal Free Hospital—everyone was apologetic, but the hospital was overcrowded and places were simply not to be had. I was about to give up in disgust and go back to Baker Street when I heard 'Ho! Doctor Watson!' and I turned to see Dr. Moore Agar walking towards me.

Both Holmes and I had consulted Agar as a personal physician, although it had been some time since either of us had need of him. After exchanging ritual greetings, I asked him if he still had his practice in Harley Street.

'Yes I do, doctor, and it is doing quite well. What brings you to the Foundling Hospital?'

I explained my plight.

'I see,' Agar said. 'Well, the Foundling Hospital would not accept a child with an active case of consumption in any case. However, I have some friends in the administration of Sick Children's Hospital 'round the corner in Great Ormond Street. Let me discuss this with them and I'll get back to you this afternoon or in the morning. Are you still in Baker Street?'

I assured that I was and left in much better spirits.

I returned to Baker Street to find Holmes lounging on the sofa amongst the piles of newspapers from last night.

'I have had an interesting afternoon,' said Holmes. I raised an eyebrow to encourage him to continue. 'I thought it might be profitable to surveil the Tiberian club to see if there was any indication of criminal activity, so I spent the afternoon as a beggar in King Street. Unfortunately, there was no traffic of persons going in or out, but there was one curious incident.' He paused for dramatic effect.

I indulged him. 'And the curious incident was?'

'They accepted a rather large delivery of ice around four o'clock.'

'Ice?' I was incredulous! 'Ice, in this weather?'

'Precisely.'

'What do you make of it?'

'I have told you previously that it is a capital mistake to theorize in advance of the data. So, I propose to get data. I have also previously remarked to you that one cannot gain greater knowledge of the popular culture of London by an activity other than the perusal of the agony column.' He handed me a copy of last night's edition of the *London Evening Standard,* in which an ad had been circled.

Thomas A. Burns, Jr.

AN OPPORTUNITY is available, [it ran] *for any hard-working Englishman who seeks funds to improve his situation. Reply to this ad with the basis for yr. need. Will reply in this column with a meeting place in two days if yr. reason is acceptable.*

'If this is targeting the poor,' I remarked, 'it seems remarkably inefficient. Most of the members of that class are illiterate, are they not?'

'Yes Watson, most but not all. Some of the literate poor make a decent living serving as modern day town criers, if you will, bringing the attention of their illiterate brethren to advertisements such as this one and serving as a go-between for replies. I have sent a reply, so we shall see if it bears fruit on Wednesday evening.'

The next day, Tuesday, I received the following in the noon post:

> *Dear Dr. Watson,*
>
> *You will be happy to learn that the Sick Children's Hospital will accept the boy you found as a patient as long as someone will be responsible for his expenses, which they estimate as approximately £300. I have been doing rather well of late, so I will pick up half of the cost if you and Holmes can shoulder the other half. If this is agreeable to you, you may bring the boy around to them this afternoon.*
>
> *Yrs. truly,*
> *M. Agar, M.D.*

Neither Holmes nor I were wealthy men, but I felt sure that between the two of us, we could bear the burden, especially in the light of Agar's generous offer. So, I informed Mrs. Hudson that she should make her charge presentable for transportation, and I took Little Cedric on his 'first ever ride in a hansom cab' (actually, it was his second, but he was asleep during his first). After delivering him into the care of the good doctors of Great Ormond Street, I repaired back to 221-B.

I found Holmes in a fine humour, so I took the opportunity to inform him that he was £75 poorer as the result of my afternoon's activities.

'Ah, it is well, then, that I took in five shillings and sixpence in alms yesterday.' was his philosophical response. 'But look here! I have received a reply from our scoundrels.' He handed me a folded copy of today's paper.

> *Poorboy, [it ran] we agree your need is great. Pls meet*
> *our rep. in the Bear and Staff, Leicester Sq. at 7 sharp,*
> *tonight. Wear a red ribbon on your coat.*

'I have just enough time to don my disguise,' said Holmes.

'Aren't you just a bit worried that you may be putting your head in the lion's mouth?' I asked somewhat testily.

'Not at all, dear fellow, when I will have you and your trusty revolver by my side. You will be sampling the pubkeeper's best in the Bear and Staff when this meeting occurs, and I will trust in you not to let me out of your sight until this affair is brought to a successful conclusion.'

So it was that I found myself in that venerable old watering hole that Wednesday evening with my foot on the rail, inhaling the aroma of pipe smoke, hops and old wood. An excellent pint of ale stood before me on the bar. I savoured it slowly, having no wish to dull my reflexes, given my imminent duty. A bit later, Holmes entered in his costermonger's garb with an incongruous crimson ribbon on his coat pocket and sauntered up to the bar.

'I'll 'av me a pint o' bitter, barman.'

'Oh, youse will, will youse?' The barman replied in an unkind tone. 'Let's see yer dosh, mate.'

Holmes glared at the barman. 'I've a good mind t'take me custom elsewhere.' He reached in a pocket and flung tuppence onto the bar.

'A pint's thruppence and a hae',' said the barman. Holmes was digging in his pockets for more coins when another voice said, 'Here's a bob, Steve. Give my friend a pint o' bitter and me the same.' A shilling rang on the bar.

Shreeve must have been sitting in the shadows in the corner, as I didn't see him when I came in. But he was here now, standing behind Holmes. The barman instantly became contrite. 'Sorry, yer ludship. I dinna know 'e was wit' you.'

The barman poured two pints from the pitcher on the bar and gave Shreeve his change, which he ignored. Holmes snatched it up greedily. They retired to a corner table across the room. Since there was no need for me to know the details of their conversation, I did not try to hear; rather, I simply observed them out of the corner of my eye so I could follow them if and when they left.

About fifteen minutes later, the pints were finished and Holmes and Shreeve exited the pub. I waited a moment, finished my drink and followed. When I emerged onto Bear Street, I saw them just rounding the corner into Leicester Square. I followed, and when I arrived at the corner I spied them walking diagonally across the green. I tried to keep a consistent distance between us to avoid observation, but they seemed to be engaged in an animated conversation and Shreeve appeared to be paying little attention to his back trail. As I passed the statue of the Bard in the centre of the square, they were entering Spur Street, which was much darker than the square due to a dearth of streetlights. It was also more deserted, so I allowed them get a little further ahead of me before following them into Panton Street, which they traversed before turning south on the Haymarket. The Haymarket was much more crowded than the side streets even at this hour, and a chill went up my spine, as I had difficulty identifying the pair amongst the crowd. However, I was fairly certain that they were making for the Tiberian club, so I hurried down to Charles Street, ignoring the entreaties of the ladies of the evening on the way, and spotted the pair halfway down, heading toward St. James Square. I waited until they reached Regent Street, then followed again, keeping a full block between us.

They crossed St. James Square and headed into King Street, so now I was sure they were going to the Tiberian. I gave them time to get there, then hurried down and stationed myself near the old Junior Army and Navy Club building, across the street from the fine old Georgian townhouse that housed the Tiberian.

By this time Holmes and Shreeve had vanished, so I was forced to conclude that they had gone inside. I reckoned to give Holmes about an hour before taking any action. I hunkered down inside my greatcoat, wrapped my scarf tightly around my face, pulled the flaps of my cap over my ears and waited.

After a time, the lights in the first-floor windows overlooking King Street came on. The floor-to-ceiling windows were easily ten feet above street level, much too high for me to peer inside from the street, but I had taken the precaution of bringing one of Holmes' powerful monoculars along in my pocket. I focused on the window and looked into a dining room—I saw Holmes at the table with Shreeve, Teddy Grenville and a third man whom I did not recognize. Holmes, Shreeve and Teddy sat down then the unknown man left the room. He returned a few moments later carrying a covered tray which he placed on the table, then he removed the cover and passed out plates of food. He then procured a bottle of wine and served the others before he sat down to partake of the meal along with them.

Deuced generous of Teddy to wine and dine a costermonger who answered an ad from the agony column, I thought.

The men, including Holmes, ate and drank with seeming relish. Teddy was holding forth in a seeming diatribe when Holmes suddenly collapsed face first onto the table. Teddy and Shreeve jumped up as if they were waiting for this and hustled Holmes' limp body out of the room, one on either side of him.

I knew that I had no time to go for aid. I drew my Webley Bull Dog, hurried across the street and rattled the front door knob. It was locked, of course. A single strike with my shoulder convinced me that the door was stout enough to resist entry by that means, so I placed the barrel of the pistol next to the lock and fired two shots that reverberated loudly throughout the stony cavern of King Street. I sincerely hoped that someone would report the noise to the authorities. Another shoulder strike was enough to breech the door.

I rushed inside shouting 'Holmes! Holmes!' If any of the occupants had shown themselves I would have shot them down without a thought. But none did, so I raced through the house, throwing open doors looking for my friend. I found myself in the dining room in which I saw Holmes fall. The remnants of the night's dinner were still on the plates—beefsteak, mash, vegetables. A dark red stain marked Holmes place, where his wine glass had overturned. I pushed through the swinging doors into the kitchen where I was confronted with an anomalous sight. A man sitting at the counter, weeping uncontrollably, looked up as I entered. It was not Shreeve or Teddy, but the third man, the fellow whom I did not know. He did not seem to notice the revolver I pointed at him.

'I can't do it anymore,' he said.

'Do what? Where's Holmes, man! What have you done with him?'

'I can't do it anymore!' He shouted. Now his eyes fixed on the revolver in my hand, then glowed with a malevolent light. He snatched a knife from the counter and the stool on which he sat overturned with a clatter as he charged me. I had no choice. I shot twice and brought him down.

My physician's instincts commanded me to render aid as a rapidly spreading crimson pool appeared beneath him, but my reason told me I had no time. Instead, I broke my revolver and extracted the empty shells, then reloaded the cylinder with cartridges from my pocket. I felt that Holmes was in deadly danger somewhere in this house. I had to find him!

I found myself back at the front door. A staircase led to the upper floors of the townhouse, and a door under the stairs likely concealed steps to the basement. Up or down? Down, I decided. Nefarious activities were best conducted in the depths of the earth.

There was indeed a flight of stone steps behind the heavy door, but the downward passage was as black as sin beyond a small area illuminated by the light in the hallway. I glanced around and saw a candle in a stand on a side table. I seized it and lit it from the gas, then cautiously made my way down the stony staircase with the candle in one hand and the pistol in the other. At the bottom of the stairs was a dank stone passage that stank of sewer gas. Light blazed from an open doorway at the end.

Even now, sitting in my warm, safe rooms in Baker Street, I hesitate to describe what I saw in that horrible chamber. But I must, if I am to exorcize the demons that possess me!

I blew out my candle and set it down on the floor of the passage, then crept silently down the passage towards the door. I heard metal rattle against stone, then voices from within.

'Pick 'is feet up, will yer? That's it! He's a big 'un, so the chain needs t'be tight.'

I peered around the corner into the room and the sight froze my blood.

Yellow light from a lantern on the stone floor revealed a man, Teddy it was, who, stripped to the waist, was wrapping a chain about the ankles of another man who was prostrate on the floor. Holmes! Shreeve, in a similar state of *déshabillé*, held Holmes' legs so Teddy could do the deed. The chain ran upward to a block hanging from the ceiling, allowing a body to be hoisted aloft.

The lantern light also glinted off a metal surgeon's table, a rack of wicked knives mounted on the wall and several copper tubs on the opposite side of the room. Arms, legs and heads protruded from the gleaming chunks of ice that filled them. The bodies of men! The realization of what the meat on the plates in the dining room must have been washed over me like an icy wave. I stepped into the doorway, and as the two scoundrels turned to face me with wide eyes and their mouths forming shocked o's, I fired deliberately four times, two bullets for each of them. I examined the bodies and determined that the final bullet in the cylinder was unnecessary.

***

Ten Steps from Baker Street

The next evening, I sat in Baker Street with Holmes and Athelney Jones. The former looked distinctly unwell in his mouse grey dressing gown and slippers. He was out of bed against my express orders, but he insisted that he wanted to bring this affair to a close as quickly as possible. I could not blame him.

'… and the Captain said that no charges will be brought against you, Dr. Watson, for shooting those rogues in King Street. I doubt there won't be any trouble from the Duke neither, as he would have no wish to see any of this in the papers.'

'Not one of my better efforts, I am afraid,' Holmes admitted. 'During my meeting with Shreeve, he intimated that I was being recruited for a party of thugs who were going to "teach a lesson" to another nobleman who had disparaged him in public. He invited me to the Tiberian for dinner as a show of good faith before giving me the money. Naturally, I suspected some kind of double-cross was in the offing.'

'I knew that either Shreeve or Teddy—I suspect the latter—had murdered poor Rosey to get the money back. My suspicions were confirmed when I saw this hanging on the wall of the dining room.' Holmes picked up a curious, lozenge-shaped blade of beaten bronze about a foot long, with a sharp point and a broad middle. 'I should think that the coroner will find that this fits the wounds on Mabel Copley's corpse very well. After I noticed it, I was contriving a means to absent myself from the premises without alarming my hosts when dinner was served. I noticed the meat had an unusual appearance, so I didn't eat any. The only reason to secure large quantities of ice, especially in the winter time, would be to preserve something, and I was beginning to get an inkling of just what might have happened to Cedric Copley. I did, however, sip the wine, so as not to arouse their apprehension that I was on to them.

My suspicions were confirmed when Teddy began to brag. After poor Copley responded to the post in the agony column and informed the blackguards of Little Cedric's plight, they offered him a hundred guineas for his left arm! They assured him it would be removed by a competent surgeon for scientific purposes and that his chances of survival were high. Copley wisely demanded payment in advance and gave the money to Rosey. Of course, when he reported to the Tiberian Club to fulfil his part of the bargain, the bounders killed him out of hand and butchered him in that hellish abattoir in the basement. By this time, I knew I was in trouble, but unfortunately, I did not foresee the laudanum in the wine. I shudder to think of my fate had the good doctor not arrived when he did. I must confess this was one time that my powers failed me—I did not deduce that I was destined to become part of the bill of fare at the Tiberian myself.'

'How could you have?' I said. 'Cannibalism is associated with primitive areas, not with the greatest city in the modern world.'

'That is not entirely true,' Holmes said. 'While most documented cases of contemporary cannibalism have been so-called cases of survival cannibalism, such as that documented by Chase among the survivors of the ill-fated American whale-ship *Essex* and with the Donner party and Alfred Packer in the United States, cannibalism has also been associated with several killing sprees, the most notable being that of our own Saucy Jack in 1888. The repulsive Bean family of Galloway in the 1400's also comes to mind—the *Newgate Calendar* documents they had 'the legs, hands, arms and feet of men, women and children suspended in rows like dried beef' when their caverns were raided by a party in command of a personage no less than James I. And just three years ago, the infamous parliamentarian Henry Labouchere was acquitted of libel after accusing the duc de Vallombrasa of feeding the French Army on the corpses of its own dead.'

Holmes paused to take a drink of his brandy and soda—I noticed he was drinking quite a bit more than usual since his rescue from the Tiberian—then continued, 'Given the state of some of the more impoverished communities here in London, I suspect cannibalism occurs here more often than the authorities would like to admit, especially in winter. It has also been reported in several tribes in the Natal where Teddy Grenville was stationed, and he likely acquired his taste for human flesh during that time. Besides, the practice would have appealed to that perverse instinct of his to flout society's taboos.'

'There is a particular variety of lordling.' Holmes went on 'who whether as a consequence of ennui, privilege, or simply a general disdain for the rules of civilized society, takes a perverse delight in violating those rules whenever the occasion offers. Such defiance tends to breed on itself, so the rebellious behaviour becomes increasingly egregious with time. We English like to think that heredity is a significant determinant of a man's character, and in most cases I believe that it is, but just as when endeavouring to produce pure-bred animals from good stock, throwbacks arise that have none of the desirable characteristics that breeder is trying to attain. In the case of a dog or a bull, the throwback would be culled so the undesirable traits do not sully the line. When this occurs in a man, the situation becomes more complex. Social ostracism can be effectively employed to isolate miscreants and remove them from polite society, but that often results in an association of pariahs such as the one we saw in this case.'

An uncomfortable silence descended on the room. Athelney Jones and I had an unspoken agreement not to discuss what Holmes had faced at the Tiberian, and my friend seemed grateful for our discretion. Afterwards, he had looked drained and ashen-faced, and had gone to consult with Dr. Agar the following afternoon. I haven't told Holmes as yet, but I've been investigating some rural areas that might be appropriate for a little holiday as soon as the weather breaks and I've nearly settled on a place in Cornwall. I'm sure I can co-opt Dr. Agar into my little scheme to get Holmes some much needed rest.

As I wrote at the outset, I think that no good can come of releasing the details of this distressing affair to the public, so I am off to Charing Cross in the morning to bury it in one of the deepest vaults in London. May it remain there until the One who lords over all of us makes his triumphant return!

Thomas A. Burns, Jr.

The Witch of Ellenby

'I am afraid, Watson, that I shall have to go.'

'Go, Holmes? Go where?'

'To Cumberland. To the Lakes.'

I have said previously that my friend Sherlock Holmes was remarkably unappreciative of the beauties of nature, preferring instead entrenchment in London, vigilant as a spider in its web, anticipating the slightest vibration along its strands.

Neither did he believe in the venerable English tradition of holidays, because going on holiday meant absconding from one's work, and for Holmes, to work was to live.

The morning of May 1, 1899 had dawned gloriously in London—the slight predawn chill in the air was rapidly expunged by the rising sun, giving promise to the notion that the severities of the English winter were but a memory at last. It was the perfect time to turn one's thoughts to the countryside, and where to better than the Lake District, which quite possibly harbours the most stunningly beautiful landscape in all of England. However, knowing Holmes as I did, I strongly suspected that this proposed excursion had a more sombre purpose than mere tourism.

'See what you make of this, Watson,' Holmes said, tossing me an envelope that had arrived in the first morning post.

In the early days of my association with Holmes, I would have immediately removed the letter from the envelope and begun reading, but now, I took time for scrutiny. The envelope was of rich parchment, ecru in colour. A high rag content was indicated by strands I could see when I held it to the window. If further proof of the high station of the sender was necessary, it was provided by the coat of arms embossed in the upper left-hand corner—gules, a pale Or with three torteaux. As I am not a trained herald, I would need *Burke's* to identify the owner, or I could simply look at the sender's name. The envelope was addressed in black ink (a woman's hand) to Sherlock Holmes, Esq., 221B Baker Street, NW1.

I removed and unfolded the several sheets of paper inside. The top sheet was written in strong male copperplate hand. I read:

35, George's Street, Hanover Square, May 1, 1899

Re: Witchcraft

My Dear Mr. Holmes:

This letter is to assure you that you may rely absolutely upon the account which accompanies it, written by our governess Rachael Hodgson, as factual. Miss Hodgson has been in my employ for the last two years, and has proven herself capable, level-headed, and not given to flights of fancy. I trust her implicitly, as evidenced by the fact that I have entrusted her with the care of our children. I do hope that you will be able to help her with her present difficulties. Do not concern yourself with your fee, as I will guarantee payment of any reasonable charges.

I am, sir, yours sincerely,

The Rt Hon. The Viscount Porter, GCVO

A second letter inside was neatly written in a simpler roundhand script, the same female hand as on the envelope.

April 30, 1899

My Dear Mr. Holmes,

I am Rachael Hodgson, late of the village of Ellenby in the Lake District, now governess for the family of Lord Porter in London. I am taking the extraordinary step of writing to engage you to assist me with a matter involving my aunt, Miss Griselda Hodgson.

Auntie G is a spinster who lives in our ancestral home in Ellenby. She has supported her frugal lifestyle for many years by selling herbal medicines, which she brews herself from foraged materials. She has always been a bit simple-minded, but capable of fulfilling her own meagre requirements for life and well-being. I try to visit her once or twice a year to ensure that she is getting on.

Auntie G has a querulous disposition and has had sporadic altercations with some townspeople, but never anything serious. Lately she has become embroiled in a feud with Mrs. Adele Pennington, the wife of Squire Rayner Pennington, because one of Auntie's tinctures provoked an adverse reaction in the lady. Auntie is reported to have laid a curse on Mrs. Pennington. Such behaviour is unfortunately typical and would usually be discounted by those who knew Auntie, except that shortly thereafter, Mrs. Pennington fell ill. Her symptoms progressed until, at present, her very life is feared for. The town Doctor, who has had some problems with alcohol, could find no medical explanation for her condition.

The town gossip holds Auntie responsible for Mrs. Pennington's illness, saying she cast an 'evil eye' on the lady, and the word witchcraft is being bandied about. Because I fear for Auntie G's safety, I have gone home to Ellenby to be with her.

I realise you are not a doctor, Mr. Holmes, but I would be grateful if you could come up to Ellenby and provide a mundane explanation for the decline of the Squire's wife. I greatly fear what might befall my aunt if you cannot.

Yr. obd't servant,

Rachael Hodgson

'I am not familiar with Ellenby, but a glance at my *Baedeker* should set that aright,' said Holmes, retrieving the weighty volume from the shelf and paging through it. 'Ah! Here 'tis. No wonder I do not know it. Ellenby is a small village of some 300 souls on the shores of Mereswater. It is accessible from the town of Windermere, which in turn may be reached by a branch of the London and Northwestern line. Mr. Bradshaw will provide us specific directions and departure times.' He turned to me. 'Watson, there is little time for delay. Pack your bags for an extended excursion.'

I have long ago ceased to take umbrage at such peremptory demands, knowing how much Holmes has come to rely on my assistance. So, I retired to my room and before long, my Gladstone and portmanteau were packed with enough clothes for a week. I donned my Harris tweed flat cap, draped my Norfolk jacket over my arm, and felt prepared for any vagaries of weather the Cumberland climate might offer. Returning to the sitting room with my luggage, I tucked a copy of *Swallow*, by that excellent storyteller Henry Rider Haggard, into the commodious pocket of my Norfolk. Holmes had two bags as well, along with his Inverness and beloved deerstalker. To accommodate our luggage, he had ordered a four-wheeler for our trip to Euston Station.

It was scarcely a mile to the depot along Marylebone and Euston Roads. We had little time to enjoy the splendid Spring weather before we were passing beneath the great Doric arch that guards the terminal. Holmes summoned a porter for our bags, then we descended the grand staircase into the concourse to purchase tickets. The atmosphere inside was close with tobacco and coal smoke as well as the miasma of humanity, so I was grateful we had only a short wait before boarding.

'Surely the Viscount will not object to first-class accommodation for so long a journey,' said Holmes as we entered our compartment. It was not long before the train lurched, then settled down to a smooth glide along the rails.

The trip to our first point of embarkation, Oxenholme near Kendal, consumed nearly six hours, because of numerous stops along the way. We passed through Hertfordshire, Buckinghamshire, Northamptonshire, Warwickshire, Staffordshire and Cheshire, before arriving at the northern industrial city of Manchester for a protracted layover. Holmes had lapsed into one of those deep brown studies to which he was prone. I amused myself in turn with Haggard's rousing story of the Boer Trek of 1836, and enjoyment of the ever-changing panoply of the English countryside.

The train lurched again and we were off northward, this time for a much shorter ride to Oxenholme, a hamlet that comprised a railway station and a few scattered houses. We changed trains for the last leg of our passage to Windermere village, on the banks of the lake of the same name. Windermere is the largest lake in England, a so-called 'ribbon lake' because it curls between the bosom of the surrounding hills, its banks handsomely forested and draped with a necklace of rustic villas.

While not yet dusk when we arrived at Windermere Station, it was so late in the day that no more coaches were scheduled to travel to Mereswater—instead, we took an omnibus to the nearest hotel, and hired a dogcart to carry us to Ellenby. I rode in front with the driver while Holmes lounged in back with the luggage. Our route took us along the banks of Windermere, then through the charming village of Ambleside before entering a pristine forest, where we passed burbling becks that fed the mighty lake from the north. The trees gradually disappeared as we ascended the fells, giving way to open country and affording spectacular views of the glistening lakes twisting amongst the emerald fields and the budding copses.

'By Jove, Holmes, isn't this absolutely grand?' I said, and receiving no answer, I glanced in back to find my companion slumbering peacefully, his head propped on a bag.

Topping a col, we descended back into the woods, dimmer and more foreboding than before—ruddy beams of light filtered through the branches overhead, signalling the proximity of dusk, and a damp, cool hand lay upon the land. The setting sun had painted the sky a deep crimson by the time we rolled up in front of the Fells, the sole inn/public house in Ellenby. It was a two-story stone building swathed in strands of ivy, the largest in the square. Because of the lateness of the hour, we decided to secure lodging first, then send word to Miss Hodgson, advising her of our presence and inquiring whether a visit tonight or in the morning would suit her.

After signing the register, we stepped back outside, where we had noticed several boys skylarking. Holmes hailed one of them:

'Halloa, you lad! Do you know the Hodgson house?'

The youths froze, staring at us with wide eyes, then scattered to the winds as one.

'That bodes ill indeed,' I said.

We returned to the public room, its round wooden tables filled with taciturn provincials who regarded us with accusatory eyes. Holmes addressed the innkeeper, who was plying a cloth on the shiny wooden bar, doing his best to ignore us.

'My name is Sherlock Holmes. I would like to send a message to Miss Rachael Hodgson, informing her of my presence here.'

The innkeeper turned to us with a look bordering on hostility. 'Ah canna stop tha',' he said with a thick northern accent, looking Holmes up and down. 'But they'll be nobbut a place 'ere fer aw what's 'ankled up wi' witches.'

Without a word, Holmes turned on his heel and returned to the reception area, where we had left our bags. I followed.

'It seems we must find other accommodation,' he said. 'Perhaps Miss Hodgson can provide it.'

'But how shall we locate her?' I said. 'The villagers seem disinclined to aid us.'

'You know my methods, Watson. Apply them.'

We took up our luggage and exited back to the square. Darkness was rapidly encroaching, and our dogcart had departed to return to Windermere. I foresaw a vile evening ahead indeed if we had to sleep rough.

Holmes looked about, then said, 'Perhaps the local constabulary can aid us.' He set out across the square at a lope. We approached another two-story building of roughcast grey stone, its bright green wooden door papered with ragged handbills, and bars securing the windows on the upper floor. Holmes worked the latch and entered.

We found ourselves in a lamplit room with unfinished stone walls and a crude plank floor. A tall wooden counter with a gate at the far end divided the chamber into a narrow walkway that ended in a casement window and a much larger area containing a desk, filing cabinets, an over-stuffed sofa, easy chairs, and a compact kitchen. Waves of heat rolled from a pot-bellied stove, and the odour of coal fumes was nearly overpowering.

A flight of stairs in the far corner led upward. A female voice filtered down. 'You cannot do this, Weed! Auntie has done nothing wrong. You cannot lock her up like a common criminal!'

Repairing down the walkway and entering the office through the gate, we ascended. We entered a large room that comprised the entire second floor, yellow with light from a lantern hanging from the ceiling. One side seemed dedicated to storage, filled with barrels, sacks, crates and various pieces of furniture thrown higgledy-piggledy on top. A wall of iron bars divided the other side into four cells. A man and a woman stood in front of one, in which an older woman was imprisoned.

The man was a most singular individual. He was of impressive height and girth—he must have been nearly 7 feet tall and 25 stone—I wondered how he had been able to negotiate the narrow staircase. His heavy blue woollen uniform marked him as the town constable. He was saying to the woman, 'Ah'm tellin' thee, Rache, ah'm doon it fer 'er own guid.' He noticed us and turned our way 'Guid evenin', gennleman! Ah'm Constable Weedon Trelawney. 'Ow kin ah aid thee?'

'Good evening, Constable. My name is Sherlock Holmes.' He addressed the young woman. 'Miss Hodgson, we have come in response to your letter. I wish to offer you my humble assistance.'

Rachael Hodgson had shoulder-length sandy hair and looked much too young to be entrusted as governess to a noble family, although I was to learn later that she was twenty-five years of age. She had an amiable, round face and bright blue eyes—she would have been a comely lass except for her agitated state, evidenced by her flushed complexion and wild hair. I could see a resemblance between her and the incarcerated woman—the same rotund facial features—but her aunt's were drawn and haggard, doubtless due to stress.

'Mr. Holmes!', she cried. 'Can you not make him see reason? He has locked Auntie up in a cell!'

'Aye, a ruffian 'e is!' screeched the old woman. 'Ah'll gi'e thoo the evil eye, Weedon Trelawney, and t'cleppets'll shri'el up lak a wether's!' I did not know what the old woman said, but Rachel brought a fist to her open mouth and looked at her aunt with horror.

'Constable, can you explain yourself?' asked Holmes.

Trelawney glowered at us, but acquiesced. 'They's bin threats made against Missus 'odgson,' he said. 'Ah canna protect her and Rache if they's in their 'ouse.'

'Perhaps the constable is correct, Miss Hodgson,' I said in a conciliatory tone. Her face contorted and tears began as her aunt shrieked unintelligibly. Suddenly angry, I began, 'Constable, I must say that this is deplorable…'

Holmes cut me off. 'No, Watson. As you said, it may be for the best. Please conduct Miss Hodgson downstairs.'

I did as Holmes asked. He and the constable followed, the harridan squawking curses in our wake.

Holmes addressed our client, 'Perhaps we should see you home, Miss Hodgson, and hear your account. We can see about getting your Auntie out tomorrow. By the way, the innkeeper seems unwilling to accept our custom. Could we prevail upon you to put us up for the duration of our stay?'

'I am sorry to tell you, Mr. Holmes, Auntie's cottage is very tiny. There would be no room for two gentlemen to stay there with a lady.'

As my heart sunk to the floorboards, the constable spoke up. 'Wot's that? Jackie Lad would nae 'av thine custom? Ah'll mak talk wi' 'im. Thoo'll 'ae beds fer the nacht! Thoo gan yam, Rache. We'll mak talk in da mornin'.'

Given the constable's assurances, we left our luggage with him and accompanied Miss Hodgson home.

The Hodgson cottage was miniscule indeed, a limewashed white clay building with a thatched roof, known as a dabbin by the locals. It had one room on the ground floor, with a ladder though an opening in the ceiling leading to a loft. After Miss Hodgson had gone round lighting oil lamps and candles, we could see that the downstairs room was as tidy and compactly arranged as any ship's galley, with a diminutive kitchen in one corner. A glass-fronted cabinet against a kitchen wall contained a myriad of labelled jars and bottles, and an assortment of various sized cauldrons and a balance reposed on top. A sitting area near the front door was furnished with a padded rocking chair and an overstuffed sofa —a pillow and rumpled bedclothes on the latter indicated that Miss Hodgson slept there. Heat was provided by a coal-fired cooking stove in the kitchen, which imbued the cottage with a heavy atmosphere.

Miss Hodgson waved us to a pub table covered with a green checked cloth. 'Can I make you some tea, gentlemen, or perhaps something stronger? Auntie G brews her own damson wine.' She considered a moment, then thought to ask. 'Have you eaten this evening?'

'Tea will be fine, Miss Hodgson,' said Holmes. 'And no, we have had nothing since luncheon on the train, hours ago.'

'That will never do,' Miss Hodson said as she placed a kettle on the stove. In short order, the table was replete with a meat pie, a coil of cooked sausages, a wedge of cheese and a loaf of bread. A bowl of mustard and a jar of pickles completed the feast.

'Now Miss Hodgson, please state your case,' said Holmes as he began filling a plate. 'Omit no detail, however unimportant it may seem to you.'

'My mother died birthing me, gentlemen, and my da' had long since skedaddled,' she began. 'I was raised by Auntie G. in this very cottage. She was not always like she is now. Oh, always a bit odd, to be sure, but it is only in the last few years that she has claimed to have magical powers.'

'What kind of powers?' I asked.

'She has always made her living as the village midwife, as well as by brewing tinctures and extracts to treat the villagers' minor ailments. But some years ago, she went off on one of her forays into the country to collect plants, mushrooms and other things she needed to craft her little potions. She was gone for nearly a week, and everyone was worried that she had tumbled from a fell. Weed, that is, Constable Trelawney, organised search parties, but no one could find her. Then she suddenly reappeared, bruised, covered in muck, her clothes in tatters, babbling nonsense. She…'

Holmes interrupted. 'What do you mean, babbling nonsense?'

'She spoke of bright lights and strange beings who had taken her, and subjected her to unspeakable things, then released her back into the wild. Weed said that she had probably taken a fall, hit her head and become delirious. In time, she recovered physically, but she was never right mentally afterwards. When I was in my teens, she began to claim to have arcane powers.' She paused for a sip of her tea, then went on. 'It was also around then that her spats with some of the villagers began to escalate.'

'What was the nature of these spats?' asked Holmes.

'Have you ever lived in a small village, Mr. Holmes?' Holmes nodded. 'Then you know that from time to time, people in such close quarters can antagonise each other. Little things can set it off—a chance remark on the street, a jostle in the marketplace, and before long, a real row is ensuing. Some in town thought Auntie was going soft, 'nick't at t'heid', as they say round here, because she professed supernatural abilities. Many tended to treat her as if she were a child, which she greatly resented. She would usually respond to such slights with threats to bring all sorts of evil down on the offender. Most folk realised that this was simply a result of her injures, and that she was harmless.'

'So, what transpired with the squire's wife?' Holmes inquired.

'You must understand that I got this second-hand, from Weed. Apparently, the good lady was feeling puny, and came to Auntie seeking a remedy for her ills. That was unusual, because Auntie and the Squire have not been attuned for years.'

'Could Mrs. Pennington not have consulted the doctor?' I asked.

'Apparently she did, but whatever he prescribed was of no help. Auntie gave her something but she continued to get worse, publicly laying the blame for her decline at Auntie's door. The two of them had a right barney at the market, complete with slapping and hair-pulling. Auntie was heard to threaten Mrs. Pennington—'A curse be t' thee and thine!', she said. When the lady became ill enough that she had to take to her bed several days later, rumours began circulating that Auntie had given her the evil eye.'

'And how did you learn of this in London?' asked Holmes.

'I had a wire from Weed informing me. He said that I should try to come home and see if I could smooth things over.'

'I do not suppose you know what your aunt prescribed for the squire's wife?' Holmes asked. Miss Hodgson shook her head.

'How was it that you came to find employment in London?' I asked. 'Is that not unusual for a young woman raised in these parts?' Holmes gave me a baleful glare for changing the subject, but I had long since grown used to his ways and did not care.

'It was a teacher, Dr. Watson, Miss Deborah Jones, who thought I deserved better than to settle down in Ellenby as a farmer's wife. She worked with me since I was a little girl to cure me of the Lakeland manner of speaking and taught me things that would make me attractive as a governess—literature, history, music and the like. It is well that she did, because after her accident, Auntie could not earn as much as previously. It is my salary that keeps her comfortable here in her old age.'

Holmes brought her back to her narrative. 'What did you do after arriving in Ellenby?'

'I went to visit Squire Pennington, with whom I'd always had a good relationship when I lived here. He assured me that he did not blame Auntie for his wife's illness, but other than saying so in public, he was powerless to control any gossip that might be spread.'

Having finished his repast, Holmes reached into his pocket for his briar and tobacco, then asked, 'May I smoke?'

'By all means.'

He glanced at the ceiling pensively as he tamped shag into his pipe with his thumb, then he struck a Vesta and applied the flame to the bowl. When it was drawing to his satisfaction, he asked, 'Do you know the nature of the ailment for which the Squire's wife sought treatment?'

'No, Mr. Holmes. We did not discuss it.'

'And what does your Aunt have to say about all of this?'

Miss Hodgson smiled ruefully. 'Although she claims that the medicine she dispensed was efficacious, Auntie is only too happy to credit Mrs. Pennington's present state to her magic.'

Holmes asked, 'Will you give me leave to look round?' On Miss Hodgson's nod, he went to the kitchen cabinet and examined the containers within. Removing one, he carefully inspected the label. He replaced it and turned away with a grim expression.

He asked, 'How long ago was it that Mrs. Pennington consulted your aunt?'

'I am not entirely sure. Perhaps the beginning of last week?'

'Do you know if she has had any other clients since?'

'I do not, Mr. Holmes.'

'Well, Watson,' Holmes said abruptly, 'I think it is time to take our leave, and hope that the constable has had his chat with the innkeeper. Miss Hodgson, thank you very much for feeding two hungry travellers.'

Miss Hodgson nodded, and we quit the stuffy cottage for the cool of the evening.

I had been associated with Holmes long enough that I knew when something was troubling him. 'What is it, old man?'

'My perusal of Auntie G's medicaments revealed that she has many dangerous elixirs. Many of them might be responsible for Mrs. Pennington's condition.'

'Do you think Miss Hodgson's aunt deliberately poisoned the Squire's wife?'

'How many times must I tell you that it is a cardinal error to theorize without data? I merely mention it as a possibility, and one that would make Miss Hodgson sorry indeed that she engaged us, should it be true.'

No one was in the reception area when we returned to The Fells, so we entered the public room, which was even more crowded than earlier. The bustle of conversation immediately ceased at our entry.

'Weed tells me ah mus' gi'e t' a bed,' said the innkeeper. 'Thoo'll find 'un upstairs.'

He turned back to his perpetual bar cleaning.

It was apparent the churl was going to obey the letter of the law and that we would get no assistance with our bags. Returning to the reception area, we saw that upper floor at the top of the stairs was unlit, so we appropriated a couple of candles before ascending.

I spent a restless night. Although there was a fireplace in the room I had chosen, there was no fire, and I was d___d if I was going to go downstairs and ask the landlord for one. The bed was lumpy, the coverings musty, and a draft that penetrated the window casing managed to make that Jezail bullet throb just as it had when it first became part of my anatomy. I reckoned it was about five in the morning when the first light peeped through the glass. The sun rose soon afterwards. A jug and wash bowl stood on a stand at the end of the bed, but I had no delusions that hot water would be provided for my morning ablutions. My father's watch informed me that it was nearly seven a.m. I gave up the hope of any more sleep.

Holmes was already in the public room when I descended, attacking a plate of cold sausages, hard bread and cheese. The innkeeper sullenly provided the same for me, but grunted negatively when I inquired about coffee.

'If thoo wan' suthin' t'wash it doon wi', thoo can 'ae a tippenny ale.'

I am ashamed to say I took him up on it.

After Holmes had lighted his post-prandial pipe, he said, 'I fancy a visit to the Squire is in order, Watson. Perhaps we will have a better reception there.'

The square was empty when we exited the inn, and Holmes immediately stuck off down the road toward the lake at a fast pace, causing me to hurry after him.

'How do you know that the Squire's house is this way?', I asked.

'We did not pass it on the way into town,' he said, and I felt like an ass.

A cool breeze blustered down from the fells as we walked, but the rapidly ascending sun gave promise of a fine mellow day. Most of the buildings surrounding the square were stone with slate roofs, giving way to more plebeian thatched clay dabbins as we approached the village perimeter. Rounding a bend, we were confronted by a stone wall, which we followed until we arrived at black cast iron gate. A bronze plaque adjacent to the gate announced that this was Mereswater House. Holmes lifted the latch and we entered. Closing it behind us, we proceeded up a gravel drive through a copse until we came upon a fine old farm house in a clearing. The house had stepped gables and a wing on either side, all constructed of local stone and slate rubble. Holmes strode confidently up to the front door and rapped sharply on the jamb with the head of his stick. A moment later a woman in a striped grey dress, white lace apron and cap opened the door.

Holmes extended his card. 'Sherlock Holmes to see Squire Pennington, if you please.'

She took it in a white-gloved hand. 'Come in and wait in the parlour, gennlemen, and I'll see if the Squire is takin' callers.'

As I followed her through the foyer, Holmes, behind me, shouted, 'Watson, stop!' It was well that I obeyed, for a feathered shaft flew in front of me, arcing to the floor and skittering into the wall. I turned to see a boy of seven or eight standing in a doorway with a bow in his hand, busily nocking another arrow. As I glared at him, he said, 'Hold, varlet! I am Robin of Locksley and I do not gi'e thee leave to pass!'

'Gan wi' thoo, Ray, or ah'll tell thy da!' the maid admonished him. He smirked and disappeared into the room behind him.

She conducted us into a room in the east wing, furnished with chintz-covered chairs and a daybed flanking a stone fireplace. French doors afforded a fine view of the garden outside and the sparkling Mereswater beyond. An easel next to the doors held a covered canvas.

'I'll tell the Squire you're 'ere,' said the maid.

I began to examine the framed photographs adorning the walls—family pictures and views of the lakes. Holmes had thrown back the sheet on the painting.

'The Squire's wife is a handsome woman,' he said. 'Of course, a tactful artist will always flatter his subject.'

I turned to view a partially completed, full-length portrait. Holmes was correct— Mrs. Pennington was a striking lady with long auburn hair curled round her bosom, accentuated by a brilliant green, floor-length gown. The painting of her figure looked to be nearly complete, with only the background, apparently the parlour doors and the garden, unfinished.

A cultured voice spoke from behind us. 'I'd rather that not be viewed until it can be unveiled for my wife when she's well.'

Holmes let the cover drop, then we turned to greet Squire Pennington.

He was a tall, thin, austere-looking chap with sharp angular features, dressed in mismatched tweeds and a black and white houndstooth vest. Piercing blue eyes glared at us from under a mane of unruly, light brown hair. Even though I knew I'd never seen him before, his face was eerily familiar. He seemed less than delighted to welcome us into his home.

'Pardon me if I have intruded,' said Holmes. 'I was merely trying to while away the time as we waited.'

'Well, I am here now,' The Squire said. 'Kindly state your business.'

'This portrait is very good, you know,' Holmes went on as if he had not heard. 'That is a singular green gown. Who was the artist?'

'A local woman. Deborah Jones. Please state your business.'

'We have come to inquire about the health of Mrs. Pennington,' said Holmes.

Apparently, the news of our arrival and our purpose had travelled rapidly throughout the small town. 'You can tell the elder Miss Hodgson that Adele is very ill, and that I intend to hold her responsible after I have seen to my wife's recovery,' the Squire replied.

Holmes frowned. 'Miss Rachael Hodgson is under the impression that you do not blame her aunt for your wife's condition. Did you change your mind?'

'I did indeed, Mr. Holmes, as Adele's condition worsened and that horrible old termagant prattled about the village that she accomplished the deed with her black magic.'

'Surely an educated man like yourself does not believe that,' I said.

'Perhaps not,' rejoined the Squire, 'but the old witch could have certainly given my wife some hellish potion to make her sick.'

'Dr. Watson is well-regarded among London physicians. Perhaps he might discover something your local doctor has overlooked.'

'That will not be necessary,' said the Squire. 'I have the utmost confidence in Dr. Phillip.'

I could not resist. 'Even though he has a drinking problem?'

Thomas A. Burns, Jr.

Pennington spitted me with that aquiline glare of his. 'If you repeat that canard outside of this house, I shall advise Dr. Phillip to sue you for slander.' He turned his back in dismissal. 'Billie will see you out.'

It is slander only if untrue was on the tip of my tongue, but before I could get it out, Holmes said, 'Quite. Come, Watson. If Squire Pennington is satisfied with the care that his wife is receiving, it is not our place to interfere. Good day, Squire. We can see ourselves out.'

Holmes opened the French doors and we exited to the garden. As we walked into the woods, approaching Mereswater, I sputtered to Holmes, 'How could you let that insufferable ass speak to us that way?'

'It is his home, Watson. In it, I am sure that he can speak to us in any way that he likes.' He hesitated, then, 'Just as sure as I am that he is poisoning his wife. It is vital that we get back into that house so you can examine the lady.'

'Poisoning his wife! How do you…'

'I thought we would walk back to the village along the lakeshore,' Holmes said. 'It will provide a nice change of scenery.'

So, it was going to be that way, was it?

'I have said previously that the English countryside is more conducive to hellish cruelty and hidden wickedness than the meanest of London's streets,' Holmes continued as we walked along the trail. 'The utter remoteness and isolation of a village such as Ellenby can act as the accomplices of the murderer, the abuser and the thief. Add to that the power and prestige of a man of a prominent social class, and you have a dire situation indeed. Hello! What have we here?'

We had encountered a singular construct. Someone had hammered two wooden posts made from rough-cut logs waist-high into the ground about two feet apart, a yard from the water, then lashed a crosspiece between them with a hempen rope. I could conceive of no earthly use for such a structure.

'Those logs were recently cut from yon felled tree,' said Holmes, pointing to a prone sapling nearly thirty feet long, which lay in the weeds to the side of the path, 'and the project seemed to require the assistance of five men, at least,' he continued after scrutinising the ground.

He resumed his examination of the forest, then turned round, giving his attention to the shore and the water beyond. 'I wonder…,' he said, then 'Watson, we must hurry. There is bad business afoot.'

211

We quick-marched back to the public house. Upon entering, we heard raised voices from the barroom.

'We're nae gonna suffer a witch in our village, eh?' The speaker was a stout man with brown, curly hair whom I had not seen before, in his thirties and wearing a blacksmith's apron. He had climbed up on a large, carved armchair the public room, and was addressing a crowd of perhaps a dozen townsmen.

'Shut yer mush, Joss Ferrier!' Constable Weed spoke up from the back of the room where he towered over the throng. 'Missus 'odgson ma' be bak yam, but she's still under ma care. Thoo'll nae 'urt her! Now be off wi' thoo afore ah clap thoo in irons.' The crowd grumbled as the erstwhile rabble rouser glared at the policeman, but he showed the inestimable good sense to get down from the chair and quit the common room.

Holmes and I took a table and were able to prevail upon the publican to serve us a ploughman's lunch, largely a duplicate of breakfast. As I was about to tuck in, Holmes nudged me with his foot and surreptitiously pointed towards the bar. Billie, Squire Pennington's maid, was handing a pitcher to Jackie Lad, presumably to be filled with ale.

Holmes raised his voice. 'Oh, Billie! Might I have a word?'

The woman glanced our way, indecision rife on her face. Few of her class could resist Holmes' commanding manner though, so she guardedly approached us.

'Sit down, Billie.'

'I don't know as I should, sir. The Squire'll be cross wi' me.'

'You do love your mistress, do you not, Billie?' Holmes asked in a low voice. She nodded her assent. 'Then please sit down, if you would see her well again.' Elbows on the table, she clasped her white-gloved hands before her like a supplicant. 'Now Billie, to save your mistress, it is vital that Dr. Watson and I get in to see her without the Squire's knowledge. Do you care for her sufficiently to make that possible?'

Her mouth popped open and her eyes became wide. 'I don't know, sir! I 'eard the Squire forbid it! I could lose my position…'

'Your mistress will likely perish if you refuse us, Billie,' Holmes snapped. 'Is that what you want?' Her lips became a thin white line and tears ran down her cheeks. She shook her head. 'Good. Now when does Squire Pennington retire for the evening?'

'He generally goes to 'is chamber after 'is cigar and brandy,' she said.

'Can you show a light, and let us in by the parlour doors after he does so tonight?' Another hesitant nod. 'Excellent! We shall await your signal in the forest behind

Mereswater House.' Holmes reached forward and took her hand, and when she withdrew it, he held on to her glove, peeling it from her hand. The livid flesh beneath was mottled with dark, crusty lesions. 'Dreadfully sorry!' he said. 'How clumsy of me.' Appalled, she leapt up from the table and dashed out of the pub, leaving behind a full pitcher of ale on the bar.

I stared at my companion, aghast. 'Holmes! Those were arsenical lesions!'

'Yes, Watson. They were.'

***

After luncheon, Holmes informed me that he had to do some investigating that would not accommodate a companion, so he was going to leave me on my own for a while. 'Perhaps you can walk about and meet some townspeople, and see if you can extract any helpful information.' Having served as Holmes' *amanuensis* as long as I had done, I was used to such treatment. I readily assented.

Ellenby was really not much of a village. It did not even have a church, so it was technically a hamlet. Most of the activity was in the town square, which contained, in addition to the Fells and the constabulary, a bakery, a greengrocer and a general merchandise market. Several roads, lined with private residences, led from the square. Due to our hasty departure from London, I found that I was running low on tobacco, so I decided to visit the market and try to replenish my supply. I knew a custom blend would likely not be available, but a tin of commercial shag or Navy cut would fill the bill nicely.

The market was in a small stone building two doors away from the inn. A little bell tinkled as I opened the door, announcing my arrival. There were only two people inside—the proprietress, a stout woman in an apron and cap who stood behind the wooden counter, waiting on another lady. Both looked my way at the sound of the bell, and I must confess that the beauty of the customer nearly took my breath away.

She wore a simple grey dress and a hooded cape, but it draped her Rubenesque form like a gown on a noblewoman. Her red hair, blazing like a mountain sunset, poured over her shoulders in a fiery cascade. Vivacious jade eyes, over a pert nose and a full mouth with dazzling white teeth, regarded me questioningly, imploring me to introduce myself.

'Good afternoon, Miss, I am, err…'. Those green eyes bored into mine, her vibrant smile leaving me as nonplussed as a schoolboy on the carpet in front of a favourite teacher.

'Oh, I know who you are,' she said.

'You do?'

'Of course! Ellenby is a small village, there are no secrets here. You are Sherlock Holmes, the great detective!'

She smiled ravishingly as my heart tumbled from my chest and bounced across the hardwood floor.

'Err, not exactly, Miss. I am Doctor John Watson, Mr. Holmes' associate.'

Her face fell. 'Oh. I am so sorry, Doctor, that I mistook you for your famous partner.'

'Quite all right,' I muttered. 'Happens all the time.'

'I am Miss Deborah Jones,' she said.

'Oh! Rachel Hodgson's teacher!'

'Not anymore. Miss Hodgson has found employment in London. But I remain the village schoolmistress.'

I studied her elegant features, and could barely detect a hint that she might have tutored Rachel Hodgson. She hid her age admirably.

She continued, 'So you must tell me all about what has brought you and Mr. Holmes to Ellenby.'

'Quite so!' I replied. I spied the familiar green can of Skipper's Navy Cut behind the counter. 'I will just purchase some tobacco, and then we can talk.'

The doorbell tinkled as the clerk handed me the can. I turned to see Squire Pennington entering the shop.

Miss Jones brightened. 'Hello, Rayner,' she said.

'Deborah.' He turned his glance to me. 'And Dr. Watson.'

I turned back to the counter and gave the clerk a shilling. After receiving my change, I again regarded the pair.

The Squire had an evil look about him. 'Oh, do as you will,' he snarled at Miss Jones, then stalked outside, slamming the door in his wake. I raised an eyebrow.

'Rayner invited me to walk with him, but I told him that I was already taken.'

I held the door open so she could precede me. 'I hope I didn't interrupt a previous appointment.'

'His wife's illness has been difficult for him,' she said. 'Sometimes it helps him to just talk. But we mustn't neglect visitors to our humble village. I'll see him later.'

'Where would you like to go?' I asked her. 'The public house?'

'I hardly think that would be appropriate,' she said. 'If you'd care for a short walk, I can show you an overlook with a fine view of the dale and the surrounding fells.'

I assented, so she led me off at a brisk pace to a path that climbed the pike behind the village. She had neither stick nor staff, but she ran up that twisty, narrow track like a mountain goat. I, on the other hand, had a difficult time remaining upright, even with the aid of my stick, because a treacherous coating of roundish gravel covered the trail, and threatened to take my shoes from beneath me. Mostly, I kept my eyes on the path at my feet, but once I glanced up to see the craggy peak towering so far above me, and my heart sank—my wounds were already paining me—however would I be able to follow this lissom wench to the top? However, I rounded a bend to find her perched on a rocky shelf. She smiled at me and patted the stone.

'This is as far as we need to go,' she said. 'Come and sit beside me.'

I sat, then began to apologise for my poor physical condition, but she sat up and schussed me by placing a finger on my lips, then indicated the expanse of the valley below with a wave of her arm. 'Feast your eyes on the Lakes, Doctor. Have you ever seen such a sight?'

I could scarcely breathe as I beheld the vista that stretched before me. The afternoon sun shone over the peak behind us, bathing the scattered groves that dotted the emerald valley in a soft buttery light, the cottages of Ellenby nestled comfortably in their verdant bosom. The argent expanse of Mereswater glimmered beyond, winding amongst the knolls like a silvery cord. I turned my glance to the achingly beautiful woman sitting beside me, and for the first time in ages my heart ached for my Mary, cruelly taken from me so many years ago. I longed to put an arm around Miss Jones and draw her close, but that was sheer foolishness—we had just met and she would surely be repulsed by such an imposition. She must have felt my gaze though, because she turned her grass-coloured eyes to mine, and before I realised what she intended, she leaned forward and placed a soft kiss on my lips.

I sat there like an idiot, stunned by her rashness. Her expression transformed from one of affection to disappointment. 'I am sorry, Doctor,' she said. 'I shouldn't have done that. Perhaps we should go.'

I said to her, 'Not at all.'

She was silent for a moment, then, 'It's lonely for a spinster in such a small village.'

'Then why remain?'

'For the children,' she smiled. 'I came here originally because they had no one to teach them.'

'It was a fine thing that you did for Miss Hodgson.'

'She was a delightfully bright child. I couldn't bear to see her wasting away in a backwater like this, as a brood mare for some illiterate bumpkin.'

'I say!' I ejaculated, again taken aback by her frankness. I hesitantly contradicted my earlier statement. 'Perhaps we should be getting back to the village? Holmes may require my assistance.'

Thankfully, she ignored my suggestion. 'What has he discovered about Mrs. Pennington's condition? Does he actually think that Griselda Hodgson cast a spell on her?'

'No,' Abruptly, I realised that she might be pumping me for information, and that anything I said might become the talk of the town. 'I really shouldn't discuss Holmes' investigation...'

Her face fell, and my heart with it. Why did I so desperately want to please this woman? 'Well, if you can't tell me...' she continued.

'I really should not,' I said

***

Deborah and I walked back down the mountain in silence, holding hands a good part of the way to steady each other on the slippery path. When we reached the outskirts of town, she took both of my hands in hers and looked deeply into my eyes with those mesmerizing, verdant orbs.

'I must say, John, that I had a most enjoyable afternoon. Please do call on me again before you go back to London. And if you find it in your heart to let me assist you and Mr. Holmes...'

'I will speak with him about it,' I said, and she smiled. 'I must go.'

That entrancing smile remained in my head all the way back to the Fells.

I found Holmes in the public room, smoking his briar and nursing a pint. He looked up at me and said, 'Did you learn anything of note from Miss Jones?'

I was d___d if I was going to ask him how he had perceived that. For all I knew, he may have been following the two of us until we started up the mountain path. 'Possibly,' I answered him. I gave him a brief account of my afternoon's adventures, *sans* my personal feelings.

'Very interesting,' was his comment when I had finished. He hesitated, then said, 'I know that you did not say anything to that woman about our surmises, Watson, and I thank you. There are deep waters here, and I do not mean Mereswater.'

This time I had to ask. 'How do you know she questioned me about our activities?'

Holmes smiled. 'Watson, your eyes have been a window to your gentle soul all the years I have known you.' After a moment of silence, he continued, 'We should have an early dinner and get ready. I want to be in the woods behind Mereswater House at dusk.'

***

So it was that we found ourselves crouched behind some bushes in the rain, as the rubicund sky slowly faded to deep purple. The lights of Mereswater House beckoned me, because I knew warmth and dryness could be found within. The French doors of the parlour, however, remained dark. I knew we would have no welcome from the owner there.

I pulled the collar of my Norfolk jacket more tightly about my neck. Holmes, in his cape and deerstalker, was more appropriately dressed for the weather. 'I hope Billie has not lost her courage,' I said. Holmes did not reply.

Good British wool is an amazing material. Because of its lanolin content, it requires hours to become saturated even in a downpour, and it confers warmth even when soaked. But wet wool is hardly comfortable and its smell is truly odious. I had experienced enough of these nocturnal vigils with Holmes so that I knew better than to say anything about the discomfort—while quiet conversation might help me pass the time, it would simply irritate him. Thus, it was a great relief when at last, we saw the light of a candle flickering in the parlour.

Billie had the French doors opened when we arrived. In a low voice, Holmes commanded, 'Take us to your mistress at once!'

We followed her out into the lamp-lit foyer and up the curved staircase. She turned and held a finger to her lips, then led us down a hallway with closed doors on either side, to a room at the end. She ushered us inside, where the sweet smell of a woman's *boudoir* mingled with the sour scent of sickness that I knew so well.

Billie lit a lamp on a round table next to the canopied bed, then whispered, 'The old 'un's chamber is right through that door,' indicating a portal on the other side of the room. 'I'll leave tha' now.'

Holmes took the candle holder from her before she could leave with it. After the door to the corridor had closed, he motioned towards the bed. 'See to the lady, Watson, while I look around,' he whispered.

I parted the curtains enclosing the bed and beheld a pitiable sight indeed. The woman lying there bore little resemblance to the green-gowned lady in the portrait downstairs—her face was pale, wizened, covered with crusty half-healed lesions, and her auburn hair was thin and faded. Her eyes were closed and she was still, scarcely breathing. I reached down and pressed two fingers to the side of her neck, finding a barely perceptible pulse.

Meanwhile, Holmes was searching the armoire and the chests of drawers. 'It's not here,' he muttered. 'What has the fiend done with it?'

Suddenly, Adele Pennington's eyes snapped open and her features transformed into a mask of dread. She began breathing rapidly and shallowly, and her already mottled skin took on a bluish tint. Then her gaze became fixed, and she gave a long, rattling exhalation that I had heard too many times before on the battlefield.

'There is nothing more to see to, Holmes,' I said angrily, in a normal voice. 'Mrs. Pennington is dead.'

Holmes immediately appeared at my side. 'Hush!' he whispered, indicating the door to the Squire's room, behind which a clatter arose. He glanced quickly about, then grabbing the bed curtain, he ripped it and removed a ragged piece about three inches square. This he soaked in the dregs of a cup on the bedtable, before stuffing the scrap into an envelope taken from a pocket. He dashed over to the window and tore it open. 'Hurry, Watson! The devil has heard us!' He put a leg over the sill to step on the sloping roof beyond.

With my wounds from Afghanistan already throbbing from hours in the cold and damp, I realised there was no way that I was going to escape from this house by sliding down a roof and jumping to the ground, so I resolved to remain and do my best to see that Holmes could flee with his evidence. As he vanished outside, I extinguished the bedside lamp. I did not have long to wait before the door to the hallway burst open and Squire Pennington confronted me, his dark form backlit from the lighted corridor, aiming a fowling piece at my midsection. If he fired at this distance, it would surely tear me in half! I steeled myself to meet my God.

***

Several hours later, I found myself occupying the elder Miss Hodgson's former quarters in the Ellenby Constabulary. Because the Squire Pennington had to hold me at gunpoint while Billie went for the constable, he could not pursue Holmes.

'Thoo'll be gan t' Carlisle in a day or two t' gae t' th' dock fer burglary, Dr. Watson,' Constable Trelawney was saying. 'And wi' most of the gadgees in Ellenby huntin 'im, thy Mr. 'olmes won't be free for lang.'

I trusted that Holmes would be able to evade most of the men of Ellenby for as long as he wanted to. But I knew that I was in serious trouble. Billie had refused to say that she had admitted us to Mereswater House, implicating us as burglars, which carried a sentence of years of hard labour.

I spent a wretched night in that small stony cell, my clothes drying slowly on my back. Very little heat from the coal stove downstairs was able to penetrate up there, so I shivered miserably until dawn. Other than to bring me a breakfast very similar to the one I had in the public house and a pot of hellishly strong tea, I saw nothing of the constable after he locked me away. Lunch was more of the same.

The afternoon seemed interminable. It was warm now—indeed, the attic had become almost uncomfortably hot when I heard a noise on the stairs. Then Deborah appeared, carrying a covered basket.

'My poor John!' Even in my present wretched state, a thrill passed through me at the sight of her. 'What have they done to you? Burglary, indeed,' she snorted, tossing her fine head like a spirited mare. She turned to regard Constable Trelawney, whose great bulk was emerging from the staircase. 'Constable, please open this cell so I can give Dr. Watson the victuals I prepared for him.'

'You shouldn't have…' I began.

'Bosh and nonsense!' She cut me off. 'You shouldn't be in here so I had to.' She cast an evil glare at the constable once more.

He obediently unlocked the cell to allow her to pass the basket inside. She contrived to stroke my hand as she did so, sending a line of fire up my arm.

Trelawney relocked the door, saying 'Miss Jones, ah 'av other business…'

'So attend to it, Constable,' she snapped. 'Do you think I'm going to rip these bars off and fly away with him?'

'I'll gi'e thoo ten minutes.' The constable returned downstairs.

She stared at me earnestly with those green, green eyes. 'Mr. Holmes came to me last night,' she said. 'He's at my cottage now. He wants me to tell you to be strong— he's going to Carlisle to get the sample from the bedroom tested. He hopes to be back in a few days to have you freed.'

My effort last night was not in vain, then. 'Thank you for telling me. It will make my imprisonment easier.'

We spent the rest of her time just chatting. I placed my hand on a bar and she covered it with hers, stroking my knuckles with her thumb to comfort me. By the time Trelawney returned for her, she had me totally bewitched.

I nibbled from her basket to while away the time as the sun sank slowly outside my barred window. The constable returned just before nightfall to light the overhead lantern so I should not have to sit in the dark, and I thanked him for his kindness.

Night had fully embraced the land when I heard another hubbub on the stairs. I was shocked to see Sherlock Holmes appear and hurry towards my cell.

'Up Watson, up! There is deviltry afoot!'

Holmes unlocked my cell and threw open the door, then wheeled back to the stairs.

'What?'

'A mob has descended on Miss Hodgson's house,' he said over his shoulder. 'They have taken her! To be tried as a witch!'

My wounds were still paining me. I struggled to keep up with him as we hurried below.

Standing at a gun rack, Holmes removed a rifle and tossed it to me, followed by a box of ammunition.

'Load quickly,' Holmes said. 'The constable has gone ahead, but there may be too many for him.'

'Where did he go?' I asked.

'To the banks of Mereswater.'

I followed him as best I could out into the square and down the road toward the Squire's house. Before we had gone that far, he veered off into the woods. I lost sight of him for a moment, and was worried that I'd be left behind, but then I saw his shadowy form rushing towards the orangey glow of a fire ahead. A threatening growl of angry men throbbed through the dark.

Thomas A. Burns, Jr.

I burst into a smoky clearing on the lakeshore where a bonfire begot shadowy fingers that waved over the massed crowd. Something whirled above me and I heard a woman scream, then I spied a long, thick pole with a chair on the end, a struggling figure within it. It reeled above the lake, then descended into the icy waters with a splash.

The crack of a rifle split the air.

'Back, you rabble,' shouted Holmes. 'Back, or my next bullet will find the body of a man!'

The crowd turned as one in Holmes' direction. I could see that three farmers held Trelawney fast—he must have unwisely rushed into the throng. I brought my rifle to my shoulder and added my voice. 'Release the constable, or I will shoot!' My eye caught motion and I saw someone raising a rifle at Holmes. I shifted targets and squeezed off a round. The fellow went down. 'Hold, I say! I have no wish to injure anyone else.'

The pair seizing the constable let him go. 'Thoo gadgees gae' Miss 'odgson outta t'lake,' he shouted in his stentorian voice. 'Now!'

A half dozen men jumped up and grabbed the end of the long pole suspended in the air, its centre resting on the curious structure that we had discovered the other morning, which acted as a fulcrum. It was an old-fashioned dunking chair! They hauled downwards and the end erupted from the lake, the sodden, unmoving body of the victim still tied into the chair, as the water cascaded to whence it came. They pushed the shaft sideways and swung the woman's body over the bank, then they lowered her to the ground.

My shot had cooled the ardour of the crowd considerably, so I was happy to drop my weapon and return to my nobler calling. I rushed over to examine Miss Hodgson. She wasn't breathing!

'Get me a knife! We must free her from this d___d chair!'

We soon had her face first on the ground. I straddled her, placed my hands on her shoulder blades and began pumping for all I was worth, to expel the lake water from her lungs. After a few minutes hard labour, I was rewarded when she began gasping and coughing.

Meantime, Holmes had taken centre stage in front of the fire. 'You lot have nearly perpetrated a grievous injustice,' he declaimed. 'Miss Griselda Hodgson is no witch!'

A voice from the crowd shouted, 'She murdered the Squire's wife w' her evil eye!'

'She did nothing of the kind,' said Holmes. 'Squire Pennington murdered his wife. He poisoned her with arsenic!'

The Squire emerged from the crowd, his rage causing him to lapse into his childhood vernacular. 'Gan then, tha' lyin' dog! I'll sue thee for libel!'

Holmes reached inside his Inverness and produced a mass of cloth, its brilliant green folds sparkling in the firelight. He shook it in the Squire's face. 'You murdered her, I say, with this noxious garment! You made her wear it daily under the guise of sitting for her anniversary portrait. The results of a Marsh test in the police laboratory at Carlisle will be sufficient to send you to the gallows.'

The look of horror on the Squire's livid face as he stared at the garment in Holmes' hands attested to his guilt.

***

A week later, we were again ensconced in Baker Street, Holmes in his mouse grey dressing gown and me with a towel over my head, trousers rolled up to my knees, and my feet immersed in a steaming basin of Epsom salts provided by Mrs. Hudson. I had not escaped unscathed from that rainy night in the woods and my subsequent incarceration in a chilly jail cell.

He tossed a telegram he was holding onto the table. 'The Marsh test of the dress and the contents of the cup in Adele Pennington's bedchamber both came back positive,' he said. 'As I said before, the Squire will hang.'

'Good,' I sniffed. 'Perfidious dog, murdering the mother of his son. But how did he ever poison her with a dress?'

'Some years ago, these emerald ball gowns became all the rage on the continent,' Holmes said. 'No one had seen their like before—until that time, such a brilliant green hue in an article of clothing could simply not be attained. But then the clothing manufactures happened on a dye that had been synthesised in the 18th century by the German chemist Carl Wilhelm Scheele, which gave gratifying results. Unfortunately, it was a compound of cupric hydrogen arsenite.

'Of course, there were incidents among women who wore such gowns, skin rashes mostly. The workers who manufactured the clothes suffered more greatly because of prolonged contact with the raw dye, and there were even some deaths.'

'How in the world could they allow such clothing to be sold?'

'The law is still *caveat emptor*, Watson. But word of mouth was sufficient to at least limit the damage from the toxic garments. And, truth be told, the effects were generally not catastrophic if a gown was worn only for a few hours at a ball.

'Now, our man the Squire set up an entirely different situation. Using the pretext of the portrait sitting, he had his wife wear the gown for hours a day, day after day. She would become hot and sweaty posing in the sun in front of the parlour window, more and more poison leaching from the cloth, solubilising in her perspiration, facilitating its entry into her system. He could monitor the progress of his scheme by watching her get sicker and sicker.'

Holmes rose and went to the mantel for his meerschaum and the Persian slipper. 'Her deteriorating condition drove Adele Pennington to consult Griselda. My examination of the medicament cabinet in her dabbin that first night suggested that she had prescribed oil of pennyroyal, a treatment for nausea and an upset stomach, but also associated with deleterious systemic effects. Regardless of Mrs. Pennington's opinion, I think that Griselda had tried to do her best by her patient. But she could not resist gaining a reputation for infamy when the Squire's wife labelled her as a witch.'

Holmes had his pipe going to his satisfaction, so he went back to his chair. 'When we arrived on the scene inquiring about his wife's health, the Squire contrived to hurry her along to Paradise by adding a tot of rat poison to her bedtime cup of milk. Once he knew I had seen the unfinished painting, he also took the precaution of getting rid of the green dress.

'The Squire was an evil, evil man, Watson. Not only did he murder his wife, but I also believe that he was responsible for Griselda's present condition.'

'How do you mean?'

'Surely you have noticed the resemblance between the Squire and our client.'

I digested that for a moment, then realised what must have happened to Griselda on that ill-fated foraging trip so many years ago. 'Did you inform Rachael?'

'No. Some truths are best left untold.'

I came back to another point that had been bothering me. 'The green dress, Holmes. Wherever did you find it?'

My friend regarded me with a sympathetic expression. 'Watson, I must ask you to brace yourself. I have to tell you that the true perpetrator of this crime has escaped justice, at least for now.'

I was suddenly wary. 'What do you mean?'

'I have not yet discussed the Squire's motive for the murder of his wife. I am afraid he shared it with a Hebrew king.'

'What do you mean?' I said again, fearful this time.

'The Squire was engaged in an adulterous affair. With Miss Jones.'

'With Deborah? That is not possible!' I shouted.

'I am afraid it is, old fellow. I found the arsenical dress in her hope chest.'

I sat there as if poleaxed. It could not be! I thought she was like my Mary…

'I am so sorry, Watson,' Holmes said softly.

I took a moment to compose myself. I would not have my voice break when addressing Holmes. When I was ready, I asked, 'How did you know?'

'I suspected when you told me of the meeting between Miss Jones and the Squire in the market. You told me they addressed each other by their first names. Now that is not uncommon in Ellenby among childhood friends, but everyone addressed Pennington as 'Squire' and moreover, Miss Jones was not a village native. So, their informality likely meant only one thing.

'I took a chance and went to her after I left you at Mereswater House. I gambled that she would not betray me to Trelawney until after she discovered how much I knew. Naturally, I feigned ignorance of her involvement. I prevailed upon her to take a specious message to you, searched her cottage after she left, and found the dress. Apparently, she realized it was missing while we were rescuing the elder Miss Hodgson, and lost no time in decamping.'

I had received a note from Deborah the day after Griselda Hodgson was rescued from the mob, telling me that she was upset by the affair and had gone to spend some time with her mother in Cardiff. I had no reason to question it. Now it was apparent that she knew that Holmes had found her out.

'So, for the second time in my illustrious career, I find myself bested by a woman,' Holmes said. 'I would not be surprised if the entire nefarious scheme was hers. Miss Deborah Jones was truly the Witch of Ellenby.

'

Thomas A. Burns, Jr.

Acknowledgements

I want to thank the following people who were instrumental in the completion and publication of *10 Steps from Baker Street*.

If not for that eminent Sherlockian David Markham, these stories would have never seen print. He acted as editor for many of them and was always gracious and encouraging.

Mr. Steve Emecz first published many of these tales in various volumes of *The MX Book of New Sherlock Holmes Stories*. This is a worthy project that serves to finance a school in the United Kingdom for special needs children, *Stepping Stones*, which has been established at Undershaw, a former residence of Sir Arthur Conan Doyle.

Mr. Derrick Belanger also first published some of these stories through his company Belanger Books.

The participants in our monthly *Five Miles from Anywhere* meetings have made many helpful suggestions.

My beta readers Craig Chapman, Paul Crockett, Skip Dyer and Samuel Leeman Munk also provided many helpful suggestions and encouraged me to see this project through. And special thanks to Ms. Elizabeth Hamilton-Smyth of the UK for helping me eliminate many Americanisms.

About the Author

As a kid, I started reading mysteries with the Hardy Boys, Ken Holt and Rick Brant, then graduated to the classics by authors such as A. Conan Doyle, Erle Stanley Gardner, John Dickson Carr, and Rex Stout, to name a few. I have written fiction as a hobby all of my life, starting in marble-backed copybooks in grade school. I built a career as a technical and science writer and as an editor for nearly thirty years in academia, industry and government. Now that I'm truly on my own as a freelance science writer and editor, I'm excited to publish my own mystery series as well.

Follow me on Facebook at https://www.facebook.com/3MDetectiveAgency/, on Twitter @3Mdetective, Instagram at 3mdetective, Tumblr at nataliemcmasters or email me at tom@3mdetectiveagency.com.

Be sure to visit the 3M Detective Agency website at https://www.3mdetectiveagency.com/contact/ and subscribe to my newsletter to get all the news about Nattie and the 3M gang.